A SPELL WORSE THAN DEATH

Bink was 25, but he had always been treated as a child because he had no magic. Now he was an exile from the magic land of Xanth. And he and the strange girl Fanchon were captives of the notorious Evil Magician Trent.

The Evil Magican was, in many respects, the opposite of the popular image—he was handsome, strong and urbane. Yet Bink knew better than to let fair words deceive him.

"Fanchon, stand forth," Trent said.

Fanchon stepped forth, open cynicism on her face. Trent did not gesture or chant. He merely glanced at her.

She vanished. In her place was a struggling, baleful lizardlike thing with wings. It was a basilisk.

"Bink, stand forth," Trent said, exactly as before.

By Piers Anthony
Published by Ballantine Books:

THE MAGIC OF XANTH
  A Spell For Chameleon
  The Source Of Magic
  Castle Roogna
  Centaur Aisle
  Ogre, Ogre
  Night Mare

THE APPRENTICE ADEPT
  Book One: Split Infinity
  Book Two: Blue Adept
  Book Three: Juxtaposition

A SPELL
FOR CHAMELEON

Piers Anthony

A Del Rey Book

BALLANTINE BOOKS • NEW YORK

Contents

XANTH

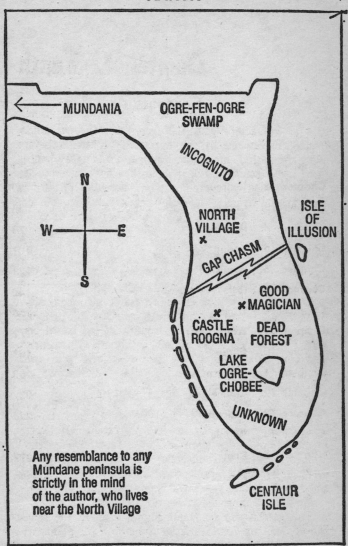

← MUNDANIA

OGRE-FEN-OGRE SWAMP

INCOGNITO

N
W — E
S

NORTH VILLAGE ✕

ISLE OF ILLUSION

GAP CHASM

GOOD ✕ MAGICIAN

✕ CASTLE ROOGNA

DEAD FOREST

LAKE OGRE-CHOBEE

UNKNOWN

CENTAUR ISLE

Any resemblance to any Mundane peninsula is strictly in the mind of the author, who lives near the North Village

Chapter 1. Xanth

A small lizard perched on a brown stone. Feeling threatened by the approach of human beings along the path, it metamorphosed into a stingray beetle, then into a stench-puffer, then into a fiery salamander.

Bink smiled. These conversions weren't real. It had assumed the forms of obnoxious little monsters, but not their essence. It could not sting, stink, or burn. It was a chameleon, using its magic to mimic creatures of genuine threat.

Yet as it shifted into the form of a basilisk it glared at him with such ferocity that Bink's mirth abated. If its malice could strike him, he would be horribly dead.

Then abruptly a silent moth hawk swooped down from the sky and caught the chameleon in its beak. There was a thin scream of anguish as the lizard convulsed; then it dangled limply as the hawk ascended. The chameleon, despite all its pretensions, was dead. Even while trying to threaten Bink, it had been destroyed by another agency.

This realization continued to percolate through Bink's emotion. The chameleon was harmless—but most of untamed Xanth was not. Was this some twisted omen, a small suggestion of a dire fate awaiting him? Omens were serious business; they always came true, but usually were misinterpreted until too late. Was Bink fated to die brutally—or was some enemy of his?

He had, so far as he knew, no enemies.

The golden sun of Xanth shone through the magic Shield, striking sparkles from the trees. All plants had

1

their enchantments, but no spell could eliminate the need for light, water, and healthy soil. Instead, magic was used to make these necessities of the vegetable kingdom more available, and to protect the plants from destruction, unless they were overpowered by stronger magic or simple bad luck, like the chameleon.

Bink looked at the girl beside him as she stepped through a slanting sunbeam. He was no plant, but he too had needs, and even the most casual inspection of her made him aware of this. Sabrina was absolutely beautiful—and her beauty was completely natural. Other girls managed to enhance their appearance by cosmetics or padding or specialized spells, but beside Sabrina all other females looked somewhat artificial. She was no enemy!

They came to Lookout Rock. This was not a particularly lofty promontory, but its situational magic made it seem more elevated than it was, so that they could look down on a quarter slice of Xanth. This was a land of multicolored vegetation, small pretty lakes, and deceptively quiet fields of flowers, ferns, and crops. Even as Bink watched, one of the lakes expanded slightly, making itself seem cooler and deeper, a better place for a swim.

Bink wondered briefly about this, as he often did. He had an unruly mind, which constantly pestered him with questions for which there were no ready answers. As a child he had driven parents and friends almost to distraction with his "Why is the sun yellow?" "Why do ogres crunch bones?" "Why can't sea monsters cast spells?" and similarly infantile prattle. No wonder he had soon been hustled away to centaur school. Now he had learned to control his mouth, but not his brain, and so he let it run on in silence.

Animate spells he could understand, such as those of the unfortunate chameleon; they facilitated comfort, survival, or image for living creatures. But why should inanimate things have magic? Did a lake care who swam in it? Well, maybe so; a lake was an ecological unit, and the community of living things within it might have a mutual interest in promoting it. Or a freshwater dragon might be responsibile, luring in prey. Dragons were the most varied and dangerous life forms of Xanth; species occupied air, earth, and water, and a number breathed fire. One thing they all had in common: good appetite. Pure chance might not bring in enough fresh meat.

But what about Lookout Rock? It was bare, without even lichen, and hardly beautiful. Why should it want company? And if it did, why not make itself more handsome, instead of remaining gray and drab? People did not come here to admire the rock, but to admire the rest of Xanth. Such a spell seemed self-defeating.

Then Bink stubbed his toe on a sharp fragment of stone. He was standing on a cracked-rock terrace, formed generations ago by the breaking up of a pretty-colored boulder and—

There it was! That other boulder, which must have been close to Lookout Rock and of similar size, had been fragmented to make this path and terrace, losing its identity. Lookout Rock had survived. Nobody would break it up, because it would make an ugly path, and its unselfish magic made it useful as it stood. One minor mystery solved.

Still, there were philosophical considerations, his insatiable mind insisted. How could an inanimate thing think or have feelings? What was survival to a rock? A boulder was merely the fragment of a prior layer of rock; why should it have a personal identity if the bedrock didn't? Still, the same question could be asked of a man: he had been formed from the tissues of the plants and animals he consumed, yet he had a separate—

"What did you wish to talk to me about, Bink?" Sabrina inquired demurely.

As if she didn't know. But as his mind formed the necessary words, his mouth balked. He knew what her answer had to be. No one could remain in Xanth after his twenty-fifth birthday unless he demonstrated a magic talent. Bink's own critical birthday was barely a month away. He was no child now. How could she marry a man who was so soon to be exiled?

Why hadn't he thought of that before bringing her out here? He could only embarrass himself! Now he had to say something to her, or suffer further embarrassment, making it awkward for her as well. "I just wanted to see your—your—"

"See my *what?*" she inquired with an arch lift of eyebrow.

He felt the heat starting up his neck. "Your holograph," he blurted. There was much more of her he longed to see, and to touch, but that could come only after marriage. She was that sort of girl, and it was part of her appeal. The girls who had it didn't need to put it on casual display.

Well, not quite true. He thought of Aurora, who certainly had it, yet who—

"Bink, there *is* a way," Sabrina said.

He glanced sidelong at her, then quickly away, confused. She couldn't be suggesting—

"The Good Magician Humfrey," she continued blithely.

"What?" He had been on quite a different track, no credit to his willful mind.

"Humfrey knows a hundred spells. Maybe one of them—I'm sure he could find out what your talent is. Then everything would be all right."

Oh. "But he charges a year's service for a single spell," Bink protested. "I have only a month." But that was not quite accurate; if the Magician identified a talent for Bink, then he would not be exiled, and he would have a year available. He was deeply touched by Sabrina's faith in him. She did not say what others said: that he had no magic. She did him the immense courtesy of choosing to believe that his magic merely remained undiscovered.

Perhaps it was that faith that had first attracted him

to her. Certainly she was beautiful and intelligent and talented, a prize by any definition. But she could have been much less in all categories and still been his—

"A year is not so long," Sabrina murmured. "I would wait."

Bink stared down at his hands, pondering. His right hand was normal, but he had lost the middle finger of his left hand in a childhood accident. It had not even been the result of inimical magic; he had been playing with a cleaver, holding down a stalk of coilgrass while he chopped, pretending it was the tail of a dragon. After all, a boy could not start to practice too early for the serious side of life. The grass had twitched out of his grip as he swung, and he had grabbed for it, and the cleaver had come down hard on his extended finger.

It had hurt, but the worst of it was that because he was not supposed to play with the cleaver, he had not dared scream or tell of his injury. He had controlled himself with extreme effort and suffered in silence. He had buried the finger, and managed to hide his mutilation by keeping his hand closed for several days. When the truth finally came out, it was too late for a restorative spell; the finger was rotted and could not be reattached. A strong-enough spell could have attached it—but it would have remained a zombie finger.

He had not been punished. His mother, Bianca, believed he had learned his lesson—and he had, he had! Next time he played with a cleaver on the sly he would watch where his fingers were. His father seemed privately pleased that Bink had shown so much courage and tenacity in adversity, even in his wrongdoing. "The lad's got nerve," Roland had said. "Now if only he had magic—"

Bink jerked his eyes away from the hand. That had been fifteen years ago. Suddenly a year seemed short indeed. One year of service—in exchange for a lifetime with Sabrina. It was a bargain.

Yet—suppose he had no magic? Was he to pay a year of his life to verify the certainty of being thrust into the drear realm of the null-talented? Or would it be better to accept exile, preserving the useless hope that he did have a latent talent?

Sabrina, respecting his flurry of contemplation, began her holograph. A haze of blue appeared before her, hanging over the slope. It expanded, thinning at the edges, intensifying in the center, until it was two feet in diameter. It looked like thick smoke, but did not dissipate or drift.

Now she began to hum. She had a good voice—not a great one, but right for her magic. At the sound, the blue cloud quivered and solidified, becoming roughly spherical. Then she changed her pitch, and the outer rim turned yellow. She opened her mouth, singing the word "girl," and the colors assumed the shape of a young lass in a blue dress with yellow frills. The figure was three-dimensional, visible from all sides with differing perspective.

It was a fine talent. Sabrina could sculpt anything— but the images vanished the moment her concentration stopped, and never had any physical substance. So this was, strictly speaking, useless magic. It did not improve her life in any material fashion.

Yet how many talents really did help their people? One person could make a leaf of a tree wither and die as he looked at it. Another could create the odor of sour milk. Another could make insane laughter bubble up from the ground. These were all magic, no question about it—but what use were they? Why should such people qualify as citizens of Xanth while Bink, who was smart, strong, and handsome, was disqualified? Yet that was the absolute rule: no nonmagical person could remain beyond his quarter-century mark.

Sabrina was right: he had to identify his talent. He had never been able to find it on his own, so he should pay the Good Magician's price. Not only would this preserve him from exile—which really might be a fate worse than death, since what was the point in life without magic?—and win him Sabrina, a fate considerably better than death. It would also redeem his battered self-respect. He had no choice.

"Oh!" Sabrina exclaimed, clapping her hands to her pert derriere. The holograph dissolved, the blue-dressed girl distorting grotesquely before she vanished. "I'm on fire!"

Bink stepped toward her, alarmed. But even as he moved, there was loud juvenile laughter. Sabrina whirled furiously. "Numbo, you stop that!" she cried. She was one of those girls who was as appealing in anger as in joy. "It's not funny."

It was, of course, Numbo who had given her a magical hotseat, a fiery pain in the posterior. Talk about a useless talent! Bink, his fists clenched so tightly that his thumb jammed into the stub of his missing finger, strode toward the grinning youth standing behind Lookout Rock. Numbo was fifteen, cocky and annoying; he needed a lesson.

But Bink's foot struck a loose rock, which turned his ankle long enough to cost him his balance. It didn't hurt, but it interrupted his forward progress. His hand swung forward—and his fingers touched an invisible wall.

There was another shout of laughter. Bink hadn't crashed headlong into the wall, thanks to the providential stone under his foot, but evidently someone thought he had.

"You too, Chilk," Sabrina said. That was Chilk's talent: the wall. It was a kind of complement to Sabrina's talent; instead of being visible without substance, it had substance without visibility. It was only six feet square; and, like so many talents, it was strictly temporary—but it was hard as steel in the first few moments.

Bink could dodge around it and run the kid down—but he was sure to get caught several times by that remanifesting wall, and suffer more damage than he could do to the boy. It wasn't worth it. If only he had a talent of his own, such as Numbo's hotseat, he could make the joker sorry regardless of the wall. But he didn't, and

Chilk knew it. Everyone knew it. That was Bink's big problem. He was fair game for all the pranksters, because he couldn't strike back—not magically, and it was deemed crass to do it physically. Right now he was quite ready to be crass, however.

"Let's get out of here, Bink," Sabrina said. There was disgust in her voice, nominally directed at the intruders, but Bink suspected part of it applied to him. An impotent kind of rage began building up—one he had felt many times before, and had never gotten used to. He had been balked from proposing to her by the lack of a talent, and he could not stay here, for the same reason. Not here at Lookout Rock or here in Xanth. Because he didn't fit.

They walked back down the path. The jokers, getting no further rise from their prey, went in search of other mischief. The landscape no longer seemed so lovely. Maybe he'd be better off away from here. Maybe he should take off now, not waiting to be officially exiled. If Sabrina really loved him, she'd come with him—even Outside, into Mundania.

No, he knew better than that. Sabrina loved him—but she loved Xanth, too. She had such a sweet shape, such kissable lips, that she could find another man much more easily than she could adjust to the rigors of life among the unmagical. For that matter, he could find another girl more easily than . . . what he faced. So probably, objectively, he'd be better off going alone.

So why didn't his heart agree?

They passed the brown stone where the chameleon had perched, and he shuddered.

"Why don't you ask Justin?" Sabrina suggested as they approached the village. It was dusk, closing in faster here than up at Lookout Rock. The village lamps were coming on.

Bink glanced across at the unique tree she indicated. There were many kinds of trees in Xanth, a number of them vital to the economy. Beerbarrel trees were tapped for drink, and oilbarrel trees for fuel, and Bink's own footwear came from a mature shoe tree east of the village. But Justin Tree was something special, a species never sprouted from seed. Its leaves were shaped like flat hands, and its trunk was the hue of tanned human flesh. This was scarcely surprising, since it had once been human.

In an instant that history flashed across Bink's mind—part of the dynamic folklore of Xanth. Twenty years ago there had been one of the greatest of the Evil Magicians: a young man named Trent. He had possessed the power of transformation—the ability to change any living thing into any other living thing, instantly. Not satisfied with his status of Magician, granted in recognition of the awesome strength of his magic, Trent had sought to use his power to preempt the throne of Xanth. His procedure had been simple and most direct: he transformed anyone who opposed him into something that could not oppose him. The worst threats he converted to fish—on dry land, allowing them to flop until they died. The mere nuisances he changed to animals or plants. Thus several intelligent animals owed their status to him; though they were dragons, two-headed wolves, and land-octopi, they retained the intelligence and perspective of their human origins.

Trent was gone now—but his works remained, for there was no other transformer to change them back. Holographs, hotseats, and invisible walls were qualifying talents, but transformation was of a different order. Only once in a generation did such power manifest in an individual, and it seldom manifested twice in the same form. Justin had been one of Magician Trent's annoyances—no one remembered exactly what he had done—so Justin was a tree. No one had the ability to change him back into a man.

Justin's own talent had been voice projection—not the parlor trick that was ventriloquism, or the trivial talent of insane laughter, but genuine comprehensible ut-

terance at a distance without the use of vocal cords. He
retained this talent as a tree, and as he had a great deal
of time for thought, villagers often came to this tree for
advice. Often it was good advice. Justin was no genius,
but a tree had greater objectivity about human problems.

It occurred to Bink that Justin might actually be better off as a tree than he had been as a man. He liked
people, but it was said that in his human form he had
not been handsome. As a tree he was quite stately, and
no threat to anyone.

They veered to approach Justin. Suddenly a voice
spoke directly in front of them: "Do not approach,
friends; ruffians are lurking."

Bink and Sabrina drew up short. "Is that you, Justin?" she asked. "Who is lurking?"

But the tree could not hear as well as it could speak,
and did not answer. Wood did not seem to make the
best ears.

Bink, angry, took a step toward it. "Justin is public
scenery," he muttered. "Nobody has a right to—"

"Please, Bink!" Sabrina urged, pulling back on his
arm. "We don't want any trouble."

No, she never wanted any trouble. He would not go
so far as to call this a fault in her, but at times it became annoyingly inconvenient. Bink himself never let
trouble bar him from a matter of principle. Still, Sabrina was beautiful, and he had caused her trouble
enough already tonight. He turned to accompany her
away from the tree.

"Hey, no fair!" a voice exclaimed. "They're going
away."

"Justin must've tattled," another cried.

"Then let's chop down Justin."

Bink halted again. "They wouldn't!" he said.

"Of course they wouldn't," Sabrina agreed. "Justin is
a village monument. Ignore them."

But the voice of the tree came again, a bit misplaced
in relation to Bink and Sabrina—evidence of poor con-

centration. "Friends, please fetch the King quickly. These ruffians have an axe or something, and they've been eating locoberries."

"An axe!" Sabrina exclaimed in sheer horror.

"The King is out of town," Bink muttered. "Anyway, he's senile."

"And he hasn't summoned more than a summer shower in years," Sabrina agreed. "Kids didn't dare make so much mischief when he had his full magic."

"*We* certainly didn't," Bink said. "Remember the hurricane flanked by six tornadoes he summoned to put down the last wiggle spawning? He was a real Storm King then. He—"

There was the ringing sound of metal biting into wood. A scream of sheer agony erupted from the air. Bink and Sabrina jumped.

"That's Justin!" she said. "They're doing it."

"No time for the King anyway," Bink said. He charged toward the tree.

"Bink, you *can't!*" Sabrina cried after him. "You don't have any magic."

So the truth came out, in this moment of crisis. She didn't really believe he had a talent. "I've got muscle, though!" he yelled back. "You go for help."

Justin screamed again as the blade struck a second time. It was an eerie wooden noise. There was laughter—the merry mirth of kids out on a lark, having no care at all what consequences their actions might have. Loco? This was mere insensitivity.

Then Bink was there. And—he was alone. Just when he was in the mood for a good fight. The malicious pranksters had scattered.

He could guess their identities—but he didn't have to. "Jama, Zink, and Potipher," Justin Tree said. "Oooo, my foot!"

Bink squatted to inspect the cut. The white wood-wound was clearly visible in contrast to the shoelike bark of the base of the tree trunk. Driblets of reddish sap were forming, very much like blood. Not too serious for a tree this size, but surely extremely uncomfortable.

"I'll get some compresses for that," Bink said. "There's some coral sponge in the forest near here. Yell if anyone bothers you while I'm gone."

"I will," Justin said. "Hurry." Then, as an after-thought: "You're a great guy, Bink. Much better than some who—uh—"

"Than some who have magic," Bink finished for him. "Thanks for trying to spare my feelings." Justin meant well, but sometimes spoke before he thought. It came from having a wooden brain.

"It isn't fair that louts like Jama are called citizens, while you—"

"Thanks," Bink said gruffly, moving off. He agreed completely, but what was the use talking about it? He watched out for anyone lurking in the bushes, waiting to bother Justin when the tree was unprotected, but saw nobody. They were really gone.

Jama, Zink, and Potipher, he thought darkly—the village troublemakers. Jama's talent was the manifesta-tion of a sword, and that was what had chopped Justin's trunk. Anyone who could imagine that such vandalism was funny—

Bink remembered one of his own bitter experiences with that bunch, not so many years ago. Intoxicated by locoberries, the three had lurked in ambush along one of the paths beyond the village, just looking for mis-chief. Bink and a friend had walked into that trap, and been backed up against the cloud of poison gas that was Potipher's magic talent, while Zink made mirage-holes near their feet and Jama materialized flying swords for them to duck. Some sport!

Bink's friend had used his magic to escape, animating a golem from a stick of wood that took his place. The golem had resembled him exactly, so that it fooled the pranksters. Bink had known the difference, of course, but he had covered for his friend. Unfortunately, though the golem was immune to poison gas, Bink was not. He had inhaled some of it, and lost consciousness even as help arrived. His friend had brought Bink's mother and father—

Bink had found himself holding his breath again as the poison cloud enveloped him. He saw his mother tugging at his father's arm, pointing Bink's way. Bianca's talent was replay: she could jump time back five seconds in a small area. This was very limited but deviously powerful magic, for it enabled her to correct a just-made mistake. Such as Bink's breath of poison gas.

Then his breath had whooshed out again, making Bianca's magic useless. She could keep replaying the scene indefinitely, but *everything* was replayed, including his breath. But Roland looked, piercingly—and Bink had frozen.

Roland's talent was the stun gaze: one special glance and what he looked at was frozen in place, alive but immobile until released. In this manner Bink had been prevented from breathing the gas a second time, until his rigid body had been carried out.

As the stun abated, he had found himself in his mother's arms. "Oh my baby!" she cried, cradling his head against her bosom. "Did they hurt you?"

Bink came to an abrupt stop by the bed of sponge, his face flushing even now with the keen embarrassment of the memory. Had she had to do that? Certainly she had saved him from an early death—but he had been the laughingstock of the village for an interminable time thereafter. Everywhere he went, kids exclaimed "My baby!" in falsetto, and sniggered. He had his life—at the expense of his pride. Yet he knew he could not blame his parents.

He had blamed Jama and Zink and Potipher. Bink had no magic, but, perhaps for that reason, he was the huskiest boy in the village. He had had to fight as long as he could remember. He was not especially well coordinated, but he had a lot of raw power. He had gone after Jama privately and demonstrated convincingly that the fist was swifter than the magic sword. Then Zink, and finally Potipher; Bink had hurled him into his

own gas cloud, forcing him to dissolve it very suddenly.
Those three had not sniggered at Bink thereafter; in
fact, they tended to avoid him—which was why they
had scattered when he charged the tree. Together they
could have overcome him, but they had been well con-
ditioned by those separate encounters.

Bink smiled, his embarrassment replaced by grim
pleasure. Perhaps his manner of dealing with the situation had been immature, but there had been a lot of
satisfaction in it. Down underneath he knew it had been
his irritation at his mother that motivated him, dis-
placed to people like Jama—but he did not regret it. He
did love his mother, after all.

But in the end his only chance to redeem himself had
been to find his own magic talent, a good strong one
like that of his father, Roland. So no one would dare to
tease him or laugh at him or baby him, ever again. So
that pure shame would not drive him from Xanth. And
that had never happened. He was known contemp-
tuously as the "Spell-less Wonder."

He stooped to gather several good, strong sponges.
These would abate Justin Tree's discomfort, for that
was their magic: they absorbed agony and spread a
healing comfort. A number of plants and animals—he
was not quite sure in which category the sponges fit—
had similar properties. The advantage of the sponges
was that they were mobile; plucking them would not kill
them. They were tough; they had migrated from the water when the corals did, and now thrived on land. Probably their magic healing properties had been developed
to facilitate their lives in the new medium. Or maybe
before the migration, since coral was cutting stuff.

Talents tended to run in schools, with one overlapping another; thus many variants of each type of magic
showed up in the plant and animal kingdoms. But
among people, magic varied extremely widely. It
seemed that individual personality had more to do with
it than heredity, though the strongest magic tended to
turn up in particular family lines. As if strength of

magic was hereditary, while type of magic was environmental. Yet there were other factors—

Bink could fit a lot of reflection into a passing moment. If reflection were magic, he'd be a Magician. But right now he'd better concentrate on what he was doing, or he'd be in trouble.

Dusk was intensifying. Dismal shapes were rising out of the forest, hovering as if seeking prey. Eyeless and formless, they nevertheless conducted themselves with a disquieting awareness, orienting on Bink—or seeming to. More magic was unexplained than was safely catalogued. A will-o'-the-wisp caught Bink's nervous eye. He started to follow the half-glimpsed light, then abruptly caught himself. The lure of the wisp was sheer mischief. It would lead him into the wilderness and lose him there, prey to the hostile magic of the unknown. One of Bink's childhood friends had followed the wisp and never returned. Warning enough!

Night transformed Xanth. Regions like this one that were innocent by day became horrors as the sun sneaked down. Specters and shades came out, questing for their ghastly satisfactions, and occasionally a zombie ripped free of its grave and marched clumsily about. No sensible person slept outdoors, and every house in the village had repulsion spells against the supernatural. Bink did not dare use the shortcut back to Justin Tree; he would have to go the long way, following the looping but magically protected trails. This was not timidity but necessity.

He ran—not from fear, for there was no real danger on this charmed route, and he knew the paths too well to stray accidentally from them, but in order to reach Justin more swiftly. Justin's flesh was wood, but it hurt every bit as much as normal flesh. How anyone could be so crass as to chop at Justin Tree . . .

Bink passed a field of sea oats, hearing the pleasant swish and gurgle of their oceanic tides. When harvested, they made excellent foamy broth, except that it tended to be rather salty. The bowls could only be filled halfway; otherwise the broth's continuing sea waves slopped over.

He remembered the wild oats he had planted as an adolescent. Sea oats were restless, but their cousins the wild oats were hyperactive. They had fought him savagely, their stems slashing across his wrists as he tried to harvest a ripe ear. He had gotten it, but had been uncomfortably scratched and abraded before getting clear of the patch.

He had planted those few wild seeds in a secret plot behind his house, and watered them every day, the natural way. He had guarded the bad-tempered shoots from all harm, his anticipation growing. What an adventure for a teenaged male! Until his mother, Bianca, had discovered the plot. Alas, she had recognized the species instantly.

There had been a prompt family hassle. "How could you?" Bianca demanded, her face flaming. But Roland had labored to suppress his admiring smile. "Sowing wild oats!" he murmured. "The lad's growing up."

"Now, Roland, you know that—"

"Dear, it isn't as if there's any real harm in it."

"No harm!" she exclaimed indignantly.

"It is a perfectly natural urge for a young man—" But her furious expression had halted Bink's father, who feared nothing in Xanth but was normally a peaceable man. Roland sighed and turned to Bink. "I gather you *do* know what you were doing, son?"

Bink felt excruciatingly defensive. "Well—yes. The nymph of the oats—"

"Bink!" Bianca snapped warningly. He had never seen her so angry before.

Roland held up his hands, making peace. "Dear— why don't you let us work this out, man-to-man? The boy's got a right."

And so Roland had betrayed his own bias; when his man-to-man chat was with Bink, it was with a *boy*.

Without another word, Bianca had stalked out of the house.

Roland turned to Bink, shaking his head in a gesture that was only nominally negative. Roland was a powerful, handsome man, and he had a special way with gestures. "Genuine wild oats, culled thrashing from the stem, sown by the full moon, watered with your own urine?" he inquired frankly, and Bink nodded, his face at half heat. "So that when the plants mature, and the oat nymph manifests, she will be bound to you, the fertilizer figure?"

Bink nodded grimly.

"Son, believe me, I comprehend the attraction; I sowed wild oats myself when I was your age. Got me a nymph, too, with flowing green hair and a body like the great outdoors—but I had forgotten about the special watering, and so she escaped me. I never saw anything so lovely in my life—except your mother, of course."

Roland had sown wild oats? Bink had never imagined such a thing. He remained silent, afraid of what was coming.

"I made the mistake of confessing about the oats to Bianca," Roland continued. "I fear she became somewhat sensitized on the subject, and you caught the brunt. These things happen."

So his mother was jealous of something that had happened in his father's life before he married her. What a pitful of concepts Bink had stumbled into, unwittingly.

Roland's face became serious. "To a young man, inexperienced, the notion of a lovely, nude, captive nymph may be phenomenally tempting," he continued. "All the physical attributes of a real woman, and none of the mental ones. But, son, this is a juvenile dream, like finding a candy tree. The reality really would not be all you anticipated. One quickly becomes surfeited, tired of unlimited candy, and so it also is with—with a mindless female body. A man can not love a nymph. She might as well be air. His ardor rapidly turns to boredom, and to disgust."

Still Bink dared not comment. He would not have become bored, he was sure.

Roland understood him, too well. "Son, what you need is a real live girl," he concluded. "A figure with a personality, who will talk back to you. It is far more challenging to develop a relationship with a complete woman, and often extremely frustrating." He glanced meaningfully at the door through which Bianca had departed. "But in the long run it is also far more rewarding. What you sought in the wild oats was a shortcut—but in life there are no shortcuts." He smiled. "Though if it had been up to me, I'd have let you try the shortcut. No harm in it; no harm at all. But your mother—well, we have a conservative culture here, and the ladies tend to be the most conservative—especially the pretty ones. It's a small village—smaller than it used to be—so everybody knows his neighbor's business. So we are circumscribed. Know what I mean?"

Bink nodded uncertainly. When his father laid down the law, however circumspectly, that was final. "No more oats."

"Your mother—well, she was caught by surprise by your growing up. The oats are out—she's probably rooting them up right this instant—but you still have a lot of good experience ahead of you. Bianca might like to think of you as a little boy forever, but even she can't balk nature. Not for more than five seconds! So she'll simply have to go along with it."

Roland paused, but Bink was silent again, unsure of what his father was leading up to.

"There's a girl due to move here from one of the lesser villages," Roland continued. "Theoretically this is for proper schooling, since we have the best centaur schoolmaster in Xanth. But I suspect the underlying reason is that there simply aren't many eligible boys in her village. I understand she has not yet discovered her magic talent, and she's about your age—" He paused to glance meaningfully at Bink. "I think she could use a handsome, healthy young man to show her around and warn her of local hazards. I understand she is extremely smart and pretty, and soft-spoken—a rare combination."

Then Bink began to understand. A girl—a real girl—for him to get to know. One who would not be prejudiced by his lack of magic. And Bianca would not be able to disapprove, though privately she might dislike the fact of Bink's newly masculine drives. His father had given him a viable option. Suddenly he realized he could do without wild oats.

"Her name is Sabrina," Roland said.

A light ahead brought Bink back to the present. Someone was standing by Justin Tree, holding a magic lamp. "It is all right, Bink," Justin's voice said in the air beside him. "Sabrina brought help, but it wasn't needed. Did you get the sponge?"

"I got it," Bink said.

So his little adventure had been no adventure at all. Just like his life. As Sabrina helped him pack the sponge around Justin's wound, Bink realized that he had decided. He could not go on this way, a nonentity; he would go to see the Good Magician Humfrey and learn what his own magic talent was.

He glanced up. His eyes caught those of Sabrina, glowing by the light of the lamp. She smiled. She was even more lovely now than she had been when he first met her, so many years ago, when they had both been adolescents, and she had always been true to him. There was no question: Bink's father had been correct about the advantages—and frustrations—of a real live girl. Now it was up to Bink to do what he had to do—to become a real live man.

Chapter 2. Centaur

Bink set off on foot, wearing a stuffed knapsack and bearing a good hunting knife and a home-cut staff. His mother had urged him to let them hire a guide for him, but Bink had had to refuse; the "guide" would really be a guard to keep him safe. How would he ever live that down? Yet the wilderness beyond the village had 'its hazards for the traveler unfamiliar with it; few people hiked it alone. He really would have been better off with a guide.

He could have had transport on a winged steed, but that would have been expensive, and risky in its own fashion. Griffins were often surly creatures. He preferred to make his own way on the secure ground, if only to prove that he could, despite the fancied snickers of the village youths. Jama wasn't snickering much at the moment—he was laboring under the mortification spell the village Elders had put on him for his attack on Justin Tree—but there were other snickerers.

At least Roland had understood. "One day you'll discover that the opinions of worthless people are worthless," he had murmured to Bink. "You have to do it your own way. I comprehend that, and wish you well—on your own."

Bink had a map, and knew which path led to the castle of the Good Magician Humfrey. Rather, which path *had* led there; the truth was that Humfrey was a crotchety old man who preferred isolation in the wilderness. Periodically he moved his castle, or changed the approaches to it by magical means, so that one never could be sure of finding it. Regardless, Bink intended to track the Magician to his lair.

The first leg of his journey was familiar. He had spent his whole life in the North Village and explored most of its surrounding bypaths. Hardly any dangerous flora or fauna remained in the immediate vicinity, and those that were potential threats were well known.

He stopped to drink at a water hole near a huge needle cactus. As he approached, the plant quivered, making ready to fire on him. "Hold, friend," Bink said commandingly. "I am of the North Village." The cactus, restrained by the pacification formula, withheld its deadly barrage. The key word was "friend"; the thing certainly was not a friend, but it had to obey the geis laid on it. No genuine stranger would know this, so the cactus was an effective guard against intruders. Animals below a certain size it ignored. Since most creatures had to have water sooner or later, this was a convenient compromise. Some areas had been ravaged occasionally by wild griffins and other large beasts, but not the North Village. One experience with an irate needler more than sufficed as a lesson for the animal lucky enough to survive it.

Another hour's swift march brought him to less-familiar territory, by definition less safe. What did the people of this area use to guard their water holes? Unicorns trained to impale strangers? Well, he would find out soon enough.

The rolling hills and small lakes gave way to rougher terrain, and strange plants appeared. Some had tall antennas that swiveled to orient on him from a distance; others emitted subtly attractive crooning noises, but had branches bearing powerful pincers. Bink walked at a safe distance around them, taking no unnecessary risks. Once he thought he spied an animal about the size of a man, but it had eight spiderlike legs. He moved on rapidly and silently.

He saw a number of birds, but these were of little concern. Since they could fly, they had little need for

defensive magic against man, so he had no cause to be
wary of them—unless he saw any big birds; those might
consider him prey. Once he spied the monstrous form
of a roc in the distance, and cowered down, letting it
wing on without seeing him. So long as the birds were
small, he actually preferred their company, for the insects and bugs were at times aggressive.

In fact, a cloud of gnats formed around his head,
casting a mass sweat spell that made him even more
uncomfortable. Insects had an uncanny ability to dis-
cern those with no magic for defense. Maybe they
merely used trial and error, getting away with whatever
they could. Bink looked about for bug-repellent weeds,
but found none. Weeds were never where one wanted
them. His temper was getting short as the sweat
streamed down his nose and into his eyes and mouth.
Then two little sucker-saps swooped in, sucking up the
gnats, and he had relief. Yes, he liked little birds!

He made about ten miles in three hours, and was tiring. He was in good condition generally, but was not
used to sustained marching with a heavy pack. Every so
often he got a twinge from the ankle he had turned at
Lookout Rock. Not a bad twinge, for it turned out to be
a minor hurt; just enough to keep him cautious.

He sat on a hillock, first making sure it contained no
itch ants, though it did have a needle cactus. He approached this very cautiously, uncertain as to whether it
had been tamed by the spell. "Friend," he said, and just
to make sure he spilled a few drops of water from his
canteen onto the soil for its roots to taste. Apparently it
was all right; it did not let fly at him. Even wild things
often responded to common courtesy and respect.

He broke out the lunch lovingly packed by his
mother. He had food for two days—enough to get him
to the Magician's castle under ordinary circumstances.
Not that things in Xanth were usually ordinary! He
hoped to extend that by staying overnight with some
friendly farmer. He would need food for the return trip,
too, and in any event did not relish the notion of sleep-

ing outdoors. Night brought out special magic, and it could be ugly. He did not want to find himself arguing cases with a ghoul or ogre, since the case would most likely be the proper disposition of his human bones: whether they should be consumed live, while the marrow was fresh and sweet, or crunched after being allowed to age for a week after death. Different predators had different tastes.

He bit into the cressmato sandwich. Something crunched, startling him, but it was not a bone, just a flavorstem. Bianca certainly knew how to make a sandwich. Roland always teased her about that, claiming she had mastered the art under the tutelage of an old sandwitch. Yet it was unfunny to Bink, for it meant he was still dependent on her—until he finished what she had prepared and foraged for himself.

A crumb dropped—and vanished. Bink looked around and spied a chipmouse chewing busily. It had conjured the crumb ten feet, avoiding the risk of close approach. Bink smiled. "I wouldn't hurt you, chip."

Then he heard something: the pounding of hooves. Some big animal was charging, or a mounted man approached. Either could mean trouble. Bink stuffed a chunk of wingcow cheese into his mouth, suffering a brief vision of the cow flying up to graze on the treetops after being relieved of her load of milk. He closed up his pack and shrugged his arms into the straps. He took his long staff in both hands. He might have to fight or run.

The creature came into sight. It was a centaur, the body of a horse with the upper torso of a man. He was naked, in the manner of his kind, with muscular flanks, broad shoulders, and an ornery visage.

Bink held his staff before him, ready for defense but not aggressively so. He had little confidence in his ability to outfight the massive creature, and no hope of outrunning him. But maybe the centaur was not unfriendly, despite appearances—or did not know that Bink had no magic.

The centaur pulled up close. He held his bow ready, an arrow nocked. He looked formidable indeed. Bink had developed a lot of respect for centaurs in school. This was obviously no elder sage, however, but a youthful brute. "You are trespassing," the centaur said. "Move off this range."

"Now wait," Bink said reasonably. "I'm a traveler, following the established path. It's a public right-of-way."

"Move off," the centaur repeated, his bow swinging around menacingly.

Bink was normally a good-natured fellow, but he had a certain ornery streak that manifested in times of stress. This journey was vitally important to him. This was a public path, and he had had his fill of deferring to magical menaces. The centaur was a magical creature, having no existence in the Mundane world beyond Xanth, by all accounts. Thus Bink's aggravation against magic was stirred up again, and he did something foolish.

"Go soak your tail!" he snapped.

The centaur blinked. Now he looked even huskier, his shoulders broader, his chest deeper, and his equine body even more dynamic than before. Obviously he was not accustomed to such language, at least not directed at him, and the experience startled him. In due course, however, he made the requisite mental and emotional adjustments, signaled by an awe-inspiring knotting of oversized muscles. A deep red, almost purple wash of color ascended from the hairy horse base up through the bare stomach and scarred chest, accelerating and brightening as it funneled into the narrower neck and finally dying the head and ugly face explosively. As that inexorable tide of red rage ignited his ears and penetrated to his brain, the centaur acted.

His bow swung about, the nocked arrow drawing back. As it bore on Bink, the arrow let fly.

Naturally, Bink wasn't there. He had had ample opportunity to read the storm signals. As the bow moved, he ducked under. Then he straightened up right under the centaur's nose and brought his staff around in a hard swing. It fetched the creature a smart rap on the shoulder, doing no actual harm. But it had to sting severely.

The centaur emitted a bellow of sheer impassioned rage. He whipped his bow around with his left hand while his right hand dived for the quiver of arrows hanging on his equine shoulder. But now Bink's staff was tangled in his bow.

The creature threw down the bow. The action ripped the staff out of Bink's hands. The centaur made a huge fist. Bink scurried around to the rear as that fist swung at him. But the rear of the centaur was no safer than the front; one leg licked back violently. Through a freak of timing, it missed Bink and clubbed into the trunk of the needle cactus.

The cactus responded with a barrage of flying needles. Even as the hoof struck, Bink threw himself flat on the ground. The needles overshot him and plunked into the handsome posterior of the centaur. Once more Bink had lucked out: he was miraculously untouched by either hoof or needles.

The centaur neighed with truly amazing volume. Those needles *hurt;* each one was two inches long, and barbed, and a hundred of them decorated the glistening surface, tacking the tail to the donkey, as it were. Had the creature been facing the cactus, he could have been blinded or killed as the barbs punctured his face and neck; he was lucky, too, though he hardly seemed to appreciate his fortune at the moment.

Now there were no bounds to the centaur's anger. An unholy contortion of utter rage ravaged his homely face. He did a massive prance, his hindquarters rising and descending in an arc, bringing his front part abruptly adjacent to Bink. Two crushingly powerful arms shot out, and two horny hands closed about Bink's relatively puny neck. Slowly they tightened, with viselike deliberation. Bink, lifted off the ground so that his feet dangled,

was helpless. He knew he was about to be strangled; he
could not even plead for mercy, for his air and much of
his blood were cut off.

"Chester!" a female voice cried.

The centaur stiffened. This did Bink no good.

"Chester, you put that man down this instant!" the
voice said peremptorily. "Do you want an interspecies
incident?"

"But, Cherie," Chester protested, his color abating
several shades. "He's an intruder, and he asked for it."

"He's on the King's path," Cherie said. "Travelers
are immune to molestation; you know that. Now let him
go!"

The lady centaur hardly seemed to be in a position to
enforce her demand, but Chester slowly bowed to her
authority. "Can't I just squeeze him a little?" he begged,
squeezing a little. Bink's eyeballs almost popped out of
their sockets.

"If you do, I'll never run with you again. Down!"

"Aaaww . . ." Reluctantly Chester eased off. Bink
slid to the ground, reeling. What a fool he had been to
tangle with this brute!

The female centaur caught him as he swayed. "Poor
thing!" she exclaimed, cushioning his head against a
plush pillow. "Are you all right?"

Bink opened his mouth, gagged, and tried again. It
seemed that his crushed throat would never unkink.
"Yes," he croaked.

"Who are you? What happened to your hand? Did
Chester—"

"No," Bink said hastily. "He didn't bite off my finger. That's a childhood injury. See, it's long since healed
over."

She inspected it carefully, running her surprisingly
delicate fingers over it. "Yes, I see. Still . . ."

"I—I am Bink of the North Village," he said. He
turned his head to face her—and discovered the nature
of the pillow he rested against. *Oh no, not again!* he
thought. *Will I* always *be babied by women?* Centaur

females were smaller than the males, but still stood somewhat taller than human beings. Their humanoid portions were somewhat better endowed. He jerked his head away from her bare front. It was bad enough being babied by his mother, let alone a lady centaur. "I am traveling south to see the Magician Humfrey."

Cherie nodded. She was a beautiful creature, both as horse and as human, with glossy flanks and a remarkable human forefigure. Her face was attractive, only very slightly long of nose in the equine manner. Her brown human hair trailed all the way down to her saddle region, balancing her similarly flowing tail. "And this ass waylaid you?"

"Well—" Bink looked at Chester, again noting the rippling muscle beneath the deadly glower. What would happen when the filly departed? "It was—it was a misunderstanding."

"I'll bet," Cherie said. But Chester relaxed a trifle. Evidently he did not want to tangle with his girlfriend. Bink could readily appreciate why. If Cherie was not the loveliest and spunkiest centaur of the herd, she was surely close to it.

"I'll just be moving on now," Bink said. He could have done this at the outset, allowing Chester to run him off in a southerly direction. He had been as much to blame for the altercation as the centaur. "Sorry about the problem." He held out his hand to Chester.

Chester showed his teeth, which were more like horse's teeth than human ones. He made a big fist.

"Chester!" Cherie snapped. Then, as the centaur guiltily relaxed his fist: "What happened to your flank?"

The male's complexion darkened again, but not precisely with rage this time. He trotted his damaged posterior around to avoid the inquiring gaze of the female. Bink had almost forgotten about the needles. They must still be hurting—and it would hurt more to yank them all out. What a pain in the tail! A most awkward locale to discuss in mixed company. He almost felt sympathy for the surly creature.

Chester suppressed his assorted reactions and with fine discipline took Bink's hand. "I hope everything comes out all right in the end," Bink said, with a smile that became a bit broader than intended. In fact, he feared it resembled a smirk. And abruptly he knew he shouldn't have chosen those particular words or that particular expression on this particular occasion.

Something homicidal reddened the whites of the centaur's eyes. "Quite all right," he gritted through the grinding of clenched teeth. His hand began to squeeze—but his eyes were not yet so bloodshot as to miss the filly's glare. The fingers relaxed unwillingly. Another close call. Bink could have had his fingerbones pulped in that grip.

"I'll give you a lift," Cherie decided. "Chester, put him on my back."

Chester put his hands under Bink's elbows and hoisted him like a feather. For a moment Bink feared he would be thrown fifty feet . . . but Cherie's fair eye was still on them, and so he landed safely and gently on the lady's back.

"Is that your staff?" she inquired, glancing at the tangled staff and bow. And Chester, without even being directed, lifted the staff and returned it to Bink, who tucked it slantwise between his back and his pack for easy transport.

"Put your arms around my waist, so you won't fall off when I move," Cherie said.

Good advice. Bink was inexperienced at riding, and there was no saddle. Very few honest horses remained in Xanth. Unicorns were very touchy about being mounted, and the winged horses were almost impossible to catch or tame. Once, when Bink was a child, a horsefly had been singed by a dragon, losing its flight feathers, and had had to prostitute itself so far as to give the villagers short rides in exchange for food and protection.

The moment it had recovered, it had flown away. That had been Bink's only prior riding experience.

He leaned forward. The staff interfered, preventing him from bending his back sufficiently. He reached back to draw it out—and it fell out of his hands to the ground. There was a snort from Chester that sounded suspiciously like humor. But the centaur picked it up and returned it to him. Bink tucked it under his arm this time, leaned forward again, and hugged Cherie's slender waist, heedless of Chester's renewed glower. Some things were worth the risk—such as getting out of here in a hurry.

"You go to the vet and get those needles out of your—" Cherie began, speaking over her shoulder to the male.

"Right away!" Chester interrupted. He waited for her to start, then turned and cantered off in the direction he had come from, a little awkwardly. Probably each motion inflamed his hindquarters more.

Cherie trotted down the path. "Chester is really a good creature at heart," she said apologetically. "But he does tend to be a bit arrogant, and he gets his tail all knotted up when balked. We've had some trouble with outlaws recently, and—"

"Human outlaws?" Bink asked.

"Yes. Kids from the north, doing mischief magic, gassing our livestock, shooting swords into trees, making dangerous pits seem to appear under our feet, that sort of thing. So naturally Chester assumed—"

"I know the culprits," Bink said. "I had a scrape with them myself. They've been grounded now. If I had known they were coming down here—"

"There just doesn't seem to be much discipline on the range these days," she said. "According to the Covenant, your King is supposed to keep order. But recently—"

"Our King is getting old," Bink explained. "He's losing his power, and there's a lot of trouble cropping up. He used to be a major Magician, a storm brewer."

"We know," she agreed. "When the fireflies infested our oatfields, he generated a storm that rained five days and drowned them all. Of course, it also ruined our crops—but the flies were doing that already. Every day new fires! At least we were able to replant without further molestation. We are not forgetting the help he rendered. So we don't want to make an issue of it—but I don't know how much longer stallions like Chester are going to put up with these annoyances. That's why I wanted to talk with you—maybe when you go home, if you could call things to the attention of the King—"

"I don't think that would work. I'm sure the King wants to keep order; he just doesn't have the power any more."

"Then perhaps it is time for a new King."

"He's getting senile. That means he hasn't got the sense to step down, and won't admit there's any problem."

"Yes, but problems don't go away by being ignored!" She made a delicate feminine snort. "Something has to be done."

"Maybe I can get some advice from Magician Humfrey," Bink said. "It's a serious business, deposing a King; I don't think the Elders would go for it. He did do good work in his prime. And there's really nobody to replace him. You know that only a great Magician can be King."

"Yes, of course. We centaurs are all scholars, you know."

"Sorry, I forgot. Our village school is run by a centaur. I just wasn't thinking of that, in the wilderness."

"Understandable—though I'd call this range, not wilderness. I specialize in humanoid history, and Chester studies horsepower applications. Others are legal scholars, experts in natural sciences, philosophers—" She broke off. "Now hang on. There's a trench up ahead I've got to hurdle."

Bink had been relaxing, but now he leaned forward again and clasped his hands tightly around her waist.

She had a sleek, comfortable back, but it was too easy to slide off. However, if she weren't a centaur, he would never have had the nerve to assume such a position!

Cherie picked up speed, galloping down the hill, and the motion made him bounce alarmingly. Peering ahead under her arm, he saw the trench. Trench? It was a gorge, some ten feet across, rushing up at them. Now he was more than alarmed; he was frightened. His hands became sweaty, and he began to slide off the side. Then she leaped with a single mighty spasm of her haunches and sailed up and across.

Bink slipped further. He had a glimpse of the stony bottom of the trench; then they landed. The jolt caused him to slide around even more. His arms scrambled desperately for a more secure hold—and wandered into distinctly awkward territory. Yet if he let go—

Cherie caught him around the waist and set him on the ground. "Easy," she said. "We made it."

Bink blushed. "I—I'm sorry. I started to fall, and just grabbed—"

"I know. I felt your weight shift as I leaped. If you had done it on purpose, I'd have dropped you into the trench." And in that instant she looked uncomfortably like Chester. He believed her: she could drop a man into a trench if she had reason to. Centaurs were tough creatures!

"Maybe I'd better walk now."

"No—there's another trench. They've been opening up recently."

"Well, I could climb down one side and up the other, carefully. It would take longer, but—"

"No—there are nickelpedes at the bottom."

Bink quailed. Nickelpedes were like centipedes, but about five times as large and considerably more deadly. Their myriad legs could cling to vertical rock faces, and their pincers could gouge out disks of flesh an inch across. They inhabited shadowed crevices, not liking direct sunlight. Even dragons hesitated to walk through ditches known to be infested by nickelpedes, and for good reason.

"The cracks have been opening up recently," Cherie continued as she kneeled to permit Bink to mount her again. He picked up his dropped staff and used it to help him climb. "I'm afraid there's big magic brewing somewhere, spreading throughout Xanth, causing discord in animal, vegetable, and mineral. I'll get you across that next trench; then it's beyond centaur territory."

It hadn't occurred to him that there would be such barriers. They didn't show on his map. The trail was supposed to be clear and reasonably safe throughout. But the map had been made years ago, and these cracks in the ground were new, Cherie said. Nothing in Xanth was permanent, and travel was always somewhat risky. He was lucky he had obtained the lady centaur's help.

The landscape changed, as if the trench separated one type of place from another. Before it had been rolling hills and fields; now it was forest. The path became narrower, crowded by huge mock-pine trees, and the forest floor was a red-brown carpet of mock needles. Here and there were patches of light green ferns, which seemed to thrive where weeds could not, and regions of dark green moss. A cold wind gusted through, tousling Cherie's hair and mane, carrying strands back against Bink. It was quiet here, and there was a pleasant piney smell. He felt like dismounting and lying down in a bed of moss, just appreciating this peaceful spot.

"Don't do it," Cherie warned.

Bink jumped. "I didn't know centaurs practiced magic!"

"Magic?" she inquired, and he knew she was frowning.

"You read my mind."

She laughed. "Hardly. We do no magic. But we do know the effect these woods have on humans. It's the peace spell the trees make to protect themselves from getting chopped."

"Nothing wrong in that," Bink said. "I wasn't going to chop them anyway."

"They don't trust in your good intentions. I'll show you." She stepped carefully off the beaten trail, her hooves sinking into the soft pine-needle floor. She threaded her way between several dagger-spoked buck-spruce trees, passed a thin snake palm, which didn't even bother to hiss at her, and stopped near a tangle willow. Not too near; everyone knew better than that. "There," she murmured.

Bink looked where her hand pointed. A human skeleton lay on the ground. "Murder?" he asked, shivering.

"No, just sleep. He came to rest here, as you wished to do just now, and never got up the gumption to depart. Complete peace is an insidious thing."

"Yes . . ." he breathed. No violence, no distress—just loss of initiative. Why bother to work and eat when it was so much easier merely to relax? If a person wanted to commit suicide, this would be the ideal manner. But he had reason to live—so far.

"That's part of why I like Chester," Cherie said. "He'll never succumb to anything like this."

That was a certainty. There was no peace in Chester. Cherie herself would never succumb, Bink thought, though she was considerably more gentle. Bink felt the lassitude, despite the sight of the skeleton, but she was evidently able to resist the spell. Maybe the biology of the centaurs differed enough—or maybe she had savagery in her soul that her angelic form and pleasant words masked. Most likely a bit of both. "Let's get out of here."

She laughed. "Don't worry. I'll see you safely through it. But don't come back this way alone. Travel with an enemy, if you can find one; that's best."

"Better than a friend?"

"Friends are peaceful," she explained.

Oh. That did make sense. He'd never relax under a pine tree if he were with someone like Jama; he'd be too afraid of getting a sword in his gut. But what an ironic necessity: to locate an enemy to accompany one to walk through a peaceful forest! "Magic makes strange companions," he murmured.

This peace spell also explained why there was so little other magic here. The plants did not need individual defensive spells; no one was going to attack. Even the tangle tree had seemed quiescent, though he was sure it would make a grab when it had the chance, since that was the way it fed. Interesting how quickly magic faded when the immediate imperative of survival abated. No—there was magic, strong magic; it was the communal magic of the entire forest, with each plant contributing its modicum. If a person could figure out a way to nullify the effect in himself, perhaps with a countercharm, he could live here in absolute safety. That was worth remembering.

They threaded their way back to the path and resumed travel. Bink almost slid off his perch twice, falling asleep, each time awakening with a shock. He would never have made it out of here alone. He was glad to see the pine forest thin, shifting into hardwoods. He felt more alert, more violent, and that was good. Harder wood, harder feelings.

"I wonder who that was back there," Bink mused.

"Oh, I know," Cherie answered. "He was one of the Last Wave, who got lost, wandered in here, and decided to rest. Forever!"

"But the Lastwavers were savage!" Bink said. "They slaughtered indiscriminately."

"All Waves were savage, when they came, with one exception," she said. "We centaurs know; we were here before the First Wave. We had to fight all of you—until the Covenant. You didn't have magic, but you had weapons and numbers and vicious cunning. Many of us died."

"My ancestors were First Wave," Bink said with a certain pride. "We always had magic, and we never fought the centaurs."

"Now don't get aggressive, human, just because I

took you out of the peace pines," she cautioned. "You do not have our knowledge of history."

Bink realized that he'd better moderate his tone if he wanted to continue the ride. And he did want to continue; Cherie was pleasant company, and she obviously knew all the local magic, so that she was able to avoid all threats. Last and most, she was giving his tired legs a good rest while bearing him forward rapidly. Already she had taken him a good ten miles. "I'm sorry. It was a matter of family pride."

"Well, that's no bad thing," she said, mollified. She made her way delicately across a wooden trestle over a bubbling brook.

Suddenly Bink was thirsty. "May we stop for a drink?" he asked.

She snorted again, a very horselike sound. "Not here! Anyone who drinks from that water becomes a fish."

"A fish?" Suddenly Bink was twice as glad to have this guide. He surely would have drunk otherwise. Unless she was merely telling him that to tease him, or trying to scare him away from this area. "Why?"

"The river is trying to restock itself. It was cleaned out by the Evil Magician Trent twenty-one years ago."

Bink remained a bit skeptical about inanimate magic, especially of that potency. How could a river desire anything? Still, he remembered how Lookout Rock had saved itself from being broken up. Better to play it safe and assume that some features of the landscape could cast spells.

Meanwhile, the reference to Trent preempted his attention. "The Evil Magician was here? I thought he was a phenomenon of our own village."

"Trent was everywhere," she said. "He wanted us centaurs to support him, and when we balked—because of the Covenant, you know, not to interfere in human business—he showed us his power by changing every fish in this river into a lightning bug. Then he departed.

I think he figured that those shocking buggers would force us to change our minds."

"Why didn't he change the fish into a human army, and try to conquer you that way?"

"No good, Bink. They might have had the bodies of men, but their minds would have remained fish. They would have made very wishy-washy soldiers, and even if they had been good soldiers, they would hardly have served the man who had put them under that enchantment. They would have attacked Trent."

"Um, yes. I wasn't thinking. So he transformed them into lightning bugs and got well away from there so they couldn't shock him. So they went for the next best thing."

"Yes. It was a bad time for us. Oh, those bugs were a pain! They pestered us in clouds, scorching us with their little lightning bolts. I've still got scars on my—" She paused, grimacing. "On my tail." It was obviously a euphemism.

"What did you do?" Bink inquired, fascinated, glancing back to see whether he could locate the scars. What he could see seemed flawless.

"Trent was exiled soon after that, and we got Humfrey to abate the spell."

"But the Good Magician isn't a transformer."

"No, but he told us where to find repellent magic to drive off the flies. Denied our electrocooked flesh, the scourge soon died out. Good information is as good as good action, and the Good Magician certainly had the information."

"That's why I'm going to him," Bink agreed. "But he charges a year's service for a spell."

"You're telling us? Three hundred head of centaur— one year each. What a job!"

"All of you had to pay? What did you have to do?"

"We are not permitted to tell," she said diffidently.

Now Bink was doubly curious, but he knew better than to ask again. A centaur's given word was inviolate. But what could Humfrey have needed done that he could not do himself via one of his hundred spells? Or at least by means of his good information? Humfrey was basically a divinator; anything he didn't know, he could find out, and that gave him enormous power. Probably the reason the village Elders had not asked the Good Magician what to do about their senile King was that they knew what he would answer: depose the King and install a new, young, fresh Magician instead. That they obviously weren't ready to do. Even if they could find such a young Magician to serve.

Well, there were many mysteries and many problems in Xanth, and it was hardly given to Bink to know of them all or to solve any. He had learned long ago to bow, however ungraciously, to the inevitable.

They were past the river now, and climbing. The trees were closing in more thickly, their great round roots ridging across the path. No hostile magic threatened; either the centaurs had cleaned out the area, the way the villagers had cleaned out Bink's home region, or Cherie knew this path so well that she avoided spells automatically, without seeming to. Probably some of both.

Life itself, he thought, involved many alternate explanations for perplexing questions, and was generally "some of both." Few things were hard and fast in Xanth.

"What was that history you know that I don't?" Bink inquired, becoming bored by the trail.

"About the Waves of human colonization? We have records of them all. Since the Shield and the Covenant, things have quieted down; the Waves were terrors."

"Not the Firstwavers!" Bink said loyally. "We were peaceful."

"That's what I mean. You are peaceful now, except for a few of your young hoodlums, so you assume your ancestors were peaceful then. But my ancestors found it otherwise. They would have been happier had man never discovered Xanth."

"My teacher was a centaur," Bink said. "He never said anything about—"

"He'd have been fired if he had told you the truth."

Bink felt uneasy. "You're not teasing me, are you? I'm not looking for any trouble. I have a very curious mind, but I've already had more trouble than I care for."

She turned her head around to fix him with a gentle stare. Her torso twisted from the human waist to facilitate the motion. The torque was impressive; her midsection was more limber than that of a human girl, perhaps because it was harder for a centaur to turn her whole body around. But if she had a human lower section to match the upper section, what a creature she would be!

"Your teacher didn't lie to you. A centaur never lies. He merely edited his information, on orders from the King, so as not to force on the impressionable minds of children things their parents did not want them to hear. Education has ever been thus."

"Oh, I wasn't implying any slight on his integrity," Bink said quickly. "I liked him, as a matter of fact; he was the only one who didn't get fed up with all my questions. I learned a lot from him. But I guess I didn't ask about history much. I was more preoccupied with something he couldn't tell me—but at least he did tell me about the Magician Humfrey."

"What is your question for Humfrey, if I may ask?"

What difference did it make? "I have no magic," he confessed. "At least, I seem to have none. All through my childhood I was at a disadvantage because I couldn't use magic to compete. I could run faster than anybody else, but the kid who could levitate still won the race. Stuff like that."

"Centaurs get along perfectly well without magic," she pointed out. "We wouldn't take magic if it were offered."

Bink did not believe that, but did not make an issue of it. "Humans have a different attitude, I guess. When I got older, it got worse. Now I will be exiled if I don't show some magic talent. I'm hoping Magician Humfrey can—well, if I do have magic, it means I can stay and marry my girl and have some pride. Finally."

Cherie nodded. "I suspected it was something like that. I suppose if I were in your situation I could choke down the necessity of having magic, though I really think your culture's values are distorted. You should base your citizenship on superior qualities of personality and achievement, not on—"

"Exactly," Bink agreed fervently.

She smiled. "You really should have been a centaur." She shook her head so that her hair flung out prettily. "You have undertaken a hazardous journey."

"Not more hazardous than the one to the Mundane world that will otherwise be forced on me."

She nodded again. "Very well. You have satisfied my curiosity; I'll satisfy yours. I'll tell you the whole truth about the human intrusion into Xanth. But I don't expect you to like it much."

"I don't expect to like the truth about myself much," Bink said ruefully. "I might as well know whatever there is to know."

"For thousands of years Xanth was a comparatively peaceful land," she said, assuming the somewhat pedantic tone he remembered from his school days. Probably every centaur was at heart a teacher. "There was magic, very strong magic—but no unnecessary viciousness. We centaurs were the dominant species, but, as you know, we have absolutely no magic. We *are* magic. I suppose we migrated here from Mundania originally—but that was so long ago it is lost even to our records."

Something tripped over in Bink's mind. "I wonder if that really is true—about magic creatures not being able to work spells? I saw a chipmouse conjure a crumb of bread—"

"Oh? Are you sure it wasn't a chip*munk*? That is a natural creature, according to our taxonomy, so it might work magic."

"You tax animals?" Bink asked, amazed.

"Taxonomy," she repeated with an indulgent smile. "The classification of living things, another centaur specialty."

Oh. Bink considered, embarrassed. "I thought it was a chipmouse, but I'm not quite certain now."

"Actually, we're not quite certain either," she admitted. "It may be that some magical creatures can work magic. But, as a general rule, a creature either *does* magic or *is* magic, not both. Which is just as well—think of the havoc a dragon Magician could make!"

Bink thought of it. He shuddered. "Let's get back to the history lesson," he suggested.

"About a thousand years ago the first human tribe discovered Xanth. They thought it was just another peninsula. They moved in and cut down the trees and slaughtered the animals. There was more than enough magic here to repulse them, but Xanth had never been subjected to such callous, systematic ravage before, and we did not quite believe it. We thought the humans would leave soon.

"But then they realized that Xanth was magic. They saw the animals levitating and the trees moving their branches. They hunted the unicorns and griffins. If you wonder why those big animals hate people, let me assure you they have good reason: their ancestors would not have survived if they'd tried to be friendly. The First-wavers were nonmagical creatures in a land of spells, and after they got over the initial shock they liked it."

"Now that's wrong!" Bink exclaimed. "Humans have the very strongest magic. Look at all the great Magicians. You yourself told me just now how Evil Magician Trent changed all the fish—"

"Pipe down before I buck you off!" Cherie snapped. Her tail swished menacingly past Bink's ear. "You don't know the quarter of it. Of course humans have magic now. That's part of their problem. But not at the start."

Bink backed down again. It was increasingly easy to do; he liked this centaur lady very well. She was answering questions he hadn't even thought to ask yet. "Sorry. This is new to me."

"You remind me of Chester. I'll bet you're awful stubborn, too."

"Yes," Bink said contritely.

She laughed, and it sounded a bit like neighing. "I do like you, human. I hope you find your"—she pursed her lips distastefully—"magic." Then she flashed a sunny smile, and as quickly sobered. "Those Firstwavers had no magic, and when they found out what magic could do they were fascinated but a bit afraid of it. A number of them perished in a lake that had a drown spell, and some ran afoul of dragons, and when they met the first basilisk—"

"Are there still basilisks?" Bink inquired worriedly, abruptly remembering the omen of the chameleon. It had stared at him in the guise of a basilisk just before it died, as if its spell had backfired. He had yet to be sure of the meaning of that sequence.

"Yes, there are—but not many," she answered. "Both humans and centaurs labored to stamp them out. Their glance is fatal to us too, you know. Now they hide, because they know that the first intelligent creature killed that way will bring an avenging army of mirror-masked warriors down on them. A basilisk is no match for a forewarned man or centaur; it's just a small winged lizard, you know, with the head and claws of a chicken. Not very intelligent. Not that it usually needs to be."

"Say!" Bink exclaimed. "Maybe that's the missing factor—intelligence. A creature can do magic or be magic or be smart—or any two of the three, but never all three. So a chipmouse might conjure, but not a smart dragon."

She turned her head about again to face him. "That's a novel idea. You're pretty smart yourself. I'll have to think about it. But until we verify it, don't go into the central wilderness unprotected; there just might be a smart spell-throwing monster in there."

"I won't go into the wilderness," Bink promised. "At least, I won't stray from the cleared path through it, until I get to the Magician's castle. I don't want any lizards looking death at me."

"Your ancestors were more aggressive," Cherie remarked. "That's why so many of them died. But they conquered Xanth, and formed an enclave where magic was banned. They liked the country and the uses of magic, you see, but they didn't want it too close to home. So they burned the forest there, killed all magical animals and plants, and built a great stone wall."

"The ruins!" Bink exclaimed. "I thought those old stones were from an enemy camp."

"They are from the First Wave," she insisted.

"But I am descended from—"

"I said you wouldn't like this."

"I don't," he agreed. "But I want to hear it. How can my ancestors have—"

"They settled in their walled village and planted Mundane crops and herded Mundane cattle. You know—beans and wingless cows. They married the women they had brought along or that they could raid from the closest Mundane settlements, and had children. Xanth was a good land, even in that region expunged of magic. But then something amazing happened."

Cherie turned to face him again, glancing obliquely in a manner that would have been most fetching in a human girl. In fact, it was fetching in a centaur girl, especially if he squinted so as to see only her human portion: splendidly fetching, despite his knowledge that centaurs lived longer than humans, so that she was probably fifty years old. She looked twenty—a twenty that few humans ever achieved. No halter would hold this filly!

"What happened?" he asked, catering to her evident desire for an intellectual response. Centaurs were good storytellers, and they did like a good audience.

"Their children came up magic," she said.

Aha! "So the Firstwavers *were* magic!"

"No, they were not. The land of Xanth is magic. It's an environmental effect. But it works much better with children, who are more formative, and it works best with babies conceived and birthed here. Adults, even of long residence, tend to suppress the talents they have, because they 'know better.' But children accept what is. So not only do they have more natural talent, they use it with more enthusiasm."

"I never knew that," he said. "My folks have much more magic than I do. Some of my ancestors were Magicians. But me—" He sobered. "I'm afraid I was a terrible disappointment to my parents. By rights I should have had very strong magic, maybe even have been a Magician myself. Instead . . ."

Cherie discreetly did not comment. "At first the humans were shocked. But soon they accepted it, and even encouraged the development of special talents. One of the youngsters had the ability to transform lead into gold. They ravaged the hills, searching for lead, and finally had to send a mission to obtain it from Mundania. It was almost as if lead had become more valuable than gold."

"But Xanth has no dealings with the Mundane world."

"You keep forgetting: this is ancient history."

"Sorry again. I wouldn't interrupt so much if I weren't so interested."

"You are an excellent audience," she said, and he felt pleased. "Most humans would refuse to listen at all, because it is not a complimentary history. Not to your kind."

"I'd probably be less open-minded if I didn't face exile myself," he admitted. "About all I have to work with is my brain and body, so I'd better not fool myself."

"A commendable philosophy. You are, incidentally, getting a longer ride than I planned, because you pay such good, responsive attention. At any rate, they got the lead out—but paid a hideous price. Because the

Mundanes of Mundania learned about the magic. They were true to their type: greedy and rapacious. The notion of cheap gold sent them into a frenzy. They invaded, stormed the wall, and killed all the First Wave men and children."

"But—" Bink protested, horrified.

"These were the Secondwavers," Cherie said gently. "They saved the Firstwaver women, you see. Because the Second Wave was an all-male army. They thought there was a machine to convert the lead into gold, or an alchemical process organized by a secret formula. They didn't really believe in magic; that was just a convenient term to describe the unknown. So they didn't realize that the lead was converted into gold by the magic of a child—until too late. They had destroyed what they had come for."

"Horrible!" Bink said. "You mean I am descended from—"

"From the rape of a First Wave mother. Yes—there is no other way you can authenticate your lineage. We centaurs had never liked the Firstwavers, but we were sorry for them then. The Secondwavers were worse. They were literal pirates, rapacious. Had we known, we would have helped the Firstwavers fight them off. Our archers could have ambushed them—" She shrugged. Centaur archery was legendary; no need to belabor the point.

"Now the invaders settled," she continued after a pause. "They sent their own archers all over Xanth, killing—" She broke off, and Bink knew how keenly she felt the irony of her kind being prey to the inferior archery of human beings. She gave a little shudder that almost dislodged him, and forced herself to continue. "Killing centaurs for meat. Not until we organized and ambushed their camp, putting shafts through half of them, did they agree to let us alone. Even after that, they did not honor their agreement very well, for they had precious little sense of honor."

"And their children had magic," Bink continued,

seeing it now. "And so the Thirdwavers invaded and killed off the Secondwavers——"

"Yes, this happened after several generations, though it was every bit as vicious when it came. The Second-wavers had become tolerably good neighbors, all things considered, by then. Again, only the women were saved—and not many of them. Because they had been in Xanth all their lives, their magic was strong. They used it to eliminate their rapist husbands one by one in ways that could not be directly traced to the women. But their victory was their defeat, for now they had no families at all. So they had to invite in more Mundanes——"

"This is ghastly!" Bink said. "I am descended from a thousand years of ignominy."

"Not entirely. The history of man in Xanth is brutal, but not without redeeming values, even greatness. The Second Wave women organized, and brought in only the finest men they could locate. Strong, just, kind, intelligent men, who understood the background but came more from principle than from greed. They promised to keep the secret and to uphold the values of Xanth. They were Mundanes, but they were noble ones."

"The Fourthwavers!" Bink exclaimed. "The finest of them all."

"Yes. The Xanth women were widows and victims of rape and finally murderesses. Some were old, or scarred physically and emotionally by the campaign. But they all had strong magic and iron determination; they were the survivors of the cruel upheaval that had wiped out all other humans in Xanth. These qualities were quite evident. When the new men learned the whole truth, some turned about and returned to Mundania. But others liked marrying witches. They wanted to have children with potent magic, and they thought it might be hereditary, so they regarded youth and beauty as secondary. They made excellent husbands. Others wanted the potentials of the unique land of Xanth developed and protected; they were the environmentalists, and magic was the most precious part of the environment. And not all the Fourthwavers were men; some were carefully selected young women, brought in to marry the children, so that there would not be too much inbreeding. So it was a settlement, not an invasion, and it was not rooted in murder but based on sound commercial and biological principles."

"I know," Bink said. "That was the Wave of the first great Magicians."

"So it was. Of course, there were other Waves, but none so critical. The effective dominance of human beings in Xanth dates from that Fourth Wave. Other invasions killed many and drove more into the backwoods, but the continuity was never broken. Just about every truly intelligent or magical person traces his ancestry to the Fourth Wave; I'm sure you do too."

"Yes," Bink agreed. "I have ancestors from the first six Waves, but I always thought the First Wave lineage was the most important."

"The institution of the Magic Shield finally stopped the Waves. It kept all Mundane creatures out and all Xanth creatures in. It was hailed as the salvation of Xanth, the guarantor of utopia. But somehow things didn't improve much. It is as if the people exchanged one problem for another—a visible threat for an invisible one. In the past century Xanth has been entirely free from invasion—but other threats have developed."

"Like the fireflies and the wiggles and Bad Magician Trent," Bink agreed. "Magical hazards."

"Trent was not a *bad* Magician," Cherie corrected him. "He was an *Evil* Magician. There's a distinction— a crucial one."

"Um, yes. He was a good Evil Magician. Lucky they got rid of him before he took over Xanth."

"Certainly. But suppose another Evil Magician appears? Or the wiggles manifest again? Who will save Xanth this time?"

"I don't know," Bink admitted.

"Sometimes I wonder whether the Shield was really a

good idea. It has the net effect of intensifying the magic in Xanth, preventing dilution from outside. As if that magic were building up toward an explosion point. Yet I certainly wouldn't want to return to the days of the Waves!"

Bink had never thought of it that way. "Somehow I find it hard to appreciate the problems of the concentration of magic in Xanth," he said. "I keep wishing there were just a little more. Enough for me, for my talent."

"You might be better off without it," she suggested. "If you could just obtain a dispensation from the King—"

"Ha!" Bink said. "I'd be better off living like a hermit in the wilderness. My village won't tolerate a man without a talent."

"Strange inversion," she murmured.

"What?"

"Oh, nothing. I was just thinking of Herman the Hermit. He was exiled from our herd some years back for obscenity."

Bink laughed. "What could be obscene to a centaur? What did he do?"

Cherie drew up abruptly at the edge of a pretty field of flowers. "This is as far as I go," she said tersely.

Bink realized that he had said the wrong thing. "I didn't mean to offend—I apologize for whatever—"

Cherie relaxed. "You couldn't know. The odor of these flowers makes centaurs do crazy things; I have to stay clear except in real emergencies. I believe Magician Humfrey's castle is about five miles south. Keep alert for hostile magic, and I hope you find your talent."

"Thanks," Bink said gratefully. He slid off her back. His legs were a bit stiff from the long ride, but he knew she had gained him a day's travel time. He walked around to face her and held out his hand.

Cherie accepted it, then leaned forward to kiss him— a motherly kiss on his forehead. Bink wished she had

not done that, but he smiled mechanically and started
walking. He heard her hooves cantering back through
the forest, and suddenly he felt lonely. Fortunately, his
journey was nearly over.

But still he wondered: what had Herman the Hermit
done that the centaurs considered obscene?

Chapter 3. Chasm

Bink stood at the brink, appalled. The path
had been sundered by another trench—no, not a trench,
but a mighty chasm, half a mile across and seemingly of
bottomless depth. Cherie the centaur could not have
known of it, or she would have warned him. So it must
be of very recent formation—perhaps within the past
month.

Only an earthquake or cataclysmic magic could have
formed such a canyon so rapidly. Since there had been
no earthquakes that he knew of, it had to be magic.
And that implied a Magician—of phenomenal power.

Who could it be? The King in his heyday might have
been able to fashion such a chasm by using a rigidly
controlled storm, a channeled hurricane—but he had no
reason to, and his powers had faded too much to manage anything like this now. Evil Magician Trent had
been a transformer, not an earthmover. Good Magician
Humfrey's magic was divided into a hundred assorted
divinatory spells; some of those might tell him how to
create such a gross channel, but it was hardly conceivable
that Humfrey would bother to do it. Humfrey never did
anything unless there was a fee to be earned from it. Was
there another great Magician in Xanth?

Wait—he had heard rumors of a master of illusion. It was far easier to make an apparent chasm than a genuine one. That could be an amplification of Zink's pretend-hole talent. Zink was no Magician, but if a real Magician had this type of talent, this was the kind of effect he might create. Maybe if Bink simply walked out into this chasm, his feet would find the path continuing on . . .

He looked down. He saw a small cloud floating blithely along, about five hundred feet down. A gust of cool dank wind came up to brush him back. He shivered; that was extraordinarily realistic for an illusion!

He shouted: "Hallooo!"

He heard the echo following about five seconds after: "Allooo!"

He picked up a pebble and flipped it into the seeming chasm. It disappeared into the depths, and no sound of its landing came back.

At last he kneeled and poked his finger into the air beyond the brim. It met no resistance. He touched the edge, and found it material and vertical.

He was convinced, unwillingly. The chasm was real.

There was nothing to do but go around it. Which meant he was not within five miles of his destination, but within fifty—or a hundred, depending on the extent of this amazing crevice.

Should he turn back? The villagers certainly should be advised of this manifestation. On the other hand, it might be gone by the time he brought anyone else back here to see it, and he would be labeled a fool as well as a spell-less wonder. Worse, he would be called a coward, who had invented a story to explain his fear of visiting the Magician and gaining absolute proof of his talentlessness. What had been created magically could be abolished magically. So he had better try to get around it.

Bink looked somewhat wearily at the sky. The sun was low in the west. He had an hour or so of diminishing daylight left. He'd better spend it trying to locate a

house in which to spend the night. The last thing he
wanted was to sleep outside in unfamiliar territory, at
the mercy of strange magic. He had had a very easy trip
so far, thanks to Cherie, but with this emergency detour
it would become much more difficult.

Which way to turn—east or west? The chasm seemed
to run interminably in both directions. But the lay of
the land was slightly less rugged to the east, making a
gradual descent; maybe it would approach the bottom
of the chasm, enabling him to cross it. Farmers tended
to build in valleys rather than on mountains, so as to
have ready sources of water and be free of the hostile
magic of high places. He would go east.

But this region was sparsely settled. He had seen no
human habitations along the path so far. He walked increasingly swiftly through the forest. As dusk came, he
saw great black shapes rising out of the chasm: vastly
spreading leathery wings, cruelly bent beaks, glinting
small eyes. Vultures perhaps, or worse. He felt horribly
uneasy.

It was now necessary to conserve his rations, for he
had no way of knowing how far they would have to
stretch. He spotted a breadfruit tree and cut a loaf from
it, but discovered the bread was not yet ripe. He would
get indigestion eating it. He had to find a farmhouse.

The trees became larger and more gnarled of trunk.
They seemed menacing in the shadows. A wind was rising, causing the stiff, twisted branches to sigh. Nothing
ominous about that; these effects weren't even magical.
But Bink found his heart beating more rapidly, and he
kept glancing back over his shoulder. He was no longer
on the established trail, so his comparative security was
gone. He was going deeper into the hinterland, where
anything could happen. Night was the time of sinister
magic, and there were diverse and potent kinds. The
peace spell of the pines was only an example; there
were surely fear spells and worse. If only he could find
a house!

Some adventurer he was! The moment he had to go

a little out of his way, the instant it got dark, he started reacting to his own too-creative imagination. The fact was, this was not the deep wilderness; there would be few real threats to a careful man. The true wilds were beyond the Good Magician's castle, on the other side of the chasm.

He forced himself to slow down and keep his gaze forward. Just keep walking, swinging the staff over to touch anything suspicious, no foolish—

The end of the staff touched an innocuous black rock. The rock burst upward with a loud whirring noise. Bink scrambled back, falling on the ground, arms thrown up protectively before his face.

The rock spread wings and flapped away. "Koo!" it protested reproachfully. It had been only a stone dove, folded into its rock shape for camouflage and insulation during the night. Naturally, it had reacted when poked—but it was quite harmless.

If stone doves nested here, it was bound to be safe for him. All he had to do was stretch out anywhere and sleep. Why didn't he do just that?

Because he was foolishly terrified of being alone at night, he answered himself. If only he had some magic, then he would feel more secure. Even a simple confidence spell would serve.

He spied a light ahead. Relief! It was a yellow square, nearly certain indication of human habitation. He was almost tearfully pleased. He was no child, no adolescent, but he might as well be, here in the forest and off the bounds of his map. He needed the comfort of human companionship. He hurried toward the light, hoping it would not turn out to be some illusion or trap sponsored by an inimical being.

It was real. It was a farm at the edge of a small village; now he could see other squares of light farther down the valley. Almost joyfully, he knocked on the door.

It opened grudgingly to show a homely woman in a soiled apron. She peered at him suspiciously. "I don't know you," she grumped, edging the door closed again.

"I am Bink of the North Village," he said quickly. "I have traveled all day, and was balked by the chasm. Now I need lodging for the night. I will perform some reasonable service for the favor. I'm strong; I can chop wood or load hay or move rocks—"

"You don't need magic to do those things," she said.

"Not with magic! With my hands. I—"

"How do I know you're not a wraith?" she demanded.

Bink held out his left hand, wincing. "Prick me; I bleed." It was a standard test, for most nocturnal supernatural creatures had no blood, unless they had recently fed on some living creature. Even then they had none that would flow.

"Oh, come on, Martha," a man's gruff voice called from inside. "There hasn't been a wraith in these parts for a decade, and they don't do no harm anyway. Let him in; if he eats, he's human."

"Ogres eat," she muttered. But she cracked the door open far enough for Bink to squeeze through.

Now Bink saw the farm's guardian animal: a small werewolf, probably one of their children. There were no true werewolves or other weres that he knew of; all were humans who had developed the talent. Such changelings were increasingly frequent, it seemed. This one had the large head and flattish face typical of the type. A real werewolf would have been indistinguishable from a canine until it changed; then it would have been a wolfish man. Bink put out his hand as it slunk up to sniff him, then patted it on the head.

The creature metamorphosed into a boy about eight years old. "Did I scare you, huh?" he begged.

"Terrified," Bink agreed.

The lad turned toward the man. "He's clean, Paw," he announced. "No smell of magic on him."

"That's the trouble," Bink murmured. "If I had magic, I wouldn't be traveling. But I meant what I said. I can do good physical work."

"No magic?" the man inquired as the woman poured Bink a steaming bowl of stew. The farmer was in his mid-thirties, as homely as his wife, but possessed of a few deep smile-lines around his mouth and eyes. He was thin, but obviously sturdy; hard physical labor made for tough men. He flexed purple as he talked, then green, his whole body changing color smoothly: his talent. "How'd you make it all the way from North Village in one day, then?"

"A lady centaur gave me a lift."

"A filly! I'll *bet* she did! Where'd you hang on to when she jumped?"

Bink smiled ruefully. "Well, she said she'd drop me in a trench if I did it again," he admitted.

"Haw! Haw! Haw!" the man brayed. Farmers, being relatively uneducated, tended to have an earthy sense of humor. Bink noticed that the homely wife wasn't laughing, and the boy merely stared uncomprehendingly.

Now the farmer got down to business. "Listen, I don't need no hand labor nowsabout. But I've got a part in a hearing coming up, and I don't want to go. Upsets the missus, you know."

Bink nodded, though he did not understand. He saw the wife nod grim agreement. What sort of thing was this?

"So if you want to work off your lodging, you can stand in for me," the farmer continued. "Won't only take 'bout an hour, no work to it 'cept to agree to anything the bailiff says. Softest job you can find, and easy for you, too, 'cause you're a stranger. Playing opposite a cute young thing—" He caught the grim look of his wife and aborted that line. "How 'bout it?"

"Anything I can do," Bink said uncertainly. What was this about playing opposite a cute young thing? He'd never find out while the wife was present. Would Sabrina object?

"Fine! There's hay in the loft, and a bucket so you

won't have to go outside. Just don't snore too loud—the
missus don't like it."

The missus didn't like a lot of things, it seemed. How
did a man ever come to marry a woman like that?
Would Sabrina turn shrewish after marriage? The idea
made him uneasy. "I won't," Bink agreed. The stew was
not very tasty, but it was filling. Good stuff to travel on.

He slept comfortably in the hay, with the wolf curled
up beside him. He did have to use the pot, and it stank
all night, having no cover—but that was much better
than going into the magic night. After that initial expression of objection to the stew, his innards settled down.
Bink really had no complaint.

He had gruel for breakfast, heated without fire. That
was the wife's talent, a useful one for a farmstead. Then
he reported to the neighbor's house a mile on down
along the chasm for the hearing.

The bailiff was a big, bluff man, above whose head a
small cloud formed when he concentrated on anything
too intently. "Know anything about it?" he inquired
after Bink explained.

"Nothing," Bink admitted. "You'll have to tell me
what to do."

"Good! It's just a sort of little playlet, to settle a
problem without ruining anybody's reputation. We call
it surrogate magic. Mind you, don't use any actual
magic."

"I won't," Bink said.

"You just agree to whatever I ask you. That's all."

Bink began to get nervous. "I don't believe in lying,
sir."

"This ain't exactly lying, boy. It's in a good cause.
You'll see. I'm s'prised you folk don't practice it in
North Village."

Bink was uneasily silent. He hoped he had not gotten
himself into something ugly.

The others arrived: two men and three young
women. The men were ordinary, bearded farmers, one
young, one middle-aged; the girls ranged from indiffer-

ent to ravishing. Bink forced his eyes away from the prettiest one lest he stare. She was the most voluptuous, striking black-haired beauty he had ever seen, a diamond in the mud of this region.

"Now the six of you sit down acrost from each other at this table," the bailiff said in his official voice. "I'll do the talking when the judge comes. Mind you, this is a play—but it's secret. When I swear you in, it's for keeps—absolutely no blabbing about the details after you get out, understand?"

They all nodded. Bink was becoming more perplexed. He now understood about playing opposite a sweet young thing—but what kind of play was this, with an audience of one, that no one was permitted to report on later? Well, so be it; maybe it *was* a kind of magic.

The three men sat in a row on one side of the table, and the three girls faced them. Bink was opposite the beautiful one; her knees touched his, for the table was narrow. They were silky smooth, sending a shiver of appreciation up his legs. *Remember Sabrina!* he told himself. He was not ordinarily swayed by a pretty face, but this was an extraordinary face. It didn't help that she wore a tight sweater. What a figure!

The judge entered—a portly man with impressive paunch and sideburns. "All stand," the bailiff said.

They all stood respectfully.

The judge took a seat at the end of the table and the bailiff moved to the far side. They all sat down.

"Do you three ladies swear to tell no truth other than that presented in this hearing, any time, anywhere, and to shut up about that?" the bailiff demanded.

"We do," the girls chorused.

"And do you three louts swear the same?"

"We do," Bink said with the others. If he was supposed to lie here, but never to talk about it outside, did that mean it wasn't really a lie? The bailiff knew what was true and what was false, presumably, so in effect—

"Now this is the hearing for an alleged rape," the

bailiff announced. Bink, shocked, tried to conceal his dismay. Were they supposed to act out a rape?

"Among these present," the bailiff continued, "is the girl who says she was raped—and the man she charges. He says it happened but it was voluntary. That right, men?"

Bink nodded vigorously along with the others. Brother! He would rather have chopped wood for his night's lodging. Here he was, possibly lying about a rape he never committed.

"This is done anonymously to protect the reputations of those involved," the bailiff said. "So's to have an advisory opinion, in the presence of the first parties, without advertising it to the whole community."

Bink was beginning to understand. A girl who had been raped could be ruined, though it was no fault of her own; many men would refuse to marry her for that reason alone. Thus she could win her case but lose her future. A man guilty of rape could be exiled, and a man accused of rape would be viewed with suspicion, complicating his own future. It was almost, he thought grimly, as serious a crime as having no magic. Getting at the truth could be a very delicate matter, not something either party would want to advertise in a public trial. Win or lose, reputations would suffer grievously. Yet how could justice be done if it never came to trial? Thus this private, semianonymous hearing. Would it suffice?

"She says she was walking down by the Gap," the bailiff said, glancing at his notes. "He came up behind her, grabbed her, and raped her. Right, girls?"

The three girls nodded, each looking hurt and angry. The vigorous head motion caused the knee of the girl facing Bink to shake, and another ripple of suggestion traveled up his leg. What an opposite lady, in what a play!

"He says he was standing there and she came up and made a suggestion and he took her up on it. Right, men?"

Bink nodded with the others. He hoped his side won; this was nervous business.

Now the judge spoke. "Was it close to a house?"

" 'Bout a hundred feet," the bailiff said.

"Then why did she not scream?"

"He said he'd push her off the brink if she made a sound," the bailiff replied. "She was frozen in terror. Right, girls?"

They nodded—and each looked momentarily terrified. Bink wondered which of the three had actually been raped. Then he corrected his thought hastily: which one had made the accusation? He hoped it wasn't the one opposite him.

"Were the two known to each other prior to the occasion?"

"Yes, Your Honor."

"Then I presume she would have fled him at the outset, had she disliked him—and that he would not have forced her if she trusted him. In a small community like this, people get to know each other very well, and there are few actual surprises. This is not conclusive, but it strongly suggests she had no strong aversion to contact with him, and may have tempted him with consequence she later regretted. I would probably, were this case to come up in formal court, find the man not guilty of the charge, by virtue of reasonable doubt."

The three men relaxed. Bink became aware of a trickle of sweat on his forehead, generated while he listened to the judge's potential decision.

"Okay, you have the judge's ifso," said the bailiff. "You girls still want to bring it to open trial?"

Grim-faced, looking betrayed, the three girls shook their heads, no. Bink felt sorry for his opposite. How could she avoid being seductive? She was a creature constructed for no other visible purpose than ra—than love.

"Then take off," the bailiff said. "Remember—no talking outside, or we'll have a *real* trial, for contempt of court." The warning seemed superfluous; the girls would hardly be talking about this one. The guilty—uh, innocent—man would also shut up, and Bink himself just wanted to get clear of this village. That left only one man who might want to talk—but if he breathed a word, all the others would know who had blabbed. There would be silence.

So it was over. Bink stood and filed out with the others. The whole thing had taken less than the promised hour, so he was well off. He'd had a night's lodging and was well rested. All he needed now was to find a route past the chasm to the Good Magician's castle.

The bailiff emerged, and Bink approached him. "Could you tell me if there is any way south from here?"

"Boy, you don't want to cross the Gap," the bailiff said firmly, the little cloud forming over his head. "Not unless you can fly."

"I'm on foot."

"There's a route, but the Gap dragon . . . You're a nice boy, young, handsome. You did a good job in the hearing. Don't risk it."

Everybody thought he was so damned young! Only good, strong, personal magic would give him real manhood in the eyes of Xanth. "I *have* to risk it."

The bailiff sighed. "Well, I can't tell you no then, son. I'm not your father." He sucked in his paunch, which was almost as impressive as that of the judge, and contemplated the cloud over his head momentarily. The cloud seemed about to shed a tear or two. Again Bink winced inwardly. Now he was getting fathered as well as mothered. "But it's complicated. Better have Wynne show you."

"Wynne?"

"Your opposite. The one you almost raped." The bailiff smiled, making a signal with one hand, and his cloud dissipated. "Not that I blame you."

The girl approached, apparently in answer to the signal.

"Wynne, honey, show this man to the southern slope of the Gap. Mind you keep clear of the dragon."

"Sure," she said, smiling. The smile did not add to her splendor, because that was impossible, but it tried.

Bink had mixed emotions. After this hearing, suppose she accused him of . . . ?

The bailiff glanced at him understandingly. "Don't worry about it, son. Wynne don't lie, and she don't change her mind. You behave yourself, difficult as that may be, and there'll be no trouble."

Embarrassed, Bink accepted the girl's company. If she could show him a quick, safe route past the chasm, he would be well ahead.

They walked east, the sun beating into their faces. "Is it far?" Bink asked, still feeling awkward for assorted reasons. If Sabrina could see him now!

"Not far," she said. Her voice was soft, somehow sending an involuntary thrill through him. Maybe it was magic; he hoped so, because he didn't like to think that he could be so easily subverted by mere beauty. He didn't know this girl!

They continued in silence for a while. Bink tried again: "What is your talent?"

She looked at him blankly.

Uh-oh. After the hearing, she could not be blamed for taking that the wrong way. "Your magic talent," he clarified. "The thing you can do. A spell, or . . ."

She shrugged noncommittally.

What was with this girl? She was beautiful, but she seemed somewhat vacuous.

"Do you like it here?" he asked.

She shrugged again.

Now he was almost certain: Wynne was lovely but stupid. Too bad; she could have made some farmer a marvelous showpiece. No wonder the bailiff had not been concerned about her; she was not much use.

They walked in silence again. As they rounded a bend, they almost stumbled over a rabbit nibbling a mushroom in the path. Startled, the creature jumped straight into the air and hung there, levitating, its pink nose quivering.

Bink laughed. "We won't hurt you, magic bunny," he said. And Wynne smiled.

They passed on under it. But the episode, minor as it was, bothered Bink in retrospect, and for a familiar reason. Why should a common, garden-variety rabbit possess the magic power of floating, while Bink himself had nothing? It simply wasn't fair.

Now he heard the strains of a lovely melody, seeming to punctuate his thoughts. He looked about and saw a lyrebird playing its strings. The music carried through the forest, filling it with a pseudo joy. Ha!

He felt the need to talk, so he did. "When I was a kid they always teased me because I had no magic," he said, not caring whether she understood. "I lost footraces to others who could fly, or put walls in my way, or pass through trees, or who could pop out in one place and in at another place." He had said as much to Cherie the centaur; he was sorry to be stuck in this groove, but some unreasonable part of his mind seemed to believe that if he repeated it often enough he would find some way to alleviate it. "Or who could cast a spell on the path ahead of them, making it all downhill, while I had to cover the honest lay of the land." Remembering all those indignities, he began to feel choked up.

"Can I go with you?" Wynne asked abruptly.

Uh-oh. Maybe she figured he could regale her with more stories indefinitely. The other rigors of travel did not occur to her. In a few miles her shapely body, obviously not constructed for brute work, would tire, and he'd have to carry her. "Wynne, I'm going a long way, to see the Magician Humfrey. You don't want to come along."

"No?" Her marvelous face clouded up.

Still conscious of the rape hearing, and wary of any possible misunderstanding, he phrased it carefully. They were now descending a tortuous path into a low section of the chasm, winding around tufts of clatterweed and clutchroot saplings. He had taken the lead, bracing with his staff, so as to be able to catch her if she lost her footing and fell; when he glanced up at her he caught distracting glimpses of her exquisite thighs. There seemed to be no part of her body that was not perfectly molded. Only her brain had been neglected. "It is dangerous. Much bad magic. I go alone."

"Alone?" She was still confused, though she was handling the path very well. Nothing wrong with her coordination! Bink found himself a bit surprised that those legs could actually be used for climbing and walking. "I need help. Magic."

"The Magician charges a year's service. You—would not want to pay." The Good Magician was male, and Wynne had only one obvious coin. No one would be interested in her mind.

She looked at him in perplexity. Then she brightened, standing upright on the path above him. "You want payment?" She put one hand to the front of her dress.

"No!" Bink yelled, almost dislodging himself from the steep slope. He already visualized a reenactment of the hearing, and a different verdict. Who would believe he had not taken advantage of the lovely idiot? If she showed him any more of her body— "No!" he repeated, more to himself than to her.

"But—" she said, clouding up again.

He was rescued by another distraction. They were near the bottom now, and Bink could see across the base to the more gentle rise of the south slope. No problem about climbing that. He was about to tell Wynne she could go home when there was an uncomfortable sound, a kind of slide-bump. It was repeated—very loud and shuddersome, without being precisely definable.

"What's that?" he asked nervously.

Wynne cupped her ear, listening, though the noise was plainly audible. With the shift in her balance, her feet lost purchase, and she began to slide down. He jumped to catch her, and eased her to the chasm floor.

What an armful she was, all softness and resilience and slenderness in miraculous proportions!

She turned her face to him, brushing back her slightly disarrayed hair, as he stood her back on her feet. "The Gap dragon," she said.

For a moment he was confused. Then he remembered that he had asked her a question; now she was answering it, with the single-mindedness of the meager intellect she had.

"Is it dangerous?"

"Yes."

She had been too stupid to tell him before he asked. And he had not thought to ask before he heard it. Maybe if he hadn't been looking at her so much—yet what man would not have looked?

Already he saw the monster coming from the west— a smoking reptilian head, low to the ground, but large. Very large. "Run!" he bawled.

She started to run—straight ahead, into the chasm.

"No!" he yelled, sprinting after her. He caught her by one arm and spun her about. Her hair swirled winsomely, a black cloud about her face.

"You want payment?" she asked.

Brother! "Run *that* way!" he cried, shoving her back toward the northern slope, since it was the closest escape. He hoped the dragon was not a good climber.

She obeyed, moving fleetly over the ground.

But the glaring eyes of the Gap dragon followed her, orienting on the motion. The creature swerved to intercept her. Bink saw she could not reach the path in time. The monster was whomping along at galloping-centaur velocity.

Bink sprinted after her again, caught her, and half hurled her back toward the south. Even in this desperate moment, her body had a limber, appealing quality that threatened to distract his mind. "That way!" he cried. "It's catching up!" He was acting as foolishly as she, changing his mind while doom closed in.

He had to divert the monster somehow. "Hey, steamsnoot!" he bawled, waving his arms wildly. "Look at me!"

The dragon looked. So did Wynne.

"Not you!" Bink yelled at her. "Get on across. Get out of the Gap."

She ran again. No one could be so stupid as not to understand the danger here.

Now the dragon's attention was on Bink. It swerved again, bearing down on him. It had a long, sinuous body and three sets of stubby legs. The legs lifted the torso and whomped it forward, causing it to slide several feet. The process looked clumsy—but the thing was traveling disconcertingly fast.

Time for him to run! Bink took off down the chasm, toward the east. The dragon had already cut him off from the north slope, and he didn't want to lead it in the direction Wynne was going. For all its awkward mode of propulsion, it could run faster than he; no doubt its speed was enhanced by magic. It was, after all, a magical creature.

But what of his theory about no creature having magic and intelligence if it was magical in itself? If that was valid, this thing would not be very smart. Bink hoped so; he'd rather try to outwit a dumb dragon than a smart one. Especially when his life depended on it.

So he ran—but already he knew this course was hopeless. This was the dragon's hunting ground, the factor that stopped people from crossing the chasm on foot. He should have known that a magically constructed chasm would not be left unattended. Someone or something did not want people crossing freely from north Xanth to south Xanth. Especially nonmagical people like him.

Bink was puffing now, out of breath, and a pain was developing in his side. He had underestimated the speed of the dragon. It was not a little faster than he was, it was substantially faster. The huge head snapped forward, and steam gushed around him.

Bink inhaled the stuff. It wasn't as hot as he had

feared, and it smelled faintly of burning wood. But it was still uncomfortable. He choked, gasped—tripped on a stone and fell flat. His staff flew out of his hands. That fatal moment of distraction!

The dragon whomped right over him, unable to stop so rapidly. It was so long and low that it couldn't fall. The metallic body shot past, inertia carrying the head beyond range. If magic enhanced the thing's speed, then there was no magic to help it brake, for what that small blessing was worth.

Bink's breath was momentarily knocked out of him by the fall. He was already desperately short of air. He gasped for more, unable to concentrate on anything else at the moment, not even on escape. While he lay, effectively paralyzed, the middle set of legs came down— right at him. They came together as though yoked, ready to heave the heavy body up and forward again. He couldn't even roll aside in time. He would be crushed!

But the massive claws of the right foot landed squarely on the rock that had tripped him. It was a big rock, bigger than it looked, and he had fallen on the lower side after stumbling on its built-up upper side. He was sprawled in a kind of erosion gully. The three claws were splayed by the rock, so that one missed him to the left, another to the right, and the middle one arched right over him, hardly touching the ground. Perhaps a ton of dragonweight on that one foot, none of it touching him. A lucky placement that could never have happened by design!

Now he had some of his breath back, and the foot was gone, already lifted for the next whomp. Had Bink been able to roll aside, he would have been caught squarely by one of the claws, and squished.

But one freak break did not mean he was out of trouble. The dragon was curling around to find him again, steaming back along its own long torso. It was marvelously supple, able to bend in a tight U-turn. Bink would have admired this quality more from a safe distance.

Snakelike, the monster could convolute into knots if it had to, reaching him wherever he tried to hide. No wonder it whomped; it had no rigid backbone.

Knowing it was futile, Bink still found himself trying to escape. He dashed under the tree-trunk-thick tail. The head followed him, the nostrils pursuing his scent as accurately as the eyes traced his motion.

Bink reversed course and leaped up over the tail, scrambling for handholds on the scales. He was in luck; some dragons had scales with serrated edges that sliced the flesh of anything that touched them; this one's scales were innocuously rounded. It was probably a survival trait in a chasm like this, though Bink wasn't sure why. Did sharp scales tend to snag on things, slowing the velocity of a low-to-the-ground monster?

He tumbled over the tail—and the dragon's head followed smoothly. No steam now; maybe the monster didn't want to heat up its own flesh. It was already savoring its conquest and repast, playing cat and mouse with him, though he'd never seen a werecat do that; possibly real cats did play that way, though there weren't many of those—or mice—around these days, for some reason.

But he was letting his mind run away with his attention again, and he couldn't afford it. Could he lead the dragon's head such a merry chase around its own body that it actually did tie itself in a knot? He doubted it, but might have to give it a try anyway. It was better than just getting swallowed.

He was back at the rock he had stumbled over. Now its position was changed; the moving weight of the dragon had dislodged it. There was a crack in the ground where it had been: a deep, dark hole.

Bink didn't like holes in the ground; no telling what might lurk in there: nickelpedes, stinglice, hoopworms, lepermud—ugh! But he had no chance at all here amid the coils of the Gap dragon. He jumped feet first into the hole.

The earth crumbled beneath his weight, but not quite enough. He sank in up to his thighs, and stuck.

The dragon, seeing him about to escape, blasted a torrent of steam. But again it was warm vapor, not burning hot, actually little more than coalesced breath. This was not after all a fire dragon, but a pseudo fire dragon. Few people were likely to get close enough to know the difference. The mist bathed Bink, soaking him down thoroughly, and turned the dirt around him to mud. Thus lubricated, he began to move again. Down.

The dragon snatched at him—but Bink popped through the constriction with a sucking sound that complemented the futile clicking of the dragon's teeth. He dropped about two feet, to solid rock. His feet stung, especially the ankle that had been turned, but he was unhurt. He ducked his head down and felt about him in the darkness. He was in a cave.

What luck! But he still wasn't safe. The dragon was clawing at the ground, gouging out huge chunks of dirt and rock, steaming the remainder into rivulets of mud. Gooey chunks splatted against the cave floor. The opening was widening, letting in more light. Soon it would be big enough for the dragon's head. Bink's doom had only been postponed.

This was no occasion for caution. Bink strode ahead, hands touching each other before him, arms bowed in a horizontal circle. If he hit a wall, he would only bruise his forearms. Better a bruise than the crunch of dragon's teeth.

He did not hit a wall. He struck a mud slick instead. His foot shot out from under, and he took a bellyflop. There was water here—real water, not dragon's breath—a trickle wending down.

Down? Down *where?* Surely to an underground river! That could account for the sudden canyon. The river could have been tunneling for centuries, and suddenly the ground above collapsed, forming the chasm. One phenomenal sinkhole. Now the river was working again—and he would surely drown if he splashed into it, for there was no guarantee that its current was slow or that there was air in its passage. Even if he swam well, he could be consumed by river monsters, the especially vicious kind that frequented dark, cold waters.

Bink clawed his way back up the slope. He found a branching passage leading up, and followed it as rapidly as possible. Soon he saw a shaft of light from above. Safe!

Safe? Not while the dragon still lurked. Bink dared not dig his way out until it left. He would have to wait, hoping the predator didn't dig this far. He hunkered down, trying not to get any more mud on him.

The sounds of the dragon's digging diminished, then ceased altogether. There was silence—but Bink wasn't fooled. Dragons were of the hide-and-pounce variety, generally. At least the landbound ones were. They could move fast when they moved, but could not keep it up long. A dragon would never successfully run down a deer, for example, even if the deer lacked escapist magic. But dragons were very good at waiting. Bink would have to stay low until he actually heard it move off.

It was a long wait, complicated by the cold discomfort of the mud and dark and his prior wetting by the dragon's breath. Plus the fact that he could not be quite sure the dragon was there. This might all be for nothing, and the dragon could be emitting steamy chuckles as it retreated silently—they could be very quiet when they wanted to—and hunted elsewhere.

No! That was what the predator wanted him to think. He dared not emerge, or even move, lest the thing hear him. That was why it was so quiet now; it was listening. Dragons had excellent senses; perhaps that was why they were so common in the wilderness regions, and so feared. They were a survival type. Apparently his scent had suffused the area, issuing from stray vents, so that it did not give away his precise location. The dragon was not about to wear itself out dig-

ging up the entire cave system. But sound or sight
would do him in.

Now that he was absolutely still, he was cold. This
was summer in Xanth, and it really did not get very
cold even in winter, for many plants had heat magic,
local weather control, or other mechanisms for comfort.
But the chasm was sparsely vegetated, and sheltered
from much of the sun, and the cool air tended to settle
and be trapped. It had taken awhile for the heat of his
exertions to dissipate, but now he was shivering. He
could not afford to shiver too violently! His legs and
feet hurt, becoming cramped. To top it off, he felt a
scratchiness in his throat. He was coming down with a
cold. This present discomfort would hardly help him to
throw that off, and he could not go to the village doctor
for a medicinal spell.

He tried to distract himself by thinking of other
things, but he did not care to rehearse yet again the assorted indignities of his bitter childhood, or the frustration of having but not being able to hold a lovely girl
like Sabrina because of his lack of magic. The notion of
lovely girls reminded him of Wynne; he would not be
human if he didn't react to her fantastic face and body!
But she was so abysmally stupid; and anyway, he was
engaged already, so he had no business thinking of her.
His efforts at self-distraction came to nothing; it was
better to suffer in mental silence.

Then he became aware of something more insidious.
It had been in evidence for some time, but he had not
been consciously aware of it because of his other con-
cerns. Even unsuccessful distractions did some good.

It was a peripheral, almost subliminal thing. A kind
of flickering, which vanished when he looked directly at
it, but became insistent at the fringe of his vision. What
was it? Something natural—or something magic? Innocent or sinister?

Then he recognized it. A shade! A half-real spirit,
ghost, or some unquiet dead, doomed to skulk in
shadow and night until its wrongs were righted or its

evil exonerated. Because the shades could not go abroad by day, or enter light, or intrude in populous places, they represented no threat to ordinary folk in ordinary circumstances. Most were bound to the place of their demise. As Roland had advised Bink, long ago: "If a shade bothers you, walk away from it." They were easy to escape; this was called "pulling the shade."

Only if an unwary person foolishly slept near the abode of a shade was he in trouble. It took a shade about an hour to infiltrate a living body, and a person could move away at any time and be free of it. Once Roland, in a fit of uncharacteristic ire, had threatened to stun an annoying trespasser and leave him in the nearest shade barrow. The man had quickly departed.

Now Bink was neither stunned nor asleep—but if he moved, the Gap dragon would pounce. If he did not move, the shade would infiltrate his body. That could be a fate worse than death—really!

All because he had tried to rescue a beautiful, vacuous girl from a dragon. In folklore, such a hero always received a most intriguing reward. In reality, the hero was as likely as not to find himself in need of rescue, as now. Well, such was real-life justice in Xanth.

The shade grew bolder, thinking him helpless or inattentive. It did not glow; it was merely a lesser darkness than that of the cave. He could see it fairly well now, by not looking at it: a vague, mannish outline, very sad.

Bink wanted to leap away, but he found the dank wall close behind him, and in any event he could not afford to take a step. No matter how silently he did it, the dragon would hear. He could walk forward, right through the shade, and all he would feel would be a momentary chill, like that of the grave. It had happened on occasion to him before; unpleasant but hardly critical. But this time the dragon would be on him.

Maybe he could run, being fully rested, and get a head start before the dragon woke. The dragon must surely be sleeping, getting its rest, while its keen ears were attuned to the quarry.

The shade touched him. Bink jerked his arm away—and the dragon stirred above. It was there, all right! Bink froze—and the dragon lost him again. The mere jerk had not been quite enough.

The dragon circled, trying to sniff him out. Its huge nose passed over the upper crack; steam jetted down. The shade retreated in alarm. Then the dragon settled in place, giving up the chase for the moment. It knew its prey would give itself away sooner or later. When it came to waiting, the dragon was much better equipped than the human.

One more reptilian twitch—and the end of the tail dropped through the crack, dangling almost to the floor. In order to escape, Bink would have to brush past it. Now what were his chances?

Suddenly Bink had an idea. The dragon was a living, if magical, animal. Why shouldn't the shade take over *its* body? A shade-dominated dragon would probably have other things on its mind than eating a hiding person. If he could just move over so as to place the dangling tail between him and the shade—

He tried, shifting his balance with tedious slowness, trying to lift one foot so as to put it forward. Silently. But the moment it lifted, it hurt, and he flinched. The dragon's tail twitched, and Bink had to freeze. This was extremely awkward, because his balance in this semi-squatting position was at best tenuous, and now both feet and ankles felt as if they were on fire.

The shade advanced again.

Bink tried to ease his foot farther forward, so as to achieve a more comfortable balance without falling over. Away from the shade! Again agony shot through him, and again the tail twitched; once more he froze, in even more discomfort. And yet again the shade moved in. He could not go on this way.

The shade touched his shoulder. This time Bink steeled himself not to flinch; he would certainly have lost his balance, and then his life. The touch was hideously cool, not cold; it made his skin crawl. What was he to do?

He controlled himself, with continuing effort. It would take an hour or so for the shade to take over his body; he could break the spell at any time before it was complete. The dragon would gobble him down in seconds. Appalling as the notion was, the shade was the better risk; at least it was slow. Maybe in half an hour the dragon would have gone away . . .

Maybe the moon would fall out of the sky and squish the dragon under green cheese, too! Why wish for the impossible? If the dragon did not go, then what? Bink just didn't know. But so far he didn't see much choice.

The shade moved in inexorably, cooling his shoulder through to chest and back. Bink felt the intrusion with barely suppressed loathing. How would it be possible to submit to this invasion of the dead? Yet he had to do it, at least for a while, lest the dragon quickly convert him to a shade himself. Or would that be preferable? At least he would die a man.

The ghastly cool essence impinged slowly on his head. Now Bink was terrified, yet frozen; he could not lean his head away any farther. The horror crept through, and he felt himself sinking, slipping, being blotted up by . . . and then he was eerily calm.

Peace, the shade said in his mind.

The peace of the pine forest, where the sleepers never woke? Bink could not protest aloud, because of the dragon's ears. But he gathered himself for a final effort, to leap away from this dread possession. He would crash past the dragon's tail before the monster could react, and take his chance with the subterranean river.

No! Friend, I can help you! the shade cried, louder but still silently.

Somehow, insidiously, Bink began to believe. The spirit actually seemed sincere. Perhaps it was just in contrast to the alternatives: consumption by dragon or drowning in river.

Fair exchange, the shade persisted. *Permit me, for one hour. I will save your life, then dissipate, my onus abated.*

It had the ring of conviction. Bink faced death anyway; if the shade could somehow save him, it would certainly be worth an hour of possession. It was true that shades dissipated once their burden was lifted.

But not all shades were honest. The criminal ones sometimes were recalcitrant, choosing not to atone for their crimes in life. Instead, they added to them in death, under cover of the new identity, ruining the reputation of the unlucky person they controlled. After all, the shade had little to lose; he was already dead. Absolution would merely consign him to oblivion or to his place in the infernal regions, depending on his faith. Small wonder some chose never to die completely.

My wife, my child! the shade pleaded. *They go hungry, they sorrow, ignorant of my status. I must tell them where the silver tree grows that I died to locate.*

The silver tree! Bink had heard of the like. A tree with leaves of pure silver, incredibly valuable—for silver was a magic metal. It tended to repel evil magic, and armor made from it resisted magic weapons. And, of course, it could even be used as money.

No, it is for my family! the shade cried. *That they may never again dwell in poverty. Do not take it for yourself!*

That convinced Bink. A dishonest shade would have promised him everything; this one promised only life, not riches. *Agreed,* Bink thought, hoping he was not making a dreadful mistake. Trust unwisely given—

Wait until merging is complete, the shade said gratefully. *I cannot help you until I become you.*

Bink hoped it was no deception. But what, really, did he have to lose? And what did the shade have to gain by a lie? If it did not save Bink, it would only share the sensation of being eaten by the dragon. Then they would both be shades—and Bink would be an angry one. He wondered what one shade could do to another. Meanwhile, he waited.

At last it was done. He was Donald, the prospector. A man whose talent was flying.

"We go!" Donald cried through Bink's lips exultantly. He put his arms up as if diving and rose straight up through the crack in the ceiling, with such power that the edges of rock and dirt were flung aside.

The sheer brightness of day blinded them as they emerged. The Gap dragon took a moment to orient on this strange occurrence, then pounced. But Donald made another effort, and shot up so swiftly that the huge teeth snapped on air. He kicked the monster on the snout, hard. "Ha, gaptooth!" he yelled. "Chew on this." And he stomped on the tender portion of the dragon's nose.

The jaws gaped open, and a cloud of steam shot out. But Donald was already zooming out of reach. The dragon had no chance to catch them before they were too high.

Up, up they sailed, straight out of the canyon, above the trees and slopes. There was no effort other than mental, for this was magic flight. They leveled off, proceeding north across Xanth.

In delayed reaction, Bink realized that he had a magic talent. By proxy, certainly—but for the first time in his life he was experiencing what every other citizen of Xanth experienced. He was performing. Now he knew how it felt.

It felt wonderful.

The sun bore down from almost straight overhead, for it was now midday. They were up amid the clouds. Bink felt discomfort in his ears, but an automatic reaction by his other self popped them, making the pain abate before it intensified. He didn't know why flying should hurt his ears; maybe it was because there wasn't enough to hear up here.

For the first time, too, he saw the full upper contours

of the clouds. From beneath they were generally flat, but from above they were elegantly if randomly sculptured. What seemed like tiny puffballs from the ground were big masses of fog in person. Donald flew through them with equanimity, but Bink didn't like the loss of vision. He was nervous about banging into something.

"Why so high?" he inquired. "I can hardly see the ground." This was an exaggeration; what he meant was that he could not make out the details he was accustomed to. Also, it would have been nice to have some of the people see him flying. He could buzz around the North Village, astounding the scoffers, qualifying for his citizenship . . . no, that would not be honest. Too bad the most tempting things were not right to do.

"I don't want to advertise," Donald said. "It could complicate things if people thought I was alive again."

Oh. Perhaps so. There could be renewed expectations, maybe debts to be paid, ones that mere silver would not abate. The shade's business was necessarily anonymous, at least so far as the community was concerned.

"See that glint?" Donald inquired, pointing down between two clouds. "That's the silver oak tree. It's so well hidden it can be spotted only from above. But I can tell my boy exactly where to find it. Then I can rest."

"I wish you could tell me where to find a magic talent," Bink said wistfully.

"You don't have one? Every citizen of Xanth has magic."

"That's why I'm not a citizen," Bink said glumly. They both spoke through the same mouth. "I'm going to the Good Magician. If he can't help me, I'll be exiled."

"I know the feeling. I spent two years exiled in that cave."

"What happened to you?"

"I was flying home, after discovering the silver tree, and a storm came up. I was so excited by the thought of riches that I couldn't wait. I risked the trip in high winds—and got blown into the Gap. The impact was so great I landed in the cave—but I was already dead."

"I didn't see any bones."

"You didn't see any hole in the ground, either. The dirt filled in over me, and then my body got washed away by the river."

"But—"

"Don't you know anything? It's the place of death that anchors the shade, not the place of the corpse."

"Oh. Sorry."

"I hung on, though I knew it was hopeless. Then you came." Donald paused. "Look, you've done me such a favor—I'll share the silver with you. There's enough on that tree for both my family and you. Only promise not to tell anyone else where it is."

Bink was tempted, but a moment's reflection changed his mind. "I need magic, not silver. Without magic, I'll be exiled from Xanth, so I won't be able to share the silver. With magic—I don't care about wealth. So if you want to share it, share it with the tree; don't take all its leaves, but just a few at a time, and some of the silver acorns that drop, so the tree can go on living in health and perhaps reproduce itself. In the long run that will be more productive anyway."

"It was a fortunate day for me when you dropped into my cave," Donald said. He banked into a curve, going down.

Bink's ears popped again as they descended. They dropped into a forest glade, then walked half a mile to an isolated, run-down farm. It took that much motion to completely eliminate the lingering cramps in Bink's legs. "Isn't it beautiful?" Donald inquired.

Bink looked at the rickety wooden fence and sagging roof. A few chickens scratched among the weeds. But to a man who had love invested here, love enough to sustain him two years after violent death, it must be the fairest of ranches. "Um," he said.

"I know it isn't much—but after that cave, it is like

heaven itself," Donald continued. "My wife and boy have magic, of course, but it isn't enough. She cures feather fade in chickens, and he makes little dust devils. She brings in barely enough to feed them. But she's a good wife, and lovely beyond belief."

Now they entered the yard. A seven-year-old boy looked up from the picture he was making in the dirt. He reminded Bink briefly of the werewolf boy he had left—was it only six hours ago? But that impression was destroyed when this boy opened his mouth. "Go 'way!" he yelled.

"Better I don't tell him," Donald said slowly, a bit taken aback. "Two years—that's a long time for that age. He doesn't recognize this body. But see how he's grown."

They knocked on the door. A woman answered: plain, in a dingy dress, her hair swept back under a soiled kerchief. In her heyday she might have been ordinary; now hard work had made her old before her time. *She hasn't changed a bit,* Donald thought admiringly. Then, aloud: "Sally!"

The woman stared at him with uncomprehending hostility.

"Sally—don't you know me? I'm back from the dead to wrap up my affairs."

"Don!" she exclaimed, her pale eyes lighting at last.

Then Bink's arms enfolded her, and his lips kissed hers. He saw her through Donald's overwhelming emotion—and she was good and lovely beyond belief.

Donald drew back, staring into the splendor of her love as he spoke. "Mark this, darling: thirteen miles north-northeast of the small millpond, beside a sharp east-west ridge, there is a silver tree. Go harvest it—a few leaves at a time, so as not to damage it. Market the metal as far away as you can, or get a friend to do it for you. Tell no one the source of your wealth. Remarry— it will make a fine dowry, and I want you to be happy, and the boy to have a father."

"Don," she repeated, tears of grief and joy in her eyes. "I don't care about silver, now that you're back."

"I'm not back! I'm dead, returning only as a shade to tell you of the tree. Take it, use it, or my struggle has been for nothing. Promise!"

"But—" she started, then saw the look on his face. "All right, Don, I promise. But I'll never love any other man!"

"My onus is abated, my deed is done," Donald said. "One more time, beloved." He bent to kiss her again— and dissipated. Bink found himself kissing another man's wife.

She knew it immediately, and jerked her face away. "Uh, sorry," Bink said, mortified. "I have to go now."

She stared at him, suddenly hard-eyed. What little joy remained in her had been wrung out by the brief manifestation of her husband. "What do we owe you, stranger?"

"Nothing. Donald saved my life by flying us away from the Gap dragon in the chasm. The silver is all yours. I will never see you again."

She softened, comprehending that he was not going to take away the silver. "Thank you, stranger." Then, on obvious impulse: "You could share the silver, if you wanted. He told me to remarry—"

Marry her? "I have no magic," Bink said. "I am to be exiled." It was the kindest way he could think of to decline. Not all the silver of Xanth could make this situation attractive to him, on any level.

"Will you stay for a meal?"

He was hungry, but not that hungry. "I must be on my way. Do not tell your son about Donald; he felt it would only hurt the boy. Farewell."

"Farewell," she said. Momentarily he saw a hint of the beauty Donald had seen in her; then that too was lost.

Bink turned and left. On the way out of the farm he saw a whirling dust devil coming toward him, product of the boy's minor malice toward strangers. Bink dodged it and hurried away. He was glad he had done this favor for the prospector, but also relieved that it was done. He had not properly appreciated before what poverty and death could mean to a family.

Chapter 4. Illusion

Bink resumed his journey—on the wrong side of the chasm. If only Donald's farm had been to the south!

Strange, how everyone here knew about the chasm and took it for granted—yet nobody in the North Village did. Could it be a conspiracy of silence? That seemed unlikely, because the centaurs didn't seem to know about it either, and they were normally extremely well informed. It had been present for at least two years, since the shade had been there that long, and probably much longer, since the Gap dragon must have spent its whole life there.

It must be a spell—an ignorance spell, so that only those people in the immediate vicinity of the chasm were aware of it. Those who departed—forgot. Obviously there had never been a clear path from the north to the south of Xanth—not in recent years.

Well, that was not his concern. He just had to get around it. He was not going to attempt to cross it again; only a phenomenal series of coincidences had saved his skin. Bink knew that coincidence was an untrustworthy ally.

The land here was green and hilly, with head-high candy-stripe ferns sprouting so thickly that it was impossible to see very far ahead. He had no beaten trail now. He got lost once, apparently thrown off by an aversion spell. Some trees protected themselves from molestation by causing the traveler to veer aside, so as to pass some distance from them. Maybe that was how the silver oak had remained undiscovered so long. If someone got into a patch of such trees, he could be bounced far afield, or even routed in a perpetual circle. It could be difficult indeed to break out of that sort of trap, because it was not at all obvious; the traveler thought he was going where he wanted to go.

Another time he encountered a very fine path going right his way, so fine that natural caution made him avoid it. There were a number of wilderness cannibal plants that made access very attractive, right up until the moment their traps sprung.

Thus it was three days before he made significant progress—but he remained in good form, apart from his cold. He found a few nosegays that helped clear his nose, and a pillbox bush with headache pills. At irregular intervals there were colorfruit trees, bearing greens, yellows, oranges, and blues. He had fair luck finding lodging each night, for he was obviously a fairly harmless type, but he also had to spend some hours in labor, earning his board. The people of this hinterland were minimally talented; their magic was of the "spot on a wall" variety. So they lived basically Mundane lives, and always needed chores done.

At last the land wound down to the sea. Xanth was a peninsula that had never adequately been mapped—obviously! the unmarked chasm proved that!—so its precise dimensions were unknown, perhaps unknowable. In general, it was an oval or oblong stretching north-south, connected to Mundania by a narrow bridge of land on the northwest. Probably it had been an island at one time, and so evolved its distinct type of existence free from the interference of the outside world. Now the Shield had restored that isolation, cutting off the land bridge by its curtain of death and wiping out the personnel of invading ships. If that weren't enough, there was said to be a number of ferocious sea monsters. Off-shore. No, Mundania did not intrude any more.

Bink hoped the sea would permit him to get around the chasm. The Gap dragon probably could not swim, and the sea monsters should not come too close to land. There should be a narrow section where neither dragon nor sea monster prevailed. Maybe a beach he could walk across, plunging into the water if the terror of the chasm charged, and onto land if magic threatened from the sea.

There it was: a beautiful thread of white sand stretching from one side of the chasm to the other. No monsters were in sight. He could hardly believe his luck—but he acted before it could change.

Bink hit the beach running. For ten paces everything was fine. Then his foot came down on water, and he fell into the brine.

The beach was illusion. He had fallen for a most elementary trap. What better way for a sea monster to catch its prey than a vanishing beach converting to deep water?

Bink stroked for the real shoreline, which he now saw was a rocky waste upon which the waves broke and spumed. Not a safe landing at all, but his only choice. He could not go back on the "beach" he had come along; it no longer seemed to exist even in illusion. Either he had somehow been borne across the water or he had been swimming without knowing it. Either way, it was not magic he cared to get tangled up in again. Better to know exactly where he was.

Something cold and flat and immensely powerful coiled around one ankle. Bink had lost his staff when the Gap dragon ran him down, and had not yet cut a new one; all he had was his hunting knife. It was a puny resource against a sea monster, but he had to try.

He drew the knife from its sheath, held his breath, and lashed in the vicinity of his ankle. What held him felt like leather; he had to saw at it to sever it. These monsters were tough all over!

Something huge and murky loomed at him under the water, reeling in the tongue he sawed at. Yard-long teeth flashed as the giant jaws opened.

Bink lost what little nerve he had left. He screamed. His head was underwater. The scream was a disaster. Water rushed into his mouth, his throat.

Firm hands were pressing his back rhythmically, forcing the water out, the air in. Bink choked and hacked and coughed. He had been rescued! "I—I'm okay!" he gasped.

The hands eased off. Bink sat up, blinking.

He was on a small yacht. The sails were of brightly colored silk, the deck of polished mahogany. The mast was gold.

Gold? Gold plate, maybe. Solid gold would have been so heavy as to overbalance the ship.

Belatedly, he looked at his rescuer, and was amazed again. She was a Queen.

At least, she looked like a Queen. She wore a platinum crownlet and a richly embroidered robe, and she was beautiful. Not as lovely as Wynne, perhaps; this woman was older, with more poise. Precise dress and manner made up for the sheer voluptuous innocence of youth that Wynne had. The Queen's hair was the richest red he had ever seen—and so were the pupils of her eyes. It was hard to imagine what a woman like this would be doing boating in monster-infested surf.

"I am the Sorceress Iris," she said.

"Uh, Bink," he said awkwardly. "From the North Village." He had never met a Sorceress before, and hardly felt garbed for the occasion.

"Fortunate I happened by," Iris remarked. "You might have had difficulties."

The understatement of the year! Bink had been finished, and she had given him back his life. "I was drowning. I never saw you. Just a monster," he said, feeling inane. How could he thank this royal creature for sullying her delicate hands on something like him?

"You were hardly in a position to see anything," she said, straightening so that her excellent figure showed to advantage. He had been mistaken; she was in no way inferior to Wynne, just different, and certainly more intelligent. More on a par with Sabrina. The manifest mind of a woman, he realized, made a great deal of difference in her appeal. Lesson for the day.

There were sailors and servants aboard the yacht, but they remained unobtrusively in the background, and Iris adjusted the sails herself. No idle female, she!

The yacht moved out to sea. Soon it bore upon an island—and what an island it was! Lush vegetation grew all around it, flowers of all colors and sizes: polka-dot daisies the size of dishes, orchids of exquisite splendor, tiger lilies that yawned and purred as the boat approached. Neat paths led from the golden pier up toward a palace of solid crystal, which gleamed like a diamond in the sun.

Like a diamond? Bink suspected it was a diamond, from the way the light refracted through its myriad faces. The largest, most perfect diamond that ever was.

"I guess I owe you my life," Bink said, uncertain as to how to handle the situation. It seemed ridiculous to offer to chop wood or pitch animal manure to earn his keep for the night; there was nothing so crude as firewood or animal refuse on this fair island! Probably the best favor he could do her was to remove his soaking, bedraggled presence as rapidly as possible.

"I guess you do," she agreed, speaking with a surprising normality. He had somehow expected her to be more aloof, as befitted pseudo-royalty.

"But my life may not be worth much. I don't have any magic; I am to be exiled from Xanth."

She guided the yacht to the pier, flinging a fine silver chain to its mooring post and tying it tight.

Bink had thought his confession would disturb her; he had made it at the outset so as not to proceed under false pretenses. She might have mistaken him for someone of consequence. But her reaction was a surprise.

"Bink, I'm glad you said that. It shows you are a fine, honest lad. Most magic talents aren't worthwhile anyway. What use is it to make a pink spot appear on a wall? It may be magic, but it doesn't accomplish anything. You, with your strength and intelligence, have more to offer than the great majority of citizens."

Amazed and pleased by this gratuitous and probably unjustified praise, Bink could make no answer. She was correct about the uselessness of spot-on-wall magic, certainly; he had often thought the same thing himself. Of course, it was a standard remark of disparagement, meaning that a given person had picayune magic. So this really was not a sophisticated observation. Still, it certainly made him feel at ease.

"Come," Iris said, taking him by the hand. She guided him across the gangplank to the pier, then on along the main path to the palace.

The smell of flowers was almost overwhelming. Roses abounded in all colors, exhaling their perfumes. Plants with sword-shaped leaves were even more common; their flowers were like simplified orchids, also of all colors. "What are those?" he inquired.

"Irises, of course," she said.

He had to laugh. "Of course!" Too bad there was no flower named "Bink."

The path passed through a flowering hedge and looped around a pool and fountain to the elaborate front portico of the crystal palace. Not a true diamond after all. "Come into my parlor," the Sorceress said, smiling.

Bink's feet balked, before the significance penetrated to his brain. He had heard about spiders and flies! Had she saved his life merely to—

"Oh, for God's sake!" she exclaimed. "Are you superstitious? Nothing will hurt you."

His recalcitrance seemed foolish. Why should she revive him, then betray him? She could have let him choke to death instead of pumping the water out of him; the meat would have been as fresh. Or she could have tied him up and had the sailors bring him ashore. She had no need to deceive him. He was already in her power—if that was the way it was. Still . . .

"I see you distrust me," Iris said. "What can I do to reassure you?"

This direct approach to the problem did not reassure him very much. Yet he had better face it—or trust to fate. "You—you are a Sorceress," he said. "You seem to have everything you need. I—what do you want with me?"

She laughed. "Not to eat you, I assure you!"

But Bink was unable to laugh. "Some magic—some people do get eaten." He suffered a vision of a monstrous spider luring him into its web. Once he entered the palace—

"Very well, sit out there in the garden," Iris said. "Or wherever you feel safe. If I can't convince you of my sincerity, you can take my boat and go. Fair enough?"

It was too fair; it made him feel like an ungrateful lout. Now it occurred to Bink that the whole island was a trap. He could not swim to the mainland—not with the sea monsters there—and the yacht's crew might grab him and tie him up if he tried to sail across.

Well, it wouldn't hurt to listen. "All right."

"Now, Bink," she said persuasively—and she was so lovely in her intensity that she was very persuasive indeed. "You know that though every citizen of Xanth has magic, that magic is severely limited. Some people have more magic than others, but their talents still tend to be confined to one particular type or another. Even Magicians obey this law of nature."

"Yes." She was making sense—but what was the point?

"The King of Xanth is a Magician—but his power is limited to weather effects. He can brew a dust devil or a tornado or a hurricane, or make a drought or a ten-day downpour—but he can't fly or transmute wood into silver or light a fire magically. He's an atmospheric specialist."

"Yes," Bink agreed again. He remembered Donald

the shade's son, who could make dust devils, those eva-
nescent swirls of dust. The boy had an ordinary talent;
the King had a major one—yet they differed in degree,
not type.

Of course, the King's talent had faded with age; perhaps all he could conjure now would be a dust devil. It
was a good thing the Shield protected Xanth!

"So if you know a citizen's talent, you know his limi-
tations," Iris continued. "If you see a man make a
storm, you don't have to worry about him forming a
magical pit under you or changing you into a cock-
roach. Nobody has multiple *fields* of talent."

"Except maybe Magician Humfrey," Bink said.

"He is a powerful Magician," she agreed. "But even
he is restricted. His talent is divination, or information;
I don't believe he actually looks into the future, just the
present. All his so-called hundred spells relate to that.
None of them are performance magic."

Bink did not know enough about Humfrey to refute
that, but it sounded correct. He was impressed with how
the Sorceress kept up with the magic of her counterpart.
Was there professional rivalry among those of strong
magic? "Yes—talents run in schools. But—"

"My talent is illusion," she said smoothly. "This
rose—" She plucked a handsome red one and held it
under his nose. What a sweet smell! "This rose, in reality, is . . ."

The rose faded. In her hand was a stalk of grass. It
even smelled grassy.

Bink looked around, chagrined. "All of this is illusion?"

"Most of it. I could show you the whole garden as it
is, but it would not be nearly as pretty." The grass in
her hand shimmered and became an iris flower. "This
should convince you. I am a powerful Sorceress. Therefore I can make an entire region seem like something it
is not, and every detail will be authentic. My roses smell
like roses, my apple pies taste like apple pies. My
body—" She paused with half a smile. "My body feels

like a body. All seems real—but it is illusion. That is, each thing has a basis in fact, but my magic enhances it, modifies it. This is my complex of talents. Therefore I have no other talent—and you can trust me to that extent."

Bink was uncertain about that last point. A Sorceress of illusion was the last type of person to be trusted, to any extent! Yet he comprehended her point now. She had shown him her magic, and it was unlikely that she would practice any other magic on him. He had never thought of it this way before, but it was certainly true that no one in Xanth mixed types of magic talents.

Unless she were an ogre, using illusion to change her own appearance, too . . . No. An ogre was a magical creature, and magical creatures did not have magical talents. Probably. Their talents *were* their existence. So centaurs, dragons, and ogres always seemed like what they were, unless some natural person, animal, or plant changed them. He had to believe that! It was possible that Iris was in collusion with an ogre—but unlikely, for ogres were notoriously impatient, and tended to consume whatever they could get hold of, regardless of the consequence. Iris herself would have been eaten by this time.

"Okay, I trust you," Bink agreed dubiously.

"Good. Come into my palace, and I will tend to all your needs."

That was unlikely. No one could give him a magic talent of his own. Humfrey might discover his talent for him—at the price of a year's service!—but that would be merely revealing what was there, not creating it.

He suffered himself to be led into the palace. It was exquisite inside, too. Rainbow-hued beams of light dropped down from the prismatic roof formations, and the crystal walls formed mirrors. These might be illusion—but he saw his own reflection in them, and he looked somehow healthier and more manly than he felt. He was hardly bedraggled at all. More illusion?

Soft pretty pillows were piled in the corners in lieu of

chairs or couches. Suddenly Bink felt very tired; he needed to lie down for a while! But then the image of the skeleton in the pine forest returned to him. He didn't know what to feel.

"Let's get you out of those wet clothes," Iris said solicitously.

"Uh, I'll dry," Bink said, not wanting to expose his body before a woman.

"Do you think I want my cushions ruined?" she demanded with housewifely concern. "You were floundering in salt water; you've got to rinse the salt off before you start itching. Go into the bathroom and change; there is a dry uniform awaiting you."

A uniform awaiting him? As though she had been expecting him. What could that mean?

Reluctantly, Bink went. The bathroom was, appropriately, palatial. The tub was like a small swimming pool, and the commode was an elegant affair of the type the Mundanes were said to employ. He watched the water circle around the bowl and drain out into a pipe below, disappearing as if by magic. He was fascinated.

There was also a shower; a spray of water, like rain, emerged from an elevated nozzle, rinsing him off. That was sort of fun, though he was not sure he would want it as a regular thing. There must be a big tank of water upstairs somewhere, to provide the pressure for such devices.

He dried with a plush towel embroidered with images of irises.

The clothing was hung on a rack behind the door: a princely robe, and knickers. Knickers? Ah, well—they were dry, and no one would see him here in the palace. He donned the uniform, and stepped into the ornate sandals awaiting him. He strapped his hunting knife on, concealing it beneath the overhang of the robe.

Now he felt better—but his cold was developing apace. His sore throat had given way to a runny nose; he had thought this was merely aggravation by the salt water he had taken in, but now he was dry and it was apparent that his nose needed no external supply of fluid. He didn't want to sniff overtly, but he had no handkerchief.

"Are you hungry?" Iris asked solicitously as he emerged. "I will fetch you a banquet."

Bink certainly was hungry, for he had eaten only sparingly from his pack since starting along the chasm, depending on foraging along the way. Now his pack was soaked with salt water; that would complicate future meals.

He lay half buried in cushions, his nose tilted back so that it wouldn't dribble forward, surreptitiously mopping it with the corner of a pillow when he had to. He snoozed a bit while she puttered in the kitchen. Now that he knew this was all illusion, he realized why she did so much menial work herself. The sailors and gardeners were part of the illusion; Iris lived alone. So she had to do her own cooking. Illusion might make for fine appearance, texture, and taste, but it would not prevent her from starving.

Why didn't Iris marry, or exchange her services for competent help? Much magic was useless for practical matters, but her magic was extraordinary. Anyone could live in a crystal palace if he lived with this Sorceress. Bink was sure many people would like that; appearance was often more important than substance anyway. And if she could make ordinary potatoes taste like a banquet, and medicine taste like candy—oh yes, it was a marketable talent!

Iris returned, bearing a steaming platter. She had changed into a housewifely apron, and her crownlet was gone. She looked less regal and a good deal more female. She set things up on a low table, and they sat crosslegged on cushions, facing each other.

"What would you like?" she inquired.

Again Bink felt nervous. "What are you serving?"

"Whatever you like."

"I mean—really?"

She made a moue. "If you must know, boiled rice. I

have a hundred-pound bag of the stuff I have to use up before the rats catch on to the illusory cat I have guarding it and chew into it. I could make rat droppings taste like caviar, of course, but I'd rather not have to. But you can have anything you want—anything at all." She took a deep breath.

So it seemed—and it occurred to Bink that she was not restricting it to food. No doubt she got pretty lonely here on her island, and welcomed company. The local farmers probably shunned her—their wives would see to that!—and monsters weren't very sociable.

"Dragon steak," he said. "With hot sauce."

"The man is bold," she murmured, lifting the silver cover. The rich aroma wafted out, and there lay two broiled dragon steaks steeped in hot sauce. She served one expertly onto Bink's plate, and the other onto her own.

Dubiously, Bink cut off a piece and put it to his mouth. It was the finest dragon steak he had ever tasted—which was not saying much, since dragons were very difficult prey; he had eaten it only twice before. It was a truism that more people were eaten by dragons than dragons eaten by people. And the sauce—he had to grab for the glass of wine she had poured for him, to quench the heat. But it was a delicious burn, converting to flavor.

Still, he doubted. "Uh—would you mind . . . ?"

She grimaced. "Only for a moment," she said.

The steak dissolved into dull boiled rice, then back into dragon meat.

"Thanks," Bink said. "It's still a bit hard to believe."

"More wine?"

"Uh, is it intoxicating?"

"No, unfortunately. You could drink it all day and never feel it, unless your own imagination made you dizzy."

"Glad to hear it." He accepted the elegant glass of sparkling fluid as she refilled it, and sipped. He had gulped down the first too fast to taste it. Maybe it was actually water, but it seemed to be perfect blue wine, the kind specified for dragon meat, full-bodied and delicately flavored. Much like the Sorceress herself.

For dessert they had home-baked chocolate-chip cookies, slightly burned. That last touch made it so realistic that he was hard put to it to preserve his disbelief. She obviously knew something about cooking and baking, even in illusion.

She cleared away the dishes and returned to join him on the cushions. Now she was in a low-cut evening gown, and he saw in more than adequate detail exactly how well-formed she was. Of course, that too could be illusion—but if it felt the same as it looked, who would protest?

Then his nose almost dripped onto the inviting gown, and he jerked his head up. He had been looking a mite *too* closely.

"Are you unhappy?" Iris inquired sympathetically.

"Uh, no. My nose—it—"

"Have a handkerchief," she said, proffering a lovely lace affair.

Bink hated to use such a work of art to honk his nose into, but it was better than using the pillows.

"Uh, is there any work I can do before I go?" he inquired uneasily.

"You are thinking too small," Iris said, leaning forward earnestly and inhaling deeply. Bink felt the flush rising along his neck. Sabrina seemed very far away—and she would never have dressed like this, anyway.

"I told you—I have to go to the Good Magician Humfrey to find my magic—or be exiled. I don't really think I have any magic, so—"

"I could arrange for you to stay, regardless," she said, nudging closer.

She was definitely making a play for him. But why would such an intelligent, talented woman be interested in a nobody like him? Bink mopped his nose again. A nobody with a cold. Her appearance might be greatly enhanced by illusion, but mind and talent were obviously genuine. She should have no need of him—for anything.

"You could perform magic that everyone would see," she continued in that dismayingly persuasive way of hers, nudging up against him. She certainly felt real— most provocatively so. "I could fashion an illusion of performance that no one could penetrate." He wished she hadn't said that while touching him so intimately. "I can do my magic from a distance, too, so there would be no way to tell I was involved. But that is the least of it. I can bring you wealth and power and comfort—all genuine, nonillusive. I can give you beauty and love. All that you might desire as a citizen of Xanth—"

Bink grew more suspicious. What was she leading up to? "I have a fiancée—"

"Even that," Iris agreed. "I am not a jealous woman. You could have her as a concubine, provided you were circumspect."

"As a concubine!" Bink exploded.

She was unshaken. "Because you would be married to me."

Bink stared at her, aghast. "Why should you want to marry a man with no magic?"

"So I could be Queen of Xanth," she said evenly.

"Queen of Xanth! You'd have to marry the King."

"Precisely."

"But—"

"One of the quaint, archaic laws and customs of Xanth is that the nominal ruler must be male. Thus some perfectly capable magical females have been eliminated from consideration. Now the present King is old, senile, and without heir; it is time for a Queen. But first there must be a new King. That King could be you."

"Me! I have no knowledge of governing."

"Yes. You would naturally leave the dull details of government to me."

Now at last it was coming clear. Iris wanted power. All she needed was a suitable figurehead, to get herself installed. One sufficiently talentless and naive to be readily managed. So he would never get delusions of actually being King. If he cooperated with her, he would be dependent on her. But it was a fair offer. It provided a viable alternative to exile, regardless of the state of his own magic.

This was the first time he had seen his magic infirmity as a potential asset. Iris did not want an independent man or legitimate citizen; she would have no lasting hold on that kind of person. She needed a magic cripple like him—because without her he would be nothing, not even a citizen.

That diminished the romantic aspect considerably. Reality always did seem to be less enticing than illusion. Yet his alternative was to plunge back into the wilderness on a mission he suspected was futile. His luck was already considerably overextended; his chances of even making it as far as the castle of the Magician Humfrey were not ideal, since he now had to trek through the fringe of the central wilderness. He would be a fool not to accept the offer of the Sorceress.

Iris was watching him intently. As he looked back at her, her gown flickered, becoming transparent. Illusion or not, it was a breathtaking sight. And what difference did it make if the flesh only seemed real? He had no doubt now of what she was offering on the immediate, personal level. She would be glad to prove how good she could make it, as she had with the meal. Because she needed his willing cooperation.

Really, it made sense. He could have citizenship and Sabrina, since obviously the Sorceress Queen would never betray that aspect . . .

Sabrina. How would she feel about the arrangement?

He knew. She would not buy it. Not for anything, not for an instant. Sabrina was very straitlaced about certain things, very proper in the forms.

"No," he said aloud.

Iris's gown snapped opaque. "No?" Suddenly she sounded like Wynne, when he had told that idiot girl she could not accompany him.

"I don't want to be King."

Now Iris's voice was controlled, soft. "You don't think I can do it?"

"I rather think you can. But it's not my sort of thing."

"What *is* your sort of thing, Bink?"

"I just want to be on my way."

"You want to be on your way," she repeated, with great control. "Why?"

"My fiancée wouldn't like it if I—"

"She wouldn't like it!" Iris was working up a substantial head of steam, like the Gap dragon. "What does she offer you that I cannot better a hundredfold?"

"Well, self-respect, for one thing," Bink said. "She wants me for myself, not to use me."

"Nonsense. All women are the same inside. They differ only in appearance and talent. They all use men."

"Maybe so. I'm sure you know more about that sort of thing than I do. But I have to be going now."

Iris reached out a soft hand to restrain him. Her gown disappeared entirely. "Why not stay the night? See what I can do for you? If you still want to go in the morning—"

Bink shook his head. "I'm sure you could convince me overnight. So I have to go now."

"Such candor!" she exclaimed ruefully. "I could give you an experience like none you have imagined."

In her artful nudity, she already stimulated his imagination far more than was comfortable. But he steeled himself. "You could never give me back my integrity."

"You idiot!" she screamed, with a startling shift of attitude. "I should have left you to the sea monsters."

"They were illusions too," he said. "You set up the whole thing, to make me beholden to you. The illusion beach, the illusion threat, all. That was your leather strap that wrapped around my ankle. My rescue was no coincidence, because I never was in danger."

"You are in danger now," she gritted. Her lovely bare torso became covered by the military dress of an Amazon.

Bink shrugged and stood up. He blew his nose. "Good-bye, Sorceress."

She studied him appraisingly. "I underestimated your intelligence, Bink. I'm sure I can improve my offer, if you will only let me know what you want."

"I want to see the Good Magician."

Now her rage burst out anew. "I'll destroy you!"

Bink walked away from her.

The crystal ceiling of the palace cracked. Fragments of glass broke off and dropped toward him. Bink ignored them, knowing they were unreal. He kept walking. He was quite nervous, but was determined not to show it.

There was a loud, ominous crunching sound, as of stone collapsing. He forced himself not to look up.

The walls shattered and fell inward. The remaining mass of the roof tumbled down. The noise was deafening. Bink was buried in rubble—and pushed on through it, feeling nothing. Despite the choking smell of dust and plaster, and the continued rumble of shifting debris, the palace was not really collapsing. Iris was a marvelous mistress of illusion, though! Sight, sound, smell, taste—everything but touch. Because there had to be something to touch, before she could convert it to feel like something else. Thus there was no solidity to this collapse.

He banged face first into a wall. Jarred more than physically, he rubbed his cheek and squinted. It was a wooden panel, with flaking paint. The real wall, of the real house. The illusion had concealed it, but now reality was emerging. Doubtless she could have made it feel like gold or crystal or even like slimy slugs, but the illusion was breaking down. He could find his way out.

Bink felt his way along the wall, tuning out the terrifying sights and sounds of the collapse, hoping she did not change the feel of the wall so that he would be deceived by that and led astray. Suppose it became a row of mousetraps or thistles, forcing his hand away?

He found the door and pulled it invisibly open. He

had made it! He turned and for a moment looked back. There was Iris, standing in the splendor of her female fury. She was a middle-aged woman running slightly to fat, wearing a worn housecoat and sloppy hair net. She had the physical qualities she had shown him via her peek-a-boo outfit, but they were much less seductive at age forty than at the illusion of age twenty.

He stepped outside. Lightning flared and thunder cracked, making him jump. But he reminded himself that Iris was mistress of illusion, not weather, and walked out into it.

Rain pelted him, and hailstones. He felt the cold splats of water on his skin, and the stones stung—but they had no substance, and he was neither wet nor bruised after the initial sensation. Iris's magic was in its prime, but there were limits to illusion, and his own disbelief in what he saw tended to reduce the impact.

Suddenly there was the bellow of a dragon. Bink jumped again. A fire-belching winged beast was bearing down on him, not a mere steamer like the Gap dragon, but a genuine flamer. Seemingly genuine; was it real or illusion? Surely the latter—but he could not take the chance. He dived for cover.

The dragon swooped low, passing him. He felt the wash of air from its motion, the blast of heat. He still didn't know for sure, but he might be able to tell from its action; real fire-belchers were very stupid, as dragons went, because the heat shriveled their own brains. If this one reacted intelligently—

It looped about almost immediately, coming at him for a second run. Bink made a feint to the right, then scooted left. The dragon was not fooled; it zeroed right in on him. That was the intellect of the Sorceress, not the animal.

Bink's heart was thudding, but he forced himself to stand upright and still, facing the menace as it came. He lifted one finger in an obscene gesture at it. The dragon opened its jaws, blowing out a tremendous cloud of fire and smoke that enveloped Bink, singeing the hair of his body—and leaving him untouched.

He had gambled and won. He had been almost certain, but his body still trembled in reaction, for none of his senses had doubted the illusion. Only his brain had defended him, preventing him from being reduced to quivering acquiescence to the will of the Sorceress, or from being herded into some genuine hazard. Illusions could kill—if one heeded them.

Bink moved out again, with more confidence. If there were a real dragon in the vicinity, there would have been no need for an illusory one; therefore all dragons here were illusion.

He stumbled. Illusion could hurt him another way, though—by covering up dangerous breaks in the terrain, forcing him to misstep or fall or drop into a well. He would have to watch his step—literally.

As he concentrated on the region near his feet, he was able to penetrate the illusion with greater facility. Iris's talent was phenomenal, but in covering the entire island it was necessarily thinly spread. His will could oppose hers in a localized area while her attention was distracted. Behind the façade of the flower gardens was the weedy wilderness of the island. The palace was a rickety shack, first cousin to the farmhouses he had met along the way. Why build a good house when illusion could do it so much easier?

His borrowed clothing, too, had changed. Now he wore a crude feminine shawl and—he verified with dismay—panties. Lacy silk girl-style panties. His fancy handkerchief was exactly what it appeared to be. Apparently the Sorceress did indulge herself in some reality, and lace hankies were what she could afford. And panties.

He hesitated. Should he go back for his own clothing? He didn't want to encounter Iris again, but to travel in the wilderness or meet people in *this* outfit—

He had a vision of walking up to the Good Magician Humfrey to ask for his boon of information.

BINK: Sir, I have come across Xanth at great peril to ask—

MAGICIAN: For a new dress? A bra? Ho, ho, ho!

Bink sighed, feeling his face redden again. He turned back.

Iris spotted him as soon as he reentered the shack. A flicker of hope lighted her face—and that briefly honest expression had more compulsion than all her illusion. Human values moved Bink. He felt like the supreme heel.

"You changed your mind?" she asked. Suddenly her voluptuous youth was back, and a section of the glittering palace formed around her.

That dashed it. She was a creature of artifice, and he preferred reality—even the reality of a shack among weeds. Most of the farmers of Xanth had nothing better, after all. When illusion became an essential crutch to life, that life lost value. "Just want my own clothes," Bink said. Though his decision was firm, he still felt like a heel for interfering with her splendid aspirations.

He proceeded to the bathroom—which he now saw was an attached outhouse. The fabulous toilet was merely the usual board with a hole sawed in it, and flies buzzed merrily below it. The bathtub was a converted horse-watering trough. How had he taken a shower? He saw a bucket; had he dumped water on his own head, not knowing it? His clothing and pack were in a pile on the floor.

He started to change—but found that the facility was really only an opening in the back wall of the shack. Iris stood watching him. Had she watched him change before? If so, he had to take it as a compliment; her approach had become much more direct and physical thereafter.

His eye fell on the bucket again. *Someone* had dumped water on him, and he was sure now that he had not done it himself. The only other person who could have done it—ouch!

But he was not about to display himself so freely to

her again, though it was obvious that he had no physical
secrets remaining! He picked up his things and headed
for the door.

"Bink—"

He paused. The rest of the house was dull wood, with
flaking paint, straw on the floor, and light showing
through the cracks. But the Sorceress herself was lovely.
She wore very little, and she looked a lush eighteen.

"What do you want in a woman?" she asked him.
"Voluptuousness?" She became extremely well endowed, with an exaggerated hourglass figure. "Youth?"
Suddenly she looked fourteen, very slender, lineless and
innocent. "Maturity?" She was herself again, but better
dressed. "Competence?" Now she was conservatively
dressed, about twenty-five, quite shapely but of a busi-
nesslike mien. "Violence?" The Amazon again, robust
but still lovely.

"I don't know," Bink said. "I'd really hate to choose.
Sometimes I want one thing, sometimes another."

"It can all be yours," she said. The alluring fourteen-
year-old reappeared. "No other woman can make this
promise."

Bink was suddenly, forcefully tempted. There were
times when he wanted this, though he had never dared
admit it openly. The Sorceress's magic was potent indeed—the strongest he had ever experienced. So it was
illusion—yet in Xanth illusion abounded, and was
quite legitimate; it was never possible to know precisely
what was real. In fact, illusion was part of Xanth reality, an important part. Iris really could bring him wealth
and power and citizenship, and she could be, for him,
any kind of woman he wanted. Or all kinds.

Furthermore, through her illusions, applied politi-
cally, she could in time create an identical reality. She
could build an actual crystal palace with all the trappings; the powers of the Queenship would make this
possible. In that light, it was reality she offered, with
her magic simply a means to that end.

But what was actually in her scheming mind? The

reality of her inner thoughts might not be sweet at all. He could never be sure he understood her completely, and therefore could never trust her completely. He was not at all sure she would make a good Queen; she was too interested in the trappings of power, instead of the welfare of the land of Xanth as a whole.

"I'm sorry," he said, and turned away.

She let him go. No more palace, no more storm. She had accepted his decision—and that, perversely, tempted him again. He could not call her evil; she was merely a woman with a need, and she had offered a deal, and was mature enough to accede to necessity, once her temper cooled. But he forced himself to keep going, trusting his logic more than his meandering feeling.

He picked his way down to the sagging wharf, where the rowboat was tied. The craft looked insecure, but it had brought him here, so it could take him away.

He got into it—and stepped into a puddle. The boat leaked. He grabbed a rusty pail and bailed it out somewhat, then sat and took the oars.

Iris must have performed quite a maneuver, to row this boat while seeming to be an idle Queen. She had a lot of plain old-fashioned practical talent to supplement her magic. She probably *could* make a good ruler of Xanth—if she ever found a man who would go along with her.

Why hadn't he cooperated? As he rowed, he considered the matter more carefully, looking back at the isle of illusion. His superficial reasons were sufficient for the moment, but not for an enduring decision. He must have some underlying rationale to which he was true, even though he gave himself some more-presentable justification. It could not just be his memory of Sabrina, evocative as that was, for Iris was as much of a woman as Sabrina, and much more magical. There had to be something else, diffuse but immense—ah, he had it! It was his love of Xanth.

He could not allow himself to become the instrument

of his homeland's corruption. Though the present King was ineffective, and many problems were developing, still Bink was loyal to the established order. The days of anarchy, or of brute might making right, were over; there were set procedures for the transfer of authority, and these had to be honored. Bink would do anything to stay in Xanth—except to betray it.

The ocean was calm. The devastating rocks of the shore had also been illusion; there was after all a small beach—but it was not where it had seemed to be, either when he thought he ran along it or after he was in the brine. A long narrow pier angled out from the side of the chasm; that was what he had run along at the beginning. Until he had simply run off the end, splashing abruptly into deep water. In more than one sense.

He beached his boat on the south shore. Now—how was he to return the boat to the Sorceress?

No way. If she didn't have another boat, she would simply have to swim for it. He regretted that, but he was not going back to that isle of illusion again. With her powers, she could probably scare away any sea creatures that threatened, and he was sure she was an adequate swimmer.

He changed into his original clothes, salty though they might be, shrugged into his knapsack, and turned his face to the west.

Chapter 5. Spring

The landscape south of the chasm was rougher than that to the north. It was not hilly, but mountainous. The tallest peaks were enchanted with white snow. The narrow passes were choked with almost impenetrable growth, forcing Bink to detour again and again. Ordinary nettles and itch bushes would have been bad, but there was no telling what magic these strange plants had. A lone tangle tree was well worth avoiding, and there were whole groves of related species. He could not risk it.

So whenever an aspect of the jungle balked him, Bink turned back and tried again farther along. He avoided the most obvious paths also; they were suspect. Thus he tramped through intermediate vegetation—the borderline between jungle and field, often in the roughest terrain of all: barren, burning rock faces; steep rocky slopes; high windswept plateaus. What even magic plants disdained was hardly worth any person's trouble—except for the traveler who wanted to stay out of trouble. One cleared area turned out to be the landing strip for a very large flying dragon; no wonder there were no other predators in that region. Bink's progress was so slow that he knew it would take him many days to reach the Good Magician's castle.

He fashioned himself a burrow in the ground, with a pile of stones for a windshield and dead brush for a blanket, and slept uncomfortably. He wondered now why he hadn't at least accepted the Sorceress's offer to stay the night; it would surely have been much more comfortable than this.

No, he knew why he had to go. He might never have left the island after that night. Not as his own man. And if he had, Sabrina would never have forgiven him. The very fact that such a night tempted him in retrospect—and not merely for the comfort of sleep—meant that it was not a night he could have afforded.

He reminded himself of that several times before he shivered himself to sleep. Then he dreamed of a diamond-crystal palace, woke with mixed emotions, and had to shiver his way to sleep again. Turning down temptation certainly wasn't much pleasure when alone on the open trail. Tomorrow he would search diligently for a blanket tree and some hotsoup gourds.

On the third morning of his south-chasm leg, he trekked along a ridge, his only feasible route westward. He had cut himself a new staff, after several tries; the first saplings he went for magicked him off by using aversion spells of assorted types. He had no doubt there were many suitable trees he never saw at all, because of their passive "do not notice me" spells. One used a physical repulsion charm directed at cutting objects; every time he slashed at it, his knife veered away.

About an hour on the way with his new staff, he was still pondering the natural selectivity of magic. The plants with the most effective spells survived best, so became more common, but how many times did stray travelers come by here with knives? Then he realized that he might make good use of that repulsion spell. If he succeeded in cutting a staff from such a tree, would it repel all attacks against him? Obviously this magic was for defense against the depredations of dragons, beavers, and such, not actual knives, and he would certainly feel safer with an anti-dragon staff. No; cutting the tree would kill it, and its magic would abate. But maybe a seed from it—

No sense consuming time going back; he should be able to locate another such tree. All he had to do was attempt to cut a new staff and note which tree repulsed his knife. He might be able to dig up a small one and take it entire, keeping it alive and effective.

He moved down the side of the ridge, testing trees. This proved to be more hazardous than anticipated; the knife's approach toward their tender bark brought out the worst in them. One dropped hard fruit on him, barely missing his head; another exhaled sleep perfume that almost stopped his journey right there. But no cutting-aversion spells, now.

One large tree had a dryad, an inhabiting wood nymph, who looked very fetching, about like Iris at fourteen, but who cursed Bink roundly in most unladylike language. "If you want to carve defenseless things, go carve your own kind!" she screamed. "Go carve the wounded soldier in the ditch, you son of a—" Fortunately she balked at completing the rhyme. Dryads were not supposed to know such language.

Wounded soldier? Bink located the ditch and explored it carefully. Sure enough, there lay a man in military apparel, blood crusted on his back, groaning piteously.

"Peace," Bink said. "I will help you, if you permit." Xanth had once needed a real army, but now the soldiers were mostly messengers for the King. Still, their costumes and pride remained.

"Help me!" the man exclaimed weakly. "I will reward you—somehow."

Now Bink felt it safe to approach. The soldier was severely wounded and had lost much blood. He was burning with the fever of infection. "I can't do anything for you myself; I'm no doctor, and if I even move you, you may expire. I will return with medication," Bink said. "I must borrow your sword." If the soldier gave up his sword, he was really sick.

"Return soon—or not at all," the man gasped, raising the hilt.

Bink took the heavy weapon and climbed out of the ditch. He approached the tree of the dryad. "I need magic," he told her. "Blood restoration, wound healing, fever abatement—that sort of thing. Tell me where I can get them, quickly, or I will chop your tree down."

"You wouldn't!" she cried, horrified.

Bink hefted the sword menacingly. At this moment he reminded himself of Jama, the village sword conjurer; the image disgusted him.

"I'll tell! I'll tell!" she screamed.

"Okay. Tell." He was relieved; he doubted that he could actually have made himself chop down her tree. That would have killed her, and to no real purpose. Dryads were harmless creatures, pretty to look at; there was no point in molesting them or their cherished tree homes.

"Three miles to the west. The Spring of Life. Its water will cure anything."

Bink hesitated. "There is something you're not telling me," he said, hefting the sword again. "What's the catch?"

"I may not reveal it," she cried. "Anyone who tells—the curse—"

Bink made as if to chop at the trunk of the tree. The dryad screamed with such utter misery that he abated the effort. He had fought to protect Justin Tree back at home; he could not ravage this one. "All right. I'll risk the curse," he said. He set off westward.

He found a path leading his way. It was not an inviting one, merely an animal run, so he felt justified in using it with caution. It seemed others knew the route to the Spring. Yet as he approached, he became increasingly nervous. What was the catch, and what was the curse? He really ought to know before he either risked himself or gave the water to the ailing soldier.

Xanth was the land of magic—but magic had its rules, and its qualifications. It was dangerous to play with magic unless the precise nature of the spell was understood. If this water really could heal the soldier, it was a most strongly enchanted Spring. For that sort of aid, there had to be a price.

He found the Spring. It was in a depression, under a giant spreading acorn tree. The tree's health augured well for the water; it could hardly be poisoned. But there could be some other menace associated with it. Suppose a river monster were hiding in it, using the water as a lure for the unwary? Injured or dying creatures would be easy prey. A false reputation for healing would attract them from many miles around.

Bink didn't have time to wait and watch. He had to help the soldier now or it would be too late. So this was a risk he simply had to take.

He moved cautiously to the Spring. It looked cool and clear. He dipped his canteen into it, keeping his other hand on the sword. But nothing happened; no grim tentacle rose from the depths to challenge him.

Viewing the filled canteen, he had another thought. Even if the water were not poisoned, it was not necessarily curative. What use to take it to the soldier, if it wouldn't do the job?

There was one way to find out. He was thirsty anyway. Bink put the canteen to his mouth and sipped.

The water was chill and good. He drank more deeply, and found it supremely refreshing. It certainly wasn't poisoned.

He dipped the canteen again and watched the bubbles rise. They distorted the view of his left hand under the water, making it seem as if he had all his fingers. He did not think much about the digit he had lost in childhood, but such a view of a supposedly complete hand teased him unpleasantly.

He lifted out the canteen—and almost dropped it. *His finger was whole!* It really was! The childhood injury had been eliminated.

He flexed it and touched it, amazed. He pinched it and it hurt. No question: his finger was real.

The Spring really *was* magic. If it could heal a fifteen-year-old amputation so cleanly and painlessly and instantly, it could heal anything!

How about a cold? Bink sniffed—and discovered that his nose was clear. It had cured his sniffles, too.

No question about it: he could recommend this Spring of Life. A true description for a potent magic. If this Spring were a person, it would be a full Magician.

Again Bink's natural caution came into play. He still did not know the nature of the catch—or of the curse. Why could no one tell the secret of this Spring? What was the secret? Obviously not the fact of its healing properties; the dryad had told him that, and he could tell it to others. The curse could not be a river monster, for none had struck. Now that Bink was whole and well, he would be much better able to defend himself. Scratch one theory.

But this did not mean there was no danger. It merely meant the threat was more subtle than he had thought. A subtle danger was the worst of all. The man who fled from the obvious menace of a flaming dragon could succumb to the hidden menace of the peace spell of the pines.

The soldier was dying. Moments were precious, yet Bink delayed. He had to ferret this out, lest he put both the soldier and himself in greater peril than before. It was said that a person should not look a gift unicorn in the mouth, lest it prove to be enchanted, but Bink always looked.

He kneeled before the Spring and stared deep into it. Looking it in the mouth, as it were. "O Spring of Life," he murmured. "I come on a mission of mercy, seeking no profit for myself, though I have indeed benefited. I conjure you to reveal your rationale, lest I inadvertently trespass." He had little confidence in this formal invocation, since he had no magic with which to enforce it, but it was all he could think of. He just couldn't accept such a wonderful gift without trying to ascertain the payment to be exacted. There was always a price.

Something swirled deep in the Spring. Bink felt the potent magic of it. It was as if he peered through a hole into another world. Oh, yes—this Spring had its own consciousness and pride! The field of its animus rose up to encompass him, and his consciousness plunged through the depths, bringing comprehension. *Who imbibes of me may not act against my interest, on pain of forfeiture of all that I bring him.*

Uh-oh. This was a self-preservation spell, plain and simple. But enormously complicated in its execution. Who defined what was or was not contrary to the interests of the Spring? Who but the Spring itself? There would obviously be no lumbering in this region, for cutting trees could damage the environment and change the climate, affecting rainfall. No mining, for that could lower the water table and pollute the Spring. Even the prohibition against revealing the rationale made sense, for people with minor injuries and complaints might not use the magic water if they knew the price in advance. The loggers and miners certainly wouldn't. But any action had extending if diminishing consequences, like the ripples of a stone dropped in a pool. In time such ripples could cover the whole ocean. Or the whole of Xanth, in this case.

Suppose the Spring decided that its interest was threatened indirectly by some action of the distant King of Xanth, such as levying a tax on lumber that caused the lumbermen to cut more wood in order to pay it. Would the Spring force all its users to oppose the King, perhaps assassinating him? A person who owed his life to the Spring might very well do it.

It was theoretically possible for this magic Spring to change the whole society of Xanth—even to become its *de facto* ruler. But the interests of one isolated Spring were not necessarily the interests of the human society. Probably the magic of the Spring could not extend to such extremes, for it would have to be as strong as the massed powers of all the other entities of Xanth. But slowly, given time, it would have its effect. Which made this an ethical question.

"I cannot accept your covenant," Bink said into the deep swirl. "I hold no animosity toward you, but I cannot pledge to act only in your interest. The interest of the whole of Xanth is paramount. Take back your benefits; I go my own way."

Now there was anger in the Spring. The unfathomable depths of it roiled. The field of magic rose up again, enveloping him. He would suffer the consequence of his temerity.

But it faded like a dissipating storm, leaving him . . . whole. His finger remained healed, and his cold was still cured. He had called the Spring's bluff—and won.

. Or had he? Maybe his benefits would not be revoked until he acted specifically against the interest of the Spring. Well, his benefits were minor; he could afford the penalty. He certainly would not be deterred from doing what he felt was right by fear of that consequence.

Bink stood, keeping the sword in his hand as he slung the strap of the canteen over his shoulder. He turned.

A chimera was crawling toward him.

Bink whipped his sword around, though he was hardly expert in its use. Chimeras were dangerous!

But in a moment he saw that the creature was in dire straits. The tongue was hanging out of its lion's head, its goat's head was unconscious, and the snake's head at the end of the tail was dragging on the ground. The creature was scraping along on its stomach toward the Spring, trailing blood.

Bink stood aside and let it pass. He held no malice even for a chimera in this state. He had never before seen a living creature suffering like this. Except the soldier.

The chimera reached the water and plunged its lion head in, drinking desperately.

The change was immediate. The goat's head snapped erect and awake, swiveling from its neck in the middle of the back to glare at Bink. The snake head hissed.

No doubt about it: the chimera was healthy again. But now it was dangerous, for this class of monster hated all things human. It took a step toward Bink, who held his sword tightly before him with both hands, knowing that flight would be futile. If he wounded it, he might escape before it dragged itself back to the Spring for a second restoration.

But abruptly the thing turned away, without attacking. Bink sighed with relief; he had put up a front, but the last thing he wanted to do was to engage in combat with such a monster, in the presence of an unfriendly Spring.

There must be a general truce in this vicinity, Bink realized. It was contrary to the interest of the Spring to have predators lurk here, so no hunting or fighting was permitted. Lucky for him!

He scrambled up the slope and headed east. He hoped the soldier had survived.

The soldier had. He was tough, as soldiers tended to be; he refused to gasp out his last until nature ripped it from him. Bink dribbled some magic water into his mouth, then poured some over the wound. Suddenly the man was well.

"What did you do?" he cried. "It is as if I never got stabbed in the back."

They walked up the hill together. "I fetched water from a magic Spring," Bink explained. He paused at the dryad's tree. "This accommodating nymph very kindly directed me to it."

"Why, thank you, nymph," the soldier said. "Any favor I can do in return—"

"Just move on," she said tightly, eyeing the sword in Bink's hands.

They moved on. "You can't act contrary to the interest of that Spring," Bink said. "Or tell anyone about the price you paid for its help. If you do, you'll be right back where you started. I figured the price was worth it, for you."

"I'll say! I was doing patrol duty, guarding a patch of the King's eyeball ferns, when somebody—hey, one drink of this elixir and the King's eyes would be perfect without those ferns, wouldn't they? I should take—" He broke off.

"I can show you where the Spring is," Bink offered. "Anybody can use it, as far as I know."

"No, it's not that. I just suddenly got the feeling—I don't think the King ought to have this water."

This simple comment had a profound impact on Bink. Did it confirm his reasoning, that the Spring's influence extended widely and selfishly? Revived health of the King might not be in the interest of the Spring, so—

But, on the other hand, if the King were cured by Spring water, then the King himself would serve the Spring's interest. Why should the Spring object to that?

Also, why had Bink himself not suffered the loss of his finger and restoration of his cold when he told the secret to the soldier? He had defied the Spring, yet paid no penalty. Was the curse a mere bluff?

The soldier extended his hand. "I'm Crombie. Corporal Crombie. You saved my life. How can I repay you?"

"Oh, I just did what was right," Bink said. "I couldn't just let you die. I'm on my way to the Magician Humfrey, to see if I have any magic talent."

Crombie put his hand to his beard, pondering. He was rather handsome in that pose. "I can tell you the direction." He closed his eyes, put out his right hand, and slowly rotated. When his pointing finger stabilized, he opened his eyes. "Magician's that way. That's my talent —direction. I can tell you where anything is."

"I already know the direction," Bink said. "West. My main problem is getting through all this jungle. There's so much hostile magic—"

"You said it," Crombie agreed heartily. "Almost as much hostile magic as there is in civilized regions. The raiders must have magicked me here, figuring I'd never get out alive and my body would never be found. My shade couldn't avenge me in the deep jungle."

"Oh, I don't know about that," Bink said, thinking of the shade Donald in the chasm.

"But now I've recovered, thanks to you. Tell you

what: I'll be your bodyguard until you reach the Magician. Is that a fair return?"

"You really don't need to—"

"Oh, but I do! Soldier's honor. You did me a good turn, I'll do you a good turn. I insist. I can help a lot. I'll show you." He closed his eyes again, extended his hand, and rotated. When he stopped, he continued: "That's the direction of the greatest threat to your welfare. Want to verify it?"

"No," Bink said.

"Well, I do. Danger never went away by being ignored. You have to go out and conquer it. Give me back my sword."

Bink gave it back, and Crombie proceeded in the direction he had pointed: north.

Bink followed, disgruntled. He did not want to seek out danger, but he knew it was not right to let the soldier walk into it in his stead. Maybe it was something obvious, like the Gap dragon. But that was no immediate threat, so long as Bink stayed out of the chasm. He fully intended to stay out.

When Crombie found himself balked by thick brush, he simply slashed it away with his sword. Bink noticed that some of the vegetation gave way before the blade actually struck; if providing a path was the best route to survival, these plants took it. But suppose the soldier hacked into a tangle tree? That could be the danger he had pointed out.

No—a tangler was deadly to the unwary, but it did not move from the place it had rooted. Since Bink had been going west, not north, no stationary thing was much of a threat to him unless it was west.

There was a scream. Bink jumped, and Crombie held his sword at the ready. But it was only a woman, cringing and frightened.

"Speak, girl!" Crombie roared, flourishing his wicked blade. "What mischief do you intend?"

"Don't hurt me!" she cried. "I am only Dee, lost and alone. I thought you came to rescue me."

"You lie!" Crombie exclaimed. "You mean harm to this man, my friend who saved my life. Confess!" And he lifted his sword again.

"For God's sake—let her be!" Bink yelled. "You made a mistake. She's obviously harmless."

"My talent's never been wrong before," Crombie said. "This is where it pointed your greatest threat."

"Maybe the threat is behind her, beyond," Bink said. "She was merely in the line of sight."

Crombie paused. "Could be. I never thought of that." He was evidently a reasonable man, under the violence. "Wait, I'll verify."

The soldier withdrew somewhat, stationing himself to the east of the girl. He shut his eyes and rotated. His pointing finger came to bear squarely on Dee.

The girl burst into tears. "I mean you no harm—I swear it. Don't hurt me!"

She was a plain girl, of strictly average face and figure, no beauty. This was in contrast to the several females Bink had encountered recently. Yet there was something vaguely familiar about her, and Bink was always unnerved by feminine distress. "Maybe it's not physical danger," he said. "Does your talent differentiate?"

"No, it doesn't," Crombie admitted, a bit defensively. "It can be any kind of threat, and she may not actually mean you harm—but sure as hell, there's something."

Bink studied the girl, whose sniffles were drying up. That familiarity—where had he seen her before? She was not from the North Village, and he really had not encountered many girls elsewhere. Somewhere on his current journey?

Slowly the notion dawned on him: a Sorceress of illusion did not have to make herself beautiful. If she wanted to keep track of him, she could adopt a completely different appearance, thinking he would never suspect. Yet the illusion would be easiest to maintain if it corresponded somewhat to her natural contours. Take off a few pounds here and there, modify the voice—

could be. If he fell for the ruse, he could be in dire danger of being led into corruption. Only the soldier's special magic gave it away.

But how could he be sure? Even if Dee represented some critical threat to him, he had to be sure he had identified the right danger. A man who stepped around a venom mouse could be overlooking a harpy on the other side. Snap judgments about magic were suspect.

A brilliant notion came to him. "Dee, you must be thirsty," he said. "Have a drink of water." And he proffered his canteen.

"Oh, thank you," she said, taking it gladly.

The water cured all ills. An enchantment was an ill, wasn't it? So if she drank, it might show her—at least momentarily—in her true guise. Then he would know.

Dee drank deeply.

There was no change.

"Oh, this is very good," she said. "I feel so much better."

The two men exchanged glances. Scratch one bright notion. Either Dee was not Iris, or the Sorceress had better control than he had supposed. He had no way of knowing.

"Now be on your way, girl," Crombie said curtly.

"I am going to see the Magician Humfrey," she said contritely. "I need a spell to make me well."

Again Bink and Crombie exchanged glances. Dee had drunk the magic water; she was well. Therefore she had no need to see the Good Magician on that score. She had to be lying. And if she were lying, what was she concealing from them?

She must have picked this particular destination because she knew Bink was going there. Yet this was still conjecture. It could be pure coincidence—or she could be an ogre in female form—a healthy ogre!—waiting for the expedient moment to strike.

Crombie, seeing Bink's indecision, made a decision of his own. "If you let her go with you, then I'm coming

too. With my hand ever on my sword. Watching her—
all the time."

"Maybe that's best," Bink agreed reluctantly.

"I bear you no malice," Dee protested. "I would do
nothing to hurt you, even were I able. Why don't you
believe me?"

Bink found it too complicated to explain. "You can
travel with us if you want to," he said.

Dee smiled gratefully, but Crombie shook his head
grimly and fingered the hilt of his sword.

Crombie remained suspicious, but Bink soon discovered he enjoyed Dee's company. She had no trace of the
personality of the Sorceress. She was such an average
girl that he identified with her to a considerable extent.
She seemed to have no magic; at least, she evaded that
subject. Perhaps she was going to the Magician in the
hope of finding her talent; maybe that was what she had
meant by needing a spell to make her well. Who was in
good shape in Xanth without magic?

However, if she were the Sorceress Iris, her ruse
would quickly be exposed by the divination of the Magician. So the truth would be known.

They stopped at the Spring of Life to refill their can-
teens, traveled half a day, then got caught by a techni-
color hailstorm. It was magic, of course, or magic-
augmented. The colors gave it away. Which meant that
there would not be any great melting or runoff. All they
had to do was take shelter from it until it passed.

But they happened to be on a barren ridge: no trees
for miles around, no caves, no houses. The land went
up and down, cut away by erosion gullies, strewn with
boulders—but there was nothing to shield them effectively from the storm.

Pelted by increasingly large hailstones, the three scurried in the direction Crombie's magic pointed: the route
to safe shelter. It came into view behind a boulder: a
monstrously spreading tentacular tree.

"That's a tangler!" Bink exclaimed in horror. "We
can't go there."

Crombie was brought up short, peering through the hail. "So it is. My talent never pointed wrong before."

Except when it accused Dee, Bink thought. He wondered just how reliable the soldier's magic really was. For one thing, why hadn't it pointed out the soldier's danger to himself, before he got stabbed in the back and left to die? But Bink did not say that out loud. There were often complexities and confusions in magic, and he was sure Crombie meant well.

"There's a hephalumph there," Dee cried. "Half eaten."

Sure enough, the huge carcass lay near the trunk orifice of the tree. Its posterior was gone, but the front end was untouched. The tree had evidently caught it and consumed as much as it could—but a hephalumph was so big that even a tangle tree could not polish it off in one meal. Now the tree was sated, its tentacles dangling listlessly.

"So it's safe after all," Bink said, wincing as an egg-sized red hailstone just missed his head. The hail was puffy and light, but it still could hurt. "It will be hours before the tree revives enough to become aggressive. Maybe even days—and even then, it'll start on the lumph first."

Still Crombie balked, understandably. "Could be an illusion, that carcass," he warned. "Be suspicious of all things—that's the soldier's motto. A trap to make us think the tree's docile. How do you think it tempted the hephalumph in there?"

Telling point. Periodic hailstorms on the ridge to drive prey to cover, and seemingly ideal cover waiting—beautiful system. "But we'll be knocked silly by hail if we don't get to cover soon," Bink said.

"I'll go," Dee said. Before Bink could protest, she plunged into the territory of the tree.

The tentacles quivered, twitching toward her—but lacked the imperative to make a real effort. She dashed up and kicked the hephalumph in the trunk—and it was solid. "No mirage," she cried. "Come on in."

"Unless she's a shill," Crombie muttered. "I tell you, she's a threat to you, Bink. If she shilled for the tangler, she could trick dozens of people into its clutches—"

The man was paranoid. Perhaps this was another useful quality for soldiers—though again, it didn't seem to have kept him out of trouble before. "I don't believe it," Bink said. "But I do believe this hailstorm! I'm going in." And he went.

He passed the outer fringe of tentacles nervously, but they remained quiescent. A hungry tangler was not a subtle plant; it normally grabbed the moment its prey was grabable.

Finally Crombie followed. The tree shuddered slightly, as if irritated by its inability to consume them, and that was all. "Well, I knew my talent told the truth. It always does," he said, somewhat weakly.

It was actually very nice here. The hailstones had grown to the size of clenched fists, but they bounced off the tree's upper foliage and piled up in a circle around it, caught by a slight depression. Predator trees tended to sit in such depressions, formed by the action of their tentacles while cleaning brush and rocks out of the way in order to have an attractive lawn for passing creatures. The refuse was tossed beyond in a great circle, so that in the course of years the land surface rose. The tangle was a highly successful type of tree, and some of them formed wells whose rims were fashioned from buried bones of past prey. They had been cleaned out near the North Village, but all children were instructed in this menace. Theoretically, a man pursued by a dragon could skirt a tangler, leading the dragon within range of the tentacles—if he had both courage and skill.

Within the shielded area there was a fine greensward rising in soft hillocks, rather like the torso of a woman. Sweet perfume odors wafted through, and the air was pleasantly warm. In short, this was a seemingly ideal place to seek shelter—and that was by design. It had certainly fooled the hephalumph. Obviously this was a good location, for the tangler had grown to enormous girth. But right now they were here rent-free.

"Well, my magic was right all the time," Crombie said. "I should have trusted it. But by the same token . . ." He glanced meaningfully at Dee.

Bink wondered about that. He believed in the soldier's sincerity, and the location magic was obviously functional. Had it malfunctioned in Dee's case, or was she really a bad if obscure threat? If so, what kind? He could not believe she meant him harm. He had suspected her of being Iris the Sorceress, but now he didn't believe that; she showed no sign of the temperament of the mistress of illusion, and personality was not something that magic could conceal for very long.

"Why didn't your magic warn you of the stab in the back?" Bink asked the soldier, making another attempt to ascertain what was reliable and what was not.

"I didn't ask it," Crombie said. "I was a damned fool. But once I see you safely to your Magician, I'll sure as hell ask it who stabbed me, and then . . ." He fingered the blade of his sword meaningfully.

A fair answer. The talent was not a warning signal; it merely performed on demand. Crombie had obviously had no reason to suspect danger, any more than Bink had reason to feel threatened now. Where was the distinction between natural caution and paranoia?

The storm continued. None of them were willing to sleep, because they did not trust the tree to that extent, so they sat and talked. Crombie told a tough story of ancient battle and heroism in the days of Xanth's Fourth Wave. Bink was no military man, but he found himself caught up in the gallantry of it, and almost wished he had lived in those adventurous times, when men of no magic were considered *men*.

By the end of that story, the storm had eased off, but the hail was piled so high that it didn't seem worthwhile to go out yet. Usually the meltoff from a magic storm was quite rapid once the sun came out again, so it was worth waiting for.

"Where do you live?" Bink asked Dee.

"Oh, I'm just a country girl, you know," she said. "No one else was going to travel through the wilderness."

"That's no answer," Crombie snapped suspiciously.

She shrugged. "It's the only answer I have. I can't change what I am, much as I might like to."

"It's the same answer I have, too," Bink said. "I'm just a villager, nothing special. I hope the Magician will be able to make me into something special, by finding out that I have some good magic talent no one ever suspected, and I'm willing to work for him for a year for that."

"Yes," she said, smiling appreciatively at him. Suddenly he felt himself liking her. She was ordinary—like him. She was motivated—like him. They had something in common.

"You're going for magic so your girl back home will marry you?" Crombie asked, sounding cynical.

"Yes," Bink agreed, remembering Sabrina with sudden poignancy. Dee turned away. "And so I can stay in Xanth."

"You're a fool, a civilian fool," the soldier said kindly.

"Well, it's the only chance I have," Bink replied. "Any gamble is worthwhile when the alternative—"

"I don't mean the magic. That's useful. And staying in Xanth makes sense. I mean marriage."

"Marriage?"

"Women are the curse of mankind," Crombie said vehemently. "They trap men into marriage, the way this tangle tree traps prey, and they torment them the rest of their lives."

"Now that's unfair," Dee said. "Didn't you have a mother?"

"She drove my worthy father to drink and loco," Crombie asserted. "Made his life hell on earth—and mine too. She could read our minds—that was her talent."

A woman who could read men's minds: hell indeed

for a man! If any woman had been able to read Bink's mind—ugh!

"Must have been hell for her, too," Dee observed.

Bink suppressed a smile, but Crombie scowled. "I ran off and joined the army two years before I was of age. Never regretted it."

Dee frowned. "You don't sound like God's gift to women, either. We can all be thankful you never touched any."

"Oh, I touch them," Crombie said with a coarse laugh. "I just don't marry them. No one of them's going to get her hooks into me."

"You're disgusting," she snapped.

"I'm smart. And if Bink's smart, he'll not let you start tempting him, either."

"I wasn't!" she exclaimed angrily.

Crombie turned away in evident repugnance. "Ah, you're all the same. Why do I waste my time talking with the likes of you? Might as well argue ethics with the devil."

"Well, if you feel that way, I'll go!" Dee said. She jumped to her feet and stalked to the edge.

Bink thought she was bluffing, for the storm, though abating, was still in force with occasional flurries. Colored hailstones were mounded up two feet high, and the sun was not yet out.

But Dee plunged out into it.

"Hey, wait!" Bink cried. He ran after her.

Dee had disappeared, hidden by the storm. "Let her go, good riddance," Crombie said. "She had designs on you; I know how they work. I knew she was trouble from the start."

Bink put his arms up over his head and face against the hail and stepped out. His feet slid out from under, skidding on hailstones, and he fell headlong into the pile. Hailstones closed in over his head. Now he knew what had happened to Dee. She was buried somewhere out here.

He had to close his eyes, for powder from crushed

stones was getting into them. This was not true ice, but coalesced vapor, magic; the stones were dry and not really cold. But they were slippery.

Something caught his foot. Bink kicked violently, remembering the sea monster near the island of the Sorceress, forgetting that it had been an illusion and that there could hardly be a sea monster here. But its grip was tight; it dragged him into an enclosure.

He scrambled to his feet as it let go. He leaped on the troll shape he saw through the film of dust.

Bink found himself flying through the air. He landed hard on his back, the creature drawing on his arm. Trolls were tough! He squirmed around and tried to grab its legs—but the thing dropped on top of him and pinned him firmly to the ground. "Ease up, Bink," it said. "It's me—Crombie."

Bink did as much of a double-take as he was able to, considering his position, and recognized the soldier.

Crombie let him up. "I knew you'd never find your way out of that mess, so I hauled you out by the one part I could reach, your foot. You had magic dust in your eyes, so you couldn't recognize me. Sorry I had to put you down."

Magic dust—of course. It distorted the vision, making men seem like trolls, ogres, or worse—and vice versa. It was an additional hazard of such storms, so that people could not see their way out of them. Probably many victims had seen the tangle tree as an innocent blanket tree. "That's okay," Bink said. "You soldiers sure know how to fight."

"All part of the business. Never charge a man who knows how to throw." Crombie raised one finger near his ear, signifying an idea. "I'll show you how to do it; it's a nonmagical talent you can use."

"Dee!" Bink cried. "She's still out there!"

Crombie grimaced. "Okay. I made her walk out; if it means so much to you, I'll help you find her."

So the man did have some decency, even with regard to women. "Do you really hate them all?" Bink asked as he girded himself to wrestle with the hail again. "Even the ones who don't read minds?"

"They all read minds," Crombie asserted. "Most of them do it without magic, is all. But I won't swear as there's no girl in the whole of Xanth for me. If I found a pretty one who wasn't mean or nagging or deceitful . . ." He shook his head. "But if any like that exist, they sure as hell wouldn't marry me."

So the soldier rejected all women because he felt they rejected him. Well, it was a good enough rationale.

Now the storm had stopped. They went out into the piled hailstones, stepping carefully so as not to take any more spills. The colored storm clouds cleared, dissipating rapidly now that their magic imperative was spent.

What caused such storms? Bink wondered. They had to be inanimate—but the course of this journey had convinced him that dead objects did indeed have magic, often very strong magic. Maybe it was in the very substance of Xanth, and it diffused slowly into the living and nonliving things that occupied the land. The living things controlled their shares of magic, channelizing it, focusing it, making it manifest at will. The inanimate things released it haphazardly, as in this storm. There had to be a lot of magic here, gathered from a large area. All wasted in a pointless mass of hailstones.

Yet not all pointless. Obviously the tangle tree benefited from such storms, and probably there were other ways in which they contributed to the local ecology. Maybe the hail culled out the weaker creatures, animals less fit to survive, facilitating wilderness evolution. And other inanimate magic was quite pointed, such as that of Lookout Rock and the Spring of Life—its magic distilled from water percolating through the entire region, intensifying its potency? Perhaps it was the magic itself that made these things conscious of their individuality. Every aspect of Xanth was affected by magic, and governed by it. Without magic, Xanth would be—the very notion filled him with horror—Xanth would be Mundane.

The sun broke through the clouds. Where the beams struck, the hailstones puffed into colored vapor. Their fabric of magic could not withstand the beat of direct sunlight. That made Bink wonder again: was the sun antipathetic to magic? If the magic emanated from the depths, the surface of the land was the mere fringe of it. If someone ever delved down deep, he might approach the actual source of power. Intriguing notion!

In fact, Bink wished that he could set aside his quest for his own personal magic and make that search for the ultimate nature of reality in Xanth. Surely, way down deep, there was the answer to all his questions.

But he could not. For one thing, he had to locate Dee.

In a few minutes all the hail was gone. But so was the girl. "She must have slid down the slope into the forest," Crombie said. "She knows where we are; she can find us if she wants to."

"Unless she's in trouble," Bink said worriedly. "Use your talent; point her out."

Crombie sighed. "All right." He closed his eyes, rotated, and pointed down the south side of the ridge.

They trotted down—and found her tracks in the soft earth at the fringe of the jungle. They followed them and soon caught up.

"Dee!" Bink cried gladly. "We're sorry. Don't risk the jungle alone."

She marched on determinedly. "Leave me alone," Dee said. "I don't want to go with you."

"But Crombie didn't really mean—" Bink said.

"He meant. You don't trust me. So keep away from me. I'd rather make it on my own."

And that was that. She was adamant. Bink certainly wasn't going to force her. "Well, if you need help or anything, call—or something—"

She went on without answering.

"She couldn't have been very much of a threat," Bink said forlornly.

"She's a threat, all right," Crombie insisted. "But no

threat's as much of a threat when it's somewhere else."

They ascended the ridge again and traveled on. In another day they came in sight of the Magician's castle, thanks to the soldier's unerring magic directional sense and ability to avoid the dangers of the wilderness. He had been a big help.

"Well, that's it," Crombie said. "I have seen you to this point safely, and I think that about squares us. I have business of my own elsewhere before I report to the King for reassignment. I hope you find your magic."

"I hope so too," Bink said. "Thanks for the throws you taught me."

"It was little enough. You'll have to practice them a lot more before they'll really serve. Sorry I got the girl mad at you. Maybe my talent was wrong about her after all."

Bink didn't care to discuss that aspect, so he just shook hands and headed for the castle of the Good Magician.

Chapter 6. Magician

The castle was impressive. It was not large, but it was tall and well designed. It had a deep moat, a stout outer wall, and a high inner tower girt with parapets and embrasures. It must have been built by magic, because it would have taken an army of skilled craftsmen a year to build it by hand.

Yet Humfrey was supposed to be a Magician of information, not of construction or illusion. How could he have magicked such an edifice?

No matter; the castle was here. Bink walked down to

the moat. He heard a horrible kind of galloping splash, and around from behind the castle came a horse, running on the water. No, not a horse—a hippocampus, or seahorse, with the head and forefeet of a horse and the tail of a dolphin. Bink knew the dolphin only from old pictures; it was a kind of magic fish that breathed air instead of water.

Bink stepped back. The thing looked dangerous. It could not follow him out onto land, but it could pulverize him in water. How was he to cross the moat? There did not seem to be any drawbridge.

Then he noted that the hippocampus wore a saddle. Oh, no! Ride the water monster?

Yet it obviously was the way to go. The Magician did not want his time wasted by anyone who wasn't serious. If he lacked the nerve to ride the seahorse, he didn't deserve to see Humfrey. It made perverse sense.

Did Bink really want the answer to his question? At the price of a year's service?

The picture of beautiful Sabrina came to his mind, so real, so evocative that all else became meaningless. He walked up to the hippocampus, waiting at the edge of the moat expectantly, and climbed onto its saddle.

The creature took off. It neighed as it sped around the moat, instead of across it. The steed was jubilant, using the water as a veritable race track, while Bink clung desperately to the saddle horn. The powerful front legs of the hippocampus terminated in flippers rather than hooves, scooping gouts of water back on either side, drenching him with the spray. The tail, curled in a muscular loop when the creature was stationary, uncoiled and threshed the water with such vigor that the saddle whipped back and forth, threatening to dislodge the rider momentarily.

"Neigh! Ne-ei-igh!" the monster sounded gleefully. It had him where it wanted him: right in the saddle, ripe for bucking off. The moment he hit the water, it would turn and devour him. What a fool he had been!

Wait—so long as he remained in the saddle, it could

not get at him. All he had to do was hang on, and in time it would tire.

Easier thought than done. The hippocampus bucked and plunged, first lifting him above the moat, then immersing him in the frothing water. It curled its tail into a spiral and rolled, dunking him again and again. Bink was afraid it would stop with him on the bottom, forcing him to let go or drown. But the saddle was firmly fixed on its backside, and its horse's head projected the same direction Bink's head did, so it had to hold its breath when he held his. The monster was exercising, while Bink was merely hanging on; it was using more energy than he, and so it had to breathe sooner. Hence it could not drown him—once he had figured this out. In fact, all he needed to do was keep his head and he would win, for whatever that was worth.

Finally the creature gave up. It flopped to the inner gate and lay still while Bink dismounted. He had conquered the first hurdle.

"Thank you, Hip," he said, making a little bow to the seahorse. It snorted and splashed quickly out of reach.

Now Bink faced a giant wooden door. It was closed, and he pounded on it with one fist. It was so solid that his hand hurt, and the sound was minimized: *dink— dink—dink!*

He drew his knife and rapped with the handle, since he had lost his new staff in the moat—with no better result. If a hollow partition made the most noise, this was indubitably solid. There was no way to force it.

Maybe the Magician was out? There should still be servants attending to the castle.

Bink was getting angry. He had made a long, hazardous journey to get here, and he was ready to pay the exorbitant price for one piddling bit of information— and the damned Good Magician lacked the courtesy even to answer the door.

Well, he would get in despite the Magician. Somehow. He would *demand* his audience.

He studied the door. It was a good ten feet tall and

five feet wide; it seemed to have been made of hand-hewn eight-by-eight posts. The thing must weigh a ton—literally. It had no hinges, which meant it had to open by sliding to one side—no, the portals were solid stone. Lifted out of the way? There were no connecting ropes to haul it up, no pulleys that he could see. There might be hidden screws set into the wood, but that seemed a lot of trouble and somewhat risky. Screws sometimes let go at inopportune moments. Maybe the whole door dropped into the floor? But that, too, was stone. So it seemed the whole mass simply had to be removed every time someone wanted access.

Ridiculous! It had to be a phony, a dummy. There would be a more sensible aperture for routine use, either magical or physical. All he had to do was find it.

In the stone? No, that would be unmanageably heavy; if it were not, it would represent a weakened place where an enemy could force entry. No point in building a substantial castle with such a liability. Where, then?

Bink ran his fingers over the surface of the huge mock-door. He found a crack. He traced it around in a square. Yes. He placed both hands against the center and shoved.

The square moved. It slid inward, and finally dropped inside, leaving a hole just big enough for a man to crawl through. Here was his entry.

Bink wasted no time. He climbed through the hole.

Inside was a dimly illuminated hall. And another monster.

It was a manticora—a creature the size of a horse, with the head of a man, body of a lion, wings of a dragon, and tail of a scorpion. One of the most ferocious magical monsters known.

"Welcome to lunch, little morsel," the manticora said, arching its segmented tail up over its back. Its mouth was strange, with three rows of teeth, one inside another—but its voice was stranger. It was something

like a flute, and something like a trumpet, beautiful in
its fashion but difficult to comprehend.

Bink whipped out his knife. "I am not your lunch,"
he said, with a good deal more conviction than he felt.

The manticora laughed, and now its tones were the
sour notes of irony. "You are not anyone else's lunch,
mortal. You have climbed nimbly into my trap."

He had indeed. But Bink was fed up with these
pointless obstacles, and also suspected that they were
not pointless, paradoxical as that might seem. If the
Magician's monsters consumed all callers, Humfrey
would never have any business, never obtain any fees.
And by all accounts the Good Magician was a grasping
man who existed principally to profit himself; he
needed those exorbitant fees to increase his wealth. So
probably this was another test, like those of the seahorse and the door; all Bink had to do was figure out
the solution.

"I can walk back out of this cage any time I want
to," Bink said boldly. He willed his knees not to knock
together with his shivering. "It isn't made to hold people my size; it holds in monsters your size. You're the
prisoner, molar-face."

"*Molar*-face!" the manticora repeated incredulously,
showing about sixty molars in the process. "Why, you
pipsqueak mortal, I'll sting you into a billion-year suffering sleep!"

Bink made for the square portal. The monster
pounced, its tail stabbing forward over its head. It was
horribly fast.

But Bink had only feinted; he was already ducking
forward, directly at the lion's claws. It was the opposite
direction from that which the monster had expected,
and the thing could not reverse in midair. Its deadly tail
stabbed into the wood of the door, and its head popped
through the square hole. Its lion's shoulders wedged
tightly against it, unable to fit through the hole, and its
wings fluttered helplessly.

Bink could not resist. He straightened up, turned,

and yelled: "You didn't think I came all the way here just to back out again, did you, you half-reared monster?" Then he planted a swift hard kick on the creature's posterior, just under the lifted tail.

There was a fluted howl of rage and anguish from the door. Then Bink was away, running down the hall, hoping that there was a man-sized exit. Otherwise—

The door seemed to explode. There was a thump behind as the manticora fell free and rolled back to its feet. It was really angry now! If there were no way out—

There was. The challenge had been to get around the monster, not to kill it; no man could kill such a creature with a knife. Bink scrambled through the barred gate as the manticora charged down the hall too late, splinters of wood falling from its tail.

Now Bink was in the castle proper. It was a fairly dark, dank place, with little evidence of human habitation. Where was the Good Magician?

Surely there would be some way to announce his presence, assuming that the ruckus with the manticora had not sufficed. Bink looked around and spied a dangling cord. He gave it one good yank and stepped back lest something drop on him. He did not quite trust this adorable castle.

A bell sounded. DONG-DONG, DONG-DONG.

A gnarled old elf trotted up. "Who shall I say is calling?"

"Bink of the North Village."

"Drink of what?"

"Bink! B-I-N-K."

The elf studied him. "What shall I say is the business of your master Bink?"

"*I* am Bink! My business is the quest for a magical talent."

"And what recompense do you offer for the invaluable time of the Good Magician?"

"The usual scale: one year's service." Then, in a

lower tone: "It's robbery, but I'm stuck for it. Your master gouges the public horrendously."

The elf considered. "The Magician is occupied at the moment; can you come back tomorrow?"

"Come back tomorrow!" Bink exploded, thinking of what the hippocampus and manticora would do to him if they got a second chance. "Does the old bugger want my business or doesn't he?"

The elf frowned. "Well, if you're going to be that way about it, come on upstairs."

Bink followed the little man up a winding staircase. The interior of the castle lightened with elevation and became more ornate, more residential.

Finally the elf showed the way into a paper-filled study. The elf seated himself at a big wooden desk. "Very well, Bink of the North Village. You have won your way through the defenses of this castle. What makes you think your service is worth the old gouging bugger's while?"

Bink started to make an angry exclamation—but cut himself off as he realized that this was the Good Magician Humfrey. He was sunk!

All he could do now was give a straight answer before he got kicked out. "I am strong and I can work. It is for you to decide whether that is worth your while."

"You are oink-headed and doubtless have a grotesque appetite. You'd no doubt cost me more in board than I'd ever get from you."

Bink shrugged, knowing it would be futile to debate such points. He could only antagonize the Magician further. He had really walked into the last trap: the trap of arrogance.

"Perhaps you could carry books and turn pages for me. Can you read?"

"Some," Bink said. He had been a reasonably apt pupil of the centaur instructor, but that had been years ago.

"You seem to be a fair hand at insult, too; maybe

you could talk intruders out of intruding with their petty problems."

"Maybe," Bink agreed grimly. Obviously, he had really done it this time—and after coming so close to success.

"Well, come on; we don't have all day," Humfrey snapped, bouncing out of his chair. Bink saw now that he was not a true elf, but a very small human being. An elf, of course, being a magical creature, could not be a Magician. That was part of what had put him off at first—though increasingly he wondered about the accuracy of that conjecture. Xanth continued to show him ramifications of magic he had not thought of before.

Apparently the Magician had accepted the case. Bink followed him to the next room. It was a laboratory, with magical devices cluttering the shelves and piled on the floor, except for one cleared area.

"Stand aside," Humfrey said brusquely, though Bink hardly had room to move. The Magician did not have an endearing personality. It would be a real chore to work for him a year. But it just might be worth it, if Bink learned he had a magic talent, and it was a good one.

Humfrey took a tiny bottle from the shelf, shook it, and set it on the floor in the middle of a pentagram—a five-sided figure. Then he made a gesture with both hands and intoned something in an arcane tongue.

The lid of the bottle popped off. Smoke issued forth. It expanded into a sizable cloud, then coalesced into the shape of a demon. Not a particularly ferocious demon; this one's horns were vestigial, and his tail had a soft tuft instead of a cutting barb. Furthermore, he wore glasses, which must have been imported from Mundania, where such artifacts were commonly used to shore up the weak eyes of the denizens there. Or so the myths had it. Bink almost laughed. Imagine a near-sighted demon!

"O Beauregard," Humfrey intoned. "I conjure thee by the authority vested in me by the Compact, tell us what magic talent this lad, Bink of the North Village of Xanth, possesses."

So that was the Magician's secret: he was a demon-summoner. The pentagram was for containing the demons released from their magic bottles; even a studious demon was a creature of hell.

Beauregard focused his lenscovered eyes on Bink. "Step into my demesnes, that I may inspect you properly," he said.

"Nuh-*uh!*" Bink exclaimed.

"You're a tough nut," the demon said.

"I didn't ask you for his personality profile," Humfrey snapped. "What's his magic?"

The demon concentrated. "He has magic—strong magic—but—"

Strong magic! Bink's hopes soared.

"But I am unable to fathom it," Beauregard said. He grimaced at the Good Magician. "Sorry, fathead; I'll have to renege on this one."

"Then get ye gone, incompetent," Humfrey snarled, clapping his hands together with a remarkably sharp report. Evidently he was used to being insulted; it was part of his life style. Maybe Bink had lucked out again.

The demon dissolved into smoke and drained back into his bottle. Bink stared at the bottle, trying to determine what was visible within it. Was there a tiny figure, hunched over a miniature book, reading?

Now the Magician contemplated Bink. "So you have strong magic that cannot be fathomed. Were you aware of this? Did you come here to waste my time?"

"No," Bink said. "I never was sure I had magic at all. There's never been any evidence of it. I hoped—but I feared I had none."

"Is there anything you know of that could account for this opacity? A counterspell, perhaps?"

Evidently Humfrey was far from omnipotent. But now that Bink knew he was a demon-conjurer, that explained it. Nobody summoned a demon without good reason. The Magician charged heavily for his service because he took a heavy risk.

"I don't know of anything," Bink said. "Except maybe the drink of magic healing water I took."

"Beauregard should not have been deceived by that. He's a pretty savvy demon, a real scholar of magic. Do you have any of that water with you?"

Bink held out his canteen. "I saved some. Never can tell when it might be needed."

Humfrey took it, poured out a drop on his palm, touched his tongue to it, and grimaced thoughtfully. "Standard formula," he said. "It doesn't bollix up informational or divinatory magic. I've got a keg of similar stuff in my cellar. Brewed it myself. Mine is free of the Spring's self-interest geis, of course. But keep this; it can be useful."

The Magician set up a pointer attached to a string, beside a wall chart with pictures of a smiling cherub and a frowning devil. "Let's play Twenty Questions."

He moved his hands, casting a spell, and Bink realized that his prior realization had been premature. Humfrey did do more than demon-summoning—but he still specialized in information. "Bink of the North Village," he intoned. "Have you oriented on him?"

The pointer swung around to indicate the cherub.

"Does he have magic?"

The cherub again.

"Strong magic?"

Cherub.

"Can you identify it?"

Cherub.

"Will you tell me its nature?"

The pointer moved to cover the devil.

"What is this?" Humfrey demanded irritably. "No, that's not a question, idiot! It's an exclamation. I can't figure why you spirits are balking." Angrily he cast the release spell and turned to Bink. "There's something mighty funny here. But it's become a challenge. I'm going to use a truth spell on you. We'll get to the heart of this."

The Magician waved his stubby arms again, muttered a vile-sounding incantation—and suddenly Bink felt strange. He had never experienced this odd type of magic before, with its gestures, words, and assorted apparatus; he was used to inherent talents that worked when they were willed to work. The Good Magician seemed to be something of a scientist—though Bink hardly understood that Mundane term, either.

"What is your identity?" Humfrey demanded.

"Bink of the North Village." It was the truth—but this time Bink said it because the spell compelled him to, not because he wanted to.

"Why did you come here?"

"To find out whether I have magic, and what it might be, so I shall not be exiled from Xanth and can marry—"

"Enough. I don't care about the sordid details." The Magician shook his head. "So you were telling the truth all along. The mystery deepens, the plot thickens. Now—what is your talent?"

Bink opened his mouth, compelled to speak—and there was an animal roar.

Humfrey blinked. "Oh—the manticora is hungry. Spell abate; wait here while I feed him." He departed.

An inconvenient time for the manticora to get hungry! But Bink could hardly blame the Magician for hastening to the feeding chore. If the monster should break out of its cage—

Bink was left to his own devices. He walked around the room, stepping carefully to avoid the litter, not touching anything. He came to a mirror. "Mirror, mirror on the wall," he said playfully. "Who is the fairest one of all?"

The mirror clouded, then cleared. A gross fat warty toad peered out. Bink jumped. Then he realized: this was a magic mirror; it had shown him the fairest one of all—the fairest toad.

"I mean, the fairest female human being," he clarified.

Now Sabrina looked out at him. Bink had been joking at first, but he should have realized that the mirror would take him seriously. Was Sabrina really the fairest girl of all? Probably not, objectively. The mirror showed her because, to Bink's prejudiced eye, she was the one. To some other man—

The picture changed. Now the girl Wynne looked out. Yes, she was pretty too, though too stupid to be worthwhile. Some men would like that very well, however. On the other hand—

Now the Sorceress Iris looked out, in her most beguiling illusion. "Well, it's about time you got around to me, Bink," she said. "I can still enable you to—"

"No!" Bink cried. And the mirror went blank.

He calmed himself, then faced the mirror again. "Can you answer informational questions too?" Of course it could; otherwise it wouldn't be here.

The mirror clouded and cleared. A picture of the cherub appeared, meaning yes.

"Why are we having so much trouble discovering my talent?"

The picture that formed this time was that of a foot, a paw—a monkey's paw.

Bink looked at it for some time, trying to figure out its meaning, but it eluded him. The mirror must have gotten confused and thrown in an irrelevant image.

"What is my talent?" he asked at last.

And the mirror cracked.

"What are you doing?" Humfrey demanded behind him.

Bink jumped guiltily. "I—seem to have broken your mirror," he said. "I was just—"

"You were just asking stupidly direct questions of an instrument designed for subtlety," Humfrey said angrily. "Did you actually think the mirror could reveal what the demon Beauregard balked at?"

"I'm sorry," Bink said lamely.

"You're a lot more trouble than you're worth. But you are also a challenge. Let's get on with it." The Magician made his gesture and incantation again, restoring the truth spell. "What is your—"

There was a crash. The glass had fallen out of the cracked mirror. "I wasn't asking you!" Humfrey yelled at it. He returned to Bink. "What—"

There was a shudder. The castle shook. "Earthquake!" the Magician exclaimed. "Everything happens at once."

He crossed the room and peered out an embrasure. "No, it's only the invisible giant passing by."

Humfrey returned once more to Bink. This time he squinted at him, hard. "It's not coincidence. Something is preventing you—or anything else—from giving that answer. Some very powerful, unidentified magic. Magician-caliber enchantment. I had thought there were only three persons of that rank alive today, but it seems there is a fourth."

"Three?"

"Humfrey, Iris, Trent. But none of these have magic of this type."

"Trent! The Evil Magician?"

"Perhaps you call him evil. I never found him so. We were friends, in our fashion. There is a kind of camaraderie at our level—"

"But he was exiled twenty years ago."

Humfrey looked slantwise at Bink. "You equate exile with death? He resides in Mundania. My information does not extend beyond the Shield, but I am sure he survives. He is an exceptional man. But without magic now."

"Oh." Bink had equated exile with death, emotionally. This was a good reminder; there was life beyond the Shield. He still did not want to go there, but at least it diminished the specter.

"Though it galls me exceedingly, I dare not push the question further. I am not properly protected against interference magic."

"But why would anyone try to prevent me from knowing my own talent?" Bink asked, bewildered.

"Oh, you know it. You just can't tell it—even to yourself. The knowledge is buried deep inside you. And there, it seems, it is going to remain. I simply am not prepared to take the risk involved for a mere one-year service; I'd almost certainly take a loss on that contract."

"But why would a Magician—I mean, I'm nobody! How could it benefit anybody else to stop me from—"

"It might not be a person at all, but a thing placing a geis on you. A geis of ignorance."

"But why?"

Humfrey grimaced. "Lad, you grow repetitive. Your talent could represent some threat to some powerful special interest. As a silver sword is a threat to a dragon, even though it may not be near that dragon. So that entity protects itself by blocking off your knowledge of your talent."

"But—"

"If we knew that, we'd know your talent," Humfrey snapped, answering the unformed question.

Still Bink persisted. "How can I demonstrate my talent, then, so I can stay in Xanth?"

"You do seem to have a problem," Humfrey remarked, as if it were of only academic importance. He shrugged. "I'd answer if I could, but I can't. There is of course no charge for my service, since I was unable to complete it. I will send a note with you. Perhaps the King will allow you to remain after all. I believe the bylaws specify that each citizen shall be possessed of magic, not that he actually has to demonstrate it in public. On occasion the demonstration is suspended. I remember one young man who was able to change the color of his urine at will, for example. An affidavit was accepted in lieu of public display."

Failure seemed to have mellowed the Magician considerably. He served Bink a pleasant meal of brown bread and milk—from his private breadfruit orchard and deerfly stable, respectively—and chatted almost sociably. "So many people come here and waste their questions," he confided. "The trick is not necessarily to find the answer, but to find the correct question. Yours is the first real challenge I've had in years. The last one was—let me think—the amaranth. This farmer wanted to know how to develop a really superior plant for greens and grain, so he could feed his family better, and bring in a little income for the comforts of life. I located the magic amaranth for him, and now its use has spread all over Xanth, and beyond it too, for all I know. It is possible to make bread from it that is almost indistinguishable from the real thing." The Magician pulled out a drawer and brought out a special loaf. "See, this has no stem; it was baked, not budded." He broke off a chunk for Bink, who was glad to accept it. "Now that was the kind of question to ask. The answer benefited the whole country of Xanth as well as the individual. Too many desires are of the monkey's-paw variety, in contrast."

"The monkey's paw!" Bink exclaimed. "When I asked the magic mirror, it showed me—"

"It would. The image derives from a Mundane story. They thought it was fiction. But here in Xanth there is magic like that."

"But what . . . ?"

"Do you want to invest a year's service after all?"

"Uh, no, not for that." Bink concentrated on chewing the new bread. It was tougher than true bread.

"Then have it free. It simply means a type of magic that brings you more grief than good, though it grants what you technically ask. Magic you are better off without."

Was Bink better off not knowing his talent? That was what the mirror had seemed to tell him. Yet how could exile, which would deprive him of it entirely, be better than knowledge? "Do many people come with questions, stupid or otherwise?"

"Not so many now that I built this castle and hid it.

Only the really determined find their way here now. Like you."

"How did you build it?" So long as the Magician was talking . . .

"The centaurs built it. I told them how to rid themselves of a local pest, and they served me for a year. They are very skilled craftscreatures, and did a fine job. Periodically I foul up the routes here, applying spells of misdirection, so as not to be pestered by casual querists; it's a good location."

"The monsters!" Bink exclaimed. "The hippocampus, the manticora—they're serving their year's service, discouraging idle questioners?"

"Of course. Do you think they'd stay here for the mere pleasure of it?"

Bink wondered. He remembered the unholy glee with which the seahorse had flung itself about. Still, it would naturally prefer the open sea to a mere moat.

He had finished the bread. It *had* been almost as good as real bread. "With your powers of information, you could—why, you could be King."

Humfrey laughed, and there was nothing whining or bitter about it. "Who in his right mind would want to be King? It's a tedious, strenuous job. I am not a disciplinarian, but a scholar. Most of my labor is in making my magic safe and specific, refining it for greater applicability. Much remains to be done, and I am getting old. I can't waste time with diversions. Let those who wish the crown take it."

Disconcerted, Bink cast about for someone who wanted to rule Xanth. "The Sorceress Iris—"

"The trouble with dealing in illusion," Humfrey said seriously, "is that one begins to be deluded oneself. Iris doesn't need power half so much as she needs a good man."

Even Bink could see the truth in that. "But why doesn't she marry?"

"She's a Sorceress, a good one. She has powers you have not yet glimpsed. She requires a man she can respect—one who has stronger magic than she does. In all Xanth, only I have more magic than she—and I'm of another generation, really too old for her, even if I had any interest in marriage. And of course we would be a mismatch, for our talents are opposite. I deal in truth, she in illusion. I know too much, she imagines too much. So she conspires with lesser talents, convincing herself that it can somehow work out." He shook his head. "It is too bad, really. With the King fading, and no Heir Apparent, and this alternate requirement that the crown go only to a full Magician, it is entirely possible that the throne will be subject to her machinations. Not every young man has your integrity or loyalty to Xanth."

Bink felt a chill. Humfrey knew about Iris's offer, about their encounter. The Magician did not merely answer questions for a fee, he kept track of what was going on in Xanth. But he did not, it seemed, bother to interfere. He just watched. Maybe he investigated the background of specific seekers while the seahorse, wall, and manticora delayed them, so that by the time one won through, Humfrey was ready. Maybe he saved the information, in case someone came to ask "What is the greatest danger facing Xanth?", whereupon he could collect his fee for answering.

"If the King dies, will you take the crown?" Bink asked. "As you said, it will have to go to a powerful Magician, and for the good of Xanth—"

"You pose a question almost as awkward as the one that brought you here," the Good Magician said ruefully. "I do have a certain modicum of patriotism, but I also have a policy against interfering with the natural scheme of things. There is some substance to the concept of the monkey's paw; magic does have its price. I suppose if there were absolutely no alternative I would accept the crown—but first I would search most diligently for some superior Magician to assume the chore. We have not had a top talent appear in a generation; one is overdue." He gazed speculatively at Bink. "There

seems to be magic of that caliber associated with you—
but we cannot harness it if we cannot define it. So I
doubt you are the heir to the throne."

Bink exploded with incredulous, embarrassed laughter. "Me? You insult the throne."

"No, there are qualities in you that would honor the
throne—if you only had identified, controllable magic.
The Sorceress may have chosen better than she knew,
or intended. But evidently there is countermagic that
balks you—though I am not sure the source of that
countermagic would make a good King either. It is a
strange matter, most intriguing."

Bink was tempted by the notion of being a potent
Magician, becoming King, and ruling Xanth. Oddly, it
quickly turned him off. He knew, deep inside, that he
lacked the qualities required, despite Humfrey's remarks. This was not merely a matter of magic, but of
basic life style and ambition. He could never sentence a
man to death or exile, however justified that sentence
might be, or lead an army into battle, or spend all day
deciding the altercations of citizens. The sheer responsibility would soon weigh him down. "You're right. No
sensible person would want to be King. All I want is to
marry Sabrina and settle down."

"You are a most sensible lad. Stay the night, and on
the morrow I will show you a direct route home, with
protections against the hazards on the way."

"Nickelpede repellent?" Bink asked hopefully, remembering the trenches Cherie the centaur had hur-
dled.

"Precisely. You will still have to keep your wits
about you; no route is safe for a stupid man. But two
days' travel on foot will suffice."

Bink stayed the night. He found he rather liked the
castle and its denizens; even the manticora was affable
now that the Magician had given the word. "I would
not really have eaten you, though I admit to being
tempted for a moment or three when you booted me in

the . . . tail," it told Bink. "It is my job to scare off those who are not serious. See, I am not confined." It pushed against the bars, and the inner gate swung open. "My year is almost up, anyway; I'll almost be sorry to have it end."

"What question did you bring?" Bink inquired somewhat nervously, trying not to brace himself too obviously for flight. In an open space, he was no possible match for the manticora.

"I asked whether I have a soul," the monster said seriously.

Again Bink had to control his reaction. A year's service for a philosophical question? "What did he tell you?"

"That only those who possess souls are concerned about them."

"But—but then you never needed to ask. You paid a year for nothing."

"No. I paid a year for everything. Possession of a soul means that I can never truly die. My body may slough away, but I shall be reborn, or if not, my shade will linger to settle unfinished accounts, or I shall reside forever in heaven or hell. My future is assured; I shall never suffer oblivion. There is no more vital question or answer. Yet that answer had to be in the proper form. A simple yes or no answer would not have satisfied me; it could be a blind guess, or merely the Magician's offhand opinion. A detailed technical treatise would merely have obfuscated the matter. Humfrey phrased it in such a way that its truth was self-evident. Now I need never doubt again."

Bink was moved. Considered that way, it did make sense. Humfrey had delivered good value. He was an honest Magician. He had shown the manticora—and Bink himself—something vital about the nature of life in Xanth. If the fiercest conglomerate monsters had souls, with all that implied, who could condemn them as evil?

Chapter 7. Exile

The path was broad and clear, with no impinging magic. Only one thing chilled Bink: a region with small wormlike holes in the trunks of trees and surrounding rocks. Holes that wiggled straight through from one side to another. The wiggles had been here!

But he calmed himself. The wiggles had not passed recently, of course; that menace had been abolished. But where they had infested, it was horrible, for the little flying worms had drilled magically through anything that got in their way, including animals and people. A tree could survive a few neat holes, but a person could bleed to death, assuming he did not die outright from the holing of some vital organ. The mere thought made Bink wince. He hoped the wiggles never spawned again in Xanth—but there was no certainty about that. There was no certainty about anything where magic was involved.

He walked faster, made nervous by the old wiggle scars. In half an hour Bink reached the chasm—and there, sure enough, was the impossible bridge the Good Magician had told him of. He verified its existence by tossing a handful of dirt and observing the pattern of its fall into the depths; it guided around one section. Had he known of this on the way over—but of course that was the thing about information. Without it, a person suffered enormous complications. Who would have thought there was an invisible bridge all the way across?

Yet his long detour had not been an entire loss. He had participated in the rape hearing, and helped the shade, and witnessed some fantastic illusions, and rescued Crombie the soldier, and generally learned a lot more about the land of Xanth. He wouldn't care to do it all over again, but the experience had made him grow.

He stepped out onto the bridge. There was one thing about it, the Magician had warned him: once he started across, he could not turn back, or it would dematerialize, dropping him into the chasm. It was a one-way ramp, existing only ahead of him. So he walked across boldly, though the gulf opened out awesomely beneath him. Only his hand on the invisible rail reassured him.

He did risk a look down. Here the base of the chasm was extremely narrow—a virtual crack rather than a valley. The Gap dragon could not run here. But there seemed to be no way to climb down the steep cliff-slope; if the fall did not kill a person, starvation and exposure would. Unless he managed to straddle the narrowest part of the crack and walk east or west to a better section—where the dragon could then catch him.

Bink made it across. All it took was knowledge and confidence. His feet safely on land, he looked back. There was no sign of the bridge, of course, and no obvious approach to it. He was not about to risk another crossing.

The nervous release left him thirsty. He saw a spring to one side of the path. The path? There had been none a moment ago. He looked back toward the chasm, and there was no path. Oh—it led away from the bridge, not toward it. Routine one-way magic. He proceeded to the spring. He had water in his canteen, but it was Spring of Life water, which he avoided drinking, saving it for some future emergency.

A driblet of water emerged from the spring to flow along a winding channel and finally trickle down into the chasm. The channel was richly overgrown with strange plants, species that Bink had never observed before: a strawberry runner bearing beechnuts, and ferns with deciduous leaves. Odd, but no threat to his welfare. Bink looked around carefully for predator beasts that might lurk near a water hole, then lay down to put his mouth to the waiting pool.

As he lowered his head, he heard a fluting cry above him. "You'll be sooorry!" it seemed to say.

He glanced up into the trees. A birdlike thing perched there, possibly a variety of harpy. She had full woman-breasts and a coiled snake tail. Nothing to concern him, so long as she kept her distance.

He bent his head again—and heard a rustle, too close. He jumped up, drew his knife, moved a few paces, and through the trees sighted an incredible thing. Two creatures were locked in combat: a griffin and a unicorn. One was male, the other female, and they were—they were not fighting, they—

Bink retreated, profoundly embarrassed. They were two different species! How *could* they!

Disgusted, he returned to the spring. Now he noted the recent tracks of the creatures: both unicorn and griffin had come to drink here, probably within the hour. Maybe they had crossed the invisible bridge, as he had, and seen the spring, so conveniently located. So the water could hardly be poisoned—

Suddenly he caught on. This was a love spring. Anyone who drank of this water would become compellingly enamored of the first creature he encountered thereafter, and—

He glanced over at the griffin and unicorn. They were still at it, insatiably.

Bink backed away from the spring. If he had drunk from it—

He shuddered. He was no longer remotely thirsty.

"Aw, go take a drink," the harpy fluted.

Bink swept up a rock and hurled it at her. She squawked and fluttered higher, laughing coarsely. One of her droppings just missed him. There was nothing more hateful than a harpy.

Well, the Good Magician had warned him that the path home was not entirely free of problems. This spring must be one of the details Humfrey hadn't thought important enough for specific mention. Once Bink was back on the trail along which he had originally come, the hazards would be familiar, such as the peace pines—

How would he get through them? He needed an enemy to travel with, and he had none.

Then he had a bright idea. "Hey you—birdbrain!" he called up into the foliage. "Stay away from me, or I'll stuff your tail down your filthy throat!"

The harpy responded with a withering torrent of abuse. What a vocabulary she had! Bink threw another rock at her. "I'm warning you—don't follow me," he cried.

"I'll follow you to the edge of the Shield itself," she screeched. "You'll *never* get rid of me."

Bink smiled privately. Now he had a suitable companion.

He hiked on, dodging the occasional droppings the harpy hurled at him, hoping her fury would carry her through the pines. After that—well, first things first.

Soon the path merged with the one he had taken south. Curious, he sighted along the main path both ways; it was visible north and south. He looked back the way he had just come—and there was only deep forest. He took a step back along where he knew he had passed—and found himself knee-deep in glow-briers. The weeds sparkled as they snagged on his legs, and only by maneuvering with extreme caution did he manage to extricate himself without getting scratched. The harpy laughed so hard she almost fell from her perch.

There was simply no path here, this direction. But the moment he faced about again, there it was, leading cleanly through the briers to join the main route. Ah, well—why did he even bother to question such things? Magic was magic; it had no rationale except its own. Everyone knew that. Everyone except himself, at times.

He hiked all day, passing the brook where to drink was to become a fish—"Have a drink, harpy!"—but she already knew of the enchantment, and reviled him with double fury; the peace pines— "Have a nap, harpy!"; and the trench with the nickelpedes—"I'll fetch you something to eat, harpy!"—but actually he used the repellent the Good Magician had provided, and never even saw a nickelpede.

At last he stopped at a farmhouse in the centaur territory for the night. The harpy finally gave up her chase; she dared not come within range of a centaur bow. These were older centaurs, unaggressive, interested in the news of the day. They listened avidly to the narration of his experiences across the chasm and considered this to suffice for his room and board. Their grandchild colt was staying with them, a happy-go-lucky prancing tyke of barely twenty-five years—Bink's age, but equivalent to a quarter that in human terms. Bink played with him and did handstands for him; that was a trick no centaur could do, and the colt was fascinated.

Next day he traveled north again, and there was no sign of the harpy. What a relief; he would almost have preferred to risk the peace pines alone. His ears felt indelibly soiled after the day of her expletives. He passed through the remainder of the centaur area without encountering anyone. As evening approached, he reached the North Village.

"Hey! The Spell-less Wonder is back," Zink cried. A hole appeared at Bink's feet, causing him to stumble involuntarily. Zink would have made a wonderful companion for the pines. Bink ignored the other holes and proceeded toward his house. He was back, all right. Why had he bothered to hurry?

The examination was held next morning, in the outdoor amphitheater. The royal palms formed colonnades setting off the stage area. The benches were formed from the projecting convoluted knees of a giant dryland cypress tree. The back was braced by four huge honeymaple trees. Bink had always liked this formation—but now it was a place of discomfort. His place of trial.

The old King presided, since this was one of his royal offices. He wore his jewel-encrusted royal robe and his handsome gold crown and carried the ornate scepter, symbols of his power. All citizens bowed as the fanfare sounded. Bink could not help feeling a shiver of awe as the panoply of royalty manifested.

The King had an impressive white mane and a long beard, but his eyes tended to drift aimlessly. Periodically a servitor would nudge him to prevent him from falling asleep, and to remind him of the ritual.

At the start, the King performed his ceremonial magic by generating a storm. He held his palsied hands high and mumbled his invocation. At first there was silence; then, just as it seemed the magic had failed entirely, a ghostly gust of wind passed through the glade, stirring up a handful of leaves.

No one said anything, though it was evident that this manifestation could have been mere coincidence. It was certainly a far cry from a storm. But several of the ladies dutifully put up umbrellas, and the master of ceremonies quickly proceeded to the business at hand.

Bink's parents, Roland and Bianca, were in the front row, and so was Sabrina, fully as lovely as he had remembered her. Roland caught Bink's eye and nodded encouragingly, and Bianca's gaze was moist, but Sabrina's eyes were downcast. They were all afraid for him. With reason, he thought.

"What talent do you proffer to justify your citizenship?" the master of ceremonies asked Bink. He was Munly, a friend of Roland's; Bink knew the man would do everything he could to help, but he was duty-bound to follow the forms.

Now it was upon him. "I—I can't show it," Bink said. "But I have the Good Magician Humfrey's note that I do have magic." He held out the note with a trembling hand.

The man took it, glanced at it, and passed it to the King. The King squinted, but his eyes were so watery that he evidently could not read it.

"As Your Majesty can see," Munly murmured discreetly, "it is a message from Magician Humfrey, bearing his magic seal." This was a picture of a flippered creature balancing a ball on its snout. "It states that this person possesses an undefined magical talent."

Something like fire lighted the old monarch's ashy eye momentarily. "This counts for naught," he mumbled. "Humfrey is not King; I am!" He let the paper drop to the ground.

"But—" Bink protested.

The master of ceremonies glanced at him warningly, and Bink knew it was hopeless. The King was foolishly jealous of the Magician Humfrey, whose power was still strong, and would not heed the message. But, for whatever reason, the King had spoken. Argument would only complicate things.

Then he had an idea. "I have brought the King a present," Bink said. "Water from a healing Spring."

Munly's eyes lighted. "You have magic water?" He was alert to the possibilities of a fully functional King.

"In my canteen," Bink said. "I saved it—see, it healed my lost finger." He held up his left hand. "It also cured my cold, and I saw it help other people. It heals anything, instantly." He decided not to mention the attached obligation.

Munly's talent was the conjuration of small objects. "With your permission—"

"Granted," Bink said quickly.

The canteen appeared in the man's hand. "This is it?"

"Yes." For the first time, Bink had real hope.

Munly approached the King again. "Bink has brought a gift for Your Majesty," he announced. "Magic water."

The King took the canteen. "Magic water?" he repeated, hardly seeming to comprehend.

"It heals all ills," Munly assured him.

The King looked at it. One swallow, and he would be able to read the Magician's message, to brew decent storms again—and to make sensible judgments. This could reverse the course of Bink's demonstration.

"You imply I am sick?" the King demanded. "I need no healing! I am as fit as I ever was." And he turned the canteen upside down, letting the precious fluid pour out on the ground.

It was as if Bink's life blood were spilling out, not mere water. He saw his last chance ruined, by the very senility he had thought to alleviate. On top of that, now he had no healing water for his own emergencies; he could not be cured again.

Was this the retribution of the Spring of Life for his defiance of it? To tempt him with incipient victory, then withdraw it at the critical moment? Regardless, he was lost.

Munly knew it too. He stooped to pick up the canteen, and it vanished from his hand, returned to Bink's house. "I am sorry," he murmured under his breath. Then, loudly: "Demonstrate your talent."

Bink tried. He concentrated, willing his magic, whatever it might be, to break its geis and manifest. Somehow. But nothing happened.

He heard a sob. Sabrina? No, it was his mother, Bianca. Roland sat with stony face, refusing by his code of honor to let personal interest interfere. Sabrina still would not look at him. But there were those who did: Zink, Jama, and Potipher were all smirking. Now they had reason to feel superior; none of them were spell-less wonders.

"I cannot," Bink whispered. It was over.

Again he hiked. This time he headed westward, toward the isthmus. He carried a new staff and a hatchet and his knife; and his canteen had been refilled with conventional water. Bianca had provided more excellent sandwiches, flavored by her tears. He had nothing from Sabrina; he had not seen her at all since the decision. Xanth law did not permit an exile to take more than he could conveniently carry, and no valuables, for fear of attracting unwanted attention from the Mundanes. Though the Shield protected Xanth, it was impossible to be too safe.

Bink's life was essentially over, for he had been exiled from all that he had known. He was in effect an orphan. Never again would he experience the marvels of magic. He would be forever bound, as it were, to the ground, the colorless society of Mundania.

Should he have accepted the offer of the Sorceress Iris? At least he could have remained in Xanth. Had he but known . . . He would not have changed his mind. What was right was right, and wrong was wrong.

The strangest thing was that he did not feel entirely despondent. He had lost citizenship, family, and fiancée, and faced the great unknown of the Outside—yet there was a certain quixotic spring to his step. Was it a counterreaction buoying his spirit so that he would not suicide—or was he in fact relieved that the decision had at last been made? He had been a freak among the magic people; now he would be among his own kind.

No—that wasn't it. He had magic. He was no freak. Strong magic, Magician-caliber. Humfrey had told him so, and he believed it. He merely was unable to utilize it. Like a man who could make a colored spot on the wall—when there was no wall handy. Why he should be magically mute he did not know—but it meant that he was right, the decision of the King wrong. Those who had not stood by him were better off apart from him.

No—not that either. His parents had refused to compromise the law of Xanth. They were good, honest people, and Bink shared their values. He had refused a similar compromise when tempted by the Sorceress. Roland and Bianca could not help him by accompanying him into an exile they did not deserve—or by trying to help him stay by cheating the system. They had done what they felt was right, at great personal sacrifice, and he was proud of them. He knew they loved him, but had let him go his own way without interference. That was part of his buried joy.

And Sabrina—what then of her? She too had refused to cheat. Yet he felt she lacked the commitment of his parents to principle. She would have cheated, had she had sufficient reason. Her surface integrity was because she had not been moved strongly by Bink's misfortune. Her love had not been deep enough. She had loved him for the magic talent she had been convinced he had, as the son of strongly talented parents. The loss of that potential talent had undercut that love. She had not really wanted him as a person.

And his love for her was now revealed as similarly shallow. Sure, she was beautiful—but she had less actual personality than, say, the girl Dee. Dee had walked off because she had been insulted, and stuck by her decision. Sabrina would do the same, but for a different reason. Dee had not been posturing; she had really been angry. With Sabrina it would have been more contrived, with more art and less emotion—because she had less emotion. She cared more about appearances than the reality.

Which reminded Bink of the Sorceress Iris again—the ultimate creature of appearances. What a temper she had! Bink respected temper; it was a window to the truth at times when little else offered. But Iris was too violent. That palace-destruction scene, complete with storm and dragon . . .

Even stupid whatshername—the lovely girl of the rape hearing—Wynne, that was her name—she had feelings. He had, he hoped, enabled her to escape from the Gap dragon. There had not been much artifice in her. But Sabrina was the perfect actress, and so he had never really been sure of her love. She had been a picture in his mind, to be summoned in time of need, just to look at. He had not actually wanted to marry her.

It had taken exile to show him his own motives. Whatever it was that he wanted in a girl, ultimately, Sabrina lacked. She had beauty, which he liked, and personality—which was not the same as character—and attractive magic. All these things were good—very good—and he had thought he loved her. But when the crisis came, Sabrina's eyes had been averted. That said it all. Crombie the soldier had spoken truly: Bink would have been a fool to marry Sabrina.

Bink smiled. How would Crombie and Sabrina have gotten along together? The ultimately demanding and suspicious male, the ultimately artful and protean female. Would the soldier's inherent ferocity constitute a challenge to the girl's powers of accommodation? Would they, after all, have fashioned an enduring relationship? It almost seemed they might. They would either have an immediate and violent falling out or a similarly spectacular falling in. Too bad they couldn't meet, and that he could not be present to observe such a meeting.

The whole of his Xanth experience was passing glibly through his mind now that he was through with it. For the first time in his life, Bink was free. He no longer needed magic. He no longer needed romance. He no longer needed Xanth.

His aimlessly roving eye spotted a tiny dark spot on a tree. He experienced a sudden shudder. Was it a wiggle wound? No, just a discoloration. He felt relief—and realized that he had been fooling himself, at least to this extent. If he no longer needed Xanth, he would not care about things like the wiggles. He *did* need Xanth. It was his youth. But—he could not have it.

Then he approached the station of the Shield man, and his uncertainty increased. Once he passed through the Shield, Xanth and all its works would be forever behind him.

"What are you up to?" the Shield man asked him. He was a big, fat youth with pale features. But he was part of the vital net of magic that formed the barrier to outside penetration of Xanth. No living creature could pass the Shield, either way—but since no inhabitant of Xanth wanted to depart, its net effect was to stop all Mundane intrusions. The touch of the Shield meant death—instant, painless, final. Bink didn't know how it worked—but he didn't know how any magic worked, really. It just was.

"I have been exiled," Bink said. "You have to let me through the Shield." He would not, of course, attempt to cheat; he would leave as directed. Had he been inclined to try to avoid exile, it would not have worked; one villager's talent was spot location of individuals, and he was now tuned to Bink. He would know if Bink remained on this side of the Shield today.

The youth sighed. "Why do all the complications have to come in my shift? Do you know how difficult it is to open up a man-sized hole without bollixing the whole damn Shield?"

"I don't know anything about the Shield," Bink admitted. "But I was exiled by the King, so—"

"Oh, very well. Now look—I can't go with you to the Shield; I have to stay here at my station. But I can make an opening spell that will cancel out one section for five seconds. You be there, and you step through on schedule, because if it closes on you, you're dead."

Bink gulped. For all his thoughts about death and exile, now that it had come to the test, he did want to live. "I know."

"Right. The magic stone doesn't care who dies." Meaningfully the youth tapped the boulder he leaned against.

"You mean that dingy old stone is it?" Bink asked.

"Shieldstone. Sure. The Magician Ebnez located it nearly a century ago, and tuned it to form the Shield. Without it, we'd still be subject to invasion by the Mundanes."

Bink had heard of the Magician Ebnez, one of the great historical figures. In fact, Ebnez was in Bink's family tree. He had been able to adapt things magically. In his hands a hammer could become a sledgehammer, or a piece of wood could become a section of window-frame. Whatever existed became whatever was needed—within certain limits. He could not adapt air into food, for example, or make a suit of clothing out of water. But it had been amazing what he could do. So he had adapted a potent deathstone into the Shieldstone, killing at a set distance instead of up close, and thereby he had fashioned the salvation of Xanth. What a proud achievement!

"Okay, now," the youth said. "Here's a timestone." He tapped it against the larger rock, and the small piece fractured into two segments, each fading from the original red to white. He handed one fragment to Bink. "When this goes red, you step across; they're synched. The opening will be right in front of the big beechnut tree—and for only five seconds. So you be ready, and move—on red."

"Move on red," Bink agreed.

"Right. Now *move*; sometimes these timestones heal fast. I'll be watching mine, so as to time the spell; you watch yours."

Bink moved. He ran along the path to the west. Usually a fractured timestone took half an hour or so to heal—but it varied somewhat with the quality of the stone, the surrounding temperature, and assorted unknown factors. Maybe it was inherent in the original piece, because the two fragments always changed color together, precisely, even if one were in the sunshine and the other buried in a well. But, again, what use to seek a rationale for magic? What was, was.

And would be no more—for him. None of this had meaning in Mundania.

He hove in sight of the Shield—or rather, its effect. The Shield itself was invisible, but there was a line of dead vegetation where it touched the ground, and the corpses of animals that had been so foolish as to try to cross that line. Sometimes jumpdeer got confused and sprang through to the safe ground on the other side— but they were already dead. The Shield was invisibly thin, but absolute.

Occasional Mundane creatures blundered into it. A detail walked the line each day on the Xanth side, checking for corpses, hauling them out of the Shield when they were partway across, giving them safe burial. It was possible to handle something that lay across the Shield, so long as the living person did not touch it himself. Nevertheless, it was a grisly chore, sometimes assigned as punishment. There were never any human Mundanes, but there was always the fear that there might one day be some, with all the complications that would entail.

Ahead was the spreading beechnut tree. One branch reached out toward the Shield—and the tip of that branch was dead. Wind must have made it sway across. It helped identify the spot where he should cross.

There was an odor associated with this line of death, too. Probably it was the decay of many tiny creatures: worms in the earth, bugs flying through the Shield, rotting where they fell. This was the region of death.

Bink glanced down at the stone he held—and sucked in his breath in shock. *It was red!*

Had it just now changed—or was he already too late? His life depended on the answer.

Bink launched himself at the Shield. He knew the sensible thing to do was return to the Shield tender and explain why he had balked—but he wanted this done with. Maybe it had been the actual change of the stone's color that had attracted his attention, in which case he did have time. So he took the foolish course, and tried for it.

One second. Two. Three. He'd better have the whole five, because he wasn't there yet. The Shield seemed close, but it took time to make the supposedly instant decision and abolish inertia and get up speed. He was passing the beechnut tree at a dead run—maybe literally dead—going too fast to stop. Four seconds—he was crossing the line of death. If it closed on his trailing leg, would all of him die, or just the leg? Five—he felt a tingle. Six—no, time was up, stop counting, start panting. He was through; was he alive?

He rolled in the dirt, kicking up dry leaves and small bones. Of course he was alive! How could he worry about it otherwise? As with the manticora, concerned about his soul: if he had none, he wouldn't—

Bink sat up, shaking something dead out of his hair. So he had made it. That tingle must have been an effect of the turned-off Shield, since it hadn't hurt him.

Now it was done. He was free of Xanth forever. Free to make his own life, without being ridiculed or mothered or tempted. Free to be himself.

Bink put his face in his hands and cried.

Chapter 8. Trent

After a time he got up and walked on, into the dread world of the Mundanes. It really did not look much different: the trees were similar, the rocks unchanged, and the ocean shore he paralleled was exactly like an ocean shore. Yet an intense nostalgia gripped him. His prior euphoria had been but the swing of the pendulum, providing a false buoyancy. Better if he had died in the crossing.

Well, he could still go back. Just step across the line. Death would be painless, and he could be buried in Xanth. Was that what other exiles had done?

He revolted against the notion. He had called his own bluff. He loved Xanth, and missed it terribly already— but he did not want to die. He would simply have to make his way among the Mundanes. Others had surely done it before him. Maybe he would even be happy there.

The isthmus was mountainous. Bink sweated as he climbed the steep pass. Was this the counterpart to the chasm, a ridge that rose as high above the land as the chasm sank beneath it? Did a ridge dragon run along the heights? No, not in Mundania. But possibly such geography did have something to do with the magic. If the magic quality washed down from the height, concentrating in the depth—no, that didn't seem to make much sense. Most of it would have washed into the ocean and been hopelessly diluted.

For the first time he wondered what Mundania was really like. Was it actually possible to survive without magic? It would not be nearly as nice as Xanth, but the absence of spells should represent a formidable challenge, and there should be some decent places in it. The people should not be evil; after all, his ancestors had come from Mundane stock. Indications were that language and many customs were the same.

He heaved himself over the rise of the pass, braced for his first real glimpse of the new world—and suddenly he was surrounded by men. An ambush!

Bink whirled to run. Maybe he could trick them into plunging into the Shield, and be rid of them the easy way—not that he wanted to be responsible for their death. Anyhow, he had to try to escape them.

But as he turned, his body responding somewhat slower than his thoughts, he found a man behind him, blocking the way with drawn sword.

The sensible thing to do was to give up. They had him outnumbered and surrounded, and they could have put an arrow into his back if they had wanted to kill him outright. If all they wanted to do was rob him, he had almost nothing to lose.

But being sensible had never been Bink's strong point. Not when he was under pressure, or surprised. Reflecting after the fact, he was very sensible and intelligent, but that wasn't much use at this stage. If only he'd had a talent like that of his mother, only stronger, so that he could turn time back a couple of hours and replay all his crises to better advantage—

Bink charged the man with the sword, swinging his staff to block the blade. But someone tackled him,

bringing him down hard before he took two steps.
Bink's face struck the dirt, and he took a mouthful. Still
he fought, twisting about to get at the man who held
him.

Then they were all on him, bearing him down. Bink
had no chance; in moments he was tied and gagged.

A man thrust his tough face close to Bink's eyes as
two others held him erect. "Now get this, Xanth—if
you try any magic, we'll knock you out and carry you."

Magic? They didn't know that Bink had none he
could use—or that if he had, it would be no good out
here beyond the Shield. But he nodded, showing he understood. Maybe they would treat him better if they
thought he could somehow strike back.

They marched him down the other side of the pass
and to a military camp on the mainland beyond the
isthmus.

What was an army doing here? If it were an invasion
of Xanth, it could not succeed; the Shield would kill a
thousand men as readily as one.

They brought him to the main tent. Here, in a
screened enclosure, sat a handsome man in his forties,
wearing some sort of green Mundane uniform, a sword,
a neat mustache, and an emblem of command. "Here is
the spy, General," the sergeant said respectfully.

The General glanced at Bink, appraising him. There
was dismaying intelligence in that cool study. This was
no bandit thug. "Release him," he said quietly. "He is
obviously harmless."

"Yes, sir," the sergeant said respectfully. He untied
Bink and removed his gag.

"Dismissed," the General murmured, and without a
word the soldiers were gone. They were certainly disciplined.

Bink chafed at his wrists, trying to rub the pain out,
amazed at the General's confidence. The man was well
formed, but not large; Bink was younger and taller and
surely stronger. If he acted quickly, he might escape.

Bink crouched, ready to jump at the man and knock

him down. Suddenly the General's sword was in his hand, pointing at Bink. The man's draw had been a blur; the weapon had jumped to his hand as if by magic, but that obviously could not be the case here. "I would not advise it, young man," the General said, as if warning him not to step on a thorn.

Bink staggered, trying to brake without falling on the point of the sword. He did not succeed. But as his chest bore on that blade, the sword retreated, returning to its scabbard. The General, now on his feet, caught Bink by his elbows and stood him back upright. There was such precision and power in the action that Bink knew he had grossly underestimated this man; he had no chance to overcome him, with or without the sword.

"Be seated," the General said mildly.

Cowed, Bink moved awkwardly to the wooden chair and sat on it. Now he was conscious of his own dirty face and hands, the disorganization of his apparel, in contrast to the impeccable neatness of the General.

"Your name?"

"Bink." He did not give his village, since he was no longer affiliated with it. What was the purpose of this question, anyway? He was a nonentity regardless of his name.

"I am the Magician Trent. Perhaps you know of me."

It took a moment for the import to register. Then Bink didn't believe it. "Trent? He's gone. He was—"

"Exiled. Twenty years ago. Precisely."

"But Trent was—"

"Ugly? A monster? Crazy?" The Magician smiled, showing none of these traits. "What stories do they tell of me today in Xanth?"

Bink thought of Justin Tree. The fish of the stream, turned to lightning bugs to harass the centaurs. The opponents who had been transformed to water forms and left to die on land. "You—he was a power-hungry spell-caster who tried to usurp the throne of Xanth when I was but a child. An evil man whose evil still lives after him."

Trent nodded. "This is a kinder repute than is normally accorded the loser in a political contest. I was about your present age when I was banished. Perhaps our cases are similar."

"No. I never killed anyone."

"They accuse me of that too? I transformed many, but I did that instead of killing. I have no need to kill, since I can render an enemy harmless by other means."

"A fish on land still dies!"

"Oh, so that is how they put it. That would indeed be murder. I did transform enemies to fish—but always in water. On land I utilized only land forms. Possibly some subsequently died, but that was the doing of predators in the normal course of nature. I never—"

"I don't care. You abused your magic. I am not at all like you. I—had no magic."

The fair eyebrow lifted expressively. "No magic? Everybody in Xanth has magic."

"Because they exile those who don't have it," Bink said, with a flash of bitterness.

Trent smiled, and it was a surprisingly winning expression. "Nevertheless, our interests may be parallel, Bink. How would you like to return with me to Xanth?"

For an instant wild hope flared in his breast. Return! But immediately he quashed it. "There is no return."

"Oh, I wouldn't say that. To every act of magic there is a countermagic. It is merely a matter of invoking it. You see, I have developed a counter to the Shield."

Again Bink had to take stock of his reactions. "If you had that, you could have gone into Xanth already."

"Well, there is a certain small problem of application. You see, what I have is an elixir distilled from a plant that grows on the very fringe of the magical zone. The magic extends somewhat beyond the Shield, you understand—otherwise the Shield itself wouldn't work, for it is magic and cannot operate beyond the magic demesnes. This plant, which seems to be of basically Mundane stock, competes at the fringe with the magical plants of Xanth. It is very difficult to compete with magic, so it evolved a very special property: it suppresses magic. Do you appreciate the significance?"

"Suppresses magic? Maybe that's what happened to me."

Trent studied him with that disquieting calculation. "So you feel you were wronged by the present administration? We do have something in common."

Bink wanted no common ground with the Evil Magician, however winning the man's aspect might be. He knew that Evil could put on an extremely fair face; otherwise how would Evil ever have survived in the world so long? "What are you getting at?"

"The Shield is magic. Therefore the elixir should nullify it. But it does not, because the source of the Shield is not touched. It is necessary to reach the Shieldstone itself. Unfortunately, we do not know precisely where that stone is now, and there is not enough elixir to blanket the entire peninsula of Xanth, or even a significant fraction of it."

"Makes no difference," Bink said. "Your knowing where the Shieldstone is would not bring it within your reach."

"Ah, but it would. You see, we have a catapult, with a sufficient range to drop a bomb anywhere in nearby Xanth. We have it mounted on a ship that can sail right around Xanth. So it is very likely that we could drop a container of elixir on the Shieldstone—if we only had the precise coordinates."

Now Bink understood. "The Shield would collapse!"

"And my army would overrun Xanth. Of course, the magic-damping effect would be temporary, for the elixir dissipates readily—but a mere ten minutes would suffice to get the bulk of my army across the line. I have been drilling the men in swift short-range mancuvers. After that it would be merely a matter of time until the throne was mine."

"You would return us to the days of conquest and ravage," Bink said, horrified. "The Thirteenth Wave, worse than all the rest."

"By no means. My army is disciplined. We shall exert precisely that force that is necessary, no more. My magic will probably eliminate most resistance anyway, so there need be very little violence. I do not wish to ruin the kingdom I am to rule."

"So you haven't changed," Bink said. "You're still hungry for illicit power."

"Oh, I have changed," Trent assured him. "I have become less naive, more educated and sophisticated. The Mundanes have excellent educational facilities and a broader world view, and they are ruthless politicians. I will not this time underestimate the determination of my opposition or leave myself foolishly vulnerable. I have no doubt I will make a better King than I would have twenty years ago."

"Well, count me out."

"But I must count you in, Bink. You know where the Shieldstone is located." The Evil Magician leaned forward persuasively. "It is important that the shot be precise; we have only a quarter pound of elixir, and that is the labor of two years' work. We have virtually denuded the fringe region of the source plants; our supply is irreplaceable. We dare not guess at the location of the Shieldstone. We require a precise map—a map that only you can draw."

So there it was. Trent had posted his men to ambush any travelers from Xanth, so that they could update him on the precise position of the Shieldstone. That was the only piece of information the Evil Magician needed to initiate his wave of conquest. Bink had merely happened to be the first exile to walk into the trap. "No, I won't tell you. I won't help overthrow the legitimate government of Xanth."

"Legitimacy is commonly defined after the fact," Trent remarked. "Had I been successful twenty years ago, I would now be the legitimate King, and the present monarch would be a reviled outcast noted for drowning people irresponsibly. I presume the Storm King still governs?"

"Yes," Bink said shortly. The Evil Magician might try to convince him that it all was merely palace politics, but he knew better.

"I am prepared to make you a very handsome offer, Bink. Virtually anything you might desire in Xanth. Wealth, authority, women——"

He had said the wrong thing. Bink turned away. He would not want Sabrina on that basis anyway, and he had already turned down what amounted to a similar offer by the Sorceress Iris.

Trent steepled his fingers. Even in that minor mannerism there was implied power and ruthlessness. The Magician's plans were too finely meshed to be balked by a willful exile. "You may wonder why I choose to return to Xanth, after two decades and evident success in Mundania. I have spent some time analyzing that myself."

"No," Bink said.

But the man only smiled, refusing to be ruffled, and again Bink had the uneasy feeling that he was being skillfully maneuvered, that he was about to play into the hands of the Magician no matter how he tried to fight it. "You should wonder, lest you allow your outlook to be unconscionably narrow—as mine was when I emerged from Xanth. Every young man should go abroad into the Mundane world for a period of a year or two at least; it would make him a better citizen of Xanth. Travel of any type tends to broaden one." Bink could not argue with that; he had learned a great deal in his two-week tour of Xanth. How much more would a year in Mundania teach him? "In fact," the Magician continued, "when I assume power I shall institute such a policy. Xanth cannot prosper cut off from the real world; in isolation is only stagnation."

Bink could not restrain his morbid curiosity. The Magician had intelligence and experience that appealed insidiously to Bink's own intellect. "What is it like out there?"

"Do not speak with such distaste, young man. Mundania is not the evil place you may imagine. That is part of the reason the citizens of Xanth need more exposure to it; the ignorance of isolation breeds unwarranted hostility. Mundania is in many respects more advanced, more civilized than Xanth. Deprived of the benefits of magic, the Mundanes have had to compensate in ingenious ways. They have turned to philosophy, medicine, and science. They now have weapons called guns that can kill more readily than an arrow or even a deadly spell; I have trained my troops in other weapons, because I do not wish to introduce guns into Xanth. They have carriages that carry them across the land as fast as a unicorn can run, and boats that row across the sea as swiftly as a sea serpent can swim, and balloons that take them as high in the air as a dragon can fly. They have people called doctors who heal the sick and wounded without the use of a single spell, and a device consisting of little beads on columns that multiplies figures with marvelous speed and accuracy."

"Ludicrous!" Bink said. "Even magic can't do figures for a person, unless it is a golem, and then it has really become a person."

"This is what I mean, Bink. Magic is marvelous, but it is also limited. In the long run, the instruments of the Mundanes may have greater potential. Probably the basic life style of the Mundanes is more comfortable than that of many Xanths."

"There probably aren't as many of them," Bink muttered. "So they have no competition for good land."

"On the contrary. There are many millions of people there."

"You're never going to convince me of anything, telling such tall stories," Bink pointed out. "The North Village of Xanth has about five hundred people, counting all the children, and that's the largest one. There can't be more than two thousand people in the whole kingdom. You talk of thousands of thousands of people, but I know the Mundane world can't be much larger than Xanth!"

The Evil Magician shook his head in mock sadness. "Bink, Bink! None so blind as those who will not see."

"And if they really have balloons flying through the air, carrying people, why haven't they flown them over Xanth?" Bink demanded hotly, knowing he had the Magician on the run.

"Because they don't know where Xanth is—don't even believe it exists. They don't believe in magic, so—"

"Don't believe in magic!" The humor had never been very funny, and it was getting worse.

"The Mundanes never did know very much about magic," Trent said seriously. "It appears a great deal in their literature, but never in their daily lives. The Shield has closed off the border, as it were, so no truly magic animal has been seen in Mundania in about a century. And it may be to our interest to keep them ignorant," he continued, frowning. "If they ever get the notion Xanth is a threat to them, they might use a giant catapult to lob in firebombs—" He broke off, shaking his head as though at some horrible thought. Bink had to admire the perfection of the mannerism, which was as apt as any his father, Roland, employed. He could almost believe there was some fantastic threat lurking. "No," the Magician concluded, "the location of Xanth must remain secret—for now."

"It won't remain secret if you send all Xanth youths out into Mundania for two years."

"Oh, we would put an amnesia spell on them first, and revoke it only after they returned. Or at least a geis of silence, so no Mundane could learn from them about Xanth. Thus they would acquire Mundane experience to augment their Xanth magic. Some trusted ones would be permitted to retain their memories and freedom of speech Outside, so they could act as liaisons, recruiting qualified colonists and keeping us informed. For our own safety and progress. But overall—"

"The Fourth Wave again," Bink said. "Controlled colonization."

Trent smiled. "You are an apt pupil. Many citizens choose not to comprehend the true nature of the original colonizations of Xanth. Actually, Xanth never was very easy to locate from Mundania, because it seems to have no fixed geographic location. Historically, people have colonized Xanth from all over the world, always walking across the land bridge directly from their own countries—and all would have sworn that they migrated only a few miles. Furthermore, all comprehended one another's speech in Xanth, though their original languages were entirely different. So it would appear that there is something magical about the approach to Xanth. Had I not kept meticulous notes of my route, I would never have found my way back this far. The Mundane legends of the animals that departed from Xanth in bygone centuries show that they appeared all over the world, rather than at any specific site. So it seems to work in reverse, too." He shook his head as if it were a great mystery—and Bink was hard put to it not to become hopelessly intrigued by the concept. How could Xanth be everywhere at once? Did its magic extend, after all, beyond the peninsula, in some peculiar fashion? It would be easy to get hooked by the problem!

"If you like Mundania so well, why are you trying to get back into Xanth?" Bink demanded, trying to distract himself from temptation by focusing on the Magician's contradictions.

"I don't like Mundania," Trent said, frowning. "I merely point out that it is not evil, and that it has considerable potential and must be reckoned with. If we do not keep aware of it, it may become aware of us—and that could destroy us. Right along with itself. Xanth represents a haven, like none other known to man. A provincial, backward haven, to be sure—but there is no other place quite like it. And I—I am a Magician. I belong in my land, with my people, protecting them from the horrors arising, which you are not equipped even to imagine. . . ." He lapsed into silence.

"Well, no Mundane tales are going to make me tell you how to get into Xanth," Bink said firmly.

The Magician's eyes focused on Bink as if only now was he becoming aware of his presence. "I would prefer not to have to employ coercion," Trent said softly, "You know my talent."

Bink felt a shiver of extremely ugly apprehension. Trent was the transformer—the one who changed men into trees—or worse. The most potent Magician of the past generation—too dangerous to be allowed to remain in Xanth.

Then he felt relief. "You're bluffing," he said. "Your magic can't work outside Xanth—and I'm not going to let you into Xanth."

"It is not very much of a bluff," Trent said evenly. "The magic, as I mentioned, extends slightly beyond the Shield. I can take you to that border and transform you into a toad. And I shall do it—if I have to."

Bink's relief tightened back into a knot in his stomach. Transformation—the notion of losing his lifelong body without actually dying had an insidious horror. It terrified him.

But he still could not betray his homeland. "No," he said, his tongue feeling thick in his mouth.

"I don't understand, Bink. You surely did not leave Xanth voluntarily. I offer you the chance to get your own back."

"Not that way."

Trent sighed, with seemingly genuine regret. "You are loyal to your principles, and I cannot fault you for that. I had hoped it would not come to this."

Bink had hoped so too. But he seemed to have no choice. Except to watch his chance to make a break for it, risking his life to escape. Better a clean death in combat than to become a toad.

A soldier entered, reminding Bink faintly of Crombie—mainly a matter of bearing, not appearance—and stood at attention. "What is it, Hastings?" Trent inquired mildly.

"Sir, there is another person through the Shield."

Trent hardly showed his elation. "Really? It seems we have another source of information."

Bink felt a new emotion—but hardly a comfortable one. If there were another exile from Xanth, the Magician could get his information without Bink's help. Would he let Bink go—or turn him into a toad anyway, as an object lesson? Remembering Trent's reputation of past times, Bink had little confidence that he would be freed. Anyone who balked the Evil Magician, in whatever trifling manner, was in for it.

Unless Bink gave him the information now, redeeming himself. Should he? Since it could make no difference to the future of Xanth . . .

He saw Trent pausing, looking at him expectantly. Suddenly Bink caught on. This was a setup, a fake announcement, to make him talk. And he had almost fallen for it.

"Well, you won't be needing me, then," Bink said. One thing about being turned into a toad—he couldn't tell the Magician anything at all in that form. He imagined a potential dialogue between man and toad:

MAGICIAN: Where is the Shieldstone?

TOAD: *Croak!*

Bink almost smiled. Trent would transform him only as a last resort.

Now Trent returned to the messenger. "Bring the other one here; I will question him immediately."

"Sir—it is a woman."

A woman! Trent seemed mildly surprised, but Bink was amazed. This was not what he expected in a bluff. There was certainly no woman being exiled—and no man either. What was Trent trying to do?

Unless—oh, no!—unless Sabrina had after all followed him out.

Dismay tore at him. If the Evil Magician had her in his power—

No! It could not be. Sabrina did not really love him; the exile and her reaction to it had proved that. She would not give up all she had to follow him out. It simply was not in her nature. And he didn't really love her; he had already decided that. So this had to be a complex ruse on the part of the Magician.

"Very well," Trent said. "Bring her in."

It couldn't be a bluff, then. Not if they actually brought her in. And if it were Sabrina—it couldn't be, he was quite absolutely positively certain of that—or was he projecting, attributing his own attitudes to her? How could he really know what was in her heart? If she had followed him, he couldn't let her be changed into a toad. Yet with all of Xanth at stake—

Bink threw up his hands, mentally. He would just have to play it as it came. If they had Sabrina, he was lost; if it were an ingenious bluff, he had won. Except that he would be a toad.

Perhaps being a toad would not be so bad. No doubt flies would taste very good, and the lady toads would look as good as human girls did now. Maybe the great love of his life was waiting in the grass, warts and all . . .

The ambush detail arrived, half carrying a struggling woman. Bink saw with relief that it was not Sabrina, but a marvelously ugly female he had never seen before. Her hair was wild, her teeth gnarled, her body sexually shapeless.

"Stand," Trent said mildly, and she stood, responsive to his easy air of command. "Your name?"

"Fanchon," she said rebelliously. "Yours?"

"The Magician Trent."

"Never heard of you."

Bink, caught by surprise, had to cough to conceal his snort of laughter. But Trent was unperturbed. "This puts us on an even footing, Fanchon. I regret the inconvenience my men have caused you. If you will kindly inform me of the location of the Shieldstone, I shall pay you well and send you on your way."

"Don't tell him!" Bink cried. "He means to invade Xanth."

She wrinkled her bulbous nose. "What do I care about Xanth?" She squinted at Trent. "I could tell you—but how do I know I can trust you? You might kill me as soon as you had your information."

Trent tapped his long, aristocratic fingers together. "This is a legitimate concern. You have no way of knowing whether my given word is good. Yet it should be obvious that I should bear no malice to those who assist me in the pursuit of my objectives."

"All right," she said. "Makes sense. The Shieldstone is at—"

"Traitor!" Bink screamed.

"Remove him," Trent snapped.

Soldiers entered and grabbed him and hustled him out. He had accomplished nothing except to make it harder for himself.

But then he thought of another aspect. What were the chances of another exile coming from Xanth within an hour after him? There couldn't be more than one or two exiles a year; it was big news when anyone left Xanth. He had heard nothing about it, and no second trial had been scheduled.

So—Fanchon was not an exile. She was probably not from Xanth at all. She was an agent, planted by Trent, just as Bink had first suspected. Her purpose was to convince Bink that she was telling Trent the location of the Shieldstone, tricking him into confirming it.

Well, he had figured out the scheme—and so he had won. Do what he might, Trent would not get into Xanth.

Yet there was a nagging uncertainty . . .

Chapter 9. Transformer

Bink was thrown into a pit. A pile of hay broke his fall, and a wooden roof set on four tall posts shaded him from the sun. Other than that, his prison was barren and bleak indeed. The walls were of some stonelike substance, too hard to dig into with his bare hands, too sheer to climb; the floor was packed earth.

He walked around it. The wall was solid all around, and too high for him to surmount. He could almost touch the top when he jumped and reached up—but a lattice of metal bars across the top sealed him in. He might, with special effort, get high enough to catch hold of one of those bars—but then all he would be able to do would be to hang there. It might represent exercise, but it wouldn't get him out. So the cage was tight.

He had hardly come to this conclusion before soldiers came to stand at the grate, shaking rust onto him. They stood in the shade of the roof while one of them squatted down to unlock the little door set in that grate and swing it up and open. Then they dropped a person through. It was the woman Fanchon.

Bink jumped across, wrapping his arms around her before she hit the straw, breaking her fall. They both sprawled in the hay. The door slammed shut, and the lock clicked.

"Now, I know my beauty didn't overwhelm you," she remarked as they disentangled.

"I was afraid you'd break a leg," Bink said defensively. "I almost did, when they threw me in here."

She glanced down at her knobby knees, showing beneath her dull skirt. "A break couldn't hurt the appearance of either leg."

Not far off the mark. Bink had never seen a more homely girl than this one.

But what was she doing here? Why should the Evil Magician throw his stooge in the den with his prisoner? This was no way to trick the captive into talking. The proper procedure would be to tell Bink she had talked, and offer him his freedom for confirming the information. Even if she were genuine, she still should not have been confined with him; she could have been imprisoned separately. Then the guards would tell each one that the other had talked.

Now, if she had been beautiful, they might have thought she could vamp him into telling. But as she was, not a chance. It just didn't seem to make sense.

"Why didn't you tell him about the Shieldstone?" Bink inquired, not certain with what irony he intended it. If she were a fake, she could not have told—but she also should not have been dumped in here. If she were genuine, she must be loyal to Xanth. But then, why had she said she would tell Trent where the Shieldstone was?

"I told him," she said.

She had told him? Now Bink hoped she was phony.

"Yes," she said, looking him straight in the eye. "I told him how it was set under the throne in the King's palace in the North Village."

Bink tried to assess the ramifications of this statement. It was the wrong location—but did she know this? Or was she trying to trick him into a reaction, a revelation of its real location—while the guards listened? Or was she a true exile, who knew the location and had lied about it? That would account for Trent's reaction. Because if Trent's catapult lobbed an elixir bomb on the palace of Xanth, not only would it fail to disrupt the Shield, it would alert the King—or at least the more alert ministers, who were not fools—to the nature of the threat. The damping out of magic in that vicinity would quickly give it away.

Had Trent actually lobbed his bomb—and had he now lost all hope of penetrating Xanth? The moment the threat was known, they would move the Shieldstone to a new, secret location, so that no information from exiles would be valid. No—if that had happened, Trent would have turned Fanchon into a toad and stepped on her—and he would not have bothered to keep Bink prisoner. Bink might have been killed or released, but not simply kept. So nothing that drastic had happened. Anyway, there had not been time for all that.

"I see you don't trust me," Fanchon said.

A fair analysis. "I can't afford to," he admitted. "I don't want anything to happen to Xanth."

"Why should you care, since you got kicked out?"

"I knew the rule; I was given a fair hearing."

"Fair hearing!" she exclaimed indignantly. "The King didn't even read Humfrey's note or taste the water from the Spring of Life."

Bink paused again. How would she know that?

"Oh, come on," she said. "I passed through your village only hours after your trial. It was the talk of the town. How the Magician Humfrey had authenticated your magic, but the King—"

"Okay, okay," Bink said. Obviously she had come from Xanth, but he still wasn't sure how far he could trust her. Yet she must know the Shieldstone's location—and hadn't told it. Unless she had told it—and Trent didn't believe her, so was waiting for corroboration from Bink? But she had announced the wrong location; no purpose in that, regardless. Bink could challenge her on it, but that would still not give away the right location; there were a thousand potential spots. So probably she meant what she said: she had tried to fool Trent, and had not succeeded.

So the balance in Bink's mind shifted; now he believed she was from Xanth and she had not betrayed it. That was what the available evidence suggested. How complex could Trent's machinations become? Maybe he had a Mundane machine that could somehow pick up news from inside the Shield. Or—more likely!—he had a magic mirror set up in the magic zone just outside the Shield, so he could learn interior news. No—in that case he could have ascertained the location of the Shieldstone directly.

Bink felt dizzy. He didn't know what to think—but he certainly wasn't going to mention the key location.

"I wasn't exiled, if that's what you're thinking," Fanchon said. "They don't yet ban people for being ugly. I emigrated voluntarily."

"Voluntarily? Why?"

"Well, I had two reasons."

"What two reasons?"

She looked at him. "I'm afraid you would not believe either one."

"Try me and see."

"First, the Magician Humfrey told me it was the simplest solution to my problem."

"What problem?" Bink was hardly in a good mood.

She gave him another straight look that amounted to a stare. "Must I spell it out?"

Bink found himself reddening. Obviously her problem was her appearance. Fanchon was a young woman, but she was not plain, not homely, but ugly—the living proof that youth and health were not necessarily beauty. No clothing, no makeup could help her nearly enough; only magic could do it. Which seemed to make her departure from Xanth nonsensical. Was her judgment as warped as her body?

Faced with the social necessity of changing the subject, he fixed on another objection, an aspect of his thought: "But there's no magic in Mundania."

"Precisely."

Again his logic stumbled. Fanchon was as difficult to talk with as to look at. "You mean—magic makes you—what you are?" What a marvel of tact he demonstrated!

But she did not chide him for his lack of social grace. "Yes, more or less."

"Why didn't Humfrey charge you—his fee?"

"He couldn't stand the sight of me."

Worse and worse. "Uh—what was your other reason for leaving Xanth?"

"That I shall not tell you at this time."

It figured. She had said he wouldn't believe her reasons, and he had believed the first one, so she wouldn't tell him the other. Typically female logic.

"Well, we seem to be prisoners together," Bink said, glancing around the pit again. It remained as dismal as ever. "Do you think they're going to feed us?"

"Certainly," Fanchon said. "Trent will come around and dangle bread and water at us, and ask which one would like to give him the information. That one will be fed. It will become increasingly difficult to turn him down as time passes."

"You have a gruesomely quick comprehension."

"I am gruesomely smart," she said. "In fact, it is fair to say I am as smart as I am ugly."

Yes indeed. "Are you smart enough to figure out how to get out of here?"

"No, I don't think escape is possible," she said, shaking her head in a definite yes.

"Oh," Bink said, taken aback. Her words said no, her gesture said yes. Was she crazy? No—she knew the guards were listening, though they were out of sight. So she sent them one message while sending Bink another. Which meant she had figured out an escape already.

It was now afternoon. A shaft of sunlight spilled through the grate, finding its route past the edge of the roof. Just as well, Bink thought; it would get unbearably dank in here if the sun never reached the bottom.

Trent came to the grate. "I trust you two have made your acquaintance?" he said pleasantly. "Are you hungry?"

"Now it comes," Fanchon muttered.

"I apologize for the inconvenience of your quarters,"

Trent said, squatting down with perfect aplomb. It was as if he were meeting them in a clean office. "If you both will give me your word not to depart these premises or interfere with our activities in any way, I shall arrange a comfortable tent for you."

"Therein lies subversion," Fanchon said to Bink. "Once you start accepting favors, you become obligated. Don't do it."

She was making extraordinary sense. "No deal," Bink said.

"You see," Trent continued smoothly, "if you were in a tent and you tried to escape, my guards would have to put arrows in you—and I don't want that to happen. It would be most uncomfortable for you, and would imperil my source of information. So it is vital that I have you confined by one means or another. By word or bond, as it were. This pit has the sole virtue of being secure."

"You could always let us go," Bink said. "Since you aren't going to get the information anyway."

If that ruffled the Evil Magician, he did not show it. "Here is some cake and wine," Trent said, lowering a package on a cord.

Neither Bink nor Fanchon reached for it, though Bink suddenly felt hungry and thirsty. The odors of spice wafted through the pit temptingly; obviously the package contained fresh, good things.

"Please take it," Trent said. "I assure you it is neither poisoned nor drugged. I want you both in good health."

"For when you change us into toads?" Bink asked loudly. What did he have to lose, really?

"No, I am afraid you have called my bluff on that. Toads do not speak intelligibly—and it is important to me that you speak."

Could the Evil Magician have lost his talent in the course of his long Mundane exile? Bink began to feel better.

The package touched the straw. Fanchon shrugged and squatted, untying it. Sure enough—cake and wine.

"Maybe one of us better eat now," she said. "If nothing happens in a few hours, the other eats."

"Ladies first," Bink said. If the food were drugged and she were a spy, she wouldn't touch it.

"Thank you." She broke the cake in half. "Pick a piece," she said.

"You eat that one," Bink said, pointing.

"Very nice," Trent said from above. "You trust neither me nor each other. So you are working out conventions to safeguard your interests. But it really is unnecessary; if I wanted to poison either of you, I would merely pour it on your heads."

Fanchon took a bite of cake. "This is very good," she said. She uncorked the wine and took a swig. "This too."

But Bink remained suspicious. He would wait.

"I have been considering your cases," Trent said. "Fanchon, I will be direct. I can transform you into any other life form—even another human being." He squinted down at her. "How would you like to be beautiful?"

Uh-oh. If Fanchon were not a spy, this would be a compelling offer. The ugly one converted to beauty—

"Go away," Fanchon said to Trent, "before I throw a mudball at you." But then she thought of something else. "If you're really going to leave us here, at least give us some sanitary facilities. A bucket and a curtain. If I had a lovely posterior I might not mind the lack of privacy, but as it is I prefer to be modest."

"Aptly expressed," Trent said. He gestured, and the guards brought the items and lowered them through the hole in the grate. Fanchon set the pot in one corner and removed pins from her straggly hair to tack the cloth to the two walls, forming a triangular chamber. Bink wasn't sure why a girl of her appearance should affect such modesty; surely no one would gawk at her exposed flesh regardless of its rondure. Unless she really was extremely sensitive, with her remarks making light of what remained a serious preoccupation. In that case it did make sense. A pretty girl could express shock and distress if someone saw her bare torso, but privately she would be pleased if the reaction were favorable. Fanchon had no such pretense.

Bink was sorry for her, and for himself; it would have made the confinement much more interesting if his companion had been scenic. But actually he was grateful for the privacy, too. Natural functions would otherwise have been awkward. So he was full circle; she had defined the problem before he ever started thinking it out. She obviously did have a quicker mind.

"He's not fooling about making you beautiful," Bink said. "He can—"

"It wouldn't work."

"No, Trent's talent—"

"I know his talent. But it would only aggravate my problem—even if I were willing to betray Xanth."

This was strange. She did not want beauty? Then why her extraordinary sensitivity about her appearance? Or was this some other ploy to get him to tell the location of the Shieldstone? He doubted it. She obviously was from Xanth; no Outsider could have guessed about his experience with the water of the Spring of Life and the senile King.

Time passed. Evening came. Fanchon suffered no ill effects, so Bink ate and drank his share of the meal.

At dusk it rained. The water poured through the lattice; the roof provided some shelter, but enough slanted in to wet them down thoroughly anyway. But Fanchon smiled. "Good," she whispered. "The fates are with us tonight."

Good? Bink shivered in his wet clothing, and watched her wonderingly. She scraped with her fingers in the softening floor of the pit. Bink walked over to see what she was up to, but she waved him away. "Make sure the guards don't see," she whispered.

Small danger of that; the guards weren't interested. They had taken shelter from the rain, and were not in

sight. Even if they had been close, it was getting too
dark to see.

What was so important about this business? She was
scooping out mud from the floor and mixing it with the
hay, heedless of the rain. Bink couldn't make any sense
of it. Was this her way of relaxing?

"Did you know any girls in Xanth?" Fanchon inquired. The rain was slacking off, but the darkness protected her secret work—from Bink's comprehension as
well as that of the guards.

It was a subject Bink would have preferred to avoid.
"I don't see what—"

She moved over to him. "I'm making bricks, idiot!"
she whispered fiercely. "Keep talking—and watch for
any lights. If you see anyone coming, say the word 'chameleon.' I'll hide the evidence in a hurry." She glided
back to her corner.

Chameleon. There was something about that word—
now he had it. The chameleon lizard he had seen just
before starting on his quest to the Good Magician—his
omen of the future. The chameleon had died abruptly.
Did this mean his time was come?

"Talk!" Fanchon urged. "Cover my sounds!" Then,
in conversational tone: "You did know some girls?"

"Uh, some," Bink said. Bricks? What for?

"Were they pretty?" Her hands were blurred by the
night, but he could hear the little slaps of mud and rustle of hay. She could be using the hay to contribute fiber to the mud brick. But the whole thing was crazy.
Did she intend to build a brick privy?

"Or not so pretty?" she prompted him.

"Oh. Pretty," he said. It seemed he was stuck with
this topic. If the guards were listening, they would pay
more attention to him talking about pretty girls than to
her slapping mud. Well, if that was what she wanted—
"My fiancée, Sabrina, was beautiful—is beautiful—and
the Sorceress Iris seemed beautiful, but I met others
who weren't. Once they get old or married, they—"

The rain had abated. Bink saw a light approaching. "Chameleon," he murmured, again experiencing inner tension. Omens always were accurate—if understood correctly.

"Women don't have to get ugly when they marry," Fanchon said. The sounds had changed; now she was concealing the evidence. "Some start out that way."

She certainly was conscious of her condition. This made him wonder again why she had turned down Trent's offer of beauty. "I met a lady centaur on my way to the Magician Humfrey," Bink said, finding it difficult to concentrate even on so natural a subject as this in the face of the oddities of his situation. Imprisoned in a pit with an ugly girl who wanted to make bricks! "She was beautiful, in a statuesque kind of way. Of course she was basically a horse—" Bad terminology. "I mean, from the rear she—well, I rode her back—" Conscious of what the guards might think he was saying—not that he should even care what they thought—he eyed the approaching light. He saw it mainly by reflections from the bars. "You know, she was half equine. She gave me a ride through centaur country."

The light diminished. It must be a guard on routine patrol. "False alarm," he whispered. Then, in conversational tone: "But there was one really lovely girl on the way to the Magician. She was—her name was . . ." He paused to concentrate. "Wynne. But she was abysmally stupid. I hope the Gap dragon didn't catch her."

"You were in the Gap?"

"For a while. Until the dragon chased me off. I had to go around it. I'm surprised you know of it; I had thought there was a forget spell associated with it, because it was not on my map and I never heard of it until I encountered it. Though how it is that I remember it, in that case—"

"I lived near the Gap," she said.

"You lived there? When was it made? What is its secret?"

"It was always there. There is a forget spell—I think the Magician Humfrey put it there. But if your associations are really strong, you remember. At least for a while. Magic only goes so far."

"Maybe that's it. I'll never forget my experience with the dragon and the shade."

Fanchon was making bricks again. "Any other girls?"

Bink had the impression she had more than casual interest in the matter. Was it because she knew the people of the chasm region? "Let's see—there was one other I met. An ordinary girl. Dee. She had an argument with the soldier I was with, Crombie. He was a woman-hater, or at least professed to be, and she walked out. Too bad; I rather liked her."

"Oh? I thought you preferred pretty girls."

"Look—don't be so damned sensitive!" he snapped. "You brought up the subject. I liked Dee better than— oh, never mind. I'd have been happier talking about plans to escape."

"Sorry," she said. "I—I knew about your journey around the chasm. Wynne and Dee are—friends of mine. So naturally I'm concerned."

"Friends of yours? Both of them?" Pieces of a puzzle began to fit together. "What is your association with the Sorceress Iris?"

Fanchon laughed. "None at all. If I were the Sorceress, do you think I would look like this?"

"Yes," Bink said. "If you tried beauty and it didn't work, and you still wanted power and figured you could somehow get it through an ignorant traveler—that would explain why Trent couldn't tempt you with the promise of beauty. That would only ruin your cover— and you could be beautiful any time you wanted to be. So you might follow me out in a disguise nobody would suspect, and of course you would not help another Magician take over Xanth—"

"So I'd come right out here into Mundania, where there is no magic," she finished. "Therefore no illusion."

That gutted his case. Or did it? "Maybe this is the way you actually look; I may never have seen the real Iris, there on her island."

"And how would I get back into Xanth?"

For that Bink had no answer. He responded with bluster. "Well, why did you come here? Obviously the nonmagic aspect has not solved your problem."

"Well, it takes time—"

"Time to cancel out magic?"

"Certainly. When dragons used to fly out over Mundania, before the Shield was set up, it would take them days or weeks to fade. Maybe even longer. Magician Humfrey says there are many pictures and descriptions of dragons and other magic beasts in Mundane texts. The Mundanes don't see dragons any more, so they think the old texts are fantasy—but this proves that it takes a while for the magic in a creature or person to dissipate."

"So a Sorceress could retain her illusion for a few days after all," Bink said.

She sighed. "Maybe so. But I'm not Iris, though I certainly wouldn't mind being her. I had entirely different and compelling reasons to leave Xanth."

"Yes, I remember. One was to lose your magic, whatever it was, and the other you wouldn't tell me."

"I suppose you deserve to know. You're going to have it out of me one way or another. I learned from Wynne and Dee what sort of a person you were, and—"

"So Wynne did get away from the dragon?"

"Yes, thanks to you. She—"

A light was coming. "Chameleon," Bink said.

Fanchon scrambled to hide her bricks. This time the light came all the way to the pit. "I trust you have not been flooded out down there?" Trent's voice inquired.

"If we were, we'd swim away from here," Bink said. "Listen, Magician—the more uncomfortable you make us, the less we want to help you."

"I am keenly aware of that, Bink. I would much prefer to provide you with a comfortable tent—"

"No."

"Bink, I find it difficult to comprehend why you should be so loyal to a government that treated you so shabbily."

"What do you know about that?"

"My spies have of course been monitoring your dialogues. But I could have guessed it readily enough, knowing how old and stubborn the Storm King must be by now. Magic manifests in divers forms, and when the definitions become too narrow—"

"Well, it doesn't make any difference here."

The Magician persisted, sounding quite reasonable in contrast to Bink's unreason. "It may be that you do lack magic, Bink, though I hardly think Humfrey would be wrong about a thing like that. But you have other qualities to recommend you, and you would make an excellent citizen."

"He's right, you know," Fanchon said. "You do deserve better than you were given."

"Which side are you on?" Bink demanded.

She sighed in the dark. She sounded very human; it was easier to appreciate that quality when he couldn't see her. "I'm on your side, Bink. I admire your loyalty; I'm just not sure it's deserved."

"Why don't you tell him where the Shieldstone is, then—if you know it?"

"Because, with all its faults, Xanth remains a nice place. The senile King won't live forever; when he dies they'll have to put in the Magician Humfrey, and he'll make things much better, even if he does complain about the time it's wasting him. Maybe some new or young Magician is being born right now, to take over after that. It'll work out somehow. It always has before. The last thing Xanth needs is to be taken over by a cruel, Evil Magician who would turn all his opposition into turnips."

Trent's chuckle came down from above. "My dear, you have a keen mind and a sharp tongue. Actually, I prefer to turn my opponents into trees; they are more durable than turnips. I don't suppose you could concede, merely for the sake of argument, that I might make a better ruler than the present King?"

"He's got a point, you know," Bink said, smiling cynically in the dark.

"Which side are you on?" Fanchon demanded, mimicking the tone Bink had used before.

But it was Trent who laughed. "I like you two," he said. "I really do. You have good minds and good loyalty. If you would only give that loyalty to me, I would be prepared to make substantial concessions. For example, I might grant you veto power over any transformations I made. You could thus choose the turnips."

"So we'd be responsible for your crimes," Fanchon said. "That sort of power would be bound to corrupt us very soon, until we were no different from you."

"Only if your basic fiber were not superior to mine," Trent pointed out. "And if it were not, then you would never have been any different from me. You merely have not yet been subjected to my situation. It would be best if you discovered this, so as not to be unconscious hypocrites."

Bink hesitated. He was wet and cold, and he did not relish spending the night in this hole. Had Trent been one to keep his word, twenty years ago? No, he hadn't; he had broken his word freely in his pursuit of power. That was part of what had defeated him; no one could afford to trust him, not even his friends.

The Magician's promises were valueless. His logic was a tissue of rationalization, designed only to get one of the prisoners to divulge the location of the Shieldstone. Veto power over transformations? Bink and Fanchon would be the first to be transformed, once the Evil one had no further need of them.

Bink did not reply. Fanchon remained silent. After a moment Trent departed.

"And so we weather temptation number two," Fanchon remarked. "But he's a clever and unscrupulous man; it will get harder."

Bink was afraid she was right.

Next morning the slanting sunlight baked the crude bricks. They were hardly hard yet, but at least it was a start. Fanchon placed the items in the privacy cubicle so that they could not be seen from above. She would set them out again for the afternoon sun, if all went well.

Trent came by with more food: fresh fruit and milk. "I dislike putting it on this footing," he said, "but my patience is wearing thin. At any time they might move the Shieldstone routinely, rendering your information valueless. If one of you does not give me the information I need today, tomorrow I shall transform you both. You, Bink, will be a cockatrice; you, Fanchon, a basilisk. You will be confined in the same cage."

Bink and Fanchon looked at each other with complete dismay. Cockatrice and basilisk—two names for the same thing: a winged reptile hatched from a yolkless egg laid by a rooster and hatched by a toad in the warmth of a dungheap. The stench of its breath was so bad that it wilted vegetation and shattered stone, and the very sight of its face would cause other creatures to keel over dead. Basilisk—the little king of the reptiles.

The chameleon of his omen had metamorphosed into the likeness of a basilisk—just before it died. Now he had been reminded of the chameleon by a person who could not have known about that omen, and threatened with transformation into— Surely death was drawing nigh.

"It's a bluff," Fanchon said at last. "He can't really do it. He's just trying to scare us."

"He's succeeding," Bink muttered.

"Perhaps a demonstration would be in order," Trent said. "I ask no person to take my magic on faith, when it is so readily demonstrable. It is necessary for me to perform regularly, to restore my full talent after the long layoff in Mundania, so the demonstration is quite convenient for me." He snapped his fingers. "Allow the prisoners to finish their meal," he said to the guard who reported. "Then remove them from the cell." He left.

Now Fanchon was glum for another reason. "He may be bluffing—but if they come down in here, they'll find the bricks. That will finish us anyway."

"Not if we move right out, giving them no trouble," Bink said. "They won't come down here unless they have to."

"Let's hope so," she said.

When the guards came, Bink and Fanchon scrambled up the rope ladder the moment it was dropped. "We're calling the Magician's bluff," Bink said. There was no reaction from the soldiers. The party marched eastward across the isthmus, toward Xanth.

Within sight of the Shield, Trent stood beside a wire cage. Soldiers stood in a ring around him, arrows nocked to bows. They all wore smoked glasses. It looked very grim.

"Now I caution you," Trent said as they arrived. "Do not look directly at each other's faces after the transformation. I can not restore the dead to life."

If this were another scare tactic, it was effective. Fanchon might doubt, but Bink believed. He remembered Justin Tree, legacy of Trent's ire of twenty years ago. The omen loomed large in his mind. First to be a basilisk, then to die . . .

Trent caught Bink's look of apprehension. "Have you anything to say to me?" he inquired, as if routinely.

"Yes. How did they manage to exile you without getting turned into toads or turnips or worse?"

Trent frowned. "That was not precisely what I meant, Bink. But, in the interest of harmony, I will answer. An aide I trusted was bribed to put a sleep spell on me. While I slept, they carried me across the Shield."

"How do you know it won't happen again? You can't stay awake all the time, you know."

"I spent much time pondering that whole problem in

the long early years of my exile. I concluded that I had
brought the deception upon myself. I had been faithless
to others, and so others were faithless to me. I was not
entirely without honor; I breached my given word only
for what I deemed to be sufficient cause, yet—"

"That's the same as lying," Bink said.

"I did not think so at the time. But I dare say my
reputation in that respect did not improve in my absence; it is ever the privilege of the victor to present the
loser as completely corrupt, thus justifying the victory.
Nevertheless, my word was not my absolute bond, and
in time I realized that this was the fundamental flaw in
my character that had been my undoing. The only way
to prevent repetition was to change my own mode of
operation. And so I no longer deceive—ever. And no
one deceives me."

It was a fair answer. The Evil Magician was, in many
respects, the opposite of the popular image; instead of
being ugly, weak, and mean—Humfrey fitted that description better—he was handsome, strong, and urbane.
Yet he was the villain, and Bink knew better than to let
fair words deceive him.

"Fanchon, stand forth," Trent said.

Fanchon stepped toward him, open cynicism on her
face. Trent did not gesture or chant. He merely glanced
at her with concentration.

She vanished.

A soldier swooped in with a butterfly net, slamming
it down on something. In a moment he held it up—a
struggling, baleful, lizardlike thing with wings.

It really was a basilisk! Bink quickly averted his
eyes, lest he look directly at its horrible face and meet
its deadly gaze.

The soldier dumped the thing into the cage, and another smoke-glass-protected soldier shoved on the lid.
The remaining soldiers relaxed visibly. The basilisk
scrambled around, seeking some escape, but there was
none. It glared at the wire confinement, but its gaze had
no effect on the metal. A third soldier dropped a cloth

over the cage, cutting off the view of the little monster.
Now Bink himself relaxed. The whole thing had obviously been carefully prepared and rehearsed; the soldiers knew exactly what to do.

"Bink, stand forth," Trent said, exactly as before.

Bink was terrified. But a corner of his mind protested: *It's still a bluff. She's in on it. They have rigged
it to make me think she was transformed, and that I'm
to be next. All her arguments against Trent were merely
to make her seem legitimate, preparing for this moment.*

Still, he only half believed that. The omen lent it a
special, awful conviction. Death hovered, as it were, on
the silent wings of a moth hawk, close . . .

Yet he could not betray his homeland. Weak-kneed,
he stepped forth.

Trent focused on him—and the world jumped. Confused and frightened, Bink scrambled for the safety of a
nearby bush. The green leaves withered as he approached; then the net came down, trapping him. Remembering his escape from the Gap dragon, he dodged
at the last moment, backtracking, and the net just
missed him. He glared up at the soldier, who, startled,
had allowed his smoked glasses to fall askew. Their
gazes met—and the man tumbled backward, stricken.

The butterfly net flew wide, but another soldier
grabbed it. Bink scooted for the withered bush again,
but this time the net caught him. He was scooped inside, wings flapping helplessly, tail thrashing and getting
its barb caught in the fabric, claws snarled, beak snap-
ping at nothing.

Then he was dumped out. Two shakes, three, and his
claws and tail were dislodged. He landed on his back,
wings outspread. An anguished squawk escaped him.

As he righted himself, the light dimmed. He was in
the cage, and it had just been covered, so that no one
outside could see his face. He was a cockatrice.

Some demonstration! Not only had he seen Fanchon
transformed, he had experienced it himself—and killed

a soldier merely by looking at him. If there had been any skeptics in Trent's army, there would be none now.

He saw the curling, barbed tail of another of his kind. A female. But her back was to him. His cockatrice nature took over. He didn't want company.

Angrily he pounced on her, biting, digging in with his talons. She twisted around instantly, the muscular serpent's tail providing leverage. For a moment they were face to face.

She was hideous, frightful, loathsome, ghastly, and revolting. He had never before experienced anything so repulsive. Yet she was female, and therefore possessed of a certain fundamental attraction. The paradoxical repulsion and attraction overwhelmed him and he lost consciousness.

When he woke, he had a headache. He lay on the hay in the pit. It was late afternoon.

"It seems the stare of the basilisk is overrated," Fanchon said. "Neither of us died."

So it had really happened. "Not quite," Bink agreed. "But I feel a bit dead." As he spoke he realized something that had not quite surfaced before: the basilisk was a magical creature that could do magic. He had been an intelligent cockatrice who had magically stricken an enemy. What did that do to his theory of magic?

"Well, you put up a good fight," Fanchon was saying. "They've already buried that soldier. It is quiet like death in this camp now."

Like death—had that been the meaning of his omen? He had not died, but he had killed—without meaning to, in a manner completely foreign to his normal state. Had the omen been fulfilled?

Bink sat up, another realization coming. "Trent's talent is genuine. We were transformed. We really were."

"It is genuine. We really were," she agreed somberly. "I admit I doubted—but now I believe."

"He must have changed us back while we were unconscious."

"Yes. He was only making a demonstration."

"It was an effective one."

"It was." She shuddered. "Bink—I—I don't know whether I can take that again. It wasn't just the change. It was—"

"I know. You made a hell of an ugly basilisk."

"I would make a hell of an ugly anything. But the sheer malignancy, stupidity, and awfulness—those things are foul! To spend the rest of my life like that—"

"I can't blame you," Bink said. But still something nagged at his mind. The experience had been so momentous that he knew it would take a long time for his mind to sift through all its aspects.

"I didn't think anyone could make me go against my conscience. But this—this—" She put her face into her hands.

Bink nodded silently. After a moment he shifted the subject. "Did you notice—those creatures were male and female."

"Of course," she said, gaining control of herself now that she had something to orient on. "We are male and female. The Magician can change our forms but not our sexes."

"But the basilisks should be neuter. Hatched of eggs laid by roosters—there are no parent basilisks, only roosters."

She nodded thoughtfully, catching hold of the problem. "You're right. If there are males and females, they should mate and reproduce their own kind. Which means, by definition, they aren't basilisks. A paradox."

"There must be something wrong with the definition," Bink said. "Either there's a lot of superstition about the origins of monsters, or we were not genuine basilisks."

"We were genuine," she said, grimacing with renewed horror. "I'm sure now. For the first time in my life, I'm glad for my human form." Which was quite an admission, for her.

"That means Trent's magic is all-the-way real," Bink said. "He doesn't just change the form, he really converts things into other things, if you see what I mean." Then the thing that had nagged at his mind before came clear. "But if magic fades outside Xanth, beyond the narrow magic band beyond the Shield, all we would have to do—"

"Would be to go into Mundania!" she exclaimed, catching on. "In time, we would revert to our proper forms. So it would not be permanent."

"So his transformation ability is a bluff, even though it is real," he said. "He would have to keep us caged right there, or we'd escape and get out of his power. He has to get all the way into Xanth or he really has very little power. No more power than he already has as General of his army—the power to kill."

"All he can get now is the tantalizing taste of real power," she said. "I'll *bet* he wants to get into Xanth!"

"But meanwhile, we're still in his power."

She set out the bricks, catching the limited sunlight. "What are you going to do?" she asked.

"If he lets me go, I'll travel on into Mundania. That's where I was headed before I was ambushed. One thing Trent has shown me—it is possible to survive out there. But I'll make sure to note my route carefully; it seems Xanth is hard to find from the other direction."

"I meant about the Shieldstone."

"Nothing."

"You won't tell him?"

"No, of course not," he said. "Now we know his magic can't really hurt us worse than his soldiers can, some of the terror is gone. Not that it matters. I don't blame you for telling him."

She looked at him. Her face was still ugly, but there was something special in it now. "You know, you're quite a man, Bink."

"No, I'm nothing much. I have no magic."

"You have magic. You just don't know what it is."

"Same thing."

"I followed you out here, you know."

Her meaning was coming clear. She had heard about him in Xanth, the traveler with no spell. She had known that would be no liability in Mundania. What better match—the man with no magic, the woman with no beauty. Similar liabilities. Perhaps he could get used to her appearance in time; her other qualities were certainly commendable. Except for one thing.

"I understand your position," he said. "But if you cooperate with the Evil Magician, I won't have anything to do with you, even if he makes you beautiful. Not that it matters—you can get your reward in Xanth when he takes over, if he honors his given word this time."

"You restore my courage," she said. "Let's make a break for it."

"How?"

"The bricks, dummy. They're hard now. As soon as it's dark, we'll make a pile—"

"The grate keeps us in; its door is still locked. A step won't make any difference. If just getting up there were the only problem, I could lift you—"

"There is a difference," she murmured. "We pile the bricks, stand on them, and push the whole grate up. It's not anchored; I checked that when they brought us in here. Gravity holds it down. It's heavy, but you're strong—"

Bink looked up with sudden hope. "You could prop it up after I heave. Step by step, until—"

"Not so loud!" she whispered fiercely. "They may still be eavesdropping." But she nodded. "You've got the idea. It's not a sure thing, but it's worth a try. And we'll have to make a raid on the store of elixir, so he can't use it even if someone else comes out to tell him where the Shieldstone is. I've been working it all out."

Bink smiled. He was beginning to like her.

Chapter 10. Chase

At night they piled up the bricks. Some crumbled, for the scant sunlight had not been sufficient to bake them properly, but on the whole they were surprisingly sturdy. Bink listened carefully for the guards, waiting until they took what they called a "break." Then he stepped to the top of the brick pile, braced his hands against the edge of the grate, and shoved.

As his muscles tightened, he suddenly realized that this was Fanchon's real reason for demanding the privacy curtain of the privy. It had not been to hide her unsightly anatomy, but to hide the bricks—so they would be preserved for this moment, this effort to escape. And he had never caught on.

The revelation gave him strength. He shoved hard—and the grate rose with surprising ease. Fanchon scrambled up beside him and jammed the privy pot under the lifted edge.

Ugh! Maybe some year someone would develop a pot that smelled of roses!

But it did the job. It supported the grate as he eased off. Now there was room to scramble out. Bink gave her a boost, then hauled himself up. No guards saw them. They were free.

"The elixir is on that ship," Fanchon whispered, pointing into the darkness.

"How do you know that?" Bink asked.

"We passed it on our way to the—transformation. It's the only thing that would be guarded so carefully. And you can see the catapult aboard it."

She had certainly kept her eyes open. Ugly she might be, but she was smart. He hadn't thought to survey the premises with such an analytic eye!

"Now, getting that elixir will be a problem," she continued. "I think we'd better take the whole ship. Can you sail?"

"I've never been on anything bigger than a rowboat in my life, except maybe Iris's yacht, and that wasn't real. I'd probably get seasick."

"Me too," she agreed. "We're landlubbers. So they'll never look for us there. Come on."

Well, it was better than being changed into a cockatrice.

They crept down to the beach and entered the water. Bink looked back nervously—and saw a light moving toward the pit. "Hurry!" he whispered. "We forgot to put the grate back down; they'll know we're gone right away."

At least they were both reasonably good swimmers. They shed their clothing—what had happened to it during the transformations? again, no explaining the details of magic—and stroked silently for the sailboat moored a quarter mile out. Bink was alarmed by the dark depths of the water beneath him; what type of monsters dwelled in Mundane seas?

The water was not cold, and the exertion of swimming helped warm him, but gradually Bink tired and felt chilled. Fanchon suffered similarly. The ship had not seemed far, viewed from land—but that had been walking distance. Swimming distance was quite another matter.

Then the hue and cry commenced back at the prison pit. Lights flared everywhere, moving around like fireflies—but setting no fires. Bink had an infusion of new strength. "We've got to get there fast," he gasped.

Fanchon didn't answer. She was too busy swimming.

The swim was interminable. It drained strength from Bink, making him become more pessimistic. But at last they came up to the ship. A sailor was standing on the

deck, a silhouette in the light of the moon, peering at
the shore.

Fanchon drew close to Bink. "You go—other side,"
she gasped. "I—distract."

She had guts. The sailor might put an arrow in her.
But Bink stroked laboriously around the keel, moving
to the far side. The ship was about forty feet long, large
by Xanth standards. But if any part of what Trent had
said about Mundania was true, there were much larger
ships there.

He reached up and put his fingers on the edge of the
hull. He tried to think of the name of this portion of a
ship's anatomy, but could not. He hoped there weren't
other sailors watching. He had to haul himself up slowly
over the gunwale—that was the name—so as not to
rock the boat.

Now Fanchon, with superlative timing, made a
clamor, as of someone drowning. The sailors went to
the rail—four of them in all—and Bink heaved himself
up as silently as he could. He scraped, for his muscles
felt leaden, unresponsive. His wet body slapped against
the deck, and the ship tilted back a bit under his
weight—but the sailors stood riveted to the other side,
watching the show.

Bink got to his feet and slunk up to the mast. The
sails were furled, so that it offered scant concealment;
they would see him when they turned with their lamps.

Well, he would have to act first. He felt ill equipped
to indulge in combat, his arms and feet cold and heavy,
but it was necessary. He walked silently up behind the
four, his heart pounding. They were leaning over the
rail, trying to see Fanchon, who was still making a considerable commotion. Bink put his left hand against the
back of the nearest sailor and caught the man's trouser
with his right hand. He heaved, hard and suddenly—
and the sailor went up and over with a cry of alarm.

Bink swung immediately to the next, grabbing and
shoving. The man had started to turn toward his companion's exclamation—but too late. Bink heaved, and

the sailor went over. Almost over—one hand caught the rail. The sailor clung, twisting around to face inward. Bink knocked at his fingers and finally pried them loose, and the man dropped into the water.

But the loss of time and momentum had been crucial. Now the other two were upon Bink. One wrapped an arm around Bink's shoulder, trying to choke him, while the other hovered behind.

What had Crombie said to do in a situation like this? Bink concentrated and remembered. He grabbed the man, bent his knees, leaned forward, and heaved.

It worked beautifully. The sailor sailed over Bink's shoulder and crashed on his back on the deck.

But the last one was stepping in, fists swinging. He caught Bink on the side of the head with glancing but numbing force. Bink fell to the deck himself, and the man dove on top of him. To make things worse, Bink saw one of the others climbing back aboard. He put up his feet to hold off his opponent, but this was only partially effective. The burly sailor was pushing him down, pinning him—and the other was about to join in.

The standing figure lifted a foot. Bink could not even flinch; his arms were tangled, his body held down. The foot swung—and struck the head of Bink's antagonist.

The man rolled off Bink with a groan. It was not fun, being kicked in the head. But how had the kicker missed the proper target, at such close range? The lamps had all gone into the water along with their owners; maybe in the dark a mistake—

"Help me get him over the edge," Fanchon said. "We've got to secure this ship."

And he had mistaken her for a sailor, though she was naked! Well, blame the inadequate light again. Moonlight was pretty, but in a situation like this—

But the remaining two sailors were already rising over the gunwale. Acting on a common impulse, Bink grabbed his erstwhile opponent's shoulders, and Fanchon grabbed his feet. "One—two—three—heave!" she gasped.

They heaved almost together. The man swung up and into his two companions. All three went over the edge to splash in the sea. Bink hoped they were all lively enough to swim. The fourth one lay on the deck, apparently unconscious.

"Pull up the anchor!" Fanchon ordered. "I'll get a pole." She ran to the ship's cabin, a lean figure in the moonlight.

Bink found the anchor chain and hauled on it. The thing snagged infuriatingly, because he did not know how to make it let go, but finally he got it up.

"What did you do to this guy?" Fanchon demanded, kneeling beside the fallen sailor.

"I threw him. Crombie showed me how."

"Crombie? I don't remember—"

"A soldier I met in Xanth. We got caught in a hailstorm, and I was going back after Dee, but—well, it's complicated."

"Oh yes—you did mention the soldier." She paused. "Dee? You went after her? Why?"

"She had run out into the storm and—well, I liked her." Then, to cover up what might have been taken as a slight to his present company, who had shown extreme sensitivity about such things before, he said: "What happened to the other sailors? Did they drown?"

"I showed them this," she said, pointing to a wicked-looking boathook. "They swam for shore instead."

"We'd better get moving. If we can figure out the sail."

"No. The current is carrying us out. Wind's the wrong way. We'd just mess it up, trying to handle the sails when we don't know what we're doing."

Bink looked across at the other ship. Lights were on it. "Those sailors didn't swim ashore," he said. "They went next door. They'll be coming after us—under sail."

"They can't," she said. "I told you—the wind."

But now it was unmistakable. The other sail was being spread. They *were* using the wind.

"We'd better find that elixir," she said.

"Yes." He had forgotten about it. But for that, they could have run across the land and been lost in Mundania. But could he have lived with himself, buying his own freedom while leaving Xanth subject to the siege of the Evil Magician? "We'll dump it overboard—"

"No!"

"But I thought—"

"We'll use it as hostage. As long as we have it, they won't close on us. We'll take turns standing on the deck and holding the vial over the sea so they can see us. If anything happens to—"

"Beautiful!" he exclaimed. "I never would have thought of that."

"First we have to find our hostage. If we guessed wrong about the ship, if they put the catapult on this one and the elixir on the other—"

"Then they wouldn't be chasing us," he said.

"Yes they would. They need the catapult too. And most of all, they need us."

They searched the ship. In the cabin was a chained monster of a type Bink had never seen before. It was not large, but quite horrible in other respects. Its body was completely covered with hair, white with black spots, and it had a thin tail, floppy black ears, a small black nose, and gleaming white teeth. Its four feet had stubby claws. It snarled viciously as Bink approached— but it was chained by the neck to the wall, its mad leaps cut brutally short by that tether.

"What is it?" Bink asked, horrified.

Fanchon considered. "I think it's a werewolf."

Now the creature looked halfway familiar. It did resemble a werewolf, fixed in its animal stage.

"Out here in Mundania?"

"Well, it must be related. If it had more heads, it would be like a cerberus. With only one head, I think it's a dog."

Bink gaped. "A dog! I think you're right. I've never

actually seen a dog before. Not in the flesh. Just pictures."

"I don't think there are any in Xanth today. There used to be, but they must have migrated out."

"Through the Shield?" Bink demanded.

"Before the Shield was set up, of course—though I'd thought there were references to dogs and cats and horses within the past century. I must have misremembered the dates."

"Well, it seems we have one here now. It looks vicious. It must be guarding the elixir."

"Trained to attack strangers," she agreed. "I suppose we'll have to kill it."

"But it's a rare creature. Maybe the only one left alive today."

"We don't know that. Dogs might be common in Mundania. But it is rather pretty, once you get used to it."

The dog had quieted down, though it still watched them warily. A small dragon might watch a person that way, Bink thought, if the person were just outside its striking range. With the proper break, the person might come within range . . .

"Maybe we could revive the sailor and have him tame it," Bink said. "The animal must be responsive to members of this ship's crew. Otherwise they could never get at the elixir."

"Good idea," she agreed.

The sailor had finally recovered consciousness, but he was in no condition to resume the fight. "We'll let you go," Fanchon told him, "if you tell us how to tame that dog. We don't want to have to kill it, you see."

"Who, Jennifer?" the man asked dazedly. "Just speak her name, pat her on the head, and feed her." He lay back. "I think my collarbone's broke."

Fanchon looked at Bink. "Can't make him swim, then. Trent may be a monster, but we aren't." She turned back to the sailor. "If you will give your word not to interfere with us in any way, we'll help you recover as well as we can. Deal?"

The sailor didn't hesitate. "I can't interfere with you. I can't get up. Deal."

This bothered Bink. He and Fanchon sounded just like Trent, offering better terms to a captive enemy in return for his cooperation. Were they any different from the Evil Magician?

Fanchon checked the sailor's body around the shoulders. "Yow!" he cried.

"I'm no doctor," she said, "but I think you're right. You have a broken bone. Are there any pillows aboard?"

"Listen," the sailor said as she worked on him. He was obviously trying to divert his attention from the pain. "Trent's no monster. You called him that, but you're wrong. He's a good leader."

"He's promised you all the spoils of Xanth?" Fanchon asked, with an edge to her voice.

"No, just farms or jobs for all of us," he said.

"No killing, no rapine, no loot?" Her disbelief was evident.

"None of that. This ain't the old days, you know? We just protect him and keep order in the territory we occupy, and he'll give us small land grants where nobody's settled yet. He says Xanth's underpopulated. And there'll be—he'll encourage the local gals to marry us, so we can have families. If there aren't enough, he'll bring in gals from the real world. And meanwhile, he'll transform some smart animals into gals. I thought that was a joke, but after what I hear about those cocks—" He grimaced. "I mean those basks—" He shook his head and grimaced again, in pain.

"Keep your head still," Fanchon told him, too late. "It's true about the cockatrice and basilisk; *we* were them. But animal brides—"

"Oh, it wouldn't be so bad, miss. Just temporary, until real gals arrived. If she looks like a gal and feels like a gal, I wouldn't blame her for being a bitch before. I mean, some gals are bitches—"

"What's a bitch?" Bink asked.

"A bitch? You don't know that?" The sailor grimaced again; either he was in considerable pain or it was a natural expression. "A female dog. Like Jennifer. Hell, if Jennifer had human form—"

"Enough," Fanchon muttered.

"Well, anyway, we'll get homesteads and settle in. And our kids will be magic. I tell you, it's that last that recruited me. I don't believe in magic, understand—or I didn't then—but I remember the fairy tales from when I was a little tyke, about the princess and the frog, and the mountain of glass, and the three wishes—well, look, I was a metalworker for a crooked shop, know what I mean? And I really wanted out of the rat race."

Bink shook his head silently. He understood only part of what the sailor was saying, but it did not make Mundania look very good. Stores that were built off balance, crooked? Rats that raced? Bink would want to get out of that culture, too.

"A chance to have a decent life in the country," the sailor continued, and there was no question about his dedication to his vision. "Owning my own land, making good things grow, you know? And my kids knowing magic, real magic—I guess I still don't really believe that part, but even if it's a lie, you know, it's sure nice to think about."

"But to invade a foreign land, to take what doesn't belong to you—" Fanchon said. She broke off, evidently certain that it was pointless to debate that sort of thing with a sailor. "He'll betray you the moment he doesn't need you. He's an Evil Magician, exiled from Xanth."

"You mean he really can do magic?" the man asked with happy disbelief. "I figured all this stuff was sleight of hand, you know, when I really thought about it. I mean, I believed some of the time, but—"

"He sure as hell *can* do magic," Bink put in, becoming acclimatized to the sailor's language. "We told you how he changed us—"

"Never mind about that," Fanchon said.

"Well, he's still a good leader," the sailor insisted. "He told us how he was kicked out twenty years ago because he tried to be King, and how he lost his magic, and married a gal from here and had a little boy—"

"Trent has a family in Mundania?" Bink asked, amazed.

"We don't call our country that," the sailor said. "But yes—he had a family. Until this mystery bug went around—some kind of flu, I think, or maybe food poisoning—and they both got it and died. He said science hadn't been able to save them, but magic could have, so he was going back to magicland. Xanth, you call it. But they'd kill him if he just walked in alone, even if he got by the thing he called a Shield. So he needed an army—oooh!" Fanchon had finished her work and heaved his shoulder up onto a pillow.

So they had the sailor as comfortable as was feasible, his shoulder bound up in stray cloths. Bink would have liked to hear more of the man's unique viewpoint. But time had passed, and it was apparent that the other ship was gaining on them. They traced its progress by its sail, which moved laterally, back and forth, zigzagging against the wind—and with each pass it was closer. They had been wrong about the capabilities of ships in adverse wind. How much else were they wrong about?

Bink went into the cabin. He was feeling a bit seasick now, but he held it down. "Jennifer," he said hesitantly, proffering some of the dog food they had found. The small spotted monster wagged her tail. Just like that, they were friends. Bink screwed up his courage and patted her on the head, and she did not bite him. Then, while she ate, he opened the chest she had guarded so ferociously and lifted out the vial of greenish fluid he found therein, in a carefully padded box. Victory!

"Miss," the sailor called as Bink emerged with the vial. "The Shield—"

Fanchon looked about nervously. "Is the current carrying us into *that?*"

"Yes, miss. I wouldn't interfere, but if you don't turn this boat soon, we'll all be dead. I *know* that Shield works; I've seen animals try to go through it and get fried."

"How can we tell where it is?" she asked.

"There's a glimmer. See?" He pointed with difficulty.

Bink peered and saw it. They were drifting toward a curtain of faint luminescence, ghostly white. The Shield!

The ship progressed inexorably. "We can't stop it," Fanchon cried. "We're going right through."

"Throw down the anchor!" the sailor said.

What else was there to do? The Shield was certain death. Yet to stop meant capture by Trent's forces. Even bluffing them back by means of the vial of elixir would not suffice; the ship remained a kind of prison.

"We can use the lifeboat," Fanchon said. "Give me the vial."

Bink gave it to her, then threw over the anchor. The ship slowly turned as the anchor took hold. The Shield loomed uncomfortably close—but so did the pursuing ship. Now it was clear why it was using the wind instead of the current; it was under control, in no danger of drifting into the Shield.

They lowered the lifeboat. A reflector lamp from the other ship bathed them in its light. Fanchon held the vial aloft. "I'll drop it!" she screamed at the enemy "Hit me with an arrow—the elixir drowns with me."

"Give it back," Trent's voice called from the other ship. "I pledge to let you both go free."

"Ha!" she muttered. "Bink, can you row this boat yourself? I'm afraid to set this thing down while we're in range of their arrows. I want to be sure that no matter what happens to us, they don't get this stuff."

"I'll try," Bink said. He settled himself, grabbed the oars, and heaved.

One oar cracked into the side of the ship. The other

dug into the water. The boat skewed around. "Push off!" Fanchon exclaimed. "You almost dumped me."

Bink tried to put the end of one oar against the ship, to push, but it didn't work because he could not maneuver the oar free of its oarlock. But the current carried the boat along until it passed beyond the end of the ship.

"We're going into the Shield!" Fanchon cried, waving the vial. "Row! Row! Turn the boat!"

Bink put his back into it. The problem with rowing was that he faced backward; he could not see where he was going. Fanchon perched in the stern, holding the vial aloft, peering ahead. He got the feel of the oars and turned the boat, and now the shimmering curtain came into view on the side. It was rather pretty in its fashion, its ghostly glow parting the night—but he recoiled from its horror.

"Go parallel to it," Fanchon directed. "The closer we stay, the harder it'll make it for the other ship. Maybe they'll give up the pursuit."

Bink pulled on the oars. The boat moved ahead. But he was unused to this particular form of exertion, and not recovered from his fatigue of the swim, and he knew he couldn't keep it up long.

"You're going into the Shield!" Fanchon cried.

Bink looked. The Shield loomed closer, yet he was not rowing toward it. "The current," he said. "Carrying us sideways." He had naively thought that once he started rowing, all other vectors ceased.

"Row away from the Shield," she cried. "Quickly!"

He angled the boat—but the Shield did not retreat. The current was bearing them on as fast as he could row. To make it worse, the wind was now changing— and rising. He was holding even at the moment, but he was tiring rapidly. "I can't—keep this—up!" he gasped, staring at the glow.

"There's an island," Fanchon said. "Angle toward it."

Bink looked around. He saw a black something cutting the waves to the side. Island? It was no more than a treacherous rock. But if they could anchor to it—

He put forth a desperate effort—but it was not enough. A storm was developing. They were going to miss the rock. The dread Shield loomed nearer.

"I'll help," Fanchon cried. She set down the vial, crawled forward, and put her hands on the oars, opposite his hands. She pushed, synchronizing her efforts with his.

It helped. But Bink, fatigued, was distracted. In the erratic moonlight, blotted out intermittently by the thickening, fast-moving clouds above, her naked body lost some of its shapelessness and assumed the suggestion of more feminine contours. Shadow and imagination could make her halfway attractive—and that embarrassed him, because he had no right to think of such things. Fanchon could be a good companion, if only—

The boat smashed into the rock. It tilted—rock or craft or both. "Get hold! Get hold!" Fanchon cried as water surged over the side.

Bink reached out and tried to hang on to the stone. It was both abrasive and slippery. A wave broke over him, filling his mouth with its salty spume. Now it was black; the clouds had completed their engulfment of the moon.

"The elixir!" Fanchon cried. "I left it in the—" She dived for the flooded stern of the boat.

Bink, still choking on sea water, could not yell at her. He clung to the rock with his hands, his fingers finding purchase in a crevice, anchoring the boat with his hooked knees. He suffered a foolish vision: if a giant drowning in the ocean grabbed on to the land of Xanth for support, his fingers would catch in the chasm, the Gap. Maybe that was the purpose of the Gap. Did the tiny inhabitants of this isolated rock resent the crevice that Bink's giant fingers had found? Did they have forget spells to remove it from their awareness?

There was a distant flash of lightning. Bink saw the somber mass of ragged stone: no miniature people on it. But there was a glint, as of light reflecting from a

knob in the water. He stared at it, but the lightning was
long since gone, and he was squinting at the mere memory, trying to make out the surrounding shape. For it
had been a highlight from something larger.

Lightning flashed again, closer. Bink saw briefly but
clearly.

It was a toothy reptilian creature. The highlight had
been from its malignant eye.

"A sea monster!" he cried, terrified.

Fanchon labored at an oar, finally extricating it from
its lock. She aimed it at the monster and shoved.

Thunk! The end of the oar struck the armored green
snout. The creature backed off.

"We've got to get away from here," Bink cried.

But as he spoke, another wave broke over them. The
boat was lifted and wrenched away from his feet. He
put one arm about Fanchon's skinny waist and hung on.
It seemed the fingers of his other hand would break—
but they remained wedged in the crevice, and he held
his position.

In the next trough the lightning showed small saillike
projections moving in the water. What were they?

Then another monster broke water right beside him;
he saw it in the phosphorescence that the complete
darkness had attuned his eyes to. It seemed to have a
single broad eye across its face, and a round, truncated
snout. Huge wattles were at the sides. Bink was trans-
fixed by terror, though he knew that most of the details
were really from his imagination. He could only stare at
the thing as the lightning permitted.

And the lightning confirmed his imagination. It was a
hideous monster!

Bink struggled with his terror to form some plan of
defense. One hand clung to the rock; the other held
Fanchon. He could not act. But maybe Fanchon could.
"Your oar—" he gasped.

The monster acted first. It put its hands to its face—
and lifted the face away. Underneath, was the face of
Evil Magician Trent. "You fools have caused enough

trouble! Give me the elixir, and I'll have the ship throw us a line."

Bink hesitated. He was bone-weary and cold, and knew he could not hold out much longer against storm and current. It was death to stay here.

"There's a crocodile sniffing around," Trent continued. "And several sharks. Those are just as deadly as the mythical monsters you are familiar with. I have repellent—but the current is carrying it away as rapidly as it diffuses into the water, so it's not much help. On top of that, sometimes whirlpools develop around these rocks, especially during storms. We need help now—and I alone can summon it. Give me that vial!"

"Never!" Fanchon cried. She dived into the black waves.

Trent snapped the mask back over his face and dived after her. As he moved, Bink saw that the Magician was naked except for his long sword strapped to a harness. Bink dived after him, not even thinking of what he was doing.

They met in a tangle underwater. In the dark and bubbly swirl, there was nothing but mutual mischief. Bink tried to swim to the surface, uncertain as to what foolishness had prompted him to dive here but sure that he could only drown himself. But someone had a death grip on him. He had to get up, to get his head in air so he could breathe. The water had hold of them all, carrying them around and around.

It was the whirlpool—an inanimate funnel monster. It sucked them down, spinning, into the depth of its maw. For the second time Bink felt himself drowning—and this time he knew no Sorceress would rescue him.

Chapter 11. Wilderness

Bink woke with his face in sand. Around him lay the inert tentacles of a green monster.

He groaned and sat up. "Bink!" Fanchon cried gladly, coming across the beach to him.

"I thought it was night," he said.

"You've been unconscious. This cave has magic phosphorescence, or maybe it's Mundane phosphorescence, since there was some on the rock, too. But it's much brighter here. Trent pumped the water out of you, but I was afraid—"

"What's this?" Bink asked, staring at a green tentacle.

"A kraken seaweed," Trent said. "It pulled us out of the drink, intending to consume us—but the vial of elixir broke and killed it. That's all that saved our lives. If the vial had broken earlier, it would have stopped the kraken from catching us, and we all would have drowned; later, and we would already have been eaten. As fortuitous a coincidence of timing as I have ever experienced."

"A kraken weed!" Bink exclaimed. "But that's magic!"

"We're back in Xanth," Fanchon said.

"But—"

"I conjecture that the whirlpool drew us down below the effective level of the Shield," Trent said. "We passed under it. Perhaps the presence of the elixir helped. A freak accident—and I'm certainly not going to try to reverse that route now. I lost my breathing apparatus on the way in; lucky I got a good dose of oxygen first! We're in Xanth to stay."

"I guess so," Bink said dazedly. He had gradually become accustomed to the notion of spending the rest of his life in Mundania; it was hard to abandon that drear expectation so suddenly. "But why did you save me? Once the elixir was gone—"

"It was the decent thing to do," the Magician said. "I realize you will not appreciate such a notion from my lips, but I can offer no better rationale at the moment. I never had any personal animus against you; in fact, I rather admired your fortitude and personal ethical code. You can go your way now—and I'll go mine."

Bink pondered. He was faced with a new, unfamiliar reality. Back in Xanth, no longer at war with the Evil Magician. The more he reviewed the details, the less sense any of it made. Sucked down by a whirlpool through monster-infested waters, through the invisible but deadly Shield, to be rescued by a man-eating plant, which was coincidentally nullified at precisely the moment required to let them drop safely on this beach? "No," he said. "I don't believe it. Things just don't happen this way."

"It does seem as if we were charmed," Fanchon said. "Though why the Evil Magician should have been included . . ."

Trent smiled. Naked, he was fully as impressive as before. Despite his age, he was a fit and powerful man. "It does seem ironic that the evil should be saved along with the good. Perhaps human definitions are not always honored by nature. But I, like you, am a realist. I don't pretend to understand how we got here—but I do not question that we are here. Getting to land may be more problematical, however. We are hardly out of danger yet."

Bink looked around the cave. Already the air seemed close, though he hoped that was his imagination. There seemed to be no exit except the water through which

they had come. In one nook was a pile of clean bones—
the refuse of the kraken.

It began to seem less coincidental. What better place
for an ocean monster to operate than at the exit to a
whirlpool? The sea itself collected the prey, and most of
it was killed on the way in by the Shield. The kraken
weed had only to sieve the fresh bodies out of the water.
And this highly private cave was ideal for leisurely consumption of the largest living animals. They could be
deposited here on the beach, and even given food, so
that they would remain more or less healthy until the
kraken's hunger was sufficient. A pleasant little larder
to keep the food fresh and tasty. Any that tried to escape by swimming past the tentacles—ugh! So the
kraken could have dropped the human trio here, then
been hit by the elixir; instead of split-second timing, it
became several-minute timing. Still a coincidence, but a
much less extreme one.

Fanchon was squatting by the water, flicking dry
leaves into it. The leaves had to be from past seasons of
the kraken weed; why it needed them here, with no sunlight, Bink didn't understand. Maybe it had been a regular plant before it turned magic—or its ancestors had
been regular—and it still had not entirely adapted. Or
maybe the leaves had some other purpose. There was a
great deal yet to be understood about nature. At any
rate, Fanchon was floating the leaves on the water, and
why she wasted her time that way was similarly opaque.

She saw him looking. "I'm tracing surface currents,"
she said. "See—the water is moving that way. There
has to be an exit under that wall."

Bink was impressed again with her intelligence. Every time he caught her doing something stupid, it turned
out to be the opposite. She was an ordinary, if ugly, girl,
but she had a mind that functioned efficiently. She had
plotted their escape from the pit, and their subsequent
strategy, and it had nullified Trent's program of conquest. Now she was at it again. Too bad her appearance
fell down.

"Of course," Trent agreed. "The kraken can't live in stagnant water; it needs a constant flow. That brings in its food supply and carries away its wastes. We have an exit—if it leads to the surface quickly enough, and does not pass through the Shield again."

Bink didn't like it. "Suppose we dive into that current and it carries us a mile underwater before it comes out? We'd drown."

"My friend," Trent said, "I have been pondering that very dilemma. We can not be rescued by my sailors, because we are obviously beyond the Shield. I do not like to gamble on either the current or what we may discover within it. Yet it seems we must eventually do so, for we can not remain here indefinitely."

Something twitched. Bink looked—and saw one green tentacle writhing. "The kraken's reviving!" he exclaimed. "It isn't dead!"

"Uh-oh," Trent said. "The elixir has thinned out in the current and dissipated. The magic is returning. I had thought that concentration would be fatal to a magic creature, but apparently not."

Fanchon watched the tentacles. Now others were quivering. "I think we'd better get out of here," she said. "Soon."

"But we don't dare plunge into the water without knowing where it goes," Bink objected. "We must be well below the surface. I'd rather stay here and fight than drown."

"I propose we declare a truce between us until we get free," Trent said. "The elixir is gone, and we cannot go back the way we came from Mundania. We shall probably have to cooperate to get out of here—and in the present situation, we really have no quarrel."

Fanchon didn't trust him. "So we help you get out—so then the truce ends and you change us into gnats. Since we're inside Xanth, we'll never be able to change back again."

Trent snapped his fingers. "Stupid of me to forget. Thank you for reminding me. I can use my magic now to get us out." He looked at the quivering green tentacles. "Of course, I'll have to wait until all the elixir is gone, for it voids my magic, too. That means the kraken will be fully recovered. I can't transform it, because its main body is too far away."

The tentacles lifted. "Bink, dive for it!" Fanchon cried. "We don't want to be caught between the kraken and the Evil Magician." She plunged into the water.

The issue had been forced. She was right: the kraken would eat them or the Magician would transform them. Right now, while the lingering elixir blunted both threats, was the time to escape. Still, he would have hesitated—if Fanchon had not already taken action. If she drowned, there would be no one on his side.

Bink charged across the sand, tripped over a tentacle, and sprawled. Reacting automatically, the tentacle wrapped itself around his leg. The leaves glued themselves to his flesh with little sucking noises. Trent drew his sword and strode toward him.

Bink grabbed a handful of sand and threw it at the Magician, but it was ineffective. Then Trent's sword slashed down—and severed the tentacle. "You are in no danger from me, Bink," the Magician said. "Swim, if you wish."

Bink scrambled up and dived into the water, taking a deep breath. He saw Fanchon's feet kicking ahead of him as she swam down, and saw the dark tube of the nether exit. It terrified him, and he balked.

His head popped through the surface. There was Trent, standing on the beach, parrying the converging tentacles with his sword. Fighting off the coils of the monster the man was the very picture of heroism. Yet the moment the combat was over, Trent would be a more dangerous monster than the kraken.

Bink decided. He took a new breath and dived again. This time he stroked right into the somber eye, and felt the current take him. Now there was no turning back.

The tunnel opened out almost immediately—into another glowing cavern. Bink had gained on Fanchon, and their heads broke the surface almost together. Probably she had been more cautious about navigating the exit.

Heads turned their way. Human heads, on human torsos—very nice feminine ones. Their faces were elfin, their tresses flowing in magical iridescence over slender bare shoulders and perfectly erect breasts. But the lower quarters merged into fish's tails. These were mermaids.

"What are you doing in our cave?" one of the maids cried indignantly.

"Just passing through," Bink said. Naturally, mermaids spoke the common language of Xanth. He would not have thought anything of it, had Trent not remarked on how Xanth language merged with all Mundane languages. Magic operated in so many ways. "Tell us the shortest way to the surface."

"That way," one said, pointing left. "That way," another said, pointing right. "No, that way!" a third cried, pointing straight up. There was a burst of girlish laughter.

Several mermaids plunged into the water, tails flashing, and swam toward Bink. In a moment he was surrounded. Up close, the creatures were even prettier than from afar. Each one had a perfect complexion, resulting from the natural action of the water, and their breasts floated somewhat, making them seem fuller. Maybe he had been exposed to Fanchon too long; the sight of all this loveliness gave him strange sensations of excitement and nostalgia. If he could grab them all at once—but no, they were mermaids, not his type at all.

They paid no attention to Fanchon. "He's a man!" one cried, meaning Bink was human, not merman. "Look at his split legs. No tail at all."

Suddenly they were diving under to view his legs. Bink, naked, found this distinctly awkward. They began to put their hands on him, kneading the unfamiliar musculature of his legs, a great curiosity to them. Yet why weren't they looking at Fanchon's legs too? There seemed to be more mischief than curiosity here.

Trent's head broke the water behind them. "Mermaids," he commented. "We'll get nothing from them."

So it seemed. It also seemed that the Magician could not be avoided. "I think we'd better make the truce," Bink said to Fanchon. "We have to extend some trust sometime."

She looked at the mermaids, then at Trent. "Very well," she said ungraciously. "For what it's worth—which isn't much."

"A sensible decision," Trent said. "Our long-range objectives may differ, but our short-range one matches: survival. See, here come the tritons."

As he spoke, a group of mermen appeared, swimming in from another passage. This seemed to be a labyrinth of caves and water-filled apertures.

"Ho!" a triton cried, brandishing his trident. "Skewer!"

The mermaids screamed playfully and dived out of sight. Bink avoided Fanchon's gaze; the ladies had been having entirely too much fun with him, and obviously not because of his split legs.

"Too many to fight," Trent said. "The elixir is gone. With your acquiescence, under our truce, I will change you both into fish, or perhaps reptiles, so that you can escape. However—"

"How will we change back?" Fanchon demanded.

"That is the key. I can not change myself. Therefore you will have to rescue me—or remain transformed. So we shall survive together, or suffer apart. Fair enough?"

She looked at the tritons, who were swimming determinedly toward the three, surrounding them, tridents raised. They did not look at all playful. This was obviously a gang of bullies, showing off for the applauding spectators—the mermaids, who had now reappeared on shore—taking time to put on a flashy show. "Why not change them into fish?"

"That would abate the immediate threat, could I get them all in time," Trent agreed. "But it still would not free us from the cave. I suspect we shall have to resort to magic on ourselves at some point, regardless. And we

are intruders in their cave; there is a certain proprietary
ethic—"

"All right!" she cried, as a triton heaved his three-
pointed fork. "Do it your way."

Suddenly she was a monster—one of the worst Bink
had seen. She had a huge greenish sheath around her
torso, from which arms, legs, head, and tail projected.
Her feet were webbed, and her head was like that of a
serpent.

The triton's fork struck the Fanchon-monster's
shell—and bounced off. Suddenly Bink saw the sense of
this transformation. This monster was invulnerable.

"Sea turtle," Trent murmured. "Mundane. Harmless,
normally—but the merfolk don't know that. I've made
a study of nonmagical creatures, and have developed
much respect for them. Oops!" Another trident was
flying.

Then Bink was also a sea turtle. Suddenly he was
completely comfortable in the water, and he had no fear
of the pronged spears. If one came at his face, he would
simply pull in his head. It would not retract all the way,
but the armor of the shell around it would intercept almost anything.

Something tugged at his carapace. Bink started to
dive, trying to dislodge it—then realized, in his reptilian
brain, that this was something that had to be tolerated.
Not a friend, but an ally—for now. So he dived, but
allowed the dragging weight to persist.

Bink stroked slowly but powerfully for the underwater passage. The other turtle had already entered it.
Bink didn't worry about air; he knew he could hold his
breath for as long as it took.

It did not take long. This passage slanted up to the
surface; Bink could see the moon as he broke through.
The storm had abated.

Abruptly he was human again—and swimming was
harder. "Why did you change me back?" he asked. "We
weren't to shore yet."

"When you are a turtle, you have the brain of a turtle, and the instincts of a turtle," Trent explained. "Otherwise you would not be able to survive as a turtle. Too long, and you might forget you ever were a man. If you headed out to sea, I might not be able to catch you, and so would never be able to change you back."

"Justin Tree retained his human mind," Bink pointed out.

"Justin Tree?"

"One of the men you changed into trees, in the North Village. His talent was throwing his voice."

"Oh, I remember now. He was a special case. I made him into a sapient tree—really a man in tree form, not a true tree. I can do that when I put my mind to it. For a tree it can work. But a turtle needs turtle reflexes to deal with the ocean."

Bink didn't follow all that, but he didn't care to debate it. Obviously cases differed. Then Fanchon reappeared in human form. "Well, you honored the truce," she said grudgingly. "I didn't really think you would."

"Reality must intrude sometime," Trent said.

"What do you mean by that?" she demanded.

"I said, we are not out of danger yet. I believe that is a sea serpent on its way."

Bink saw the huge head, and there was no question: the monster had seen them. It was big; the head was a yard across. "Maybe the rocks—" Bink cried, orienting on the outcropping that marked the exit from the tritons' cave.

"That thing's a huge, long snake," Fanchon said. "It could reach right down into the cave, or coil right around the rocks. We can't escape it in this form."

"I could change you into poisonous jellyfish that the serpent would not eat," Trent said. "But you might get lost in the shuffle. It also may not be wise to be transformed more than once a day; I have not been able to verify this during my exile, for obvious reasons, but I am concerned that your systems may suffer a shock each time."

"Besides which, the monster could still eat you," Fanchon said.

"You have a very quick mind," Trent agreed equably. "Therefore, I shall have to do something I dislike—transform the monster."

"You don't want to transform the sea serpent?" Bink asked, surprised. The thing was now quite close, its small red eyes fixed on the prey; saliva dripped from its giant teeth.

"It is merely an innocent creature going about its business," Trent said. "We should not enter its waters if we do not wish to participate in its mode of existence. There is a balance of nature, whether magical or mundane, that we should hesitate to interfere with."

"You have a weird sense of humor," Fanchon said sourly. "But I never claimed to understand the nuances of evil magic. If you really want to protect its life style, transform it into a little fish until we get to shore, then transform it back."

"And *hurry!*" Bink cried. The thing was now looming over them, orienting on its specific targets.

"That would not work," Trent said. "The fish would swim away and be lost. I must be able to identify the particular creature I mean to transform, and it must be within six feet of me. However your suggestion has merit."

"Six feet," Bink said. "We'll be inside it before we get that close." He was not trying to be funny; the monster's mouth was much longer than it was wide, so that as it opened to its full aperture the upper front teeth were a good twelve feet from the lower teeth.

"Nevertheless, I must operate within my limits," Trent said, unperturbed. "The critical region is the head, the seat of identity. When I transform that, the rest naturally follows. If I tried it when only the tail was within range, I would botch the job. So when it tries to take me in its mouth, it comes into my power."

"What if it goes for one of us first?" Fanchon demanded. "Suppose we're more than six feet from you?"

"I suggest you arrange to be within that radius," Trent said dryly.

Hastily Bink and Fanchon splashed closer to the Evil Magician. Bink had the distinct impression that even if Trent had had no magic, they would have been in his power. He was too self-assured, too competent in his tactics; he knew how to manage people.

The sea monster's body convulsed. Its head struck down, teeth leading. Spittle sprayed out from it in obscene little clouds. Fanchon screamed hysterically. Bink felt an instant and pervading terror. That sensation was becoming all too familiar; he simply was no hero.

But as the awful jaws closed on them, the sea serpent vanished. In its place fluttered a glowing, brightly colored insect. Trent caught it neatly in one hand and set it on his own hair, where it perched quiveringly.

"A love bug," Trent explained. "They are not good fliers, and they hate water. This one will stay close until we emerge from the sea."

Now the three swam for shore. It took them some time, for the sea remained choppy and they were tired, but no other creatures bothered them. Apparently no lesser predators intruded on the fishing territory of the sea monster. An understandable attitude—but probably within hours a host of aggressive forms would converge if the sea monster did not return. As Trent had remarked, there was always a balance of nature.

The phosphorescence became stronger in the shallows. Some of it was from glowing fish, flashing in colors to communicate with their respective kinds; most of it was from the water itself. Washes of pale green, yellow, orange—magic, of course, but for what purpose? There was so much Bink saw, wherever he went, that he did not understand. At the bottom he saw shells, some lighted around the fringes, some glowing in patterns. A few vanished as he passed over them; whether they had become truly invisible or merely doused their lights he could not tell. Regardless, they were magic, and that was familiar. Belatedly he realized that he was glad to be back among the familiar threats of Xanth!

Dawn was coming as they reached the beach. The sun pushed up behind the clouds over the jungle and finally burst through to bounce its shafts off the water. It was a thing of marvelous beauty. Bink clung to that concept, because his body was numb with fatigue, his brain locked onto the torture of moving limbs, over and over, on and on.

At last he crawled upon the beach. Fanchon crawled beside him. "Don't stop yet," she said. "We must seek cover, lest other monsters come, from the beach or jungle . . ."

But Trent stood knee-deep in the surf, his sword dangling from his handsome body. He was obviously not as tired as they were. "Return, friend," he said, flicking something into the sea. The sea monster reappeared, its serpentine convolutions much more impressive in the shallow water. Trent had to lift his feet and splash back out of the way, lest he be crushed by a hugely swinging coil.

But the monster was not looking for trouble now. It was extremely disgruntled. It gave a single honk of rage or of anguish or of mere amazement and thrashed its way toward deeper pastures.

Trent walked up the beach. "It is not fun to be a defenseless love bug when you are accustomed to being the king of the sea," he said. "I hope the creature does not suffer a nervous breakdown."

He was not smiling. There was something funny, Bink thought, about a man who liked monsters that well. But of course Trent was *the* Evil Magician of the contemporary scene. The man was strangely handsome, mannerly, and erudite, possessed of strength, skill, and courage—but his affinities were to the monsters more than to the men. It would be disastrous ever to forget that.

Odd that Humfrey, the Good Magician, was an ugly little gnome in a forbidding castle, selfishly using his magic to enrich himself, while Trent was the epitome of hero material. The Sorceress Iris had seemed lovely and sexy, but was in fact nondescript; Humfrey's good qualities were manifest in his actions, once a person really got to know him. But Trent, so far, had seemed good in both appearance and deed, at least on the purely personal level. If Bink had met him for the first time in the kraken's cave and hadn't known the man's evil nature, he would never have guessed it.

Now Trent strode across the beach, seeming hardly tired despite the grueling swim. The nascent sunlight touched his hair, turning it bright yellow. He looked in that instant like a god, all that was perfect in man. Again Bink suffered fatigued confusion, trying to reconcile the man's appearance and recent actions with what he knew to be the man's actual nature, and again finding it so challenging as to be virtually impossible. Some things just had to be taken on faith.

"I've got to rest, to sleep," Bink muttered. "I can't tell evil from good right now."

Fanchon looked toward Trent. "I know what you mean," she said, shaking her head so that her ratty hair shifted its wet tangles. "Evil has an insidious way about it, and there is some evil in all of us that seeks to dominate. We have to fight it, no matter how tempting it becomes."

Trent arrived. "We seem to have made it," he said cheerfully. "It certainly is good to be back in Xanth, by whatever freak of fortune. Ironic that you, who sought so ardently to prevent my access, instead facilitated it!"

"Ironic," Fanchon agreed dully.

"I believe this is the coast of the central wilderness region, bounded on the north by the great Gap. I had not realized we had drifted so far south, but the contour of the land seems definitive. That means we are not yet out of trouble."

"Bink's an exile, you're banished, and I'm ugly," Fanchon muttered. "We'll never be out of trouble."

"Nevertheless, I believe it would be expedient to extend our truce until we are free of the wilderness," the Magician said.

Did Trent know something Bink didn't? Bink had no magic, so he would be prey to all the sinister spells of the deep jungle. Fanchon had no apparent magic—strange, she claimed her exile had been voluntary, not forced, yet if she really had no magic she should have been banished too; anyway, she would have a similar problem. But Trent—with his skills with sword and spell, he should have no reason to fear this region.

Fanchon had similar doubts. "As long as you're with us, we're in constant danger of being transformed into toads. I can't see that the wilderness is worse."

Trent spread his hands. "I realize you do not trust me, and perhaps you have reason. I believe your security and mine would be enhanced if we cooperated a little longer, but I shall not force my company on you." He walked south along the beach.

"He knows something," Bink said. "He must be leaving us to die. So he can be rid of us without breaking his word."

"Why should he care about his word?" Fanchon asked. "That would imply he is a man of honor."

Bink had no answer. He crawled to the shade and concealment of the nearest tree and collapsed in the downy sward. He had been unconscious during part of the last night, but that was not the same as sleep; he needed genuine rest.

When he woke it was high noon—and he was fixed in place. There was no pain, only some itching—but he couldn't lift his head or hands. They were fastened to the ground by myriad threads, as if the very lawn had—

Oh, no! In the numbness of fatigue, he had been so careless as to lie in a bed of carnivorous grass! The root blades had grown up into his body, infiltrating it so slowly and subtly that it had not disturbed his sleep— and now he was caught. Once he had happened on a patch of the stuff near the North Village with an animal skeleton on it. The grass had consumed all the flesh. He had wondered how any creature could have been so stupid as to be trapped by such a thing. Now he knew.

He was still breathing, therefore he could still yell. He did so with a certain gusto. "Help!"

There was no response.

"Fanchon!" he cried. "I'm tied down. The grass is eating me up." Actually that was an exaggeration; he was not hurt, merely bound to the ground. But the tendrils continued to grow into him, and soon they would start to feed, drawing the life proteins from his flesh.

Still nothing. He realized she would not or could not help him. Probably something had put a sleep spell on her. It was obvious, in retrospect, that there were plenty of deadly threats right here at the edge of the beach; she must have fallen into another. She might be dead already.

"Help! Anybody!" he screamed desperately.

That was another mistake. All around him, in the forest and along the beach, things were stirring. He had advertised his helplessness, and now they were coming to take advantage of it. Had he struggled with the grass in silence, he might have managed in time to work his way free; he had awakened before it was ready for the kill, luckily. Maybe he had tried to turn over in his sleep, and his body had objected to the resistance strongly enough to throw off the stasis spell the grass was applying. If he struggled and failed, his demise at least would have been fairly comfortable—just a slow sinking into eternal sleep. Now by his noise he had summoned much less comfortable menaces. He could not see them, but he could hear them.

From the nearby tree came a rustle, as of meat-eating squirrels. From the beach came a scrape, as of hungry acid crabs. From the sea came a horrible kind of splashing, as of a small sea monster who had sneaked into the territory of the big sea monster Trent had transformed. Now this little one struggled to get out of the water and cross to the prey before it was gone. But the most dreadful sound of all was the pound-pound-pound of the footfalls of something deep in the forest, large and far away but moving extremely rapidly.

A shadow fell on him. "Hi!" a shrill voice cried. It was a harpy, cousin to the one he had met on the way back to the North Village. She was every bit as ugly, smelly, and obnoxious—and now she was dangerous. She descended slowly, her talons reaching down, twitching. The other harpy had seen him healthy, so had stayed well out of reach—though she might have descended had he actually drunk from the Spring of Love. Ugh! This one saw him helpless.

She had a human face and human breasts, so was in that sense female, like the mermaids. But in lieu of arms she had great greasy wings, and her body was that of a gross bird. And she was a *dirty* bird; not only were her face and breasts grotesquely shaped, grime was caked on them. It was a wonder she could fly at all. Bink had not had the opportunity—or desire—to appreciate the qualities of the prior harpy at close range; now he had a really excellent nether view. Double ugh! The mermaids had represented much that was lovely in the female form; this harpy was the ugly aspect. She made Fanchon look halfway decent in comparison; at least Fanchon was clean.

She dropped on him, claws clutching and unclutching in air, in anticipation of the glob of entrails they were about to rip out of his exposed gut. Some of the nails were broken and jagged. He caught the odor of her, a stink like none he remembered. "Oooh, you big handsome hunk of meat!" she screeched. "You look good enough to eat. I can hardly choose what to take first." And she burst into maniacal laughter.

Bink, absolutely horrified, put forth the supreme effort of his life and wrenched one arm free of the grass. Little roots trailed from it, and the separation was painful. He was lying partly on his side, one cheek anchored, so he had a very limited field of vision, but his ears continued to bring him the dreadful news of the threats about him. He struck at the harpy, scaring her off for the moment. She was of course a coward; her character matched her appearance.

Her wings fluttered heavily. A soiled feather drifted down. "Oooh, you naughty boy!" she screeched. She seemed to be unable to converse in anything less than a screech; her voice was so harsh as to be almost incomprehensible. "I'll goozle your gizzard for that." And she emitted her horrible cackle again.

But now a shadow fell on Bink, from something he could not see—but the outline was awful. He heard heavy breathing, as of some great animal, and smelled its carrion-coated breath, which for the moment overrode the stench of the harpy. It was the thing from the sea, its feet dragging as it hunched forward. It sniffed him—and the other creatures stopped moving in, afraid to stand up to this predator.

All except the harpy. She was ready to heap vilification on anything, from the safety of the air. "Get away, argus!" she screeched. "He's mine, all mine, especially his gizzard." And she dropped down again, forgetting Bink's free arm. For once Bink didn't mind. He could fight off the dirty bird, but this other thing was too much for him. Let her interfere all she wanted.

The unseen thing snorted and leaped, passing right over Bink's body with amazing agility. Now he saw it: body and tail of a large fish, four stout short legs terminating in flippers, tusked head of a boar, no neck. Three eyes were set along its torso, the middle one set lower than the others. Bink had never seen a monster quite like this before—a land-walking fish.

The harpy flew up out of the way just in time, narrowly missing being gored by the thing's semicircular horns. Another stinking feather fell. She screeched some really disgusting insults in her ire, and let fly with a gooey dropping, but the monster ignored her and turned to concentrate on Bink. It opened its mouth, and Bink made a fist to punch it in the snout—for what little good that might do—when abruptly it paused, gazing balefully over Bink's shoulder.

"Now you'll get it, argus," the harpy screeched gleefully. "Even a fishy lout like you can't ignore catoblepas."

Bink had never heard of either argus or catoblepas, but another quake of deep misgiving went through him. He felt the muzzle of the hidden monster nudge him. It was oddly soft—but such was its power that it ripped him half out of the grass.

Then the pig-snouted argus charged, furious that its meal should be taken away. Bink dropped flat again, letting the slimy flippers pass over him—and their impact dislodged more of his body. He was getting free!

The two brutes collided. "Sic 'em, monsters!" the harpy screeched, hovering overhead. In her excitement over this mischief she let fall another large squishy dropping, which just missed Bink's head. If only he had a rock to throw at her!

He sat up. One leg remained anchored—but now he had anchorage to rip out of the clutch of the demon weed. It didn't even hurt this time. He looked at the battling monsters—and saw the snakelike hair of the catoblepas twined around the head of the argus, gripping it by horns, ears, scales, and eyeballs—anything available. The body of the catoblepas was covered with reptilian scales, from its gorgon head to its cloven hooves, invulnerable to the attack of the argus. In overall shape it was like any quadruped, not all that remarkable; but that deadly writhing prehensile head hair—what a horror!

Had he really wanted to return to magic Xanth? He had so conveniently forgotten its uglier aspect. Magic had as much evil as good. Maybe Mundania would really have been better.

"Fools!" the harpy cried, seeing Bink loose. "He's getting away." But the monsters were now enmeshed in their own struggle, and paid her no attention. No doubt the winner would feast on the loser, and Bink would be superfluous.

She darted down at Bink, forgetting all caution. But he was on his feet now, and able to fight. He reached up and caught her by one wing, trying to get his hands around her scrawny throat. He would gladly have strangled her, in a sense strangling all the meanness of Xanth. But she squawked and fluttered so violently that all he got was a handful of gummy feathers.

Bink took advantage of his luck and ran away from the fray. The harpy fluttered after him for a moment, screeching such hideously foul insults that his ears burned, but soon gave up. She had no chance of overcoming him by herself. Harpies were basically carrion feeders and thieves, not hunters. It was their fashion to snatch food from the mouths of others. There was now no sign of the other creatures that had rustled and scraped toward him; they too were predators only of the helpless.

Where was Fanchon? Why hadn't she come to help him? She surely must have heard his cries for help—if she still lived. There was no way she could have been unaware of the recent fracas. So this must mean—

No! She had to be somewhere. Maybe down by the sea, catching fish, out of hearing. She had been invaluable during the past two days, and unswervingly loyal to the welfare of Xanth. Without her he could never have escaped the power of the Evil Magician. For intelligence and personality she had it all over the other girls he had met. Too bad she wasn't—

He saw her, resting against a tree. "Fanchon!" he cried gladly.

"Hello, Bink," she said.

Now his worry and speculation translated into ire. "Didn't you see me being attacked by those monsters? Didn't you hear?"

"I saw, I heard," she said quietly.

Bink was baffled and resentful. "Why didn't you help

me? You could at least have grabbed a stick or thrown
rocks. I was almost eaten alive!"

"I'm sorry," she said.

He took another step toward her. "You're *sorry!*
You just rested here doing nothing and——" He cut off,
losing the words to continue.

"Maybe if you moved me from the tree," she said.

"I'll dump you in the sea!" he cried. He strode up to
her, leaned over to grab her roughly by the arm, and
felt a sudden wash of weakness.

Now he understood. The tree had put a lethargy spell
on her, and was starting in on him. As with the carnivorous grass, it took time to take full effect; she must have
settled here to sleep, as careless in her fatigue as he had
been in his, and was now far gone. There was no actual
discomfort to alert potential prey, just a slow, insidious
draining of vitality, of strength and will, until it all was
gone. Very similar to the grass, actually, only this was
less tangible.

He fought it off. He squatted beside her, sliding his
arms under her back and legs. He really wasn't too
weak, yet; if he acted fast——

He started to lift her—and discovered that his squatting posture had given him a false sense of well-being.
He could not raise her up; in fact, he wasn't sure he
could stand alone. He just wanted to lie down and rest a
moment.

No! That would be the end. He dared not yield to
it. "Sorry I yelled at you," he said. "I didn't realize
what you were in."

"That's all right, Bink. Take it easy." She closed her
eyes.

He let go of her and backed away on his hands and
knees. "Good-bye," she said listlessly, reopening one
eye. She was almost done for.

He took hold of her feet and pulled. Another surge of
weakness came, making the job seem impossible. It was
as much emotional as physical. There was no way he
could haul her weight. He tried anyway, his stubborn-

ness prevailing over even this magic. But he failed. She was too heavy for him here.

He backed farther away—and as he left the environs of the tree his energy and will returned. But now she was beyond his reach. He stood up and took another step toward her—and lost his strength again, so that he fell to the ground. He would never make it this way.

Again he hauled himself back, sweating with the effort of concentration. Were he less stubborn, he would not have gotten this far. "I can't get you out, and I'm only wasting time," he said apologetically. "Maybe I can loop you with a rope."

But there was no rope. He walked along the trees of the edge of the jungle and spied a dangling vine. That would do nicely if he could get it loose.

He grabbed it in one hand—and screamed. The thing writhed in his grasp and looped about his wrist, imprisoning it. More vines dropped from the tree, swinging toward him. This was a land kraken, a variant of the tangle tree! He was still being fatally careless, walking directly into traps that should never have fooled him.

Bink dropped, yanking on the vine with his full weight. It stretched to accommodate him, twining more tightly about his arm. But now he spied a pointed bit of bone on the ground, remnant of prior prey; he swept it up with his free hand and poked at the vine with it, puncturing it.

Thick orange sap welled out. The whole tree shivered. There was a high keening of pain. Reluctantly the vine loosened, and he drew his arm free. Another close call.

He ran on down the beach, searching for whatever would help him. Maybe a sharp-edged stone, to cut off a vine—no, the other vines would get him. Give up that idea. Maybe a long pole? No, similar problem. This peaceful-seeming beach was a morass of danger, really coming alive; anything and everything was suspect.

Then he saw a human body: Trent, sitting crosslegged on the sand, looking at something. It seemed to be a colorful gourd; maybe he was eating it.

Bink paused. Trent could help him; the Magician could change the fatigue tree into a salamander and kill it, or at least render it harmless. But Trent himself was a greater long-term threat than the tree. Which should he choose?

Well, he would try to negotiate. The known evil of the tree might not be as bad as the uncertain evil of the Magician, but it was more immediate.

"Trent," he said hesitantly.

The man paid him no attention. He continued to stare at his gourd. He did not actually seem to be eating it. What, then, was its fascination?

Bink hesitated to provoke the man, but he did not know how long he could afford to wait. Fanchon was slowly dying; at what point would she be too far gone to be revived, even if rescued from the tree? Some risk had to be taken.

"Magician Trent," he said, more firmly. "I think we should extend the truce. Fanchon is caught, and—" He stopped, for the man was still ignoring him.

Bink's fear of the Magician began to change, much as had his attitude toward Fanchon when he thought she was malingering. It was as if the charge of emotion had to be spent one way or another, whatever the cost. "Listen, she's in trouble!" he snapped. "Are you going to help or aren't you?"

Still Trent paid no attention.

Bink, still weary from the rigors of the night and unnerved by his recent experiences, suffered a lapse of sanity. "Damn it, *answer* me!" he cried, knocking the gourd from the Magician's hands. The thing flew six feet, landing in the sand and rolling.

Trent looked up. There was no sign of anger in his countenance, just mild surprise. "Hello, Bink," he said. "What is your concern?"

"My concern!" Bink cried. "I told you three times."

Trent looked at him, puzzled. "I did not hear you."

The Magician paused thoughtfully. "In fact, I did not see you arrive. I must have been sleeping, though I had not intended to."

"You were sitting here looking at the gourd," Bink said hotly.

"Now I remember. I saw it lying on the beach, and it looked intriguing—" He broke off, glancing at his shadow. "By the sun, that was an hour ago! Where did the time go?"

Bink realized that something was amiss. He went to pick up the gourd.

"Hold!" Trent barked. "That's hypnotic!"

Bink stopped in place. "What?"

"Hypnotic. That's a Mundane term, meaning it puts you into a trance, a waking sleep. It usually takes some time to do—but of course a magic-spell hypnosis could be instant. Don't look too closely at the gourd. Its pretty colors must be intended to attract the eye; then it has— yes, I remember now—a peephole. A single glance into its fascinating innards becomes eternal. Very nice device."

"But what's the point?" Bink asked, averting his gaze. "I mean, a gourd can't eat a man—"

"But the gourd *vine* might," Trent pointed out. "Or it may be that a quiescent living body might be excellent food for its seeds to grow on. There are wasps in Mundania that sting other creatures, stunning them, and lay their eggs in the bodies. We can be sure it makes some sort of sense."

Still Bink was bemused. "How is it that you, a Magician . . . ?"

"Magicians are human too, Bink. We eat, sleep, love, hate, and err. I am as vulnerable to magic as you are; I merely have a more potent weapon with which to protect myself. If I wanted to be entirely secure, I would lock myself within a stone castle, like my friend Humfrey. My chances of survival in this wilderness would be greatly enhanced by the presence of one or two alert, loyal companions. This is why I proposed the extension of our truce—and I still feel it is a good idea. It is apparent that I need help, even if you don't." He looked at Bink. "Why did you help me, just now?"

"I—" Bink was ashamed to admit the accidental nature of that assistance. "I think we should—extend the truce."

"Excellent. Does Fanchon agree?"

"She needs help now. A—she is in thrall to a lethargy tree."

"Oho! Then I shall repay your favor by rescuing the damsel. Then we shall talk of truce." And Trent jumped up.

On the way up the beach, Bink pointed out the vine tree, and Trent whipped out his sword and neatly lopped off a length of vine. Again Bink was reminded of the skill this man had with his physical weapon; if Trent's magic were taken away entirely, he would still be dangerous. In fact, he had risen to the generalship of an army, in Mundania.

The vine twisted into shuddering convolutions like a dying serpent, oozing orange sap from the end, but it was now harmless. The tree keened again, cowed. Bink almost felt sorry for it.

They took this vine to Fanchon, looped it about her foot, and hauled her unceremoniously away from the tree. So simple with the right equipment!

"Now," Trent said briskly as Fanchon slowly recovered her vital energy. "I propose an extended truce between us, until we three escape the wilderness of Xanth. We seem to have problems separately."

This time Fanchon acquiesced.

Chapter 12. Chameleon

The first thing Fanchon did when she recovered was fetch the magic gourd Bink had told her about. "This could be useful," she said, wrapping it in a great leaf from a blanket plant.

"Now we must plan the best route out of here," Trent said. "I believe we are south of the chasm, so that will balk us if we go north—unless we remain on the coast. I don't think that is wise."

Bink remembered his experience crossing the chasm at the other side. "No, we don't want to stay on the beach," he agreed. The Sorceress Iris had complicated things there—but there could be equivalent menaces here.

"Our alternative is to cut inland," Trent said. "I am not familiar with this specific locale, but I believe Humfrey was building a castle due east of here."

"He completed it," Fanchon said.

"Fine," Bink said. "You can change us into big birds, maybe rocs, and we'll carry you there."

Trent shook his head negatively. "This is not feasible."

"But you changed us before, and we helped you. We made the truce; we wouldn't drop you."

Trent smiled. "It is not a question of trust, Bink. I trust you; I have no question at all about your basic integrity, or Fanchon's. But we are in a peculiar circumstance—"

"Fancy the Evil Magician paying a call on the Good

Magician!" Fanchon said. "What a scene that would make."

"No, you would be disappointed," Trent said. "Humfrey and I have always gotten along well. We leave each other alone professionally. I should be happy to meet him again. But he would be obliged to convey the news of my return to Xanth to the King, and once he knew my general whereabouts he would use his magic to keep track of me."

"Yes, I see the problem," she said. "No sense tipping your hand to the enemy. But we could fly somewhere else."

"We can fly nowhere," Trent insisted. "I can not afford to advertise my presence in Xanth—and neither can you."

"That's right," Bink agreed. "We're exiles. And the penalty for violating exile—"

"Is death," Fanchon finished. "I never thought— we're all in trouble."

"If you had forgotten such details two days ago," Trent observed wryly, "we would not be here now."

Fanchon looked unusually sober, as if there were some special significance to the remark. Oddly, the expression made her look less ugly than usual. Probably, Bink thought, he was merely getting used to her.

"What are we going to do?" Bink asked. "The whirlpool brought us in under the Shield; we've already agreed we can't go back that way. We can't stay here on the beach—and we can't let the citizens know we're back, even though we entered only by freak accident."

"We'll have to conceal our identities," Fanchon decided. "There are places in Xanth where we would be unknown."

"That doesn't sound like much of a life," Bink said. "Always in hiding—and if anyone asked Magician Humfrey where we were—"

"Who'd do that?" Fanchon demanded. "One year's service just to check up on someone in exile?"

"That is our only present margin of security," Trent

said. "The fact that Humfrey will not bother to check without a potential fee. However, we can worry about such things after we escape the wilderness. Perhaps by then some new avenues will have appeared. I can change you into unrecognizable forms, if necessary, and camouflage myself. It may all prove to be academic."

Because they might never make it through the wilderness, Bink thought.

They traveled along the beach until they found a region of sparse forest and field that seemed less hazardous than the rest. They spaced themselves out somewhat whenever anything dangerous appeared, so that they would not all be caught together. The selection worked well enough; at first the magic they encountered was largely innocuous, as if the concentration were all at the beach. There were spells designed to make passing animals sheer off, or color shows whose purpose was unclear. Bink had been through worse on his trip to the Good Magician's castle. Maybe the wilderness was overrated.

Fanchon spotted a fabric plant and efficiently fashioned togas for them all. The men tolerated this with good humor, having become accustomed to nudity. Had Fanchon been a provocatively proportioned woman there might have been more reason—and less desire— for bodily concealment. Still, Bink remembered how she had professed modesty in the prison pit so as to gain a private section in which to hide the bricks. She probably had her reasons this time, too.

There were several patches of spell-cast coldness, and one of heat; the clothing would have helped protect against these, but they were easy to avoid. The assorted carnivorous trees were readily spotted and bypassed; staying off attractive paths was second nature to them all now.

One region was distinctly awkward, however. It was dry and sandy, with little apparent nutrient in the soil, yet it was covered by luxuriant waist-high broad-leaved plants. The region seemed harmless, so they strode straight through the center. Then all three travelers felt a sudden and almost uncontrollable call of nature. They had to scatter, barely getting separated in time to perform.

These were very practical plants, Bink abruptly realized. Their spells compelled passing animals to deposit nutritious fluids and solids on the soil, greatly promoting plant growth. Fertilizer magic!

Farther along, one animal neither fled their approach nor acted hostile. This was a knee-high, snuffling quadruped with a greatly extended snout. Trent drew his sword as it ambled toward them, but Fanchon stopped him. "I recognize that one," she said. "It's a magic-sniffer."

"It smells by magic?" Bink asked.

"It smells magic," she said. "We used to use one on my folks' farm, to sniff out magic herbs and things. The stronger the magic, the more it reacts. But it's harmless."

"What does it feed on?" Trent asked, keeping his hand on his sword.

"Magic berries. Other magic doesn't seem to affect it one way or the other; it is just curious. It doesn't differentiate by type of spell, just intensity."

They stood and watched. Fanchon was nearest to the sniffer, so it approached her first. It snorted, making a flutelike sound. "See, I have some magic; it likes me," she said.

What magic? Bink wondered. She had never shown any talent, and never actually told him what she could do. There was still too much he did not know about her.

Satisfied, the sniffer moved on to Trent. This time its reaction was much stronger; it danced around, emitting a medley of notes. "Sure enough," Trent said, with a certain justified pride. "It knows a Magician when it smells one."

Then it came to Bink—and frisked almost as much

as it had for Trent. "So much for perception," Bink said, laughing with embarrassment.

But Trent did not laugh. "It believes you are almost as strong a magician as I am," he said, his fingers tapping his sword with unconscious significance. Then he caught himself, and seemed to be at ease again.

"I wish I were," Bink said. "But I was banished for lack of magic." Yet the Magician Humfrey had told him he had very strong magic that could not be brought out. Now his curiosity and frustration were increased by this happenstance. What kind of a talent could he have that hid itself so determinedly—or was it hidden by some outside spell?

They trudged on. They cut poles with which to poke the ground ahead for invisible barriers and pitfalls and other suspiciously unsuspect aspects of the wild. This made progress slow—but they dared not hurry. Actually, they had no reason to hurry; their only purposes were concealment and survival.

Food turned out to be no problem. They did not trust the various fruit and candy trees they saw; some might be magic, and serve the interests of their hosts rather than the interests of the consumers, though they looked similar to crop trees. But Trent merely turned a hostile thistle tree into a luxuriant multifruit tree, and they feasted on apples, pears, bananas, blackberries, and tomatoes. It reminded Bink how great was the power of a true Magician, for Trent's talent really embraced that of food conjuration as a mere subtalent. Properly exploited, the reach of his magic was enormous.

But they were still heading into the wilderness, not out of it. Illusions became bolder, more persistent, and harder to penetrate. There were more sounds, louder, more ominous. Now and then the ground shuddered, and there were great not-too-distant bellowings. Trees leaned toward them, leaves twitching.

"I think," Fanchon said, "we have not begun to appreciate the potency of this forest. Its whole innocuous permeability may have been merely to encourage us to get more deeply in."

Bink, looking nervously about, agreed. "We picked the safest-seeming route. Maybe that's where we went wrong. We should have taken the most threatening one."

"And gotten consumed by a tangle tree," Fanchon said.

"Let's try going back," Bink suggested. Seeing their doubt, he added: "Just to test."

They tried it. Almost immediately the forest darkened and tightened. More trees appeared, blocking the way they had come; were they illusions, or had they been invisible before? Bink was reminded of the one-way path he had walked from the Good Magician's castle, but this was more ominous. These were not nice trees; they were gnarled colossi bearing thorns and twitching vines. Branches crisscrossed one another, leaves sprouting to form new barriers even as the trio watched. Thunder rumbled in the distance.

"No doubt about it," Trent said. "We failed to see the forest for the trees. I could transform any in our direct path, but if some started firing thorns at us we would be in trouble regardless."

"Even if we wanted to go that way," Fanchon said, looking west. "We'd never have time to retrace it all through that resistance. Not before night."

Night—that was the worst time for hostile magic. "But the alternative is to go the way it wants us to go," Bink said, alarmed. "That may be easy now, but it surely is not our best choice."

"Perhaps the wilderness does not know us well enough," Trent said with a grim smile. "I do feel competent to handle most threats, so long as someone watches behind me and stands guard as I sleep."

Bink thought of the Magician's powers of magic and swordplay, and had to agree. The forest might be one giant spider web—but that spider might become a gnat, unexpectedly. "Maybe we should gamble that we can handle it," Bink said. "At least we'll find out what it is." For the first time, he was glad to have the Evil Magician along.

"Yes, there is always that," Fanchon agreed sourly.

Now that they had made the decision, progress became easier. The threatenings of the forest remained, but they assumed the aspect of background warnings. As dusk came, the way opened out into a clearing, within which stood an old, run-down stone fortress.

"Oh, no!" Fanchon exclaimed. "Not a haunted castle!"

Thunder cracked behind them. A chill wind came up, cutting through their tunics. Bink shivered. "I think we spend the night there—or in the rain," he said. "Could you transform it into a harmless cottage?"

"My talent applies only to living things," Trent said. "That excludes buildings—and storms."

Glowing eyes appeared in the forest behind them. "If those things rush us," Fanchon said, "you could only transform a couple before they were on us, since you can't zap them from a distance."

"And not at night," Trent said. "Remember—I have to see my subject, too. All things considered, I think we had better oblige the local powers that be and enter the castle. Carefully—and once inside, we should sleep in shifts. It is likely to be a difficult night."

Bink shuddered. The last place he wanted to spend the night was there—but he realized they had come far too deeply into the trap to extricate themselves readily. There was powerful magic here, the magic of an entire region. Too much to fight directly—now.

So they yielded, goaded by the looming storm. The ramparts were tall, but covered by moss and clinging vines. The drawbridge was down, its once-stout timbers rotting in place. Yet there was an ancient, lingering, rugged magnificence about it. "This castle has style," Trent observed.

They tapped the planks, locating a reasonably solid section on which to cross. The moat was overgrown with weeds, and its water was stagnant. "Shame to see a good castle get run down," Trent said. "It is obviously deserted, and has been for decades."

"Or centuries," Bink added.

"Why would a forest herd us into a derelict edifice?" Fanchon asked. "Even if something really horrible lurks here—what would our deaths profit the forest? We were only passing through—and we would make it much faster if the forest just left us alone. We intend it no harm."

"There is always a rationale," Trent said. "Magic does not focus without purpose."

They approached the front portcullis as the storm broke. That encouraged them to step inside, though the interior was almost black.

"Maybe we can find a torch," Fanchon said. "Feel along the walls. Usually a castle will have something near the entrance—"

Crash! The raised portcullis, which they had assumed was corroded in place, crashed down behind them. The iron bars were far too heavy to lift; the three were trapped inside. "The jaws close," Trent remarked, not seeming perturbed. But Bink could see that his sword was in his hand.

Fanchon made a half-muffled scream, clutching at Bink's arm. He looked ahead and saw a ghost. There was no question about it: the thing was a humped white sheet with dead-black eyeholes. It made a mouthless moan.

Trent's sword whistled as he stepped forward. The blade sliced through the sheet—with no visible effect. The ghost floated away through a wall.

"This castle is haunted, no question," Trent said matter-of-factly.

"If you believed that, you wouldn't be so calm," Fanchon said accusingly.

"On the contrary. It is physical menaces I fear," Trent replied. "The thing to remember about ghosts is that they have no concrete manifestation, and lack also the ability of shades to animate living creatures. Therefore they cannot directly affect ordinary people. They act only through the fear they inspire—so it is merely necessary to have no fear. In addition, this particular ghost was as surprised to see us as we were to see it. It was probably merely investigating the fall of the portcullis. It certainly meant no harm."

It was obvious that Trent was not afraid. He had not used his sword in panic, but to verify that it was a genuine ghost he faced. This was courage of a type Bink had never had; he was shivering with fear and reaction.

Fanchon had better control, now that her initial scream was out. "We could fall into quite physical pits or set off more boobytraps if we tried to explore this place in the dark. We're sheltered from the rain here— why don't we sleep right here in shifts until morning?"

"You have marvelous common sense, my dear," Trent said. "Shall we draw straws for first watch?"

"I'll take it," Bink said. "I'm too scared to sleep anyway."

"So am I," Fanchon said, and Bink felt warm gratitude for her admission. "I have not yet become blasé about ghosts."

"There is not enough evil in you," Trent said, chuckling. "Very well; I shall be first to sleep." He moved, and Bink felt something cool touch his hand. "Do you take my sword, Bink, and run it through whatever manifests. If it has no impact, relax, for it is a true ghost; if it contacts anything material, that threat will no doubt be abated by the thrust. Only take care"—and Bink heard the smile in his voice—"that you do not strike the wrong subject."

Bink found himself holding the heavy sword, amazed. "I—"

"Do not be concerned about your inexperience with the weapon; a straight, bold thrust will have authority regardless," Trent continued reassuringly. "When your watch is done, pass the blade on to the lady. When she is done, I will take my turn, being by then well rested."

Bink heard him lie down. "Remember," the Magician's voice came from the floor. "My talent is void in the dark, since I cannot see my subject. So do not wake me unnecessarily. We depend on your alertness and judgment." He said no more.

Fanchon found Bink's free arm. "Let me get behind you," she said. "I don't want you running me through by accident."

Bink was glad for her closeness. He stood peering about, sword in one sweaty hand, staff in the other, unable to penetrate the dark. The sound of the rain outside became loud; then he made out Trent's gentle snoring.

"Bink?" Fanchon said at last.

"Um."

"What kind of a man would give his enemy his sword and go to sleep?"

That question had been bothering Bink. He had no satisfactory answer. "A man with iron nerve," he said at last, knowing that that could only be part of it.

"A man who extends such trust," she said thoughtfully, "must expect to receive it."

"Well, if we're trustworthy and he isn't, he knows he can trust us."

"It doesn't work that way, Bink. It is the untrustworthy man who distrusts others, because he judges them by himself. I don't see how a documented liar and villain and schemer for the throne like the Evil Magician can be this way."

"Maybe he's not the historical Trent, but someone else, an imposter—"

"An imposter would still be a liar. But we've seen his power. Magic is never twice the same; he *has* to be Trent the Transformer."

"Yet something is wrong."

"Yes. Something is right; that's what's wrong. He trusts us, and he shouldn't. You could run him through right now, while he sleeps; even if you didn't kill him with the first thrust, he could not transform you in the dark."

"I wouldn't do that!" Bink exclaimed, horrified.

"Precisely. You have honor. So do I. It is hard to avoid the conclusion that so does he. Yet we know he is the Evil Magician."

"He must have spoken the truth before," Bink decided. "He can't make it through the wilderness alone, and he figures he'll need help to get out of this haunted castle in one piece, and he knows we can't get out alive either, so we're all on the same side and won't hurt each other. So he's serious about the truce."

"But what about when we get out of all this and the truce ends?"

Bink didn't answer. With that they were silent. But his troubled thoughts continued. If they survived the night in this dread castle, they could probably survive the day. In the morning Trent might figure the truce was over. Bink and Fanchon could guard the Magician through the night; then in the morning Trent could slay them both while they slept. If Trent had taken the first watch, he could not have done that, because he would have to slay the people who would protect him for the remainder of the evening. So it made sense to take the last watch.

No. He was not ready to believe that. Bink himself had chosen the first watch. He had to have faith in the sanctity of the truce. If that faith was misplaced, then he was lost—but he would rather lose that way than to win through dishonor. That decision gave him comfort.

Bink saw no more ghosts that night. At last he gave the sword to Fanchon. To his surprise, he managed to sleep.

He woke at dawn. Fanchon was asleep beside him, looking less ugly than he recalled—in fact, not really homely at all. He certainly was acclimatizing. Would it ever come to the point where Trent seemed noble and Fanchon beautiful?

"Good," Trent said. He was wearing his sword again.

"Now that you can look out for her, I'll have a look around the premises." He walked on down the dim hall.

They had survived the night. Bink wasn't sure in retrospect whether he had been more worried about the ghosts or the Magician. He still lacked comprehension of the motives of either.

And Fanchon—as the light brightened, he was sure her appearance had improved. She could hardly be called lovely, but she certainly was not the ugly girl he had perceived when he met her four days ago. In fact, she now reminded him of someone—

"Dee!" he exclaimed.

She woke. "Yes?"

Her response amazed him as much as the vague resemblance. He had called her Dee—but Dee was elsewhere in Xanth. Why, then, had she answered to that name as if it were her own? "I—I just thought you—"

She sat up. "You're right, of course, Bink. I knew I couldn't conceal it much longer."

"You mean you actually are . . . ?"

"I am Chameleon," she said.

Now he was totally confused. "That was only a code word we used, to alert—" And an omen . . .

"I am Fanchon-ugly," she said. "And Dee-average. And Wynne-beautiful. I change a little every day, completing the circle in the course of a month. A lunar month. It's the female cycle, you know."

Now he remembered how Dee too had reminded him of someone. "But Wynne was stupid! You—"

"My intelligence varies inversely," she explained. "That is the other facet of my curse. I range from ugly intelligence to lovely idiocy. I've been looking for a spell to turn me normal."

"A spell for Chameleon," he said musingly. What an astonishing enchantment. Yet it had to be true, for he had almost caught the similarity when he met Dee, so close to where he had lost Wynne, and now he had seen Fanchon change day by day. Chameleon—she had no magic talent; she *was* magic, like the centaurs or dragons. "But why did you follow me into exile?"

"Magic doesn't work outside Xanth. Humfrey told me I would gradually center on my normal state if I went to Mundania. I would be Dee, permanently—completely average. That seemed my best choice."

"But you said you followed me."

"I did. You were kind to Wynne. My mind may change, but my memory doesn't. You saved her from the Gap dragon at great peril to yourself, and you didn't take advantage of her when she—you know." Bink remembered the beautiful girl's willingness to disrobe. She had been too stupid to think through the likely consequence of her offer—but Dee and Fanchon, later, would have understood. "And now I know you tried to help Dee, also. She—I shouldn't have cut you off then—but we weren't as smart then as later. And we didn't know you as well. You—" She broke off. "It doesn't matter."

But it did matter! She was not one but three of the girls he had known—and one of those was excruciatingly beautiful. But also stupid. How should he react to this—this chameleon?

The concept of the chameleon, again—the magic lizard that changed its color and shape at will, mimicking other creatures. If only he could forget that omen—or be sure he understood it. He was sure this Chameleon meant him no harm, but she might in fact be the death of him. Her magic was involuntary, but it dominated her life. She had a problem, certainly—and so did he.

So she had learned that he was to be exiled for lack of magic and made her decision. Dee without magic, Bink without magic—two ordinary people with a common memory of the land of magic—perhaps the only thing to sustain them in drear Mundania. No doubt her smart phase had figured that out. What an apt couple they could make, these two demagicked souls. So she had acted—but had had no way of knowing about the ambush set by the Evil Magician.

It had been a good notion. Bink liked Dee. She was

not so ugly as to turn him off, and not so lovely as to excite his distrust after his experiences with Sabrina and the Sorceress Iris—what was the matter with beautiful women, that they could not be constant?—but also not so stupid as to make it pointless. Just a reasonable compromise, an average girl he could have loved—especially in Mundania.

But now they were back in Xanth, and her curse was in force. She was not simple Dee, but complex Chameleon, swinging from extreme to extreme, when all he wanted was the average.

"I'm not so stupid yet that I can't figure out what's going through your mind," she said. "I'm better off in Mundania."

Bink could not deny it. Now he almost wished it had worked out that way. To have settled down with Dee, raised a family—that could have been its own special brand of magic.

There was a crash. Both reacted, orienting on the sound. It had come from somewhere above.

"Trent's in trouble!" Bink said. He started down the hall, carrying his staff. "Must be stairs somewhere—" Behind his immediate consciousness he realized that this reaction indicated a fundamental change in his attitude toward the Magician. That night with the sword and the sleeping man—if evil was as evil did, Trent could not be very evil. Trust compelled trust. Maybe the Magician was only trying to manipulate Bink's attitude; regardless, that attitude had suffered a fundamental erosion.

Chameleon followed. Now that it was light, they had no fear of pitfalls, though Bink knew there could be magic ones. There was a grandly curving stone staircase beyond a palatial room. They charged up this.

Suddenly a ghost loomed up. "Ooooo!" it moaned, its great eye holes staring like holes in a dark coffin.

"Get out of my way!" Bink snapped, swinging his pole at it. The ghost, nonplused, phased out. Bink ran through its remnant, feeling the momentary chill of its presence. Trent was right: there was no need to fear the insubstantial.

Every step he took was solid; apparently there were no illusions in this old castle, just its harmless resident spooks. That was a relief after the way they had been herded into it last night.

But now there was silence upstairs. Bink and Chameleon picked their way through surprisingly opulent and well-preserved chambers, searching for their companion. At another time Bink would have admired the arrangements and tapestries of the rooms and halls at leisure, and been glad of the tight roof that had protected them from rain and weathering and rot, but right now his attention was preempted by concern. What had happened to Trent? If there were some monster lurking in this castle, summoning its victims by magic—

Then they found a kind of upstairs library. Fat old books and coiled scrolls were filed on shelves along the walls. In the center, at a polished wood table, sat Trent, poring over an open tome.

"Another peephole spell's got him!" Bink cried.

But Trent lifted his head. "No, merely the thirst for knowledge, Bink. This is fascinating."

A bit abashed, they halted. "But the crash—" Bink started.

Trent smiled. "My fault. That old chair gave way under my weight." He pointed to a tangle of wood. "Much of the furniture here is fragile. I was so interested in this library that I was thoughtless." He rubbed his backside reminiscently. "I paid for it."

"What's so fascinating about the books?" Chameleon asked.

"This one is a history of this castle," Trent explained. "It is not, it seems, just another artifact. This is Castle Roogna."

"Roogna!" Bink exclaimed. "The Magician King of the Fourth Wave?"

"The same. He ruled from here, it seems. When he died and the Fifth Wave conquered Xanth, eight hundred years ago, his castle was deserted, and finally forgotten. But it was a remarkable structure. Much of the King's nature imbued the environs; the castle had an identity of its own."

"I remember," Bink said. "Roogna's talent—"

"Was the conversion of magic to his own purposes," Trent said. "A subtle but powerful asset. He was the ultimate tamer of the forces around him. He cultivated the magic trees around here, and he built this fine castle. During his reign Xanth was in harmony with its populace. It was a kind of Golden Age."

"Yes," Bink agreed. "I never thought I'd see this famous historical place."

"You may see more of it than you want to," Trent said. "Remember how we were guided here?"

"It seems like only yesterday," Bink said wryly.

"Why were we herded here?" Chameleon demanded.

Trent glanced at her, his gaze lingering. "I believe this locale behooves you, Fanchon."

"Never mind that," she said. "I'll be a lot prettier before I'm through, more's the pity."

"She is Chameleon," Bink said. "She shifts from ugly to pretty and back again—and her intelligence varies inversely. She left Xanth to escape that curse."

"I would not regard that as a curse," the Magician commented. "All things to all men—in due course."

"You're not a woman," she snapped. "I asked about this castle."

Trent nodded. "Well, this castle requires a new resident. A Magician. It is very selective, which is one reason it has lain dormant for so many centuries. It wants to restore the years of its glory; therefore it must support a new King of Xanth."

"And you're a Magician!" Bink exclaimed. "So when you came near, everything shoved you this way."

"So it would seem. There was no malign intent, merely an overwhelming need. A need for Castle Roogna, and a need for Xanth—to make this land again what it could be, a truly organized and excellent kingdom."

"But you're not King," Chameleon said.

"Not yet." There was a very positive quality to the statement.

Bink and Chameleon looked at each other in developing comprehension. So the Evil Magician had reverted to form—assuming he had ever changed his form. They had discussed his human qualities, his seeming nobility, and been deceived. He had planned to invade Xanth, and now—

"Not ever!" she flared. "The people would never tolerate a criminal like you. They haven't forgotten—"

"So you do have prior knowledge of my reputation," Trent said mildly. "I had understood you to say you had not heard of me." He shrugged. "However, the good citizens of Xanth may not have much choice, and it would not be the first time a criminal has occupied a throne," he continued calmly. "With the powers of this castle—which are formidable—added to mine, I may not need an army."

"We'll stop you," Chameleon said grimly.

Trent's gaze touched her again, appraisingly. "Are you terminating the truce?"

That gave her pause. The end of the truce would put the two of them directly in Trent's power, if what he said about this castle was true. "No," she said. "But when it does end . . ."

There was no hint of malignancy in Trent's smile. "Yes, it seems there will have to be a settlement. I had thought if I allowed you to go your way, you would extend the same courtesy to me. But when I said the people of Xanth would not necessarily have a choice, I did not mean it precisely the way you seem to have taken it. This castle may not permit us to do other than its will. For centuries it has endured here, hanging on against inevitable deterioration, waiting for a Magician of sufficient strength to qualify. Perhaps the magic-sniffer we encountered in the forest was one of its representatives. Now it has found not one but two Magicians. It will not lightly yield them up. From here we may be bound to glory—or extinction, depending on our decision."

"Two Magicians?" she asked.

"Remember, Bink has almost as much magic as I do. That was the verdict of the sniffer, and I am not certain it was mistaken. That would place him comfortably in the Magician class."

"But I have no talent," Bink protested.

"Correction," Trent said. "To have an unidentified talent is hardly synonymous with having no talent. But even if you are talentless, there is strong magic associated with you. You may *be* magic, as is Fanchon."

"Chameleon," she said. "That's my real name; the others are merely phases."

"I beg your pardon," Trent said, making a little sitting bow to her. "Chameleon."

"You mean I'll change somehow?" Bink asked, half hopeful, half appalled.

"Perhaps. You might metamorphose into some superior form—like a pawn becoming a Queen." He paused. "Sorry—that's another Mundane reference; I don't believe chess is known in Xanth. I have been too long in exile."

"Well, I still won't help you try to steal the crown," Bink said stoutly.

"Naturally not. Our purposes differ. We may even be rivals."

"I'm not trying to take over Xanth!"

"Not consciously. But to prevent an Evil Magician from doing so, would you not consider . . . ?"

"Ridiculous!" Bink said, disgruntled. The notion was preposterous, yet insidious. If the only way to prevent Trent from—no!

"The time may indeed have come for us to part," Trent said. "I have appreciated your company, but the situation seems to be changing. Perhaps you should attempt to leave this castle now. I shall not oppose you.

Should we manage to separate, we can consider the truce abated. Fair enough?"

"How nice," Chameleon said. "You can relax over your books while the jungle tears us up."

"I do not think anything here will actually hurt you," Trent said. "The theme of Castle Roogna is harmony with man." He smiled again. "Harmony, not harm. But I rather doubt you will be permitted to depart."

Bink had had enough. "I'll take my chances. Let's go."

"You want me to come along?" Chameleon asked hesitantly.

"Unless you prefer to stay with him. You might make a very pretty Queen in a couple of weeks."

Trent laughed. Chameleon moved with alacrity. They walked to the stairs, leaving the Magician poring over his book again.

Another ghost intercepted them. This one seemed larger than the others, more solid. "Waarrningg," it moaned.

Bink stopped. "You can speak? What is your warning?"

"Dooom beeyonnd. Staay."

"Oh. Well, that's a chance we've already decided to take," Bink said. "Because we are loyal to Xanth."

"Xaaanth!" the spirit repeated with a certain feeling.

"Yes, Xanth. So we must leave."

The ghost seemed nonplused. It faded.

"It almost seems they're on our side," Chameleon commented. "Maybe they're just trying to make us stay in the castle, though."

"We can't afford to trust ghosts," Bink agreed.

They could not exit through the front gate, because the portcullis was firm and they did not understand the mechanism for lifting it. They poked through the downstairs rooms, searching for an alternate exit.

Bink opened one promising door—and slammed it shut as a host of leather-winged, long-toothed creatures stirred; they looked like vampire bats. He cracked the next open more carefully—and a questing rope twined out, more than casually reminiscent of the tree vines.

"Maybe the cellar," Chameleon suggested, spying stairs leading down.

They tried it. But at the foot, huge, baleful rats scurried into place, and they were facing, not fleeing, the intruders. The beasts looked too hungry, too confident; they surely had magic to trap any prey that entered their territory.

Bink poked his staff at the nearest, experimentally. "Scat!" he exclaimed. But the rat leaped onto the pole, climbing up toward Bink's hands. He shook it, but the creature clung, and another jumped to the staff. He thunked it against the stone floor, hard—but still they hung on, and still they climbed. That must be their magic—the ability to cling.

"Bink! Above!" Chameleon cried.

There was a chittering overhead. More rats were crowding the beams, bracing themselves to leap.

Bink threw the staff away and backed hastily up the stairs, holding on to Chameleon for support until he could get turned around. The rats did not follow.

"This castle is really organized," Bink said as they emerged on the main floor. "I don't think it intends to let us go peacefully. But we've got to try. Maybe a window."

But there were no windows on the ground floor; the outer wall had been built to withstand siege. No point in jumping from an upper turret; someone would surely break a bone. They moved on, and found themselves in the kitchen area. Here there was a back exit, normally used for supplies, garbage, and servants. They slipped out and faced a small bridge across the moat: an ideal escape route.

But there was motion on the bridge already. Snakes were emerging from the rotten planking. Not healthy, normal reptiles, but tattered, discolored things whose bones showed through oozing gaps in the sagging flesh.

"Those are zombie snakes!" Chameleon cried with genuine horror. "Waked from the dead."

"It figures," Bink said grimly. "This whole castle is waked from the dead. Rats can thrive anywhere, but the other creatures died out when the castle died, or maybe they come here to die even now. But zombies aren't as strong as real living things; we can probably handle them with our staffs." But he had lost his own staff in the cellar.

Now he smelled the stench of corruption, worse than that of the harpy. Waves of it rose from the festering snakes and the putrescent moat. Bink's stomach made an exploratory heave. He had seldom encountered genuine, far-advanced decay; usually either creatures were living or their bones were fairly neat and clean. The stages in between, of spoilage and maggot infestation and disintegration, were a part of the cycle of life and death he had chosen not to inspect closely. Hitherto.

"I don't want to try that bridge," Chameleon said. "We'll fall through—and there are zombie crocs in the water."

So there were: big reptiles threshing the slimy surface with leather-covered bones, their worm-eaten eyes gazing up.

"Maybe a boat," Bink said. "Or a raft—"

"Uh-*uh*. Even if it weren't rotten and filled with zombie bugs, it would—well, look across the water."

He looked. Now came the worst of all, walking jerkily along the far bank of the moat: human zombies, some mummified, others hardly more than animate skeletons.

Bink watched the awful things for a long moment, fascinated by their very grotesqueness. Fragments of wrappings and decayed flesh dropped from them. Some dribbled caked dirt left from their over-hasty emergence from their unquiet graves. It was a parade of putrefaction.

He thought of fighting that motley army, hacking apart already-destroyed bodies, feeling their rotting, vermin-riddled flesh on his hands, wrestling with those ghastly animations, saturated with the cloying stink of it all. What loathsome diseases did they bear, what gangrenous embraces would they bestow on him as they fell apart? What possible attack would make these moldering dead lie down again?

The spell-driven things were closing in, coming across the ragged bridge. Surely this was even worse for the zombies, for they could not voluntarily have roused themselves. They could not retire to the pleasant seclusion of the castle interior. To be pressed into service in this state, instead of remaining in the bliss of oblivion—

"I—don't think I'm ready to leave yet," Bink said.

"No," Chameleon agreed, her face somewhat green. "Not this way."

And the zombies halted, giving Bink and Chameleon time to reenter Castle Roogna.

Chapter 13. Rationale

Chameleon was now well through her "normal" phase, which Bink had known before as Dee, and moving into her beauty phase. It was not identical to the prior Wynne; her hair was lighter in color, and her features subtly different. Apparently she varied in her physical details each cycle, never exactly repeating herself, but always proceeding from extreme to extreme. Unfortunately, she was also becoming less intelligent, and was no help on the problem of escaping the castle. She was much more interested now in getting friendly with Bink—and this was a distraction he felt he could not afford at the moment.

First, his priority was to get away from here; second, he was not at all sure he wanted to associate himself in any permanent way with so changeable an entity. If only she were beautiful and bright—but no, that would not work either. He realized now why she had not been tempted by Trent's offer to make her beautiful, when they were first captured outside the Shield. That would merely have changed her phase. If she were beautiful when she was smart, she would be stupid when she was ugly, and that was no improvement. She needed to be free of the curse entirely. And even if she could be fixed permanently at the height of both beauty and brains, he would not trust her, for he had been betrayed by that type too. Sabrina—he choked off that memory. Yet even an ordinary girl could get pretty dull if she had no more than ordinary intelligence or magic . . .

Castle Roogna, now that they were not actively opposing it, was a fairly pleasant residence. It did its best to make itself so. The surrounding gardens provided a rich plenitude of fruits, grains, vegetables, and small game; Trent practiced his archery by bringing down rabbits, shooting from the high embrasures, using one of the fine bows in the castle armory. Some of the creatures were false rabbits, projecting images of themselves a bit apart from their actual locations, causing him to waste arrows, but Trent seemed to enjoy the challenge. One he nabbed was a stinker, whose magic aroma was such that there was nothing to do but bury the carcass in a hurry, very deep. Another was a shrinker; as it died it diminished in size until it was more like a mouse, hardly usable. Magic always had its little surprises. But some were good.

The kitchen did need some attention; otherwise the zombies would come in to do the cooking. Rather than permit that, Chameleon took over. Assisted by advice from the lady ghosts, who were very particular about Castle Roogna cuisine, she made creditable meals. She had no trouble with the dishes, since there was an everlasting magic fountain with aseptic properties; one rinse, and everything sparkled. In fact, having a bath in that water was quite an experience; it effervesced.

The inner partitions of the castle were as solid as the roof; there seemed to be weatherproofing spells in operation. Each person had an opulent private bedroom with costly draperies on the walls, moving rugs on the floors, quivering goose-down pillows and solid-silver chamberpots. They all lived like royalty. Bink discovered that the embroidered tapestry on the wall opposite his bed was actually a magic picture: the little figures moved, playing out their tiny dramas with intriguing detail. Miniature knights slew dragons, tiny ladies sewed, and in the supposed privacy of interior chambers those knights and ladies embraced. At first Bink closed his eyes to those scenes, but soon his natural voyeurism dominated, and he watched it all. And wished that he could—but no, that would not be proper, though he knew that Chameleon was willing.

The ghosts were no problem; they even became familiar. Bink got to know them individually. One was the gatekeeper, who had looked in on them that first night when the portcullis crashed down; another was the chambermaid; a third was the cook's assistant. There were six in all, each of whom had died inappropriately and so lacked proper burial rites. They were shades, really, but without proper volition; only the King of Xanth could absolve them, and they could not leave the castle. So they were doomed to serve here forever, unable to perform their accustomed chores. They were basically nice people who had no control over the castle itself, and constituted only an incidental part of its enchantment. They helped wherever they could, pitifully eager to please, telling Chameleon where to search for the new foods and telling Bink stories of their lives here in the Grand Old Days. They had been surprised and chagrined by the intrusion of living people at first, for they had been in isolation for centuries. But they realized it was part of the imperative of the castle itself, and now they had adjusted.

Trent spent most of his time in the library, as if seeking to master all of its accumulated knowledge. At first Chameleon spent some time there too, interested in intellectual things. But as she lost intelligence, she lost interest. Her researches changed; now she looked avidly for some spell to make her normal. When the library did not provide that, she left it, to poke around the castle and grounds. So long as she was alone, no untoward things manifested: no rats, no carnivorous vines, no zombies. She was no prisoner here, only the men. She searched for sources of magic. She ate things freely, alarming Bink, who knew how poisonous magic could be. But she seemed to lead a charmed existence—charmed by Castle Roogna.

One of her discoveries was serendipitous: a small red fruit growing plentifully on one of the garden trees. Chameleon tried to bite into one, but the rind was tough, so she took it to the kitchen to chop it in half with a cleaver. No ghosts were present; they generally appeared now only when they had business. Thus Chameleon did not have warning about the nature of this fruit. She was careless, and dropped one of the fruits on the floor.

Bink heard the explosion and came running. Chameleon, quite pretty now, was huddling in a corner of the kitchen. "What happened?" Bink demanded, looking about for hostile magic.

"Oh, Bink!" she cried, turning to him with woeful relief. Her homemade dress was in disarray, exposing her finely formed breasts above and her firm round thighs below. What a difference a few days made! She was not at the height of her loveliness, but she was quite adequate to the need.

The need? Bink found her in his arms, aware that she was eager to do any bidding he might make. It was difficult indeed to steel himself against the obvious, for she also had much of Dee in her—the aspect he had liked before he understood her nature. He could take her now, make love to her—and neither her stupid phase nor her smart phase would condemn him.

But he was not a casual lover, and he did not want to make any such commitment at this time, in this situation. He pushed her away gently, the action requiring far more effort than he cared to show. "What happened?" he asked again.

"It—it banged," she said.

He had to remind himself that her diminishing mentality was the other face of her curse. Now it was easier to hold off her lush body. A body without a mind did not appeal to him. "What banged?"

"The cherry."

"The cherry?" This was the first he had heard about the new fruit. But after patient questioning, he elicited the story.

"Those are cherry bombs!" he exclaimed, comprehending. "If you had actually eaten one—"

She was not yet so stupid as to misunderstand that. "Oh, my mouth!"

"Oh, your head! Those things are powerful. Didn't Milly warn you?" Milly was the chambermaid ghost.

"She was busy."

What would a ghost be busy with? Well, this was no time to explore that. "After this, don't eat anything unless a ghost tells you it's okay."

Chameleon nodded dutifully.

Bink picked up a cherry cautiously and considered it. It was just a hard little red ball, marked only where its stem had broken off. "Old Magician Roogna probably used these bombs in warfare. He didn't like war, as I understand it, but he never let his defenses grow soft. Any attackers—why, one man on the ramparts with a slingshot could decimate an army, lobbing these cherry bombs down. No telling what other trees there are in the arsenal. If you don't stop fooling around with strange fruits—"

"I could blow up the castle," she said, watching the

dissipating smoke. The floor was scorched, and a table had lost a leg.

"Blow up the castle . . ." Bink echoed, suddenly thinking of something. "Chameleon, why don't you bring in some more cherry bombs? I'd like to experiment with them. But be careful, very careful; don't knock or drop any."

"Sure," she said, as eager to please as any ghost. "Very careful."

"And don't eat any." That was not quite a joke.

Bink gathered cloth and string, and made bags of assorted sizes. Soon he had bag-bombs of varying power. He planted these strategically around the castle. One bag he kept for himself.

"I think we are ready to depart Castle Roogna," he said. "But first I have to talk with Trent. You stand here by the kitchen door, and if you see any zombies, throw cherries at them." He was sure no zombie had the coordination to catch such a bomb and throw it back; wormy eyes and rotting flesh necessarily had poor hand-eye integration. So they would be vulnerable. "And if you see Trent come down, and not me, throw a cherry into that pile. Fast, before he gets within six feet of you." And he pointed to a large bomb he had tied to a major support column. "Do you understand?"

She didn't, but he drilled her on it until she had it straight. She was to throw a cherry at anything she saw—except Bink himself.

Now he was ready. He went up to the library to speak with the Evil Magician. His heart beat loudly within him, now that the moment of confrontation had come, but he knew what he had to do.

A ghost intercepted him. It was Milly, the chambermaid, her white sheet arranged to resemble her working dress, her black-hole eyes somehow having the aspect of once-sultry humanity. The ghosts had become shapeless from sheer neglect and carelessness in the course of the past few centuries of isolation, but now that there was company they were shaping up into their proper forms.

Another week would have them back into people out-
lines and people colors, though of course they would
still be ghosts. Bink suspected Milly would turn out to
be a rather pretty girl, and he wondered just how she
had died. A liaison with a castle guest, then a stabbing
by the jealous wife who discovered them?

"What is it, Milly?" he asked, pausing. He had mined
the castle, but he bore no malice toward its unfortunate
denizens. He hoped his bluff would be effective, so that
it would not be necessary to destroy the home of the
ghosts, who really were not responsible for its grandiose
mischief.

"The King—private conference," she said. Her
speech was still somewhat windy, as it was hard for an
entity with so little physical substance—hardly any ec-
toplasm—to enunciate clearly. But he could make it
out.

"Conference? There's nobody here but us," he objected. "Or do you mean he's on the pot?"

Milly blushed as well as she was able to. Though as
chambermaid she had been accustomed to the chore of
collecting and emptying out the chamberpots, she felt
that any reference to a person's actual performance on
them was uncouth. It was as if the substance were completely divorced from the function. Perhaps she liked to
believe that the refuse appeared magically overnight,
untouched by human intestine. Magic fertilizer! "No."

"Well, I'm sorry, but I'll have to interrupt him," Bink
said. "You see, I don't recognize him as King, and I am
about to depart the castle."

"Oh." She put one foggily formed hand to her vague
face in feminine misgiving. "But seee."

"Very well." Bink followed her to the little chapel
room adjacent to the library. It was actually an offshoot
from the master bedroom, with no direct access to the
library. But it had, as it turned out, a small window
opening onto the library. Since the gloom of the unlit
chapel was deeper than that of the other room, it was
possible to see without being seen.

Trent was not alone. Before him stood a woman of early middle age, still handsome though the first flush of beauty had faded. Her hair was tied back and up in a functional, fairly severe bun, but there were smile lines around her mouth and eyes. And beside her was a boy, perhaps ten years old, who bore a direct resemblance to the woman, and had to be her son.

Neither person spoke, but their breathing and slight shifts of posture showed that they were alive and solid, not ghosts. How had they come here, and what was their business? Why hadn't Bink or Chameleon seen them enter? It was almost impossible to approach this castle unobserved; it was designed that way, to be readily defensible in case of attack. And the portcullis remained down, blocking off the front entry. Bink had been down by the kitchen entrance, fashioning his bombs.

But, granting that they obviously had come, why didn't they speak? Why didn't Trent speak? They all just looked at each other in eerie silence. This whole scene seemed to make no sense.

Bink studied the odd, silent pair. They were vaguely reminiscent of the widow and son of Donald the shade, the ones he had told about the silver oak so that they would not have to live in poverty any more. The similarity was not in their physical appearance, for these were better-looking people who had obviously not suffered poverty; it was in their atmosphere of quiet loss. Had they lost their man, too? And come to Trent for some kind of help? If so, they had chosen the wrong Magician.

Bink drew away, disliking the feeling of snooping. Even Evil Magicians deserved some privacy. He walked around to the hall and back to the top of the stairs. Milly, her warning completed, vanished. Apparently it required some effort for the ghosts to manifest and speak intelligibly, and they had to recuperate in whatever vacuum they occupied when off duty.

He resumed his march to the library, this time stepping heavily so as to make his approach audible. Trent would have to introduce him to the visitors.

But only the Magician was there as Bink pushed open the door. He was seated at the table, poring over another tome. He looked up as Bink entered. "Come for a good book, Bink?" he inquired.

Bink lost his composure. "The people! What happened to them?"

Trent frowned. "People, Bink?"

"I saw them. A woman and a boy, right here—" Bink faltered. "Look, I didn't mean to peek, but when Milly said you were in conference, I looked in from the chapel."

Trent nodded. "Then you did see. I did not intend to burden you with my private problems."

"Who are they? How did they get here? What did you do to them?"

"They were my wife and son," Trent said gravely. "They died."

Bink remembered the story the sailor had told of the Evil Magician's Mundane family, killed by Mundane illness. "But they were here. I saw them."

"And seeing is believing." Trent sighed. "Bink, they were two roaches, transformed into the likenesses of my loved ones. These were the only two people I ever loved or ever shall love. I miss them, I need them—if only to gaze on their likenesses on occasion. When I lost them, there was nothing left for me in Mundania." He brought an embroidered Castle Roogna handkerchief to his face, and Bink was amazed to see that the Evil Magician's eyes were bright with tears. But Trent retained his control. "However, this is not properly your concern, and I prefer not to discuss it. What is it that brings you here, Bink?"

Oh, yes. He was committed, and had to follow through. Somehow the verve had gone out of it, but he proceeded: "Chameleon and I are leaving Castle Roogna."

The handsome brow wrinkled. "Again?"

"This time for real," Bink said, nettled. "The zombies won't stop us."

"And you find it necessary to inform me? We already have our understanding about this, and I am sure I would become aware of your absence in due course. If you feared I would oppose it, it would have been to your advantage to depart without my knowledge."

Bink did not smile. "No. I feel it behooves me, under our truce, to inform you."

Trent made a little wave of one hand. "Very well. I will not claim I am glad to see you go; I have come to appreciate your qualities, as shown in the precision of your ethic that caused you to notify me of your present action. And Chameleon is a fine girl, of like persuasion, and daily more pretty. I would much prefer to have you both on my side, but since this cannot be, I wish you every fortune elsewhere."

Bink found this increasingly awkward. "This is not exactly a social leave-taking. I'm sorry." He wished now that he hadn't observed Trent's wife and son, or learned their identities; those had obviously been good people, undeserving of their fate, and Bink was wholly in sympathy with the Magician's grief. "The castle won't let us go voluntarily. We have to force it. So we have planted bombs, and—"

"Bombs!" Trent exclaimed. "Those are Mundane artifacts. There are no bombs in Xanth—and shall be none. Never, while I am King."

"It seems there were bombs in the old days," Bink said doggedly. "There's a cherry-bomb tree in the yard. Each cherry explodes on impact, violently."

"Cherry bombs?" Trent repeated. "So. What have you done with the cherries?"

"We have used them to mine the castle supports. If Roogna tries to stop us, we will destroy it. So it is better if it—lets us go in peace. I needed to tell you, so you could disarm the bombs after we're gone."

"Why tell me this? Don't you oppose my designs, and

those of Castle Roogna? If Magician and castle were destroyed, you would be the clean victor."

"Not clean. It's not the kind of victory I want," Bink said. "I—look, you could do so much good in Xanth, if you only—" But he knew it was useless. It simply was not the nature of an Evil Magician to devote himself to Good. "Here is a list of the bomb locations," he said, setting a piece of paper on the table. "All you have to do is pick up the packages and bags very carefully and take them outside."

Trent shook his head. "I don't believe your bomb threat will work to effect your escape, Bink. The castle is not intelligent per se. It only reacts to certain stimuli. It might let Chameleon go, but not you. In its perception, you are a Magician, therefore you must remain. You may have out-thought Roogna, but it will not comprehend the full nature of your ploy. Thus the zombies will balk you, as before."

"Then we shall have to bomb it."

"Exactly. You will have to set off the cherries, and all of us will be destroyed together."

"No, we'll get outside first, and heave a cherry back. If the castle cannot be bluffed—"

"It can't be bluffed. It is not a thinking thing. It merely reacts. You will be forced to destroy it—and you know I can't permit that. I need Roogna!"

Now it was getting tough. Bink was ready. "Chameleon will set off the bombs if you transform me," he said, feeling the chill of challenge. He didn't like this sort of power play, but had known it would come to this. "If you interfere in any way—"

"Oh, I would not break the truce. But—"

"You can't break the truce. Either I rejoin Chameleon alone or she heaves a cherry into a bomb. She's too stupid to do anything but follow directions."

"Listen to me, Bink! It is my given word that prevents me from breaking the truce, not your tactical preparations. I could transform you into a flea, and then transform a roach into your likeness and send that

likeness down to meet Chameleon. Once she set down
the cherry——"

Bink's face reflected his chagrin. The Evil Magician
could void the plan. Chameleon-stupid would not catch
on until too late; that nadir of intelligence worked
against him as well as for him.

"I am not doing this," Trent said. "I tell you about
the possibility merely to demonstrate that I, too, have
ethics. The end does not justify the means. I feel that
you have allowed yourself to forget this temporarily,
and if you will listen a moment you will see your error
and correct it. I cannot allow you to destroy this marvelous and historically significant edifice, to no point."

Already Bink was feeling guilty. Was he to be talked
out of a course he knew was right?

"Surely you realize," the Evil Magician continued
persuasively, "that the entire area would erupt in vengeful wrath if you did this thing. You might be outside the
castle, but you would remain in the Roogna environs,
and you would die horribly. Chameleon, too."

Chameleon, too—that hurt. That beautiful girl de-
voured by a tangle tree, ripped apart by zombies . . .
"It is a risk I must take," Bink said grimly, though he
realized the Magician was correct. The way they had
been herded to this castle—there would be no escaping
the savagery of the forest. "Maybe you will be able to
persuade the castle to let us go, rather than set off that
chain of events."

"You are a stubborn one!"

"Yes."

"At least hear me out first. If I cannot persuade you,
then what must be must be, though I abhor it."

"Speak briefly." Bink was surprised at his own temerity, but he felt he was doing what he had to. If
Trent tried to approach within six feet, Bink would take
off, to avoid transformation. He might be able to outrun
the Magician. But even so, he could not wait too long;
he was afraid that Chameleon would tire of waiting and
do something foolish.

"I really don't want to see you or Chameleon die, and of course I value my own survival," Trent said. "While I love nobody alive today, you two have been as close to me as anyone. It is almost as if fate has decreed that like types must be banned from the conventional society of Xanth. We—"

"Like types!" Bink exclaimed indignantly.

"I apologize for an invidious comparison. We have been through a great deal together in a short time, and I think it is fair to say we have saved each other's lives on occasion. Perhaps it was to associate with your like that I really returned to Xanth."

"Maybe so," Bink said stiffly, suppressing the mixed feelings he was experiencing. "But that does not justify your conquering Xanth and probably killing many entire families."

Trent looked pained, but controlled himself. "I do not pretend that it does, Bink. The Mundane tragedy of my family was the stimulus, not the justification, for my return. I had nothing remaining in Mundania worth living for, so naturally my orientation shifted to Xanth, my homeland. I would not try to harm Xanth; I hope to benefit it, by opening it up to the contemporary reality before it is too late. Even if some deaths occur, this is a small price to pay for the eventual salvation of Xanth."

"You think Xanth won't survive unless you conquer it?" Bink tried to put a sneer in his tone, but it didn't register very well. If only he had the verbal control and projection of the Evil Magician!

"Yes, actually, I do. Xanth is overdue for a new Wave of colonization, and such a Wave would benefit it as the prior ones did."

"The Waves were murder and rapine and destruction! The curse of Xanth."

Trent shook his head. "Some were that, yes. But others were highly beneficial, such as the Fourth Wave, from which this castle dates. It was not the fact of the Waves but their mismanagement that made trouble. On the whole they were essential to the progress of Xanth. But I don't expect you to believe that. Right now I'm merely trying to persuade you to spare this castle and yourself; I'm not trying to convert you to my cause."

Something about this interchange was troubling Bink increasingly. The Evil Magician seemed too mature, too reasonable, too knowledgeable, too committed. Trent was wrong—he had to be—yet he spoke with such verisimilitude that Bink had difficulty pinpointing that wrongness. "Try to convert me," he said.

"I'm glad you said that, Bink. I'd like you to know my logical rationale. Perhaps you can offer some positive critique."

That sounded like a sophisticated intellectual ploy. Bink tried to perceive it as sarcasm, but he was sure it was not. He feared the Magician was more intelligent than he, but he also knew what was right. "Maybe I can," he said guardedly. He felt as if he were walking into the wilderness, picking the most likely paths, yet being inevitably guided to the trap at the center. Castle Roogna—on the physical and intellectual levels. Roogna had lacked a voice for eight hundred years, but now it had one. Bink could no more fence with that voice than he could with the Magician's keen sword—yet he had to try.

"My rationale is dual. Part of it relates to Mundania, and part to Xanth. You see, despite certain lapses in ethics and politics, Mundania has progressed remarkably in the past few centuries, thanks to the numbers of people who have made discoveries and spread information; in many respects it is a far more civilized region than Xanth. Unfortunately, the Mundanes' powers of combat have also progressed. This you will have to take on faith, for I have no way to prove it here. Mundania has weapons that are easily capable of eradicating all life in Xanth, regardless of the Shield."

"That's a lie!" Bink exclaimed. "Nothing can penetrate the Shield!"

"Except perhaps the three of us," Trent murmured.

"But the main restriction of the Shield is against living things. You could charge through the Shield—your body would penetrate it quite readily—but you would be dead when you got there."

"Same thing."

"Not the same thing, Bink! You see, there are big guns that throw missiles which are dead to begin with, such as powerful bombs, like your cherry bombs but much worse, preset to explode on contact. Xanth is a small area, compared to Mundania. If the Mundanes were determined, they could saturate Xanth. In such an attack, even the Shieldstone would be destroyed. The people of Xanth can no longer afford to ignore the Mundanes. There are too many Mundanians; we can't remain undiscovered forever. They can and will one day wipe us out. Unless we establish relations now."

Bink shook his head in disbelief and incomprehension.

But Trent continued without rancor. "Now, the Xanth internal aspect is quite another matter. It poses no threat to Mundania, since magic is not operative there. But it does pose an insidious but compelling threat to life as we know it in Xanth itself."

"Xanth poses a threat to Xanth? This is nonsense on the face of it."

Now Trent's smile was a bit patronizing. "I can see you would have trouble with the logic of recent Mundanian science." But he sobered before Bink could inquire about that. "No, I am being unfair to you. This internal threat of Xanth is something I learned just in the past few days from my researches in this library, and it is important. This aspect alone justifies the necessity of preserving this castle, for its accumulated ancient lore is vital to Xanth society."

Bink remained dubious. "We've lived without this library for eight centuries; we can live without it now."

"Ah, but the manner of that life!" Trent shook his head as if perceiving something too vast to be expressed. He got up and moved to a shelf behind him.

He took down a book and riffled carefully through its creaking old pages. He set it down before Bink, open. "What is that picture?"

"A dragon," Bink said promptly.

Trent flipped a page. "And this?"

"A manticora." What was the point? The pictures were very nice, though they did not coincide precisely with contemporary creatures. The proportions and details were subtly wrong.

"And this?"

It was a picture of a human-headed quadruped, with hoofs, a horse's tail, and catlike forelegs. "A lamia."

"And this?"

"A centaur. Look—we can admire pictures all day, but—"

"What do these creatures have in common?" Trent asked.

"They have human heads or foreparts—except the dragon, though the one in this book has an almost human shortness of snout. Some have human intelligence. But—"

"Exactly! Consider the sequence. Trace a dragon back through similar species, and it becomes increasingly manlike. Does that suggest anything to you?"

"Just that some creatures are more manlike than others. But that's no threat to Xanth. Anyway, most of these pictures are out of date; the actual creatures don't look quite like that any more."

"Did the centaurs teach you the Theory of Evolution?"

"Oh, sure. That today's creatures are evolved from more primitive ones, selected for survival. Go back far enough and you find a common ancestor."

"Right. But in Mundania creatures like the lamia, manticora, and dragon never evolved."

"Of course not. They're magic. They evolve by magic selection. Only in Xanth can—"

"Yet obviously Xanth creatures started from Mundane ancestors. They have so many affinities—"

"All right!" Bink said impatiently. "They descended from Mundanes. What has that got to do with your conquering Xanth?"

"According to conventional centaur history, man has been in Xanth only a thousand years," Trent said. "In that period there have been ten major Waves of immigration from Mundania."

"Twelve," Bink said.

"That depends on how you count them. At any rate, this continued for nine hundred years, until the Shield cut off those migrations. Yet there are many partially human forms that predate the supposed arrival of human beings. Does that seem to be significant?"

Bink was increasingly worried that Chameleon would foul up, or that the castle would figure out a way to neutralize the cherry bombs. He was not certain that Castle Roogna could not think for itself. Was the Evil Magician stalling to make time for this? "I'll give you one more minute to make your case. Then we're going, regardless."

"How could partially human forms have evolved—unless they had human ancestors? Convergent evolution doesn't create the unnatural mishmash monsters we have here. It creates creatures adapted to their ecological niches, and human features fit few niches. There had to have been people in Xanth many thousands of years ago."

"All right," Bink agreed. "Thirty seconds."

"These people must have interbred with animals to form the composites we know—the centaurs, manticoras, merfolk, harpies, and all. And the creatures crossbred among themselves, and the composites interbred with other composites, producing things like the chimera—"

Bink turned to go. "I think your minute is up," he said. Then he froze. "They *what?*"

"The species mated with other species to create hybrids. Man-headed beasts, beast-headed men—"

"Impossible! Men can only mate with men. I mean with women. It would be unnatural to—"

"Xanth is an unnatural land, Bink. Magic makes remarkable things possible."

Bink saw that logic defied emotion. "But even if they did," he said with difficulty, "that still doesn't justify your conquering Xanth. What's past is past; a change of government won't—"

"I think this background does justify my assumption of power, Bink. Because the accelerated evolution and mutation produced by magic and interspecies miscegenation is changing Xanth. If we remain cut off from the Mundane world, there will in time be no human beings left—only crossbreeds. Only the constant influx of pure stock in the last millennium has enabled man to maintain his type—and there really are not too many human beings here now. Our population is diminishing—not through famine, disease, or war, but through the attrition of crossbreeding. When a man mates with a harpy, the result is not a manchild."

"No!" Bink cried, horrified. "No one would—would breed with a filthy harpy."

"Filthy harpy, perhaps not. But how about a clean, pretty harpy?" Trent inquired with a lift of his eyebrow. "They aren't all alike, you know; we see only their outcasts, not their fresh young—"

"No!"

"Suppose he had drunk from a love spring, accidentally—and the next to drink there was a harpy?"

"No. He—" But Bink knew better. A love spell provided an overriding compulsion. He remembered his experience with the love spring by the chasm, from which he had almost drunk, before seeing the griffin and the unicorn in their embrace. There had been a harpy there. He shuddered reminiscently.

"Have you ever been tempted by an attractive mermaid? Or a lady centaur?" Trent persisted.

"No!" But an insidious memory picture of the elegant firm mermaid breasts came to him. And Cherie,

the centaur who had given him a lift during the first leg
of his journey to see the Magician Humfrey—when he
touched her, had it really been accidental? She had
threatened to drop him in a trench, but she hadn't been
serious. She was a very nice filly. Rather, *person*. Hon-
esty compelled his reluctant correction. "Maybe."

"And surely there were others, less scrupulous than
you," Trent continued inexorably. "They might indulge,
in certain circumstances, might they not? Just for variety? Don't the boys of your village hang around the
centaur grounds on the sly, as they did in my day?"

Boys like Zink and Jama and Potipher, bullies and
troublemakers, who had caused ire in the centaur camp.
Bink remembered that too. He had missed the significance before. Of course they had gone to see the bare-
breasted centaur fillies, and if they caught one alone—

Bink knew his face was red. "What are you getting
at?" he demanded, trying to cover his embarrassment.

"Just this: Xanth must have had intercourse with—
sorry, bad word!—must have had contact with Mundania long before the date of our earliest records. Before
the Waves. Because only in Mundania is the human
species pure. From the time a man sets foot in Xanth,
he begins to change. He develops magic, and his children develop more magic, until some of them become
full-fledged Magicians —and if they remain, they inevitably become magic themselves. Or their descendants
do. Either by breaking down the natural barriers between species, or by evolving into imps, elves, goblins,
giants, trolls—did you get a good look at Humfrey?"

"He's a gnome," Bink said without thinking. Then:
"Oh, no!"

"He's a man, and a good one—but he's well along
the route to something else. He's at the height of his
magical powers now—but his children, if he ever has
any, may be true gnomes. I dare say he knows this,
which is why he won't marry. And consider Chameleon—she has no direct magic, because she has become
magic. This is the way the entire human populace of

Xanth will go, inevitably—unless there is a steady infusion of new blood from Mundania. *The Shield must come down!* The magic creatures of Xanth must be permitted to migrate outside, freely, there to revert slowly and naturally to their original species. New animals must come in."

"But—" Bink found himself fumbling with the horrors of these concepts. "If there was always—always an interchange before, what happened to the people who came thousands of years ago?"

"Probably there was some obstruction for a while, cutting off migration; Xanth could have been a true island for a thousand years or so, trapping the original prehistoric human settlers, so that they merged entirely with the existing forms and gave rise to the centaurs and other sports. It is happening again, under the Shield. Human beings must—"

"Enough," Bink whispered, fundamentally shocked. "I can't listen to any more."

"You will defuse the cherry bombs?"

Like a bolt of lightning, sanity returned. "No! I'm taking Chameleon and leaving—now."

"But you have to understand—"

"No." The Evil Magician was beginning to make sense. If Bink listened any more, he would be subverted—and Xanth would be lost. "What you suggest is an abomination. It can not be true. I can not accept it."

Trent sighed, with seemingly genuine regret. "Well, it was worth a try, though I did fear you would reject it. I still cannot permit you to destroy this castle—"

Bink braced himself to move, to get out of transformation range. Six feet—

Trent shook his head. "No need to flee, Bink; I shall not break the truce. I could have done that when I showed you the pictures, but I value my given word. So I must compromise. If you will not join me, I shall have to join you."

"What?" Bink, whose ears were almost closed to the Evil Magician's beguiling logic, was caught off guard.

"Spare Castle Roogna. Defuse the bombs. I will see you safely clear of these environs."

This was too easy. "Your word?"

"My word," Trent said solemnly.

"You can make the castle let us go?"

"Yes. This is another facet of what I have learned in these archives. I have only to speak the proper words to it, and it will even facilitate our departure."

"Your word," Bink repeated suspiciously. So far Trent had not broken it—yet what guarantee was there? "No tricks, no sudden change of mind."

"My word of honor, Bink."

What could he do? If the Magician wanted to break the truce, he could transform Bink into a tadpole now, then sneak up on Chameleon and transform her. And— Bink was inclined to trust him. "All right."

"Go and defuse your bombs. I will settle with Roogna."

Bink went. Chameleon met him with a glad little cry—and this time he was quite satisfied to accept her embrace. "Trent has agreed to get us out of here," he told her.

"Oh, Bink, I'm so glad!" she exclaimed, kissing him. He had to grab her hand to make sure she didn't drop the cherry bomb she still held.

She was growing lovelier by the hour. Her personality was not changing much, except as her diminishing intelligence caused her to be less complex, less suspicious. He liked that personality—and now, he had to admit, he liked her beauty, too. She was of Xanth, she was magic, she did not try to manipulate him for her private purposes—she was his type of girl.

But he knew that her stupidity would turn him off, just as her ugliness during the other phase had. He could live with neither a lovely moron nor an ugly genius. She was attractive only right now, while her intelli-

gence was fresh in his memory and her beauty was
manifest to his sight and touch. To believe otherwise
would be folly.

He drew away from her. "We have to remove the
bombs. Carefully," he said.

But what about the emotional bombs within him?

Chapter 14. Wiggle

The three of them walked out of Castle
Roogna without challenge. The portcullis was raised;
Trent had found the hoisting winch, oiled it, and
cranked it up with the aid of the magic inherent in its
mechanism. The ghosts appeared to bid them all fond
adieu; Chameleon cried at this parting, and even Bink
felt sad. He knew how lonely it would be for the
ghosts after these few days of living company, and he
even respected the indomitable castle itself. It did what
it had to do, much as Bink himself did.

They carried bags of fruits from the garden, and
wore functional clothing from the castle closets, stored
for eight hundred years without deterioration by means
of the potent ancient spells. They looked like royalty,
and felt like it too. Castle Roogna had taken good care
of them!

The gardens were magnificent. No storm erupted this
time. No trees made threatening gestures; instead, they
moved their limbs to be touched gently in the gesture of
parting friendship. No vicious animals appeared—and
no zombies.

In a surprisingly short time, the castle was out of
sight. "We are now beyond Roogna's environs," Trent

announced. "We must resume full alertness, for there is no truce with the true wilderness."

"We?" Bink asked. "Aren't you going back to the castle?"

"Not at this time," the Magician said.

Bink's suspicion was renewed. "Just exactly what did you say to that castle?"

"I said: 'I shall return—as King. Roogna shall rule Xanth again.' "

"And it believed that?"

Trent's gaze was tranquil. "Why should it doubt the truth? I could hardly win the crown while remaining confined in the wilderness."

Bink did not respond. The Evil Magician had never said he'd given up his plot to conquer Xanth, after all. He had merely agreed to see Bink and Chameleon safely out of the castle. He had done this. So now they were back where they had been—operating under a truce to get them all safely out of the remainder of the wilderness. After that—Bink's mind was blank.

The untamed forest did not take long to make its presence felt. The trio cut through a small glade girt with pretty yellow flowers—and a swarm of bees rose up. Angrily they buzzed the three, not actually touching or stinging, but sheering off abruptly at short range.

Chameleon sneezed. And sneezed again, violently. Then Bink sneezed too, and so did Trent.

"Sneeze bees!" the Magician exclaimed between paroxysms.

"Transform them!" Bink cried.

"I can't—achoo!—focus on them, my eyes are watering so. Achoo! Anyway, they are innocent creatures of the ah, aahh, ACHOOO!"

"Run, you dopes!" Chameleon cried.

They ran. As they cleared the glade, the bees left off and the sneezes stopped. "Good thing they weren't choke bees!" the Magician said, wiping his flowing eyes.

Bink agreed. A sneeze or two was okay, but a dozen

piled on top of one another was a serious matter. There had hardly been time to breathe.

Their noise had alerted others in the jungle. That was always the background threat here. There was a bellow, and the sound of big paws striking the ground. All too soon a huge fire-snorting dragon hove into view. It charged right through the sneeze glade, but the bees left it strictly alone. They knew better than to provoke any fire sneezes that would burn up their flowers.

"Change it! Change it!" Chameleon cried as the dragon oriented on her. Dragons seemed to have a special taste for the fairest maidens.

"Can't," Trent muttered. "By the time it gets within six feet, its fire will have scorched us all into roasts. It's got a twenty-foot blowtorch."

"You aren't much help," she complained.

"Transform me!" Bink cried with sudden inspiration.

"Good idea." Abruptly Bink was a sphinx. He retained his own head, but he had the body of a bull, wings of an eagle, and legs of a lion. And he was huge—he towered over the dragon. "I had no idea sphinxes grew this big," he boomed.

"Sorry—I forgot again," Trent said. "I was thinking of the legendary sphinx in Mundania."

"But the Mundanes don't have magic."

"This one must have wandered out from Xanth a long time ago. For thousands of years it has been stone, petrified."

"Petrified? What could scare a sphinx that size?" Chameleon wondered, peering up at Bink's monstrous face.

But there was business to attend to. "Begone, beast-ie!" Bink thundered.

The dragon was slow to adapt to the situation. It shot a jet of orange flame at Bink, scorching his feathers. The blast didn't hurt, but it was annoying. Bink reached out with one lion's paw and swiped at the dragon. It was a mere ripple of effort, but the creature was thrown sideways into a tree. A shower of rock nuts dropped on it from the angry tree. The dragon gave a single yelp of pain, doused its fire, and fled.

Bink circled around carefully, hoping he hadn't stepped on anyone. "Why didn't we think of this before?" he bellowed. "I can give you a ride, right to the edge of the jungle. No one will recognize us, and no creature will bother us!"

He squatted as low as possible, and Chameleon and Trent climbed up his tail to his back. Bink moved forward with a slow stride that was nevertheless faster than any man could run. They were on their way.

But not for long. Chameleon, bouncing around on the sphinx's horny-skinned back, decided she had to go to the bathroom. There was nothing to do but let her go. Bink hunched down so she could slide safely to the ground.

Trent took advantage of the break to stretch his legs. He walked around to Bink's huge face. "I'd transform you back, but it's really better to stick with the form until finished with it," he said. "I really have no concrete evidence that frequent transformations are harmful to the recipient, but it seems best not to gamble at this time. Since the sphinx is an intelligent life form, you aren't suffering intellectually."

"No, I'm okay," Bink agreed. "Better than ever, in fact. Can you guess this riddle? What walks on four legs in the morning, two legs at noon, and three in the evening?"

"I shall not answer," Trent said, looking startled. "In all the legends I've heard, some sphinxes committed suicide when the correct answers to their riddles were given. Those were the smaller type of sphinx, a different species—but I seem to have muddled the distinctions somewhat, and would not care to gamble on the absence of affinity."

"Uh, no," Bink said, chagrined. "I guess the riddle was from the mind of the sphinx, not me. I'm sure all sphinxes had a common ancestor, though I don't know the difference between one kind and another."

"Odd. Not about your ignorance of Mundane legends. About your riddle memory. You *are* the sphinx. I didn't move your mind into an existing body, for the original creatures have all been dead or petrified for millennia. I transformed you into a similar monster, a Bink-sphinx. But if you actually have sphinx memories, true sphinx memories—"

"There must be ramifications of your magic you don't comprehend," Bink said. "I wish I understood the real nature of magic—any magic."

"Yes, it is a mystery. Magic exists in Xanth, nowhere else. Why? What is its mechanism? Why does Xanth seem to be adjacent to *any* Mundane land, in geography, language, and culture? How is this magic, in all its multiple levels, transmitted from the geographic region to the inhabitants?"

"I have pondered that," Bink said. "I thought perhaps some radiation from the rock, or nutritional value of the soil—"

"When I am King I shall initiate a study program to determine the true story of Xanth's uniqueness."

When Trent was King. The project was certainly worthwhile—in fact, fascinating—but not at that price. For a moment Bink was tempted: with the merest swipe of his mighty forepaw he could squash the Evil Magician flat, ending the threat forever.

No. Even if Trent were not really his friend, Bink could not violate the truce that way. Besides, he didn't want to remain a monster all his life, physically or morally.

"The lady is taking her sweet time," Trent muttered.

Bink moved his ponderous head, searching for Chameleon. "She's usually very quick about that sort of thing. She doesn't like being alone." Then he thought of something else. "Unless she went looking for her spell—you know, to make her normal. She left Xanth in an effort to nullify her magic, and now that she's stuck back in Xanth, she wants some kind of countermagic. She's not very bright right now, and—"

Trent stroked his chin. "This is the jungle. I don't want to violate her privacy, but—"

"Maybe we'd better check for her."

"Umm. Well, I guess you can stand one more transformation," Trent decided. "I'll make you a bloodhound. That's a Mundane animal, a kind of dog, very good at sniffing out a trail. If you run into her doing something private—well, you'll only be an animal, not a human voyeur."

Abruptly Bink was a keen-nosed, floppy-eared, loose-faced creature, smell-oriented. He could pick up the lingering odor of anything—he was sure of that. He had never before realized how overwhelmingly important the sense of smell was. Strange that he had ever depended on any lesser sense.

Trent concealed their supplies in a mock tangle tree and faced about. "Very well, Bink; let's sniff her out." Bink understood him well enough, but could not reply, as this was not a speaking form of animal.

Chameleon's trail was so obvious it was a wonder Trent himself couldn't smell it. Bink put his nose to the ground—how natural that the head be placed so close to the primary source of information, instead of raised foolishly high as in Trent's case—and moved forward competently.

The route led around behind a bush and on into the wilderness. She *had* been lured away; in her present low ebb of intelligence, almost anything would fool her. Yet there was no consistent odor of any animal or plant she might have followed. That suggested magic. Worried, Bink woofed and sniffed on, the Magician following. A magic lure was almost certainly trouble.

But her trace did not lead into a tangle tree or gucktooth swamp or the lair of a wyvern. It wove intricately between these obvious hazards, bearing generally south, into the deepest jungle. Something obviously had led her, guiding her safely past all threats—but what, and where—and why?

Bink knew the essence, if not the detail: some will-o'-

the-wisp spell had beckoned her, tempting her ever forward, always just a little out of reach. Perhaps it had seemed to offer some elixir, some enchantment to make her normal—and so she had followed. It would lead her into untracked wilderness, where she would be lost, and leave her there. She would not survive long.

Bink hesitated. He had not lost the trail; that could never happen. There was something else.

"What is it, Bink?" Trent inquired. "I know she was following the *ignis fatuus*—but since we are close on her trail we should be able to—" He broke off, becoming aware of the other thing. It was a shuddering in the ground, as of some massive object striking it. An object weighing many tons.

Trent looked around. "I can't see it, Bink. Can you smell it?"

Bink was silent. The wind was wrong. He could not smell whatever was making that sound from this distance.

"Want me to transform you into something more powerful?" Trent asked. "I'm not sure I like this situation. First the swamp gas, now this strange pursuit."

If Bink changed, he would no longer be able to sniff out Chameleon's trail. He remained silent.

"Very well, Bink. But stay close by me; I can transform you into a creature to meet any emergency, but you have to be within range. I believe we're walking into extreme danger, or having it walk up on us." And he touched his sword.

They moved on—but the shuddering grew bolder, becoming a measured thumping, as of some ponderous animal. Yet they saw nothing. Now it was directly behind them, and gaining.

"I think we'd better hide," Trent said grimly. "Discretion is said to be the better part of valor."

Good idea. They circled a harmless beerbarrel tree and watched silently.

The thumping became loud. Extremely loud. The whole tree shook with the force of the measured vibrations. TRAMP, TRAMP, TRAMP! Small branches fell off the tree, and a leak sprang in the trunk. A thin jet of beer formed, splashing down under Bink's sensitive nose. He recoiled; even in the human state, he had never been partial to that particular beverage. He peered around the trunk—yet there was nothing.

Then at last something became visible. A branch crashed off a spikespire tree, splintering. Bushes waved violently aside. A section of earth subsided. More beer jetted from developing cracks in the trunk of their hiding place, filling the air with its malty fragrance. Still nothing tangible could be seen.

"It's invisible," Trent whispered, wiping beer off one hand. "An invisible giant."

Invisible! That meant Trent couldn't transform it. He had to see what he enchanted.

Together, silently, steeped in intensifying beer fumes, they watched the giant pass. Monstrous human footprints appeared, each ten feet long, sinking inches deep into the forest soil. TRAMP!—and the trees jumped and shuddered and shed their fruits and leaves and branches. TRAMP!—and an icecream bush disappeared, becoming a mere patina of flavored discoloration on the flat surface of the depression. TRAMP!—and a tangle tree hugged its tentacles about itself, frightened. TRAMP!—and a fallen trunk splintered across the five-foot width of the giant's print.

A stench washed outward, suffocatingly, like that of a stench-puffer or an overflowing outhouse in the heat of summer. Bink's keen nose hurt.

"I am not a cowardly man," Trent murmured. "But I begin to feel fear. When neither spell nor sword can touch an enemy . . ." His nose twitched. "His body odor alone is deadly. He must have feasted on rotten blivets for breakfast."

Bink didn't recognize that food. If that was the kind of fruit Mundane trees formed, he didn't want any.

Bink became aware that his own hackles were erect.

He had heard of such a monster, but taken it as a joke. An invisible—but not unsmellable—giant!

"If he is in proportion," Trent remarked, "that giant is some sixty feet tall. That would be impossible in Mundania, for purely physical reasons, square-cube law and such. But here—who can say nay to magic? He's looking over much of the forest, not through it." He paused, considering. "He evidently was not following us. Where is he going?"

Wherever Chameleon went, Bink thought. He growled.

"Right, Bink. We'd better track her down quickly, before she gets stepped on!"

They moved on, following what was now a well-trodden trail. Where the huge prints crossed Chameleon's traces, the scent of the giant was overlaid, so heavy that Bink's refined nose rebelled. He skirted the prints and picked up Chameleon's much milder scent on the far side.

Now a whistling descended from right angles to the path they were following. Bink looked up nervously—and saw a griffin angling carefully down between the trees.

Trent whipped out his sword and backed toward the black bole of an oilbarrel tree, facing the monster. Bink, in no condition to fight it, bared his teeth and backed toward the same protection. He was glad it wasn't a dragon; one really good tongue of fire could set off the tree explosively and wipe them all out. As it was, the overhanging branches would interfere with the monster's flight, forcing it to do combat on the ground. Still a chancy business, but it restricted the battle zone to two dimensions, which was a net advantage for Bink and Trent. Maybe if Bink distracted it, Trent could get safely within range to transform it.

The griffin settled to earth, folding its extensive glossy wings. Its coiled lion's tail twitched about, and its great front eagle's talons made streaks in the dirt. Its eagle head oriented on Trent. "Cawp?" it inquired. Bink could almost feel that deadly beak slicing through his flesh. A really healthy griffin could take on a medium-sized dragon in single combat, and this one was healthy. He nudged within transformation range.

"Follow the giant tracks, that way," Trent said to the monster. "Can't miss it."

"Bawp!" the griffin said. It turned about, oriented on the giant tracks, bunched its lion muscles, spread its wings, and launched itself into the air. It flew low-level along the channel the invisible giant had carved through the forest.

Trent and Bink exchanged startled glances. They had had a narrow escape; griffins were very agile in combat, and Trent's magic might not have taken effect in time. "It only wanted directions!" Trent said. "Must be something very strange up ahead. We'd better get there in a hurry. Be unfortunate if some part-human cult was having a ritual sacrifice."

Ritual sacrifice? Bink growled his confusion.

"You know," Trent said grimly. "Bloody altar, beautiful virgin maiden . . ."

"Rrowr!" Bink took off down the trail.

Soon they heard a commotion ahead. It was a medley of thumps, crashes, bellows, squawks, and crashes. "Sounds more like a battle than a party," Trent observed. "I really can't think what—"

At last they came in sight of the happening. They paused, amazed.

It was an astonishing assemblage of creatures, ranged in a large loose circle, facing in: dragons, griffins, manticoras, harpies, land serpents, trolls, goblins, fairies, and too many others to take in all at once. There were even a few human beings. It was not a free-for-all; all were intent on individual exercises, stamping their feet, biting at air, slamming their hooves together, and banging on rocks. In the interior of the circle, a number of creatures were dead or dying, ignored by the others. Bink could see and smell the blood, and hear their groans of agony. This was a battle, certainly—but where was the enemy? It was not the invisible giant; his prints were confined to one quadrant, not overlapping the territory of his neighbors.

"I thought I knew something about magic," Trent said, shaking his head. "But this is beyond my comprehension. These creatures are natural enemies, yet they ignore one another and do not feed on prey. Have they happened on a cache of loco?"

"Woof!" Bink exclaimed. He had spied Chameleon. She had two large flat stones in her hands and was holding them about a foot apart while she stared intently between them. Suddenly she clapped them together, with such force that they both fell out of her hands. She peered at the air above them, smiled enigmatically, picked them up, and repeated the procedure.

Trent followed Bink's gaze. "Loco!" he repeated. But Bink could smell no loco. "Her too. It must be an area spell. We'd better back off before we also fall prey to it."

They started to retreat, though Bink did not want to desert Chameleon. A grizzled old centaur cantered up. "Don't just meander around!" he snapped. "Get around to the north quadrant." He pointed. "We've suffered heavy losses there, and Bigfoot can't do it all. He can't even see the enemy. They'll break through any minute. Get some rocks; don't use your sword, fool!"

"Don't use my sword on what?" Trent demanded, with understandable ire.

"The wiggles, naturally. Cut one in half, all you have is two wiggles. You—"

"The wiggles!" Trent breathed, and Bink growled his own chagrin.

The centaur sniffed. "You been drinking?"

"Bigfoot's passage holed the beerbarrel tree we took refuge behind," Trent explained. "I thought the wiggles had been eradicated!"

"So thought we all," the centaur said. "But there's a healthy colony swarming here. You have to crush them or chew them or burn them or drown them. We can't afford to let a single one escape. Now get moving!"

Trent looked about. "Where are the stones?"

"Here. I've collected a pile." The centaur showed the way. "I knew I couldn't handle it myself, so I sent out will-o'-the-wisps to summon help."

Suddenly Bink recognized the centaur: Herman the Hermit. Exiled from the centaur community for obscenity almost a decade ago. Amazing that he had survived, here in the deepest wilderness—but centaurs were hardy folk.

Trent did not make the connection. The episode had happened after his exile. But he well knew the horror the wiggles represented. He picked up two good rocks from Herman's cache and strode toward the north quadrant.

Bink followed. He had to help too. If even one wiggle got away, there would at some later date be another swarming, perhaps not stopped in time. He caught up to the Magician. "Woof! Woof!" he barked urgently.

Trent looked straight ahead. "Bink, if I transform you here and now, the others will see, and know me for what I am. They may turn against me—and the siege against the wiggles will be broken. I think we can contain the swarm with our present creature-power; the centaur has organized the effort well. Your natural form would not be better equipped to wage this war than your present form. Wait until this is over."

Bink was not satisfied with all the arguments, but he seemed to have no choice. So he determined to make himself useful as he was. Maybe he could smell out the wiggles.

As they came up to their designated quadrant, a griffin gave a loud squawk and keeled over. It resembled the one they had directed here; it must have lost sight of its guiding will-o'-the-wisp. But all griffins looked and smelled pretty much alike to Bink. Not that it mattered, objectively; all creatures here had a common purpose. Still, he felt a certain identification. He ran to it, hoping the injury was not critical.

The creature was bleeding from a mortal wound. A wiggle had holed it through its lion's heart.

Wiggles traveled by sudden rushes along wiggle-sized magic tunnels they created. Then they paused to recuperate, or perhaps merely to contemplate philosophical matters; no one really knew the rationale of a wiggle. Therefore the killer wiggle that had gotten the griffin should be right about here. Bink sniffed and picked up its faint putrid odor. He oriented on it, and saw his first live wiggle.

It was a two-inch-long, loosely spiraled worm, hovering absolutely still in midair. It hardly looked like the menace it was. He barked, pointing his nose at it.

Trent heard him. He strode across with his two rocks. "Good job, Bink," he cried. He smashed the rocks together on the wiggle. As they came apart, the squished, dead hulk of the tiny monster dropped. One down!

Zzapp! "There's another!" Trent cried. "They tunnel through anything—even air—so we hear the collapse of the vacuum behind them. This one should be right about—there!" He smashed his stones together again, crunching the wiggle.

After that it was hectic. The wiggles were zapping determinedly outward, each in its own pattern. There was no way of telling how long they would freeze in place—seconds or minutes—or how far they would zap—inches or feet. But each wiggle went in the precise direction it had started, never shifting even a fraction, so it was possible to trace that line and locate it fairly quickly. If someone stood in front of a wiggle at the wrong time, he got zapped—and if the hole were through a vital organ, he died. But it was not feasible to stand behind a wiggle, for the closer in toward the source of the swarm one went, the more the wiggles were present. There were so many wiggles that a creature smashing one could be simultaneously holed by another. It was necessary to stand at the outer fringe of expansion and nab the leaders first.

The wiggles really seemed to be mindless, or at least indifferent to external things. Their preset wiggle courses holed anything—anything at all—in the way. If a person didn't locate a wiggle fast, it was too late, for the thing had zapped again. Yet it could be tricky to find a still wiggle, for it looked like a twisted stem from the side and a coiled stem from the end. It had to move to attract attention to itself—and then it might be too late to nab it.

"This is like standing in a firing range and catching the bullets as they pass," Trent muttered. That sounded like another Mundane allusion; evidently Mundane wiggles were called bullets.

The invisible giant operated beside Bink on the right, as his nose plainly told him. TRAMP!—and a wiggle was crushed out of existence. Maybe a hundred wiggles at once. But so was anything else that got underfoot. Bink didn't dare point out wiggles for Bigfoot; it would be his own death warrant. For all he knew, the giant was stomping randomly. It was as good a way as any.

On the left side, a unicorn operated. When it located a wiggle, it either crushed it between horn and hoof or closed its mouth over it and ground it to shreds with its equine teeth. This seemed to Bink to be a distasteful and hazardous mode of operation, because if it mistimed a wiggle—

Zzapp! A hole appeared in the unicorn's jaw. Blood dripped out. The creature made a single neigh of anguish—then trotted along the path of the zap. It located the wiggle and chomped down again, using the other side of its jaw.

Bink admired the unicorn's courage. But he had to get on with his own job. Two wiggles had just zapped within range. He pointed out the nearest for Trent, then ran to the other, afraid Trent would not reach it in time. His hound's teeth were made for cutting and tearing, not chewing, but maybe they would do. He bit down on the wiggle.

It squished unpleasantly. Its body was firm but not

really hard, and the juices squirted out. The taste was absolutely awful. There was some sort of acid—yecch! But Bink chewed carefully several times. to be sure of crushing it all; he knew that any unsquished fragment would zap away as a tiny wiggle, just as dangerous as the original. He spat out the remains. Surely his mouth would never be the same again.

Zzapp! Zzapp! Two more wiggles nearby. Trent heard one and went after it; Bink sought out the other. But even as they both oriented, a third *zzapp!* sounded between them. The pace was stepping up as the great internal mass of wiggles reached the perimeter. There were too many wiggles to keep up with! The complete swarm might number a million.

There was a deafening bellow from above. "OOAAOUGH!"

Herman the centaur galloped by. Blood trailed from a glancing wiggle-wound in his flank. "Bigfoot's hit!" he cried. "Get out of the way."

"But the wiggles are breaking out," Trent said.

"I know! We're taking heavy losses all around the perimeter. It's a bigger swarm than I thought, more dense in the center. We can't hold them anyway. We'll have to form a new containment circle, and hope that more help arrives in time. Save yourselves before the giant falls."

Good advice. A huge print appeared in Bink's territory as Bigfoot staggered. They got out of there.

"AAOOGAHH!" the giant bawled. Another print appeared, this time in toward the center of the circle. A wash of air passed as he fell, heavy-laden with the giant-aroma. "GOUGH-OOOAAAA-AAHH—" The sound arched down from a fifty-foot elevation toward the center of the wiggle swarm. The crash was like that of a petrified pine felled by magic. WHOOMP!

Herman, who had taken refuge behind the same jellybarrel tree as Trent and Bink, wiped a squirt of jelly out of his eye and shook his head sadly. "There goes a big, big man! Little hope now of containing the menace. We're disorganized and short of personnel, and the strength of the enemy is sweeping outward. Only a hurricane could get them all, and the weather's dry." Then he looked again at Trent. "You seem familiar. Aren't you—yes. Twenty years ago—"

Trent raised his hand. "I regret the necessity—" he began.

"No, wait, Magician," Herman said. "Transform me not. I will not betray your secret. I could have bashed your head in with my foot just now, had I intended you ill. Know you not why I was exiled from my kind?"

Trent paused. "I know not, for I do not know you."

"I am Herman the Hermit, punished for the obscenity of practicing magic. By summoning will-o'-the-wisps. No centaur is supposed to—"

"You mean centaurs can practice magic?"

"They could—if they would. We centaurs have existed so long in Xanth we have become a natural species. But magic is considered—"

"Obscene," Trent finished, voicing Bink's thought. So magic intelligent creatures could do magic; their inability was cultural, not genetic. "So you became a hermit in the wilderness."

"Correct. I share your humiliation of exile. But now we have a need more important than privacy. Use your talent to abolish the wiggle menace!"

"I can't transform all the wiggles. I must focus on one at a time, and there are too many—"

"Not that. We must cauterize them. I had hoped my wisps would lead in a salamander—"

"A salamander," Trent exclaimed. "Of course! But even so, the fire could not spread fast enough to burn out all the wiggles, and if it did, the fire itself would then be unstoppable, a greater menace than the wiggles. We'd merely exchange one devastation for another."

"Not so. There are certain restrictions on salamanders, and with foresight they can be controlled. I was thinking of—"

Zzapp! A hole appeared in the trunk of the tree.

Jelly oozed out like purple blood. Bink dashed out to crunch the wiggle, who fortunately had passed between them and injured no one. *Yuch!* That taste!

"They're inside the trees," Trent said. "Some are bound to land within things. Impossible to catch those ones."

Herman trotted over to a nondescript bush. He yanked several vines from it. "Salamander weed," he explained. "I have become a fair naturalist in my years of isolation. This is the one thing a salamander can't burn. It represents a natural barrier to the fire; eventually the flames are stopped by proliferating weeds. If I make a harness of this, I can carry a salamander around in a great circle just beyond the infestation—"

"But how to stop the fire before it destroys most of Xanth?" Trent asked. "We can't wait on the chance of the weeds; half of the wilderness could be ravaged before it burns itself out. We can't possibly clear a firebreak in time." He paused. "You know, that must be why your wisps summoned no salamanders. This thick forest would naturally have a salamander-repulsion spell to keep them away, because such a fire would quickly prejudice this whole environment. Still, if we start a fire—"

Herman held up one strong hand in a halt gesture. He was an old centaur, but still strong; the arm was magnificently muscled. "You know how salamander fire burns only in the direction it starts? If we form a circle of inward-burning magic fire—"

"Suddenly I comprehend!" Trent exclaimed. "It will burn itself out at the center." He looked around. "Bink?"

What else? Bink did not relish being a salamander, but anything was better than yielding Xanth to the wiggles. No person or creature would be safe if the swarms got out of control again. He came up.

Suddenly he was a small, bright amphibian, about five inches from nose to tail. Once more he remembered the omen he had seen back at the outset of this adventure: the chameleon lizard had also become a salamander—before being swallowed up by the moth hawk. Had his time finally come?

The ground he stood on burst into flame. The underlying sand would not burn, but all the material on top of it was fuel. "Climb in here," Herman said, holding a pouch he had cleverly formed of vines. "I will carry you in a great left circle. Be sure you direct your fire inward. To the left." And to make quite sure Bink understood, he pointed with his left hand.

Well, such a limit wouldn't be much fun, but—

Bink climbed into the net. The centaur picked it up and dangled it at arm's length, as well he might, for Bink was *hot*. Only the frustrating salamander-weed vines prevented him from really tearing loose.

Herman galloped. "Clear out! Clear out!" he cried with amazing volume to the straggling, wounded creatures still trying to stop the wiggles. "We're burning them out. Salamander!" And to Bink: "To the left! To the *left!*"

Bink had hoped he'd forgotten about that restriction. Ah, well, half a burn was better than none. From him a sheet of flame erupted. Everything it touched burst up anew, burning savagely. Branches, leaves, whole green trees, even the carcasses of fallen monsters—the flame consumed all. That was the nature of salamander fire— it burned magically, heedless of other conditions. No rainstorm could put it out, for water itself would burn. Everything except rock and earth—and salamander weed. Curse the stuff!

Now a hasty exodus developed. Dragons, griffins, harpies, goblins, and men scrambled out of the path of the terrible fire. Every movable form cleared out— except the wiggles, which proceeded as mindlessly as ever.

The flames spread hungrily up the great trees, consuming them with awesome rapidity. A tangle tree writhed in agony as it was incinerated, and the smell of burning beer and jelly spread. Already a swath of

scorched earth was developing, sand and ashes marking
the path they had traveled. Glorious!

Zzapp! Bink dropped to the ground. A wiggle, striking with the luck of the mindless, had holed Herman's
right hand. Good. Now Bink could get out of the net
and really go to work, setting the most magnificent
blaze in all salamander history.

But the centaur looped about and grabbed the net
with his left hand. The flames touched his fingers momentarily, and the tips shivered into ash, but he hung
on with the stubs. Damn the courage of the Hermit!
"On!" Herman cried, resuming forward speed. "To the
left."

Bink had to obey. Angrily he shot forth an especially
intense flame, hoping the Hermit would drop him again,
but it didn't work. The centaur galloped on, widening
the circle a bit, since the wiggle radius had evidently
expanded further. It was useless to burn where the wiggles had been, or where they would be; the flame had to
be where they were now. Any that zapped past the sheet
of flame and paused in an already burned spot would
survive. That made it a tricky calculation. But it was
their only chance.

The circle was almost complete; the centaur could
really move. They raced up to the broadening swath of
their starting point, pausing to let a few trapped monsters get out before being doomed. The last to go was the
great land serpent, a hundred feet of slithering torso.

Trent was there, organizing the remaining animals
into a cleanup detail to intercept any few wiggles already outside the circle of fire. Now that the great majority of wiggles were being eliminated, it was feasible
to go after those few individually. Every last one had to
be squished.

The fire closed in on the original wiggle hive. There
was a deafening groan. "AAOOGAAH!" Something
stirred invisibly.

"Bigfoot!" Trent exclaimed. "He's still alive in
there."

"I thought he was dead," Herman said, horrified. "We've already closed the circle; we can't let him out."

"He was riddled through the legs, so he fell—but he wasn't dead," Trent said. "The fall must have knocked him out for a while." He stared into the leaping flames, now outlining the form of a gargantuan man lying prone, stirring at the peripheries. The odor was of roasting garbage. "Too late now."

The doomed giant thrashed about. Flaming branches flew wide. Some landed in the jungle beyond the circle. "Catch those flames!" the centaur cried. "They can start a forest fire."

But no one could quench or move or even contain the flames. No one except Herman himself, with his weed net. He dumped Bink out and galloped toward the nearest, which was dangerously close to an oilbarrel tree.

Trent gestured hastily, and Bink was his human self again. He leaped out of the smoldering ground where his salamander self had touched. What power the Evil Magician had; he could destroy Xanth any time just by making a dozen salamanders.

Bink blinked—and saw Chameleon chasing a wiggle between the prongs of magic fire formed by thrown brands. She was too intent or too stupid to realize the danger!

He ran after her. "Chameleon! Turn back!" She paid no heed, faithful to her chore. He caught up and spun her about. "The fire's getting the wiggles. We have to get out of here."

"Oh," she said faintly. Her once-fancy dress was ragged, and dirt smudged her face, but she was excruciatingly lovely.

"Come on." He took her by the hand and drew her along.

But a determined tongue of fire had crossed behind them. They were trapped in a closing island.

The omen! Now at last it struck—at both Chameleon and him.

Herman leaped over the tongue, a splendid figure of a centaur. "Up on my back," he cried.

Bink wrapped his arms about Chameleon and heaved her up onto the Hermit's back. She was wondrously supple, slender of waist and expansive of thigh. Not that he had any business noticing such things at the moment. But his position behind her as she slid on her belly onto the centaur made the thoughts inevitable. He gave her graceful posterior one last ungraceful shove, getting her balanced, then scrambled up himself.

Herman started walking, then running, ready to hurdle the fire with his double burden.

Zzapp! A wiggle, close by.

The centaur staggered. "I'm hit!" he cried. Then he righted himself, made a convulsion of effort, and leaped.

He fell short. His front legs buckled, and the rear ones were in the flame. Bink and Chameleon were thrown forward, landing on either side of the human torso. Herman grabbed each by an arm, and with a surge of centaur strength shoved both on beyond the danger zone.

Trent charged up. "Hermit, you're burning!" he cried. "I will transform you—"

"No," Herman said. "I am holed through the liver. I am done for. Let the clean fire take me." He grimaced. "Only, to abate the agony quickly—your sword, sir." And he pointed at his neck.

Bink would have temporized, pretending misunderstanding, trying to delay the inevitable. The Evil Magician was more decisive. "As you require," Trent said. Suddenly his blade was in his hand, flashing in an arc—and the centaur's noble head flew off the body, to land upright on the ground just beyond the flame.

Bink stared, aghast. He had never before witnessed such a cold-blooded killing.

"I thank you," the head said. "You abated the agony most efficiently. Your secret dies with me." The centaur's eyes closed.

Herman the Hermit had really wanted it that way. Trent had judged correctly and acted instantly. Bink himself would have bungled it.

"There was a creature I would have been proud to have taken for a friend," Trent said sadly. "I would have saved him had it been within my power."

Little lights danced in close, centering on that dead head. At first Bink supposed they were sparks, but they did not actually burn. "The will-o'-the-wisps," Trent murmured. "Paying their last respects."

The lights dispersed, taking with them their vague impression of wonders barely glimpsed and joys never quite experienced. The fire consumed the body, then the head, and swept on into an already-burned area. Most of the remaining flame was now in the center of the circle, where the invisible giant no longer thrashed.

Trent raised his voice. "All creatures silent, in respect for Herman the Hermit, wronged by his own kind, who has died in defense of Xanth. And for Bigfoot and all the other noble creatures who perished similarly."

A hush fell on the throng. The silence became utter; not even an insect hummed. One minute, two minutes, three—no sound. It was a fantastic assemblage of monsters pausing with bowed heads in deference to the ones who had labored so valiantly against the common enemy. Bink was profoundly moved; never again would he think of the creatures of the magic wild as mere animals.

At last Trent lifted his eyes again. "Xanth is saved, thanks to Herman—and to you all," he announced. "The wiggles are exterminated. Disperse, with our gratitude, and go with pride. There is no more important service you could have performed, and I salute you."

"But some wiggles may have escaped," Bink protested in a whisper.

"No. None escaped. The job was well done."

"How can you be so sure?"

"I heard no zaps during the silence. No wiggle sits still longer than three minutes."

Bink's mouth dropped open. The silence of respect and mourning, sincere as it had been, had also been the verification that the menace had indeed been abated. Bink would never have thought of that himself. How competently Trent had assumed the difficult and demanding chore of leadership, when the centaur died. And without betraying his secret.

The assorted monsters dispersed peaceably, operating under the tacit truce of this effort. Many were wounded, but they bore their pain with the same dignity and courage Herman had, and did not snap at one another. The great land serpent slithered by, and Bink counted half a dozen holes along its length, but it did not pause. The serpent, like the others, had come to do what had to be done—but it would be as dangerous as ever in future encounters.

"Shall we resume our journey?" Trent inquired, glancing for the last time across the flat bare disk of ashes.

"We'd better," Bink said. "I think the fire is dying out now."

Abruptly he was the sphinx again, half as tall as the invisible giant and far more massive. Apparently Trent had decided multiple transformations were safe. Trent and Chameleon boarded, and he retraced the path to their cache of supplies. "And no more comfort breaks," Bink muttered in a boom. Someone chuckled.

Chapter 15. Duel

They crested a forest ridge—and abruptly the wilderness ended. The blue fields of a bluejean plantation spread out before them: civilization.

Trent and Chameleon dismounted. Bink had trudged all night, tirelessly, sleeping while his great legs worked by themselves. Nothing had bothered the party; even the fiercest things of the wilderness had some caution. Now it was mid-morning, a fine clear day. He felt good.

Suddenly he was a man again—and he still felt good. "I guess this is where we part company at last," he said.

"I'm sorry we could not agree on more things," Trent said, putting out his hand. "But I think separation will abate those differences. It has been a pleasure to know you both."

Bink took the hand and shook it, feeling oddly sad. "I suppose by definition and talent you *are* the Evil Magician—but you helped save Xanth from the wiggles, and in person you have been a friend. I can not approve your designs, but . . ." He shrugged. "Farewell, Magician."

"Same here," Chameleon said, flashing Trent a breathtaking smile that more than made up for the inelegance of her speech.

"Well, isn't this cozy!" a voice said.

All three whirled defensively—but there was nothing to see. Nothing but the ripening jeans on their green vines, and the forbidding fringe of the jungle.

Then a swirl of smoke formed, thickening rapidly. "A genie," Chameleon said.

297

But now Bink recognized the forming shape. "No such luck," he said. "That's the Sorceress Iris, mistress of illusion."

"Thank you for the elegant introduction, Bink," the now-solid-seeming woman said. She stood among the jeans, ravishing in a low-cut gown—but Bink felt no temptation now. Chameleon, at the full flush of her beauty, had a natural if magical allure that the Sorceress could not duplicate by her artifice.

"So this is Iris," Trent said. "I knew of her before I left Xanth, since she is of my generation, but we never actually met. She is certainly skilled at her talent."

"It happened I had no hankering for transformation," Iris said, giving him an arch glance. "You left quite a trail of toads and trees and bugs and things. I thought you had been exiled."

"Times change, Iris. Didn't you observe us in the wilderness?"

"As a matter of fact, I didn't. That jungle is a dreary place, with quite a number of counter-illusion spells, and I had no idea you were back in Xanth. I don't believe anyone knows, not even Humfrey. It was the huge sphinx that attracted my attention, but I could not be sure you were involved until I saw you transform it into Bink. I knew he had been exiled recently, so something was definitely amiss. How did you pass the Shield?"

"Times change," Trent repeated enigmatically.

"Yes they do," she said, nettled at being put off. She looked at each of them in turn. Bink had not realized she could project her illusions so effectively, so far afield, or perceive things from such distances. The ramifications of the powers of Magicians and Sorceresses were amazing. "Now shall we get down to business?"

"Business?" Bink asked blankly.

"Don't be naive," Trent muttered. "The bitch means blackmail."

So it was strong magic opposing strong magic. Maybe

they would cancel each other out, and Xanth would be safe after all. Bink had not anticipated this.

Iris looked at him. "Are you sure you won't reconsider my prior offer, Bink?" she inquired. "I could arrange things so that your exile would be revoked. You could still be King. The time is ripe. And if you really prefer the innocent look in women—" Suddenly another Chameleon stood before him, as beautiful as the real one. "Anything you desire, Bink—and with a mind, too."

That last little dig at the girl's stupid phase annoyed him. "Go jump in the Gap," Bink said.

The figure changed back to Iris-beautiful. It faced Chameleon. "I don't know you, my dear, but it would be a shame to see you fed to a dragon."

"A dragon!" Chameleon cried, frightened.

"That is the customary penalty for violating exile. When I notify the authorities, and they put their magic-spotters on you three and verify your status—"

"Leave her alone!" Bink said sharply.

Iris ignored him. "Now if you could only persuade your friend to cooperate," she continued to Chameleon, "you could escape that horrible fate—those dragons really like to chew on pretty limbs—and be beautiful all the time." Iris had claimed not to know Chameleon, but she had evidently figured things out. "I can make you seem as lovely in your off phase as you are right now."

"You can?" Chameleon asked, excited.

"The deceptions of the Sorceress are apt," Trent murmured to Bink, obviously with double meaning.

"The truth is not in her," Bink murmured back. "Only illusion."

"A woman is as a woman seems," Iris told Chameleon. "If she looks lovely to the eye and feels lovely to the touch, she is lovely. That is all men care about."

"Don't listen to her," Bink said. "The Sorceress just wants to use you."

"Correction," Iris said. "I want to use *you*, Bink. I bear no malice to your girlfriend—so long as you cooperate with me. I am not a jealous woman. All I want is power."

"No!" Bink cried.

Chameleon, following his lead uncertainly, echoed: "No."

"Now you, Magician Trent," Iris said. "I have not been watching you long, but you seem to be a man of your word, at least when it suits your convenience. I could make you a formidable Queen—or I can have the palace guards on the way to kill you in five minutes."

"I would transform the guards," Trent said.

"From longbow range? Perhaps," she said, raising a fair eyebrow skeptically. "But I doubt you could be King after such an incident. The whole land of Xanth would be out to kill you. You might transform a great number—but when would you sleep?"

Telling blow! The Evil Magician had been caught before when he slept. If he were exposed before he could surround himself with loyal troops, he would not be able to survive.

But why should that bother Bink? If the Sorceress betrayed the Evil Magician, Xanth would be secure— through no action of Bink's. His own hands would be clean. He would have betrayed neither his country nor his companion. He should simply stay out of it.

"Well, I might transform animals or people into my own likeness," Trent said. "It would then be very hard for the patriots to know whom to kill."

"Wouldn't work," Iris said. "No imitation will fool a magic-spotter, once it fixes on its subject."

Trent considered. "Yes, it would be very difficult for me to prevail in such circumstance. Considering this, I believe I should accept your offer, Sorceress. There are some details to work out, of course—"

"You can't!" Bink cried, shocked.

Trent gazed at him, affecting mild perplexity. "It seems reasonable to me, Bink. I desire to be King; Iris desires to be Queen. There is power enough to share, that way. Perhaps we could define spheres of influence.

It would be a marriage of pure convenience—but I have no present interest in any other kind of liaison."

"Well, now," Iris said, smiling victoriously.

"Well nothing!" Bink cried, conscious that his prior decision to stay clear of this matter was being abrogated. "You're both traitors to Xanth. I won't permit it."

"You won't permit it!" Iris laughed indelicately. "Who the hell do you think you are, you spell-less twerp?"

Obviously, her true attitude toward him had come out now that she had found another avenue for her ambition.

"Do not treat him lightly," Trent told her. "Bink is a Magician, in his fashion."

Bink felt a sudden, well-nigh overwhelming flood of gratitude for this word of support. He fought it off, knowing he could not afford to permit flattery or insult to sway him from what he knew was right. The Evil Magician could spin a web of illusion with mere words that rivaled anything the Sorceress could do with magic. "I'm no Magician; I'm just loyal to Xanth. To the proper King."

"To the senile has-been who exiled you?" Iris demanded. "He can't even raise a dust devil any more. He's sick now; he'll soon be dead anyway. That's why the time to act is now. The throne must go to a Magician."

"To a *good* Magician!" Bink retorted. "Not to an evil transformer, or a power-hungry, sluttish mistress . . ." He paused, tempted to end it there, but knew that wouldn't be entirely honest. "Of illusion."

"You dare address me thus?" Iris screamed, sounding much like a harpy. She was so angry that her image wavered into smoke. "Trent, change him into a stinkbug and step on him."

Trent shook his head, suppressing a smile. He obviously had no emotional attachment to the Sorceress, and shared a masculine appreciation for the insulting pause Bink had made. Iris had, just now, shown them all how ready she was to sell her illusion-enhanced body for power. "We operate under truce."

"Truce? Nonsense!" Her smoke now became a column of fire, signifying her righteous wrath. "You don't need him any more. Get rid of him."

Again, Bink saw how she would have treated him after he had helped her achieve power and she no longer needed him.

Trent was adamant. "If I were to break my word to him, Iris, how could you trust my word to you?"

That sobered her—and impressed Bink. There was a subtle but highly significant difference between these two magic-workers. Trent was a man, in the finest sense of the word.

Iris was hardly pleased. "I thought your truce was only until you got out of the wilderness."

"The wilderness is not defined solely by the jungle," Trent muttered.

"What?" she demanded.

"That truce would be worthless if I abridged its spirit thus suddenly," Trent said. "Bink and Chameleon and I will part company, and with luck we shall not meet again."

The man was being more than fair, and Bink knew he should accept the situation and depart—now. Instead, his stubbornness drove him toward disaster. "No," he said. "I can't just go away while you two plot to conquer Xanth."

"Now, Bink," Trent said reasonably. "I never deceived you about my ultimate objective. We always knew our purposes were divergent. Our truce covered only our interpersonal relation during the period of mutual hazard, not our long-range plans. I have pledges to fulfil, to my Mundane army, to Castle Roogna, and now to the Sorceress Iris. I am sorry you disapprove, for I want your approval very much, but the conquest of Xanth is and always was my mission. Now I ask you to part from me with what grace you can muster, for I have high respect for your motive, even though I feel the larger situation places you in error."

Again Bink felt the devastating allure of Trent's golden tongue. He could find no flaw in the reasoning. He had no chance to overcome the Magician magically, and was probably outclassed intellectually. But morally—he had to be right. "Your respect means nothing if you have no respect for the traditions and laws of Xanth."

"A most telling response, Bink. I do have respect for these things—yet the system seems to have gone astray, and must be corrected, lest disaster overtake us all."

"You talk of disaster from Mundania; I fear the disaster of the perversion of our culture. I must oppose you, in whatever way I can."

Trent seemed perplexed. "I don't believe you can oppose me, Bink. Whatever your strong magic is, it has never manifested tangibly. The moment you acted against me, I should have to transform you. I don't want to do that."

"You have to get within six feet," Bink said. "I could strike you down with a thrown rock."

"See?" Iris said. "He's within range now, Trent. Zap him!"

Yet the Magician desisted. "You actually wish to fight me, Bink? Directly, physically?"

"I don't wish to. I have to."

Trent sighed. "Then the only honorable thing to do is to terminate our truce with a formal duel. I suggest we define the locale of combat and the terms. Do you wish a second?"

"A second, a minute, an hour—whatever it takes," Bink said. He tried to quell the shaking he felt in his legs; he was afraid, and knew he was being a fool, yet he could not back down.

"I meant another person to back you up, to see that the terms are honored. Chameleon, perhaps."

"I'm with Bink!" Chameleon said immediately. She

could comprehend only a fraction of the situation, but there was no question of her loyalty.

"Well, perhaps the concept of seconds is foreign here," Trent said. "Suppose we establish an area along the wilderness border, a mile deep into the forest and a mile across. One square mile, approximately, or as far as a man might walk in fifteen minutes. And it shall be until dark today. Neither of us shall leave this area until that time, and if the issue is undecided by then, we shall declare the contest null and separate in peace. Fair enough?"

The Evil Magician seemed so reasonable—and that made Bink unreasonable. "To the death!" he said— and immediately wished he hadn't. He knew the Magician would not kill him unless he were forced to; he would transform Bink into a tree or other harmless form of life and let him be. First there had been Justin Tree; now there would be Bink Tree. Perhaps people would come to rest under his shade, to have picnic lunches, to make love. Except that now it had to be death. He had a vision of a fallen tree.

"To the death," Trent said sadly. "Or surrender." Thus he neatly abated Bink's exaggeration without hurting his pride; he made it seem as if the Magician arranged the loophole for himself, not for Bink. How was it possible for a man so wrong to seem so right?

"All right," Bink said. "You go south, I'll go north, into the forest. In five minutes we'll stop and turn and start."

"Fair enough," the Magician agreed. He held out his hand again, and Bink shook it.

"You should get out of the duel zone," Bink told Chameleon.

"No! I'm with you," she insisted. She might be stupid, but she was loyal. Bink could no more blame her for that than he could blame Trent for pursuing power. Yet he had to dissuade her.

"It wouldn't be fair," he said, realizing that it would

be futile to try to scare her by thought of the consequences. "Two against one. You have to go."

She was adamant. "I'm too dumb to go by myself."

Ouch! How true.

"Let her go with you," Trent said. "It really will make no difference."

And that seemed logical.

Bink and Chameleon set out, angling into the jungle to the northwest. Trent angled southwest. In moments the Magician was out of sight. "We'll have to figure out a plan of attack," Bink said. "Trent has been a perfect gentleman, but the truce is over, and he will use his power against us. We have to get him before he gets us."

"Yes."

"We'll have to collect stones and sticks, and maybe dig a pit for a deadfall."

"Yes."

"We have to prevent him from getting close enough to use his power of transformation."

"Yes."

"Don't just say yes!" he snapped. "This is serious business. Our lives are at stake."

"I'm sorry. I know I'm awful dumb right now."

Bink was immediately sorry. Of course she was stupid now—that was her curse. And he might be exaggerating the case; Trent might simply avoid the issue by departing, making no fight at all. Thus Bink would have made his stand, and have a moral victory—and have changed nothing. If so, Bink was the dumb one.

He turned to Chameleon to apologize— and rediscovered the fact that she was radiantly beautiful. She had seemed lovely before, in comparison with Fanchon and Dee, but now she was as he had first met her, as Wynne. Had it really been only a month ago? Now she was no stranger, though. "You're great just the way you are, Chameleon."

"But I can't help you plan. I can't do anything. You don't like stupid people."

"I like beautiful girls," he said. "And I like smart girls. But I don't trust the combination. I'd settle for an ordinary girl, except she'd get dull after a while. Sometimes I want to talk with someone intelligent, and sometimes I want to—" He broke off. Her mind was like that of a child; it really wasn't right to impose such concepts on her.

"What?" she asked, turning her eyes upon him. They had been black in her last beauty phase; now they were dark green. They could have been any color, and she would still be lovely.

Bink knew his chances of surviving the day were less than even, and his chances of saving Xanth worse than that. He was afraid—but he also had a heightened awareness of life right now. And of loyalty. And of beauty. Why hide what was suddenly in his conscious mind, however long it had developed subconsciously? "To make love," he concluded.

"That I can do," she said, her eyes brightening with comprehension. How well she understood, or on what level, Bink hesitated to ponder.

Then he was kissing her. It was wonderful.

"But, Bink," she said, when she had a chance. "I won't stay beautiful."

"That's the point," he said. "I like variety. I would have trouble living with a stupid girl all the time—but you aren't stupid all the time. Ugliness is no good for all the time—but you aren't ugly all the time either. You are—variety. And that is what I crave for the long-term relationship—and what no other girl can provide."

"I need a spell—" she said.

"No! You don't need any spell, Chameleon. You're fine just the way you are. I love you."

"Oh, Bink!" she said.

After that they forgot about the duel.

Reality intruded all too soon. "There you are!" Iris exclaimed, appearing over their makeshift bower. "Tut-tut! What have you two been doing?"

Chameleon hastily adjusted her dress. "Something

you wouldn't understand," she said with purely female insight.

"No? It hardly matters. Sex is unimportant." The Sorceress put her hands to her mouth in a megaphone gesture. "Trent! They're over here."

Bink dived for her—and passed through her image cleanly. He took a tumble on the forest floor. "Silly boy," Iris said. "You can't touch me."

Now they heard the Evil Magician coming through the forest. Bink looked frantically for some weapon, but saw only the great boles of the trees. Sharp stones might have been used against these trees—therefore all stones had been magically eliminated. Some other area might have potential weapons, but not this highly competitive wilderness, this fringe near the farms that were always in need of more cleared land.

"I have ruined you!" Chameleon cried. "I knew I shouldn't have—"

Shouldn't have made love? True enough, in one sense. They had wasted vital time, loving instead of warring. Yet there might never be another chance. "It was worth it," Bink said. "We'll have to run."

They started to run. But the image of the Sorceress appeared in front of them. "Here, Trent!" she cried again. "Cut them off before they get away."

Bink realized that they could get nowhere so long as Iris dogged them. There was no place they could hide, no surprise they could prepare, no strategic placement possible. Inevitably Trent would run them down.

Then his eye fell on an object Chameleon still carried. It was the hypnotic gourd. If he could get Trent to look into that unwittingly—

Now the Magician came into sight. Bink gently took the gourd from Chameleon. "See if you can distract him until I get close enough to shove this in his face," he said. He held the gourd behind his back. Iris probably did not realize its significance, and she would be able to do nothing once Trent was out of commission.

"Iris," the Magician called loudly. "This is supposed

to be a fair duel. If you interfere again, I shall consider our understanding terminated."

The Sorceress started to react with anger, then thought better of it. She vanished.

Trent stopped a dozen paces from Bink. "I regret this complication. Shall we start over?" he inquired gravely.

"We'd better," Bink agreed. The man was so damned sure of himself, he could give away any advantage. Maybe he wanted to wrap it up with a completely clear conscience—such as it was. But by so doing, Trent had unknowingly saved himself from possible disaster. Bink doubted he would have another opportunity to use the gourd.

They separated again. Bink and Chameleon fled deeper into the forest—and almost into the quivering arms of a tangle tree. "If only we could trick him into running into that," Bink said—but found he didn't mean it. He had somehow gotten himself into a duel he really did not want to win—and could not afford to lose. He was as dumb as Chameleon—only somewhat more complicated about it.

They spotted a noose-loop bush. The loops were up to eighteen inches in diameter, but would contract suddenly to a quarter of that when any careless animal put its head or limb through. Their fibers were so tight that only a knife or specific counterspell could alleviate the bind. Even when separated from the bush, the loops retained their potency for several days, gradually hardening in place. Careless or unlucky animals could lose feet or lives, and no creature ever bothered a noose-loop plant twice.

Chameleon shied away, but Bink paused. "It is possible to harvest and carry such loops," he said. "At the North Village we use them to seal packages tight. The trick is to touch them only on the outside. We can take some of these and lay them on the ground where Trent has to step. Or we can throw them at him. I doubt he can transform them once they're detached from the living plant. Can you throw pretty well?"

"Yes."

He walked toward the bush—and spied another wilderness threat. "Look—a nest of ant lions!" he exclaimed. "If we can put them on his scent . . ."

Chameleon looked at the foot-long, lion-headed ants and shuddered. "Do we have to?"

"I wish we didn't," Bink said. "They wouldn't actually eat him; he'd transform them first. But they might keep him so busy that we could overpower him. If we don't stop him somehow, he's very likely to conquer Xanth."

"Would that be bad?"

It was just one of her stupid questions; in her smart phase, or even her normal phase, she would never have asked it. But it bothered him. Would the Evil Magician really be worse than the present King? He put the question aside. "It is not for us to decide. The Council of Elders will choose the next King. If the crown starts being available by conquest or conspiracy, we'll be back in the days of the Waves, and no one will be secure. The law of Xanth must determine the possession of the crown."

"Yes," she agreed. Bink had surprised himself with an excellent statement of the situation, but of course it was beyond her present understanding.

Still, the notion of throwing Trent to the ant lions bothered him, so he went on searching. In the depths of his mind a parallel search was manifesting, concerning the morality of the present government of Xanth. Suppose Trent were right about the necessity of reopening Xanth to migration from outside? According to the centaurs, the human population had slowly declined during the past century; where had those people gone? Were new part-human monsters being formed even now, by magically enabled interbreeding? The very thought was like being entangled in a noose-loop bush; its ramifications were appalling. Yet it seemed to be so. Trent, as King, would change that situation. Was the evil of the Waves worse than the alternative? Bink was unable to form a conclusion.

They came to a large river. Bink had forded this in his sphinx stage, hardly noticing it, but now it was a deadly barrier. Little ripples betrayed the presence of lurking predators, and eerie mists played about the surface. Bink flipped a clod of mud into the water, and it was intercepted, just before it struck, by a giant crablike claw. The rest of the monster never showed; Bink was unable to determine whether it was a mercrab or a super crayfish or merely a disembodied claw. But he was sure he did not want to swim here.

There were a few round stones at the edge. The river did not have the same reason to be wary of stones that the trees did, but it was best to be careful. Bink poked at them gingerly with his staff to be sure they weren't magic lures; fortunately they weren't. He poked experimentally at a pleasant nearby water lily, and the flower snapped three inches off the tip of his pole. His caution was justified.

"All right," he said when they had a fair reserve of stones. "We'll try to ambush him. We'll arrange noose-loops across his likely path of retreat, and cover them over with leaves, and you can throw your loops at him and I'll throw stones. He'll duck the stones and loops, but he'll have to watch us both to do it, while retreating, so he may step into a hidden loop. It'll bind on his foot, and he'll be vulnerable while he tries to get it off, and maybe we can score. We'll get some material from a blanket tree to throw over his head, so he can't see us and can't transform us, or we can hold the hypno-gourd in front of his face. He'll have to yield then."

"Yes," she said.

They set it up. Their covered loops extended from a hungry tangle tree to the ant-lion nest, and their ambush was in an invisible bush they discovered by sheer accident. That was about the only way such a bush could be discovered. Such plants were harmless, but could be a nuisance when stumbled into. When they hid behind it, they became invisible too, so long as they kept the bush between them and the viewer. They settled down to wait.

But Trent surprised them. While they had been setting up the trap, he had been circling around, orienting on their sounds. Now he came at them from the north. Chameleon, like most girls, had to answer calls of nature frequently, particularly when she was excited. She went behind a harmless mock-tentacle banyan tree, gave one little gasp of alarm, and disappeared. As Bink turned, he saw a lovely young winged deer bound out.

The battle was upon him! Bink charged the tree, stone in one hand, pole in the other. He hoped to knock out the Magician before Trent could throw his spell. But Trent wasn't there.

Had he jumped to a conclusion? Chameleon could have scared out a hiding doe—

"Now!" the Evil Magician cried from above. He was up in the tree. As Bink looked up, Trent gestured, not making a magical gesture, but bringing his hand down within six feet so as to cast the spell effectively. Bink jumped back—too late. He felt the tingle of transformation.

He rolled on the ground. In a moment he got his hands and feet under him—and discovered he was still a man. The spell had failed! He must have made it out of range in time after all, so that only one arm was in range, not his head.

He looked back at the tree—and gasped. The Evil Magician was tangled in the prickles of a candystripe rose bush.

"What happened?" Bink asked, forgetting his own peril for the moment.

"A branch of the tree got in the way," Trent said, shaking his head as if dazed. He must have had a hard fall. "The spell transformed it instead of you."

Bink would have laughed at this freak accident, but now he remembered his own position. So the Magician had tried to turn him into a rose bush. He hefted his rock. "Sorry," he apologized—and hurled it at the handsome head.

But it bounced off the tough shell of a purple tortoise. Trent had converted the rose to the armored animal and was hidden behind it.

Bink acted without thinking. He aimed the pole like a lance, ran halfway around the tortoise, and thrust it at the Magician. But the man dodged, and again Bink felt the tingle of enchantment.

His momentum carried him beyond his enemy. He was still a man. He retreated to the invisible bush, marveling at his escape. The spell had bounced, converting the tortoise to a werehornet. The insect buzzed up angrily, but decided on escape rather than attack.

Now Trent was hot on Bink's trail. The bush became a woman-headed serpent that slithered away with an exclamation of annoyance, and Bink was exposed again. He tried to run—but was caught a third time by the magic.

Beside him a yellow toad appeared. "What is this?" Trent demanded incredulously. "I struck a passing gnat instead of you. Three times my spell has missed you. My aim can't be *that* bad!"

Bink scrambled for his staff. Trent oriented on him again, and Bink knew he could neither get out of range nor bring his weapon to bear in time. He was finished, despite all his strategy.

But the winged deer charged from the side, threatening to bowl over the Magician. Trent heard her coming, and spun to focus on her. As she reached him she became a lovely iridescent butterfly, then a very pretty wyvern. "No problem there," Trent remarked. "She's good-looking in whatever form I put her, but my spells are registering perfectly."

The small winged dragon turned on him, hissing, and suddenly she was the winged doe again. "Scat!" Trent told her, clapping his hands. Startled, the deer bounded away. She was not overly bright.

Meanwhile, Bink had taken advantage of the distraction to retreat. But he had gone toward his own carefully fashioned trap, and now he did not know precisely where the noose loops lay hidden. If he tried to cross that line, he would either trap himself or give away its presence to Trent—assuming the Magician was not already aware of it.

Trent strode toward him. Bink was cornered, victim of his own machinations. He stood unmoving, knowing the Magician would turn on him the moment he tried to act. He cursed himself for not being more decisive, but he simply did not know what to. He obviously was no duelist; he had been outmaneuvered and outmagicked from the outset of this contest. He should have left the Evil Magician alone—yet he still could not see how he could have stood by and yielded Xanth up without even token protest. This was that token.

"This time, no error," Trent said, stepping boldly toward Bink. "I know I can transform you, for I have done it many times before without difficulty. I must have been overhasty today." He stopped within range, while Bink stood still, not deigning to run again. Trent concentrated—and the magic smote Bink once more, powerfully.

A flock of funnelbirds manifested around Bink. Hooting derisively, they jetted away on their fixed wings.

"The very microbes surrounding you!" Trent exclaimed. "My spell bounced right off you—again. Now I *know* there is something strange."

"Maybe you just don't want to kill me," Bink said.

"I was not trying to kill you—only to transform you into something harmless, so that never again could you oppose me. I never kill without reason." The Magician pondered. "Something very strange here. I don't believe my talent is misfiring; something is opposing it. There has to be some counterspell operating. You have led a rather charmed life, you know; I had thought it was mere coincidence, but now—"

Trent considered, then snapped his fingers ringingly. "Your talent! Your magic talent. That's it. *You cannot be harmed by magic!*"

"But I've been hurt many times," Bink protested.

"Not by magic, I'll warrent. Your talent repels all magical threats."

"But many spells have affected me. You transformed me—"

"Only to help you—or to warn you. You may not have trusted my motives, but your magic knew the truth. I never intended to harm you before, and so my spells were permitted. Now that we are dueling and I am trying to change your status for the worse, my spells bounce. In this respect your magic is more powerful than mine—as certain prior signals have indicated indirectly."

Bink was amazed. "Then—then I have won. You cannot hurt me."

"Not necessarily so, Bink. My magic has brought yours to bay, and forced its unveiling, and thereby rendered it vulnerable." The Evil Magician drew his gleaming sword. "I have other talents than magic. Defend yourself—physically!"

Bink brought up his staff as Trent lunged. He barely parried the blade in time.

He was vulnerable—physically. Suddenly past confusions unraveled. He had never directly been harmed by magic. Embarrassed, humiliated, yes, especially in childhood. But it was evidently physical harm he was protected against. When he had run a race with another boy, and the boy had charged through trees and barriers to win, Bink had not suffered any physical damage, merely chagrin. And when he had chopped off his own finger, nonmagically, nothing had aided him there. Magic had healed that, but magic could not have made the injury. Similarly, he had been threatened by magic many times, and been terrified—but somehow had never had those threats materialize. Even when he had taken a lungful of Potipher's poison gas, he had been saved just in time. He had indeed led a charmed life—literally.

"Fascinating aspects to your magic," Trent said conversationally as he maneuvered for another opening. "Obviously it would be scant protection if its nature were widely known. So it arranges to conceal itself from discovery, by acting in subtle ways. Your escapes so often seemed fortuitous or coincidental." Yes, as when he escaped the Gap dragon. He had also been benefited by countermagic, coincidentally—as when he had been taken over by Donald the shade, enabling him to fly up out of the Gap safely.

"Your pride was never salvaged, merely your body," Trent continued, obviously taking his time about the fight while he worked out all the details, just in case. He was a meticulous man. "Maybe you suffered some discomfort, as in our entry into Xanth, whose purpose was to conceal the fact that nothing serious had happened to you. Rather than reveal itself, your talent allowed you to be exiled—because that was a legal or social matter, not really magical. Yet you were not hurt by the Shield—"

He had felt the tingle of the Shield as he dived through on his way out, and thought he had gotten safely through the opening. Now he knew he had taken the full force of the Shield—and survived. He could have walked through it at any time. But, had he known that, he might have done it—and given away his talent. So it had been concealed—from himself.

Yet now it had been revealed. And there was a flaw. "You were not hurt by the Shield either," Bink cried, striking hard with his staff.

"I was in direct contact with you when we entered," Trent said. "So was Chameleon. You were unconscious, but your talent still operated. To allow the two of us to die while you survived unscathed—that would have given it away. Or possibly a small field surrounds you, enabling you to protect those you touch. Or your talent looked ahead, and knew that if the magic of the Shield eliminated us at that time, you would be cast into the den of the kraken weed alone, and be unable to escape, and die there. You needed me and my power of transformation to survive the magical threats—so I was spared. And Chameleon, because you would not have worked with me if she had not done so. So we all survived, in order to promote your survival, and we never suspected the true cause. Similarly, your magic protected us all during our trek through the wilderness. I thought I needed you to protect me, but it was the other way around. My talent became a mere aspect of yours. When you were threatened by the wiggles and the invisible giant, you drew on my transformation of you to abate that threat, still without revealing . . ."

Trent shook his head, still parrying Bink's clumsy attacks easily. "Suddenly it becomes less amazing—and your talent more impressive. You are a Magician, with not merely the overt complex of talents but the ramifying aspects too. Magicians are not merely more powerfully talented people; our enchantments differ in quality as well as quantity, in ways seldom appreciated by normal citizens. You are on a par with Humfrey and Iris and myself. I'd really like to know your power's full nature and extent."

"So would I," Bink gasped. His efforts were winding him, without effect on the Magician. This was true frustration.

"But alas, it seems I cannot become King while a talent like that opposes me. I sincerely regret the necessity of sacrificing your life, and want you to know this was not my intent at the outset of this encounter. I would have much preferred to transform you harmlessly. But the sword is less versatile than magic; it can only injure or kill."

Bink remembered Herman the centaur, his head flying from his body. When Trent decided that killing was necessary—

Trent made a deft maneuver. Bink flung himself aside. The point of the sword touched his hand. Blood flowed; with a cry of pain, Bink dropped his staff. He could be hurt by Mundane means, obviously. Trent had aimed for that hand, testing, making absolutely sure.

This realization broke the partial paralysis that had limited the imagination of his defense. He was vulnerable—but on a straight man-to-man basis, he did have a chance. The awesome power of the Evil Magician had daunted him, but now, in effect, Trent was merely a man. He could be surprised.

As Trent set up for the finishing thrust, Bink moved with inspired competency. He ducked under the man's arm, caught it with his bloody hand, turned, bent his knees, and heaved. It was the throw that the soldier Crombie had taught him, useful for handling an attacker with a weapon.

But the Magician was alert. As Bink heaved, Trent stepped around, keeping on his feet. He wrenched his sword arm free, threw Bink back, and oriented for the killing thrust. "Very nice maneuver, Bink; unfortunately, they also know such tactics in Mundania."

Trent thrust with instant decision, and with killing force. Bink, off balance, unable to move out of the way, saw the terrible point driving straight at his face. He was done for this time!

The winged doe shot between them. The sword plunged into her torso, the point emerging from the other side, just shy of Bink's quivering nose.

"Bitch!" Trent yelled, though that was not the proper term for a female deer, winged or land-bound. He yanked free the bloody blade. "That strike was not meant for you!"

The doe fell, red blood spurting from her wound. She had been punctured through the belly. "I'll transform you into a jellyfish!" the Evil Magician continued in fury. "You'll smother to death on land."

"She's dying anyway," Bink said, feeling a sympathetic agony in his own gut. Such wounds were not immediately fatal, but they were terribly painful, and the result was the same in the long run. It was death by torture for Chameleon.

The omen! It had finally been completed. The chameleon had died suddenly. Or would die—

Bink launched himself at his enemy again, experiencing a vengeful rage he had never felt before. With his bare hands he would—

Trent stepped nimbly aside, cuffing Bink on the side of the neck with his left hand as he passed. Bink stumbled and fell, half conscious. Blind rage was no substitute for cool skill and experience. He saw Trent step up to him, raising the sword high in both hands for the final body-severing blow.

Bink shut his eyes, no longer able to resist. He had done everything he could, and lost. "Only kill her too—cleanly," he begged. "Do not let her suffer."

He waited with resignation. But the blow did not fall. Bink opened his eyes—and saw Trent putting his terrible sword away.

"I can't do it," the Magician said soberly.

The Sorceress Iris appeared. "What is this?" she demanded. "Have your guts turned to water? Dispatch them both and be done with it. Your kingdom awaits!"

"I don't want my kingdom this way," Trent told her. "Once I would have done it, but I have changed in twenty years, and in the past two weeks. I have learned the true history of Xanth, and I know too well the sorrow of untimely death. My honor came late to my life, but it grows stronger; it will not let me kill a man who has saved my life, and who is so loyal to his unworthy monarch that he sacrifices his life in defense of the one who has exiled him." He looked at the dying doe. "And I would never voluntarily kill the girl who, lacking the intelligence to be cunning, yields up her own welfare for the life of that man. This is true love, of the kind I once knew. I could not save mine, but I would not destroy

that of another. The throne simply is not worth this
moral price."

"Idiot!" Iris screamed. "It is your own life you are
throwing away."

"Yes, I suppose I am," Trent said. "But this was the
risk I took at the outset, when I determined to return to
Xanth, and this is the way it must be. Better to die
with honor than to live in dishonor, though a throne be
served up as temptation. Perhaps it was not power I
sought, but perfection of self." He kneeled beside the
doe and touched her, and she was the human Chameleon again. Blood leaked from the terrible wound in her
abdomen. "I cannot save her," he said sadly, "any more
than I could cure my wife and child. I am no doctor.
Any creature into which I might transform her would
suffer similarly. She must have help—magic help."

The Magician looked up. "Iris, you can help. Project
your image to the castle of the Good Magician Humfrey. Tell him what has happened here, and ask him for
healing water. I believe the authorities of Xanth will
help this innocent girl and spare this young man, whom
they wrongly exiled."

"I'll do nothing of the sort!" the Sorceress screamed.
"Come to your senses, man. You have the kingdom in
your grasp."

Trent turned to Bink. "The Sorceress has not suffered the conversion that experience has brought me.
She will not help. The lure of power has blinded her to
all else—as it almost blinded me. You will have to go
for help."

"Yes," Bink agreed. He could not look at the blood
coming from Chameleon.

"I will staunch her wound as well as I can," Trent
said. "I believe she will live for an hour. Do not take
longer than that."

"No . . ." Bink agreed. If she died—

Suddenly Bink was a bird—a fancy-feathered, fire-
winged phoenix, sure to be noticed, since it appeared in
public only every five hundred years. He spread his

pinions and took off into the sky. He rose high and circled, and in the distance to the east he saw the spire of the Good Magician's castle glinting magically. He was on his way.

Chapter 16. King

A flying dragon appeared. "Pretty bird, I'm going to eat you up!" it said.

Bink sheered off, but the monster was before him again. "You can't escape!" it said. It opened its toothy mouth.

Was his mission of mercy to end here, so near success? Bink pumped his wings valiantly, climbing higher, hoping the heavier dragon could not achieve the same elevation. But his wounded wing—formerly the hand Trent's sword had cut—robbed him of full lifting power and balance, forcing him to rise with less velocity. The predator paralleled him without effort, staying between him and the far castle. "Give up, dumbo," it said. "You'll never make it."

Suddenly Bink caught on. Dragons did not speak like that. Not flying fire-breathers, anyway; they lacked both the cranial capacity and the coolness of brain to talk at all. They were simply too light and hot to be smart. This was no dragon—it was an illusion spawned by the Sorceress. She was still trying to stop him, hoping that if he disappeared and Chameleon died, Trent would resume his march on the throne. Trent would have done his best, and failed; realistically, he would continue toward his goal. Thus Iris could still achieve

her dream of power through him. Naturally, she would
never confess her own part in this mischief.

Bink would rather have dealt with a real dragon. The
Sorceress's evil plot might work. Because he was a
phoenix instead of a talking bird, he could not tell anyone other than the Good Magician what was happening; others would not have the capacity to understand.
If he returned to Trent now, too much time would be
lost—and in any event, Iris could stop him there, too.
This was his own private battle, his duel with the Sorceress; he had to win it himself.

He changed course abruptly and angled directly into
the dragon. If he had guessed wrong, he would light a
fire in the belly of the fire-breather and lose all. But he
passed right through it without resistance. Victory!

Iris shouted something most unladylike at him. What
a fishwife she was when balked. But Bink ignored her
and winged on.

A cloud formed before him. Uh-oh—a storm? He
had to hurry.

But the cloud loomed rapidly larger. Blisters of black
vapor boiled out of it, swirling funnels forming below.
In moments the sheer mass of it blotted out the castle.
Ugly dark satellite clouds scudded about it, menacing as
the heads of goblins. A larger rotary pattern developed.
The whole thing looked disconcertingly formidable.

There was no hope of rising above it. His injured
wing was hurting, and the storm towered into the sky
like a giant genie. Bolts of jagged lightning danced
about, crackling loudly. There was the odor of metal
burning. Deep in the roiling bowels of it were tangled
colors and vague shapes of demonic visages. A magic
tempest, obviously, girt with colored hail: the most devastating kind.

Bink dropped lower—and the cloud circulation tightened into a single descending gray tube. A super-
tornado that would destroy him!

Then Bink almost fell out of the air with the shock of
his realization. *He could not be harmed by magic!* This

was a magic storm—therefore it could not touch him. He was being balked by a false threat.

Furthermore, there was no actual wind. This was another illusion. All he had to do was fly directly toward the castle, unswayed by optical effects. He shot straight into the cloud.

He was right again. The optical effects had been spectacular, but there was no actual storm, merely opacity and the suggestion of wetness on his feathers. Soon he would be through it, having called its bluff; then nothing could stop him from reaching the castle of the Good Magician.

But the grayness continued. How could he go to the castle when he couldn't see it? Iris couldn't fool him, but she could effectively blind him. Maybe he, personally, could not be harmed by magic—either real or illusory magic—but his talent did not seem to be concerned with the welfare of other people, no matter how Bink himself might feel about them. He would survive if Chameleon died. He might not enjoy that survival, but the technicality would have been honored.

Damn it, talent, he thought fiercely. *You'd better stop being concerned with technicalities and start being concerned with my larger welfare. I'll kill myself, physically, by Mundane means, if I find my life not worth living. I need Chameleon. So you can't save me at all if you let this hostile magic stop me from saving Chameleon. Then where will you be?*

The opacity continued. Apparently his talent was an unreasoning thing. And so, in the end, it was useless. Like a colored spot on a wall, it was magic without purpose.

He peered about, determined to fight it through himself. He had made it this far through life without any talent he had known about; he would have to make it similarly in the future. Somehow.

Had he been headed directly toward the castle? He thought so—but he could not be sure. He had been distracted by the developing cloud, trying to avoid it, and could have lost his bearings. Trent might better have transformed him into an unerring carrier pigeon. But that bird would not have been distinct enough to attract the attention of the Good Magician. Anyway, speculations on what he might have been were useless. He was what he was, and would have to prevail as he was. If he were now aimed wrong, he might never reach the castle —but he would keep trying.

He dropped down, seeking some landmark. But the cloud remained about him. He could not see a thing. If he went too low, he might crash into a tree. Had Iris won after all?

Then he emerged from the cloud floor. There was the castle. He zoomed toward it—and paused, dismayed again. This wasn't the residence of the Good Magician—this was Castle Roogna! He had become completely reversed, and flown across the wilderness to the west instead of eastward to the Good Magician. The Sorceress had surely known this, and kept up the blinding fog so that he would not discover his error until too late. How much precious time had he wasted? If he reversed course and flew straight to the proper castle now—assuming he could find it in the fog—could he possibly get help for Chameleon within the hour? Or would she be dead by the time help arrived, thanks to this delay?

He heard a faint snort. Immediately it was echoed by snorts all around him, coming from every direction. The base of the cloud dropped down to obscure his view again.

Something was funny here! He might not have paid any attention to the sound if there had not been such an obvious effort to mask its direction. Why should the Sorceress try to prevent him from landing at Castle Roogna? Was there healing water there, used to patch up zombies? Doubtful.

So the snort was important in some way. But what had caused it? There was no moat dragon at Roogna; zombies didn't snort very well anyway. Yet obviously something had made that sound—probably something all the way alive. Like a winged horse, or—

He caught on: this was not Castle Roogna but the castle of the Good Magician after all! The Sorceress had only made it look like Roogna, to turn him back. She was mistress of illusion—and he kept being deceived by the ramifications of her power. But the hippocampus of the moat had snorted, giving it away. He had been headed in the right direction after all, perhaps guided by his talent. His talent had always operated subtly; there was no reason for it to change now.

Bink headed for the remembered sound of the first snort, tuning out all others. Abruptly the fog dissipated. Apparently the Sorceress could not maintain her illusions too near the premises of the rival Magician, whose specialty was truth.

"I'll get you yet!" her voice cried from the air behind. Then she and all her effects were gone, and the sky was clear.

Bink circled the castle, which now had its proper aspect. He was shivering with reaction; how close he had come to losing his duel with the Sorceress! If he had turned back—

He found an open portal in an upper turret and angled through it. The phoenix was a powerful flier, with good control; he probably could have outdistanced a real dragon, even with his hurt wing.

It took a moment for his beady eyes to adjust to the gloom of the interior. He flapped from one room to another and finally located the Magician, poring over a massive tome. For an instant the little man reminded Bink of Trent in the Roogna library; both had serious interest in books. Had the two really been friends twenty years ago, or merely associates?

Humfrey looked up. "What are you doing here, Bink?" he inquired, surprised. He didn't seem to notice the form Bink was in.

Bink tried to talk, but could not. The phoenix was

silent; its magic related to survival from fire, not to human discourse.

"Come over here by the mirror," Humfrey said, rising.

Bink came. As he approached, the magic mirror showed a scene. Evidently this mirror was a twin to the one he had broken, for he saw no cracks to indicate repair.

The picture was of the wilderness, Chameleon lying nude and lovely and bleeding despite a crude compact of leaves and moss on her abdomen. Before her stood Trent, sword drawn, as a wolf-headed man approached.

"Oh, I see," Humfrey said. "The Evil Magician has returned. Foolish of him; this time he won't be exiled, he'll be executed. Good thing you managed to warn me; he's a dangerous one. I see he stabbed the girl and transformed you, but you managed to get away. Good thing you had the sense to come here."

Bink tried to speak again, and failed again. He danced about anxiously.

"More to say? This way." The gnomelike Magician took down a book and opened it, setting it on top of his prior volume on the table. The pages were blank. "Speak," he said.

Bink tried yet again. No sound emerged, but he saw the words forming in neat script on the pages of the book:

Chameleon is dying! We must save her.

"Oh, of course," Humfrey agreed. "A few drops of healing water will take care of that. There'll be my fee, naturally. But first we'll have to deal with the Evil Magician, which means we'll have to detour to the North Village to pick up a stunner. No magic of mine can handle Trent!"

No! Trent is trying to save her! He's not—

Humfrey's brow wrinkled. "You are saying that the Evil Magician helped you?" he asked, surprised. "That is hard to believe, Bink."

As quickly as possible, Bink explained about Trent's conversion.

"Very well," Humfrey said with resignation. "I'll take your word that he is acting in your interest in this case. But I suspect you're a bit naive, and now I don't know who's going to pay my fee. The Evil Magician is very likely to get away anyway, while we detour. But we have to try to catch him for a fair trial. He has broken the law of Xanth, and must be dealt with immediately. It would profit us nothing if we saved Chameleon while leaving Xanth in peril from the conquering lust of the transformer."

There was so much more Bink wanted to explain, but Humfrey gave him no chance. And of course he probably was being naive; once the Evil Magician had time to reconsider, he would probably revert to form. He was a serious threat to Xanth. Yet Bink knew that Trent had won the duel, and so Bink, as loser, should no longer interfere in the Magician's affairs. This was a devious but increasingly strong conviction. He hoped Trent managed to escape.

Humfrey led him down to the castle cellar, where he tapped some fluid from a barrel. He sprinkled a drop on Bink's wing, and it was instantly sound again. The rest he put in a small bottle, which he tucked into his vest pocket.

Now the Good Magician went to a closet and hauled out a plush carpet. He unrolled it, then sat cross-legged on it. "Well, get on, birdbrain!" he snapped. "You'll get lost out there by yourself, especially with Iris fooling around with the weather reports."

Bink, perplexed, stepped onto the carpet and faced the Magician. Then the rug lifted. Startled, Bink spread his wings and dug his feet deeply into the material, hanging on. It was a flying carpet.

The thing angled neatly out through a portal, then looped high up into the sky. It leveled, then accelerated. Bink, facing backward, had to furl his wings tightly and almost puncture the fabric with his claws to keep from being dislodged by the wind. He saw the castle shrink in the distance.

"Just an artifact I accepted in lieu of service some years back," Humfrey explained conversationally. He sneezed. "Never had much use for it; just collects dust. But I suppose this is an emergency." He peered at Bink, shaking his head dubiously. "You claim the Evil Magician transformed you to help you get to me quickly? Just nod your beak once for yes, twice for no."

Bink nodded once.

"But he did stab Chameleon?"

Another nod. But that was not the whole story.

"He didn't really mean to stab her? Because he was really trying to kill you, and she got in the way?"

Bink had to nod yes again. What a damning statement.

Humfrey shook his head. "It's easy to be sorry after a mistake has been made. Yet when I knew him, before his exile, he was not a man without compassion. Still, I doubt he can ever rest until he achieves his ambition— and while he remains alive and in Xanth, we can never be certain he won't. It is a difficult case. There will have to be a meticulous investigation of the facts."

Such an investigation would be the death of Trent. The old King would be determined to abolish this major threat to his declining power.

"And Trent knows what is likely to happen to him when the authorities get there, if they catch him?"

Trent surely did. Bink nodded yes again.

"And you—do you want him dead?"

Bink shook his head vehemently, no.

"Or exiled again?"

Bink had to think a moment. Then he shook his head again.

"Of course; you need him to transform you back into human form. That perhaps gives him some bargaining leverage. They might spare his life in exchange for such services. But after that, it seems likely to be exile for him—or blindness."

Blindness! But then Bink comprehended the horrible logic of it. Blind, Trent could not transform anyone; he had to see his subjects. But what a terrible fate.

"I see you don't like that notion either. Yet there are harsh realities to weigh." Humfrey pondered. "It will be difficult enough to save *your* life, since you also are an illegal immigrant. But perhaps I have a wrinkle." He frowned. "I'm really sorry to see Trent get into this scrape; he's a truly great Magician, and we've always gotten along, not interfering in each other's business. But the welfare of Xanth comes first." He smiled briefly. "After my fee, of course."

Bink didn't see much humor in it.

"Well, it will soon be out of our hands, fortunately. What will be will be."

After that he was silent. Bink watched the clouds, real ones this time; they loomed up larger and darker as the rug flew northward. Now the carpet was over the Gap, making Bink feel less secure despite his wings; it was a long way down. When the rug passed through a cloud, it dipped alarmingly; it seemed there were internal downdrafts. But Humfrey rode with seeming equanimity, eyes closed, deep in thought.

It got worse. The carpet, possessing no intelligence, zoomed straight for its preprogrammed destination, not trying to avoid the cloud banks. The clouds formed into towering mountains and awesomely deep valleys, and the drafts got worse. No illusion, this building storm; though it lacked the colors and menacing swirls of Iris's illusion-cloud, in its somber way it was just as threatening.

Then the rug dropped through the fog and came out below. There was the North Village!

The windows of the King's palace were draped in black. "I think it has happened," Humfrey remarked as they landed before the palace gate.

A village Elder came out to meet them. "Magician!" he cried. "We were about to send for you. The King is dead!"

"Well, you'd better choose his successor, then," Humfrey said acidly.

"There is no one—except you," the Elder replied.

"Lamebrain! That's no recommendation," Humfrey snapped. "What would I want with the throne? It's a big boring job that would seriously interfere with my studies."

The Elder stood his ground. "Unless you can show us another qualified Magician, the law requires that you accept."

"Well, the law can go—" Humfrey paused. "We have more pressing business. Who is caretaker during the interim?"

"Roland. He is seeing to the funeral."

Bink jumped. His father! But he knew immediately that his father would be scrupulous in avoiding any possible conflict of interest; better not even to tell him Bink was back in Xanth.

Humfrey glanced at Bink, seeming to have the same notion. "Well, I think I know just the sucker for the job," the Good Magician said. "But he has a certain technical problem to surmount first."

Bink suffered an exceedingly uncomfortable shiver of premonition. *Not me!* he tried to say, but still could not speak. *I'm no Magician, really. I know nothing of kingship. All I want to do is save Chameleon.* And let Trent get away, too.

"But first we have to settle a couple of other matters," Humfrey continued. "The Evil Magician Trent, the transformer, is back in Xanth, and a girl is dying. If we move fast, we may catch them both before it is too late."

"Trent!" The Elder was shocked. "What a time for him to show up." He ran into the palace.

Very soon they had assembled a war party. The village travel-conjurer was given the precise location, and he started popping people through.

First to go was Roland himself. With luck he would catch the Evil Magician by surprise and stun him in place, nullifying his magic. Then the others could proceed safely. Next the Good Magician went, with his vial of healing water, to save Chameleon—if she still lived.

Bink realized that if this plan was successful, Trent would never have another chance to transform anyone. If they unknowingly executed the Evil Magician before Bink was transformed, he would remain forever a phoenix. Chameleon would be alone, although well. And his father would be responsible. Was there no way out of this predicament?

Well, the plan might fail. Trent could transform Roland and Humfrey. Then Bink himself might recover his human form, but Chameleon would die. That was no good either. Maybe Trent would have escaped before Roland arrived. Then Chameleon would be cured, and Trent would survive—but Bink would remain a bird.

No matter which way it worked out, someone dear to Bink would be sacrificed. Unless Humfrey somehow managed things to make everything come out all right. Yet how could he?

One by one the Elders disappeared. Then it was Bink's turn. The conjurer gestured—

The first thing Bink saw was the body of the wolf-headed man. The creature had evidently charged, and been dispatched by Trent's singing sword. Elsewhere were a number of caterpillars that had not been here before. Trent himself stood frozen, concentrating as though in the process of casting a spell. And Chameleon—

Bink flew to her gladly. She was well! The terrible wound was gone, and she was standing, looking bewildered.

"This is Bink," Humfrey told her. "He flew to fetch help for you. Just in time, too."

"Oh, Bink!" she cried, picking him up and trying to hug him to her bare torso. Bink, as a bird with delicate plumage, did not find this as delightful as he might have in his natural form. "Change back."

"I am afraid that only the transformer can change

him back," Humfrey said. "And the transformer must first stand trial."

And what would be the result of that trial? Why hadn't Trent escaped when he had the chance?

The proceedings were swift and efficient. The Elders put questions to the frozen Magician, who of course could not answer or argue his own case. Humfrey had the travel-conjurer fetch the magic mirror—no, it was Munly, the master of ceremonies at Bink's hearing, who was himself an Elder. Bink's bird-brain was letting him get confused. Munly used his talent to conjure this small object directly to his hand from the Good Magician's castle. He held it up so that all could see the images forming within it.

In the mirror were reflected scenes from the trio's travels in Xanth. Gradually the story came out, though it did not reveal Bink's talent. It showed how the three had helped one another to survive in the wilderness; how they had stayed at Castle Roogna—there was a general exclamation about that, for no one had known this old, famous, semimythical artifact remained intact. How they had fought the wiggle swarm—and that produced another reaction! How they had finally dueled. How the Sorceress Iris had mixed in. And how—Bink felt a fury of embarrassment—he had made love to Chameleon. The mirror was merciless.

The whole sequence was clearly damning to Trent, for there were no words. *But it's not really like that,* Bink tried to cry. *He's a fine man. In many ways his rationale makes sense. If he had not spared me and Chameleon, he could have conquered Xanth.*

The picture froze on the final sequence of the duel: Trent wounding Bink, making ready to strike the final blow—and halting. *See—he spared me. He is not evil. Not any more. He is not evil!*

But no one heard him. The assembled Elders looked at one another, nodding gravely. Bink's father, Roland, was among them, and the family friend Munly, saying nothing.

Then the mirror continued, showing what had happened after Bink flew away. The monsters of the wilderness, smelling fresh blood, had converged. Trent barely had time to bandage Chameleon before these threats became pressing. He had stood before her, sword in hand, bluffing the creatures back—and transforming those who attacked anyway to caterpillars. Two wolf-heads had charged together, jaws gaping wide, slavering; one became a caterpillar while the other was cut down by the sword. Trent had killed only as necessary.

He could have run, even then, Bink cried silently. *He could have let Chameleon be taken by the monsters. He could have escaped into the magic jungle. You would never have caught him—until he caught you. He is a good man now.* But he knew there was no way he could plead this good man's case. Chameleon, of course, was too stupid to do it, and Humfrey didn't know the whole story.

At last the mirror showed the arrival of Roland, as strong and handsome in his fashion as the Evil Magician, and a few years older. He had landed facing away from Trent—and directly in front of an advancing two-headed serpent, each head a yard long. Roland, searching the wilderness before him, nervous about a nearby tangle tree, had seen neither Magician nor serpent behind him.

In the mirror, Trent charged, running at the tail of the monster, grabbing it with his bare hands, causing it to whirl on him furiously. Both heads had struck—and the thing had abruptly become another caterpillar. A two-headed caterpillar.

Roland whirled. For an instant the two men looked into each other's eyes, their deadly talents equivalent at this range. They seemed very similar to each other. Then Roland squinted, and Trent froze in place. The stun had scored before the transformation.

Or had it? *Trent never even tried to resist,* Bink thought futilely. *He could have transformed my father instead of the serpent—or simply let the serpent strike.*

"Elders, have you seen enough?" Humfrey inquired gently.

If I could have the throne of Xanth at the expense of Trent's life, I would not take it, Bink thought savagely. The trial had been a farce; they had never let Trent speak for himself, to present his eloquent thesis of the damage magic was doing to the human population of Xanth, or of the threat of a future attack from Mundania. Were they going to dispose of him the same way they had exiled Bink? Thoughtlessly, by rote law, regardless of the meaning behind the facts?

The Elders exchanged glances gravely. Each nodded slowly, affirmatively.

At least let him talk! Bink cried mutely.

"Then it would be best to release the spell," Humfrey said. "He must be free of magic for the denouement, as is our custom."

Thank God!

Roland snapped his fingers. Trent moved. "Thank you, honorable Elders of Xanth," he said politely. "You have granted me a fair presentation, and I stand ready to accept your judgment."

Trent wasn't even defending himself. This horrendously partial, silent investigation, obviously a mere ritual to justify a decision privately arrived at—how could the Evil Magician lend credibility to that?

"We find you guilty of violating exile," Roland said. "For this the set penalty is death. But we are in a unique situation, and you have changed substantially since we knew you. You always had courage, intelligence, and strong magic; now you are also possessed of loyalty, honor, and mercy. I am not unmindful that you spared the life of my son, who had foolishly challenged you, and that you protected his chosen one from the ravages of wild beasts. You have some guilt in these matters, but you expiated it. We therefore waive the set penalty and grant you leave to remain in Xanth, under two conditions."

They were not going to kill Trent. Bink almost danced for joy. But immediately he realized that there would still be stringent restrictions, to prevent Trent from ever again aspiring to the throne. Humfrey had mentioned blinding him, so that he would be unable to perform his magic. Bink had some idea of what a life without magic would be like. Trent would be forced to assume some menial occupation, working out his days in ignobility. The Elders were generally old, but not necessarily gentle; no smart citizen ever crossed them twice.

Trent bowed his head. "I thank you sincerely, Elders. I accept your conditions. What are they?"

But there was so much more to be said! To treat this fine man as a common criminal, to force his agreement to this terrible retribution—and Trent was not even protesting.

"First," Roland said, "that you marry."

Trent looked up, startled. "I can understand a requirement that I reverse all prior transformations and desist from any future exercise of my talent—but what has marriage to do with it?"

"You are presuming," Roland said grimly. And Bink thought: *Trent hasn't caught on. They have no need to make restrictions—if they blind him. He will be helpless.*

"I apologize, Elder. I will marry. What is the other condition?"

Now it comes! Bink wished he could blot out the sounds, as if by failing to hear the words of the sentence he could alleviate it. But that was not his type of magic talent.

"That you accept the throne of Xanth."

Bink's beak fell open. So did Chameleon's mouth. Trent stood as if stun-frozen again.

Then Roland bent one knee and slowly dropped to the ground. The other Elders followed, silently.

"The King, you see, is dead," Humfrey explained. "It is essential to have a good man and strong Magician in the office, one who has the demeanor of command coupled with restraint and perspective, yet who will muster savagery when necessary in the defense of Xanth. As in the event of a wiggle invasion or similar threat. One who may also provide a potential heir, so that Xanth is not again caught in the difficult situation just past. It is not necessary to like such a monarch, but we must have him. I obviously do not qualify, for I could hardly bring myself to devote the required attention to the details of governance; the Sorceress Iris would be unsuitable even if she were not female, because of her lack of restraint; and the only other person of Magician caliber has neither personality nor talent appropriate to the needs of the crown. Therefore, Xanth needs you, Magician. You can not refuse." And Humfrey, too, bent his knee.

The Evil Magician, evil no longer, bowed his head in mute acceptance. He had conquered Xanth after all.

The ceremony of coronation was splendid. The centaur contingent marched with dazzling precision, and from all over Xanth people and intelligent beasts came to attend. Magician Trent, henceforth the Transformer King, took both crown and bride together, and both were radiant.

There were of course some sly remarks at the fringe of the spectator crowd, but most citizens agreed that the King had chosen wisely. "If she's too old to bear an heir, they can adopt a Magician-caliber boy." "After all, he's the only one who can control her, and he'll never suffer from lack of variety." "And it eliminates the last real threat to the kingdom." They were not yet aware of the other formidable external and internal threats.

Bink, restored to his natural form, stood alone, contemplating the place where Justin Tree once stood. He was glad for Trent, and certain the man would make a fine King. Yet he suffered also from a certain anticlimactic disappointment. What would he, Bink, do now?

Three youths passed, one middle-aged. Zink, Jama, and Potipher. They were chastened, their eyes downcast. They knew that the days of wild nuisance were over; with the new King in power, they would have to behave—or else be transformed.

Then two centaurs trotted up. "So glad to see you, Bink!" Cherie exclaimed. "Isn't it wonderful you weren't exiled after all!" She nudged her companion. "Isn't it, Chester?"

Chester forced his face into a tortured smile. "Yeah, sure," he mumbled.

"You must come and visit us," Cherie continued brightly. "Chester speaks so often of you."

Chester made a little throttling motion with his two powerful hands. "Yeah, sure," he repeated, more brightly.

Bink changed the subject. "Did you know, I met Herman the Hermit in the wilderness," he said. "He died a hero. He used his magic—" Bink paused, remembering that the centaurs regarded magic in a centaur as obscene. That would probably change, once Trent publicized the knowledge gained from the Castle Roogna archives. "He organized the campaign that wiped out the wiggle swarm before it infested all of Xanth. I hope Herman's name will be honored among your kind in future."

Surprisingly, Chester smiled. "Herman was my uncle," he said. "He was a great character. The colts used to kid me about his exile. Now he's a hero, you say?"

Cherie's mouth tightened. "We don't discuss obscenity in the presence of a filly," she warned him. "Come on."

Chester had to accompany her. But he looked back briefly. "Yeah, sure," he said to Bink. "You come see us real soon. Tell us all about what Uncle Herman did to save Xanth."

They were gone. Suddenly Bink felt very good. Chester was the last creature he would have expected to have something in common with, but he was glad it had happened. Bink knew all about the frustration of getting teased about some supposed failing. And he did want to tell an appreciative audience about Herman the magic Hermit centaur.

Now Sabrina approached him. She was as lovely as he had ever seen her. "Bink, I'm sorry about what happened before," she said. "But now that everything is cleared up . . ."

She was like Chameleon in her beauty stage, and she was intelligent, too. A fit bride for almost any man. But Bink knew her now, too well. His talent had stopped him from marrying her—by keeping itself secret. Smart talent.

He glanced about—and spied the new bodyguard Trent had taken, on Bink's recommendation. The man who could spot anything, including danger, before it developed. The soldier was now resplendent in his imperial uniform, and impressive of demeanor. "Crombie!" Bink called.

Crombie strode over. "Hello, Bink. I'm on duty now, so I can't stay to chat. Is something the matter?"

"I just wanted to introduce you to this lovely lady, Sabrina," Bink said. "She does a very nice holograph in air." He turned to Sabrina. "Crombie is a good man and able soldier, favored by the King, but he doesn't quite trust women. I think he's just never met the right one. I believe you two should get to know each other better."

"But I thought—" she began.

Crombie was looking at her with a certain cynical interest, and she returned the glance. He was observing her physical charms, which were excellent; she was pondering his position at the palace, which was also excellent. Bink wasn't sure whether he had just done a beautiful thing or dropped a bagful of cherry bombs into the hole of a privy. Time would tell.

"Good-bye, Sabrina," Bink said, and turned away.

King Trent summoned Bink to a royal audience. "Sorry about the delay in getting back to you," he said

when they were alone. "There were some necessary pre-
liminaries."

"The coronation. The marriage," Bink agreed.

"Those too. But mainly a certain emotional readjust-
ment. The crown landed on my head rather suddenly,
as you know."

Bink knew. "If I may ask, Your Majesty—"

"Why I did not desert Chameleon and flee into the
wilderness? For you alone, Bink, I will make an answer.
Setting aside the moral considerations—which I did
not—I performed a calculation that in Mundania is
called figuring the odds. When you took flight for the
castle of the Good Magician, I judged your chances of
success to be about three to one in your favor. Had you
failed, I would have been safe anyway; there was no
point in deserting Chameleon. I knew Xanth stood in
need of a new King, for the Storm King by all accounts
was failing rapidly. The chances against the Elders finding any Magician more competent for the position than
I were also about three to one. And so on. Altogether,
my chances of obtaining the throne by sitting tight were
nine in sixteen, with only a three-in-sixteen chance of
execution. These were better odds than survival alone in
the wilderness, which I would rate at one chance in two.
Understand?"

Bink shook his head. "Those figures—I don't see—"

"Just take my word that it was a practical decision, a
calculated risk. Humfrey was my friend; I was sure he
would not betray me. He knew I had figured the
odds—but it didn't make any difference, because that is
the kind of schemer Xanth needs in a King, and he
knew it. So he went along. Not that I didn't have some
serious worries at the time of the trial; Roland certainly
made me sweat."

"Me too," Bink agreed.

"But had the odds been otherwise, I would still have
acted as I did." Trent frowned. "And I charge you not
to embarrass me by revealing that weakness to the pub-

lic. They don't want a King who is unduly swayed by personal considerations."

"I won't tell," Bink said, though privately he thought it was not much of a failing. After all, it was Chameleon he had saved.

"And now to business," the King said briskly. "I shall of course grant you and Chameleon royal dispensation to remain in Xanth without penalty for your violations of exile. No, this has nothing to do with your father; I never even realized you were the son of Roland until I saw him again and recognized the family resemblance; he never said a word about you. Fine avoidance of conflict of interest there; Roland will be an important man in the new administration, I assure you. But that's beside the point. There will not be any more exiles for anyone, or restrictions on immigration from Mundania, unless there is violence connected. Of course, this means you are released from having to demonstrate your magic talent. In all Xanth, only you and I comprehend its specific nature. Chameleon was present at the discovery, but was not in condition to assimilate it. Humfrey knows only that you have Magician-class magic. So it will remain our secret."

"Oh, I don't mind—"

"You don't quite understand, Bink. It is important that the precise nature of your talent remain secret. That is its nature; it must be a private thing. To reveal it is to vitiate it. That is why it protects itself so carefully from discovery. Probably I was permitted to learn of it only to help protect it from others, and that I intend to do. No one else will know."

"Yes, but—"

"I see you still don't follow. Your talent is remarkable and subtle. It is in its totality a thing of Magician rank, equivalent to any magic in Xanth. All other citizens, whether of the spot-on-wall variety or of Magician class, are vulnerable to those types of magic they don't themselves practice. Iris can be transformed, I can be

stunned, Humfrey can be harassed by illusion—you get
the point. Only you are fundamentally secure from all
other forms of magic. You can be fooled or shamed or
grossly inconvenienced, but never actually physically
hurt. That is exceedingly broad protection."

"Yes, but—"

"In fact, we may never know the ultimate limits of it.
Consider the manner in which you reentered Xanth—
without revealing your talent to anyone who would tell.
Our entire adventure may be no more than the manifestation of one facet of your talent. Chameleon and I may
merely have been tools to convey you back into Xanth
safely. By yourself, you might have been trapped in
Castle Roogna, or run afoul of the wiggles. So I was
there to smooth your way. It may even have protected
you from my Mundane sword, by bringing Chameleon
in to take the killing thrust. Because, you see, I had
discovered your talent in large part through my own
magic. Through its effect on my magic. Because I am a
full Magician, it could not balk me completely, as it
might a lesser power. But still it operated to protect you;
it could not completely thwart me—I was able to
wound you—so it joined me, acting to alleviate my
quarrel with you by making me King in a way you
could accept. Maybe it was your talent that changed my
mind and prevented me from killing you. Hence my
reasoning that it was your talent's decision that I be
allowed to ascertain its nature—for this knowledge has,
as you see, profoundly affected my attitude toward you
and your personal safety."

He paused, but Bink did not comment. This was
quite a concept to digest in one lump. He had thought
his talent was limited, not affecting those he cared for,
but it seemed he had underestimated it.

"So you see," Trent continued, "my throne may
merely be the most convenient agency for the promotion of your welfare. Perhaps your entire exile, and the
death of the Storm King at this time, are all part of that
magical scheme. Your exile brought me into Xanth—

without my army, in your company. I certainly am not
going to gamble that mere coincidence brought me to
this pass; your talent makes most sophisticated use of
coincidence. I don't want to go against you, and perhaps sicken and die the way my predecessor did, after
he acted against your interest. No, Bink—I wouldn't
want to be your enemy even if I weren't already your
friend. So I am becoming a conscious agent for the
preservation of your secret and the promotion of your
welfare in the best way I am able. Knowing how you
feel about Xanth, I shall try to be the best possible
King, ushering in a new Golden Age, so that you never
suffer any direct or indirect threats through my mismanagement. Now do you understand?"

Bink nodded. "I guess I do, Your Majesty."

Trent stood up, clapping him heartily on the back.
"Good! All had better be well!" He paused, thinking
of something else. "Have you decided on an occupation
yet, Bink? I can offer you anything short of the crown
itself—though even that may be in your future if—"

"No!" Bink exclaimed. Then he had to backtrack,
seeing Trent's broad grin. "I mean yes, I thought of a
job. I—you said once—" Bink hesitated, suddenly awkward.

"You don't seem to have listened very well. What
you want, you will get—if it is within my present power.
But my talent is transformation, not divination. You
must speak. Out with it!"

"Well, in the wilderness, when we were waiting for
Chameleon to—you know, just before the wiggles. We
talked about the mystery of—"

Trent raised one royal hand. "Say no more. I hereby
appoint you, Bink of the North Village, Official Re-
searcher of Xanth. Any mysteries of magic shall be
your responsibility; you shall probe wherever required
until they are fathomed to your satisfaction, and turn in
your reports directly to me for inclusion in the royal
archives. Your secret talent makes you uniquely qualified to explore the most forbidding recesses of Xanth,

for the anonymous Magician needs no bodyguard. Those recesses are long overdue for discovery. Your first assignment shall be to discover the true source of the magic of Xanth."

"I—uh, thank you, Your Majesty," Bink said gratefully. "I think I like that job much better than being King."

"Perhaps you appreciate how much that gratifies me," Trent said with a smile. "Now let's go see the girls."

The travel conjurer moved them both. Abruptly they stood at the front portal of Castle Roogna.

The drawbridge had been repaired, and now gleamed in brass and polished timbers. The moat was clean and full of water, now stocked with monsters of the finest breeds. The teeth of the portcullis glittered. Bright pennants fluttered from the highest turrets. This was a castle restored to full splendor.

Bink peered at something he thought he saw around to the side. Was it a small graveyard? Something moved there, white as a bone, with a trailing bandage. *Oh, no!*

Then the ground opened up. With a final cheery wave, the zombie sank into its resting place.

"Sleep in peace," Trent murmured. "I have kept my promise."

And if he had not, would the zombies have marched out of the wilderness to compel performance? That was one mystery Bink did not intend to explore.

They entered Roogna. All six ghosts greeted them in the front hall, every one in full human shape. Milly quickly popped off to notify the Queen of the King's arrival.

Iris and Chameleon swept up together, wearing castle tunics and slippers. The Sorceress was in her natural form, but so neatly garbed and coiffed that she was not unattractive, and Chameleon was almost back to her "center" stage, average in both appearance and intellect.

The Queen made no pretense of affection for Trent;

it had been a marriage of convenience, as anticipated. But her pleasure in the position and her excitement about the castle were obviously genuine.

"This place is marvelous!" Iris exclaimed. "Chameleon has been showing me around, and the ghosts instructed our toilettes. All the room and grandeur I ever wanted—and it's all real. And it wants so much to please—I know I'm going to love it here."

"That's good," Trent said gravely. "Now put on your pretty face; we are entertaining company."

The middle-aged woman was instantly replaced by a stunningly smooth and buxom young woman with a low décolletage. "I just didn't want to embarrass Chameleon—you know, in her 'average' phase."

"You cannot embarrass her in any phase. Now apologize to Bink."

Iris made a breathtaking curtsy to Bink. She was ready to do anything to remain Queen—and human. Trent could make her into a warty toad—or he could make her into the very figure she now resembled. He could probably make her young enough to bear a child, the heir to the throne. Trent was the master, and Iris seemed to lack even the inclination to question this. "I'm sorry, Bink, I really am. I just got carried away there during the duel, and after. I didn't know you were going to fetch the Elders, to make Trent King."

Bink hadn't known that either. "Forget it, Your Majesty," he said uncomfortably. He looked at Chameleon, so close now to Dee, the girl he had liked from the outset despite Crombie's dire warnings. A fit of shyness overcame him.

"Go ahead, get it over with," Trent muttered in his ear. "She's smart enough now."

Bink thought about how much of his adventure had centered around Chameleon's quest for a spell to make her normal—when she really was quite satisfactory, and even somewhat challenging, as she was. How many people similarly spent their lives searching for their own spells—some gratuitous benefit such as a silver tree or political power or undeserved acclaim—when all they really needed was to be satisfied with what they already had? Sometimes what they had was better than what they thought they wanted. Chameleon had thought she wanted to be normal; Trent had thought he wanted armed conquest; and Bink himself had thought he wanted a demonstrable magic talent. Everyone thought he wanted something. But Bink's real quest, at the end, had been to preserve Chameleon and Trent and himself as they were, and to make Xanth accept them that way.

He had not wanted to take advantage of Chameleon in her stupid phase. He wanted to be sure she understood the full implications, before he—before he—

Something tickled his nose. Embarrassingly, he sneezed.

Iris nudged Chameleon with her elbow.

"Yes, of course I'll marry you, Bink," Chameleon said.

Trent guffawed. Then Bink was kissing her—his ordinary, extraordinary girl. She had found her spell, all right; she had cast it over him. It was the same as Crombie's curse—love.

And at last Bink understood the meaning of his omen: he was the hawk who had carried away Chameleon. She would never get free.